CURSED

THE NEW WORLD SERIES | BOOK SIX

Stephen Llewelyn

For Sally

***Thank you for your unwavering
commitment, support and for everything you do.***

The author also wishes to acknowledge:

Mum, Dad and Bill. Thanks to Sally-Marie and Fossil Rock;
Heni, for always making the interiors look so great; and Melanie
at The Chapter House for all the reads, re-reads, marketing,
publishing, IT help and on, and on, and on...

To my long-suffering friends, thank you for a lifetime of memories
and for offering encouragement for my mad ideas. This book is
dedicated to the ones we lost so young.

Special thanks to the experts who took time out of their frantic
schedules to answer my emails and questions about our favourite
subject. Also, sci-fi legends Stephen Baxter and Simon Guerrier,
and TV naturalist Nigel Marven, for reading and offering
endorsements, not to mention their kind words of support.
My most humble thanks.

…And last but by no means least, to everyone who reads this book
and enjoyed its predecessors, my sincere thanks. There's plenty
more to come and I can't wait to share it with you. Thank you.

The crew of the USS *New World* will return soon in

THE NEW WORLD SERIES | BOOK SEVEN | COLLISION.

Almost everything that has happened on the world stage during the last few years has been written about many times in some form or other, firstly by historians and latterly by science fiction authors, too, yet it repeats time and again. I believe that imagination is more vital than ever for our future, for without imagination there is no empathy, and without empathy there is no humanity. Perhaps Isaac Asimov summed it up best:

"Individual science fiction stories may seem as trivial as ever to the blinder critics and philosophers of today, but the core of science fiction, its essence, has become crucial to our salvation, if we are to be saved at all..."

Isaac Asimov

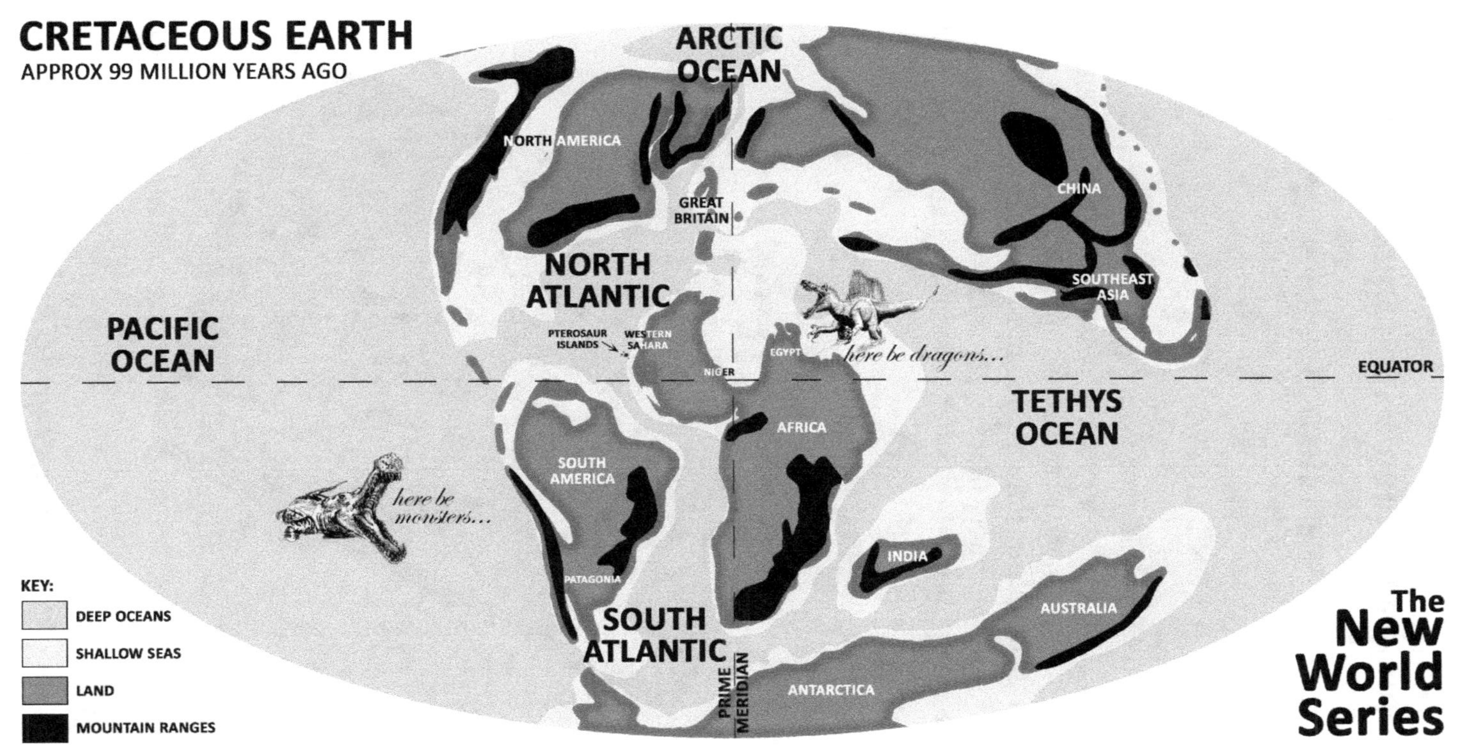

CRETACEOUS EARTH
APPROX 99 MILLION YEARS AGO
ARCTIC OCEAN
NORTH AMERICA
GREAT BRITAIN
NORTH ATLANTIC
PACIFIC OCEAN
CHINA
SOUTHEAST ASIA
PTEROSAUR ISLANDS
WESTERN SAHARA
EGYPT
NIGER
here be dragons…
EQUATOR
TETHYS OCEAN
AFRICA
SOUTH AMERICA
here be monsters…
PATAGONIA
INDIA
AUSTRALIA
SOUTH ATLANTIC
PRIME MERIDIAN
ANTARCTICA
KEY:
DEEP OCEANS
SHALLOW SEAS
LAND
MOUNTAIN RANGES
The New World Series

Your Free eBook is Waiting...

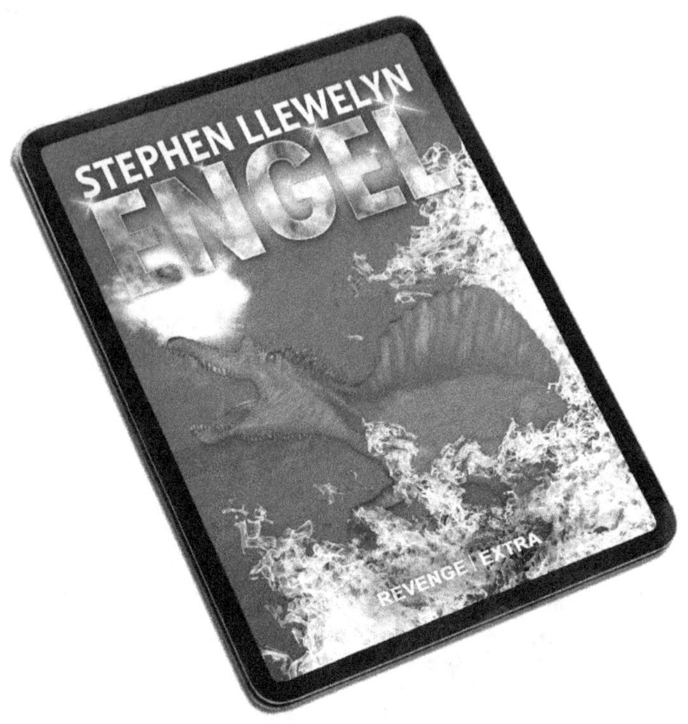

Six people alone in a Cretaceous jungle. Ordered to make a threat assessment of their environment, Corporal Heinz Engel is at a loss where to begin. Between running and hiding from a most irascible spinosaur, his team find that foolish mistakes have bloody consequences, and while their predicament brings out the best in some, others show their true colours. By the end of the mission, Engel seeks only justice.

ENGEL is set during the early chapters of REVENGE, the New World Series Book 2.

Get a free copy of ENGEL here:

www.stephenllewelyn.com/free-book

Preface

Dear readers, book six is here at last and I would like to express my continued thanks to all of you who've followed me on this journey.

This book is full of surprises. In fact, it had several for me, too, and wasn't quite the book I intended to write. If any of you remember the brief preface I wrote at the beginning of ALLEGIANCE (book three), well, lightning seems to have struck again. I changed the main theme of that book from a prehistoric virus that infected the crew, to a completely new storyline – thinking that, back in 2020, everyone was probably already fed up enough with being locked in the house because of a virus! There were also myriad titles that sprang into being on the back of the pandemic, so I decided to dramatically reduce those elements of the story and take a different path, and on that score, I have no regrets.

In the beginning, the choice to make the Nazis my bad guys was an easy one. Indeed, it's hard to imagine anyone 'badder'. They're also part of an era that carries great nostalgic value for many old enough to remember it – and can even generate a sense of anemoia in some who are not. The New World Series is set over several periods during the past and future, but that Second World War, or 'wartime', spirit of heroism and togetherness to overcome evil, has always been an important thread to these stories. Though the Nazis were by no means the world's first war criminals, it might be said that they codified conduct that was, and is, completely unacceptable – even in wartime. In CURSED, it was my intention to show them at their worst, hence the suitably dark title. Sadly, there are still regimes in the world, even in the 21st century, that seem determined to use Nazi methodology as a blueprint for their own behaviour, rather than hold it up as a shocking lesson in something that should never be repeated. If these books occasionally provide food for thought, that's great, but it has always been my hope to deliver stories primarily for escapism and entertainment. I didn't want to bring everyone down with a major epidemic storyline in ALLEGIANCE, and I don't wish to do so now with CURSED. So while this new work is not quite what I had noted in the beginning, and despite the minimising of events that would have taken us too close to real-world concerns at this time, I hope it still offers all the intrigue without grinding down the soul of the reader. Even when it seems all is in darkness, take my hand, and read on!

The fictional politics and events throughout this book were noted out a while ago and were not written to reflect current difficulties. That said, by no means do I encourage anyone to bury their head in the sand, only to take a little time for themselves where they can, to reinvigorate and imagine a better future before plunging back into doing what they must, for without imagination, surely, we are lost.

So! Despite being called CURSED, book six offers a little fun and a few positives along the way – alongside some dark and dastardly deeds, of course – as our heroes and villains slug it out, weaving their way through time...

I hope you enjoy this story as I raise my glass once again to you and to a brighter, more hopeful future for us all.

Thank you,
Stephen

Prologue

99.2 million years ago, Egypt
Dr Anne Hemmings watched and waited for Heidi's team to disappear before drawing her colleague's attention. Despite their air-conditioned environment, the equatorial sun beat down relentlessly on the black-hulled warship, causing Hemmings – or as Heidi would have it, 'Two' – to wipe perspiration from her brow.

Reid, otherwise known as 'One', leaned over her shoulder, increasing her discomfort as he spoke too close to her ear. "Is that what I think it is? In AD2122? But that's ten years into our own future!"

"I know," Hemmings agreed, leaning away from the volume. "And this one is not in Germany, either. It is due south, just a few kilometres east of what will one day be El-Shaikh Ebada in Egypt."

The balding man's forehead wrinkled in thought. Almost reverentially, he whispered, "What the hell does it mean?"

"That Heidi shot a lot of dinosaurs?" Hemmings replied, fatuously. Seeing the look of disapproval on Reid's face, she relented. "Those animals must range further than we've observed. I suppose it could mean we have more than one chance at this?" She let go a deep sigh, blowing out her cheeks. "At the moment, all we can do is log the date and coordinates, east of El-Shaikh Ebada and see what transpires. We have been tinkering with time and space for months now—"

"To save the lives of our expedition, and quite possibly the human race," Reid interjected.

Hemmings spun her seat to look him in the eye. "Yes, and we succeeded in that. But an entire world was not enough for Heidi Schultz, was it?"

{excerpt from REROUTE | Book 4}

Chapter 1 | Strange Palaeontology

Tim Norris disliked heights. They made him queasy. Nevertheless, he forced himself to look down. The drop yawed before him, making his vision swim. He took a step back from the cliff edge, instead leaning cautiously forward, so that he could still see. Below him – he groaned, covering his eyes with a hand – a good *fifty metres* below him, he could see the giant skull of Spinosaurus aegyptiacus. It was no more than three metres from where Woodsey stood, watching. He could not see his friend, merely the top of his friend's broad umbrella. Tim could not see what Woodsey was holding, either. It might have been a pick or a hammer. However, he suspected, rather uncharitably, that it was more likely a tall glass, containing something cool and refreshing.

Next to Woodsey, Morecombe Hetfield dug industriously into the cliff face. Commander retired, the man was well into his eighties, yet worked like a Trojan, despite the desert heat. Clearly displaying the benefits of an extraordinary healthcare programme, he appeared more like a fit fiftyish, these days.

Over the last decade, Tim had become close friends with Hetfield and his wife, Dr Kelly Marston. Now in the year AD2122, he led them, Woodsey, and a gaggle of students at a dig out in the Egyptian desert, near El-Shaikh Ebada.

He looked down on them, smiling as Kelly browbeat her husband to replace his hat – it had fallen from Hetfield's head again and hung uselessly on a strap about his neck. After fifty years together in the

Cretaceous, Hetfield and Marston had finally decided to tie the knot, enlisting the then-Captain Douglas to do the honours. Tim remembered their wedding. It seemed so long ago now.

He chuckled as the old man complained. He was too high up to catch the words, but he could guess. At twenty-six, Tim would have been one of the youngest ever professors of palaeontology – in his own timeline. Here, he *was* the youngest. Everything had changed since that day on a bleak hill in Northumberland.

A pang tore at his heart. It always did when memories of Rose and Henry, and everyone they left behind, resurfaced. Ten years on, yet he remembered them all so often; still hoped, one day, to reach back in time and bring them home.

Home? He shook his head at that thought, too. He could hardly remember his old home, the concrete jungle, growing out of dead soil on a world almost completely overbuilt and overused. Today was November the 5th, Guy Fawkes Day, known to others as Bonfire Night, but there would be no fireworks or celebration a quarter of the world away in Great Britain that evening. The festival now existed only in the memories of a few; just one of innumerous changes to overtake the *New World*'s crew in recent years. Adjustment had been a steep curve for all of them, still to level out, even after all this time. Tim removed his own broad-brimmed hat and wiped his brow as he glanced up at the perfect blue sky – a deception of coolness not in any way evident down on the ground.

They had chosen to dig through the winter months for the comfort of their students and staff – though in the Egyptian desert 'winter' and 'comfort' were often comparative terms. A school party, exploring the hills due east of El-Shaikh Ebada and the Nile, had discovered the fossilised dinosaur remains earlier that year. A recent rockslide had revealed elements of the skull, hind leg and tail.

In the New World Order, under which they now lived, borders and territories carried less meaning than they had in the world he remembered. Tim's students were drawn from universities, not only from all over the world, but from human colonies on *other* worlds, too. If successfully retrieved, the fossils would probably remain within one of Cairo's museums, available for study by scientists from anywhere – that was how it was done these days. Borders were more about demarcation of local district responsibility than national interest in this time. Tim had little patience with politics; he simply believed it proper and respectful to the finds themselves that they remain close to where they had lain for so long.

In his mind, he flicked back through the pages of his short life. To this day, he could not quite believe the world in which he now found himself. So strange and yet, and yet...

A cry from below brought him back to the moment. He risked another lean over the craggy precipice to see what was happening. Down on the desert sands, his people were scurrying like ants. Something was wrong. Tim sighed, pocketing the small find he had just picked up from the shale around his feet. He replaced his hat and retraced his steps, back down the rough scrambleway he had used to climb the bluff. Scouting for further fossils would just have to wait.

Woodsey was so shocked he dropped his glass. So shocked, in fact, that he did not even notice he had dropped his glass. Throwing his man-brolly aside, he ran to Morecombe Hetfield, helping the old man back to his feet. "What happened?"

Hetfield opened his mouth but could find nothing to say.

"It's gone!" Kelly called out, cutting straight to the heart of the situation.

A rumble started from the sandstone edifice. "Back away!" Woodsey yelled to the whole team, pulling the old couple with him as he retreated from the dig. Stones were falling. As yet, they were small, but Woodsey made sure everyone got well back. "What the hell...?"

"Dr Wood, what's going on?" asked one of their students, nervously.

"I'd like to know that, too!" Tim called as he scrambled and jumped down the last few metres. He ran away from the cliff to arrive breathlessly at Woodsey's side.

"Oh, mate. Am I glad *you're* here."

"Don't worry, I got down OK. The rockslide was minor."

Woodsey's expression clouded.

"I made it down safely," Tim elucidated.

Woodsey's expression cleared. "Oh, right. Yeah, nah, what I meant was, they can all hassle *you* about it now."

"About what exactly?" Tim was about to round crossly on his most annoying friend, when he stopped dead, staring. The skull jutting from the cliff face – once almost as long as a man was tall – was gone. As were all the other fossils and finds from the seam.

Hetfield was shaking his head in disbelief, still to find his voice. Eventually, he managed, "It vanished. Right in front of me."

"What did you do?" Tim asked, not sure what else to say.

"Hey, it was none o' my doin', son! I was chipping delicately around the premaxilla and up to the nares, just like you showed me, and the damned thi—"

Kelly tugged his arm. "*Language,* Hetfield!"

"—darned thing, disappeared! But that wasn't an end to it. I fell forward into a hole in the rock – that felt way too much like a sarcophagus, I can tell you – then the damned roc—"

"Mor!"

"—*darned* rock regrew itself and spat me back out, right on my a—"

"*Morecombe!*"

"It did what?" Tim asked in disbelief, but rather than wait for an answer he ran over to the base of the cliff to inspect the dig, or lack thereof, for himself.

"Dude... falling stones!" Woodsey knew his friend of old. He dashed in to pull Tim back before the falling debris dashed his valuable brains *out.*

"What do you think you're doing?" As Tim snapped at Woodsey, with little grace, a large stone hit the ground with a *thump-clack,* right where he had been standing to study the rock face. "Oh."

"Give it a minute, mate."

"Er... yeah, thanks."

"Professor Norris!" The cry came from one of their large field tents, out on the level sand about twenty metres behind them. Tim and Woodsey looked at one another. Without a word, they ran for the tent with Hetfield and Marston chuffing along after them.

Tim arrived first. Pulling the canvas aside, he burst into the finds tent to see one of his students sitting on the floor, looking like she had fallen on her backside, with hands still out in front, as if holding a non-existent basketball. "Simba! What is it? What's happened?"

Woodsey stopped just inside the tent flap and groaned. "Oh, *man.*"

Tim, kneeling at the young girl's side, spun to look up. Following Woodsey's gaze, he noted their preparation table was bare, but for a few tools and name tags. He helped the student to her feet. "Are you OK?"

"I... I..." Simba stuttered.

"It's alright, take your time."

"I'd just given the three phalanges and ungual from the middle toe of the left foot a rough clean. I... I was about to wrap them for transport when..."

"They disappeared," Tim finished for her, resignedly.

He looked to Woodsey, who glanced meaningfully at the packing crates and flight cases where most of their finds were stored prior to removal. Tim nodded and they picked a couple of the smaller cases at random. Placing them on the table, they opened them, holding their breath. "Crap!" Tim cursed.

"All gone, huh?" asked Hetfield from the door.

Woodsey nodded sombrely, while Tim placed his head in his hands, shaking it slowly. "You know what this means?"

"Yeah," Woodsey replied with a deep sigh. "No way we're gonna blag next year's budget now."

"No, you numpty! The only way these bones could have vanished..." He stopped, suddenly aware of an audience gathering at the entrance. Almost the whole team had arrived and were trying to barge their way into the tent. He nodded for Woodsey to follow him back outside. "Mor, Kelly, would you come too, please?"

They left the baffled students exchanging their own missing dinosaur stories and stepped just out of earshot.

"Those bones haven't vanished," Tim began.

"I'd beg to differ, mate," Woodsey scoffed.

"What do *you* think's happened, Tim?" asked Marston.

"They haven't vanished – they've moved to a new and unknown location."

"Of course, that's a completely different scenario, right there," Woodsey muttered.

"Will you shut up and listen a minute?" Tim spoke hotly and then lowered his voice again. "What I mean is, they still exist, just not here. Not any more."

Woodsey's eyebrows rose in bafflement. "Ergo?" he encouraged.

"*Ergo,* something must have happened in the Cretaceous to change that creature's destiny. Whatever it was must have caused it to die elsewhere. It was just a shot in a billion that we were around to see it."

"Oh, *man,*" Woodsey groaned again, rubbing his eyes wearily.

Tim nodded seriously. "I reckon I might be able to put a name to who's behind it, too."

"You suspect someone?" asked Hetfield.

Tim nodded again, closing his eyes against his worst fears.

"But I like it here," Woodsey continued with annoyance. "The air's good, there's plenty of room for everybody, and the food's great. I mean, *really* great. Just the other day, I—"

Tim cut him off. "I'm going to have to take this up with the one man who might be able to help us – to even understand it, for that matter."

Hetfield nodded. "James Douglas."

Woodsey looked astonished. "You're leaving us?"

Tim returned his look with one of his own. "Er... this is quite important, you know?"

"But what am I gonna do out here with a dozen research students, no dinosaur, and only a limited supply of beer?"

Tim searched his pockets. "Ah, here it is." He produced a small fossil, almost triangular in shape with a slight curve to one edge. It was just the tip of a large tooth. The serrations at the front and back were clear – it was the tooth of a carnivore.

"Carcharodontosaurus tooth? Or part of one?" hazarded Woodsey.

"Very good, *Doctor* Wood," Tim mocked.

Woodsey pulled a face.

"But you're quite right. I found it up on top of the bluff, right above our di— above where our dig used to be. Somewhere up in those hills is another apex predator, quite possibly a Carcharodontosaurus saharicus, as you surmised. Now, clearly, I've got to report this situation to someone, but in the meantime, I'd be very grateful if you'd keep those kids busy and not let them dwell on this."

"Some of those 'kids' are older than you, dude," Woodsey reminded him.

Tim scowled. "*Everyone* must seem mature in your world, Woodsey. At the moment we're a complete bust, so will you do me a favour and go and find us another dinosaur, please?"

1st August AD 2113, Washington DC, nine years earlier
Major-General Lisa Green was used to late night meetings at the White House; they were par for the course when she was posted close to home – and usually happened via video link when she was not. However, this meeting was different. Something very like it had happened the year before, during the summer of 2112. Sat in the very same leather chair, she had not even been able to recall why she was there. It had been something important, she remembered that much – no one ever dropped by the White House to discuss the weather[1] – but what that something was, she no longer had any idea. Chief of Staff, five-star General Marvin Faulkner had seemed equally confused at the time, and that was fortunate. Had he not, her vacant spell might well have earned her a post peeling spuds in Alaska.

"Lisa?" asked Faulkner.

"Sir?" she replied, rallying from her déjà vu.

"We've been asked to provide military support for the new colony out in the Perseus Transit. Apparently, our latest near-Earth is full of dangerous predators. I guess our wormhole specialists struck out again on finding planet Eden."

Faulkner rarely made light of anything, so Green stayed on topic. "They want us to interfere with the ecosystem there, sir?"

"No, no. Just provide some protection and support while those folks build their enclosures and safe zones. The colonists are a pretty tough breed – I don't need to tell you that, I know you've family out among the stars. They'd normally deal with the problem themselves, but apparently, some of these creatures are as big as dinosaurs – who knew? We're to take all care to subdue any creatures deemed a threat and hold them, until the project's up and running and their structures can protect our people. Then the creatures are to be set free, hopefully unharmed. You handled something similar recently, I believe."

Before she could answer, Faulkner's aide, Lieutenant-Colonel Davis Jonson, knocked and entered in a state of some agitation.

---

1   Unless that weather had a proper noun.

Surprised, Faulkner asked, "What is it, Davis? And didn't I ask you to fix us a drink?"

"Sir?"

Faulkner ran a hand over his balding pate, his face showing impatience. "Never mind. What have you?"

"Sir, we've just received a message from our people in Great Britain. Apparently, a whole bunch o' folks just appeared on a mountain somewhere, near the Anglo-Scottish border."

Faulkner looked to Green, who shrugged. He looked back to the colonel. "What's that to us?"

"No, sir. I mean literally *appeared.* They stepped out of a wormhole, sir. I've dispatched Special Agent Hemmings to liaise with the local authorities. She was already in the country, sir, and will report back directly to this office."

Faulkner blinked, ignoring the colonel's last. "They can do that? Travel without a ship? Why wasn't I informed? We don't want just anybody dropping in at the kitchen table, damn it! Find out who felt it wasn't worth passing that along to me and bust 'em down to their socks. There are such things as beachheads, you know? Now, which of the colonies did they travel from?"

Jonson was shaking his head. "No, sir. They're not from *any* of our off-world colonies. They're not from anywhere, sir."

"Make sense, Colonel, it's been a hell of a day—"

"They stepped through a wormhole?" Green interrupted.

"Yes, ma'am."

"Well then, from *where?*"

"Ma'am, sir, you're not gonna believe this."

6th November AD2122, United Nations Aeronautics and Space Administration, Canaveral USA

Douglas looked up from his desk. "Come." The door slid silently aside to reveal a jet-lagged and dishevelled-looking Tim Norris. He leapt to his feet. "Tim! Ye made excellent time. Ah didnae expect ye until tomorrow. Come in, have a seat."

The younger man's face lit up with pleasure, dispelling some of his weariness. "Captain, it's so good to see you again."

Douglas grinned broadly. "That's Training Director Douglas, now. And shouldn't Ah be calling ye Professor Norris?" He held the young man at arms' length. "Your mum told me about your professorship. Ah'm so proud of ye, laddie. Just call me James, eh?"

Tim grinned, too. "You'll always be Captain to me, sir."

They embraced and Douglas ushered Tim to a seat before taking his own. Waving a hand over a sensor in his desk, Douglas ordered some English tea from his aide. "Ah have it flown in." He winked. "Not everything's changed. The tea here tastes like dishwater recycled through the cat."

Douglas worked from a tall, diamond-shaped building, its corners honouring points of the compass. His was a tenth-floor office in the southern tip and had a three-metre-high, curved outer wall that was completely transparent. Tim was amazed by the spectacle. Not to mention the wormhole-capable spacecraft being tugged about on the tarmac below, like commercial airliners. A kilometre to his right in the southwest, he could see the Indian River, and in the distance on the left, southeast, was the Atlantic. "This is *some* office. What a view!"

Douglas chuckled. "Aye, it's a far cry from ma quarters aboard the *New World,* sure enough. Plusher, but never better, no' for me."

"It's a far cry from my tent in the desert, I know that!" Tim laughed. "The one I share with Woodsey and his snoring."

"Ah'm glad you boys stuck together." A cloud crossed Douglas' face. "Ah still think about the others..."

Tim nodded. "Me too."

"Anyhow, you were pretty vague over the comm. Can ye tell me now what it was ye needed to see me about? Not that yer visit wasnae welcome."

Tim opened his mouth to speak when the door slid open behind him. Pushing a trolley loaded down with snacks and refreshments, Mary Hutchins puffed her way in, slightly older but no less cheerful. "Young Mr Norris, what a pleasure this is."

"Actually, it's Professor Norris now, Mary," explained Douglas.

"*Nooo.* Wow! Bet your mom's so proud. And you so young, too. How is she?"

Tim's comm buzzed in his pocket. "Sorry, it's Woodsey. We've a bit of a situation at the moment. I'd better take this, forgive me, Mary. Woodsey? Yeah, it's me. Everything OK over there?"

"Not really, mate. Simba's gone missing."

"Missing? How?"

"Dunno, mate. She was last seen walking a little way into the desert. That was last night, just after dark."

"And no one queried her?"

"Dude, when someone takes themself off into the desert with a shovel, you don't make them explain themself."

"Fair enough, but surely someone noticed when she didn't return?"

"They turned in early. We all did. You know how it is, after a day walking and digging in the sun. Everybody had a couple o' cold ones and went out like a light. We didn't realise she was missing 'til dawn. We've been looking for her since."

"Dawn? And you're only telling me now?"

"Couldn't get you, mate. Assumed you were in the air."

"Right. Sorry. Have you informed the authorities?"

In his peripheral vision, Tim could see Douglas' and Mary's growing concern.

"I was just about to, but thought I'd give you one more go before I tried."

"Call them straight away, please. And, Woodsey, make sure nobody goes anywhere alone."

"They won't like that."

"I couldn't care less about their modesty. You've got the keys for the weapons case, haven't you? Good. Break out the stunners. I know we haven't come across any large predators near our dig, but we'd better not take any chances. No one goes anywhere without a companion and at least a weapon between them, got it?"

"Yeah, yeah. Don't worry, mate. She probably just got turned around in the dark and woke up somewhere unfamiliar – you know what the terrain's like here. I'll get the local authorities to help, though."

"OK. Keep me posted as soon as you hear anything, OK?"

"Yeah, yeah. Over and out, dude."

The line went dead. Tim let go an exasperated sigh.

"Problems?" asked Douglas.

"Maybe."

"Anything to do with why ye're here?"

Tim sat heavily, covering his mouth with a hand. He looked shocked. "My God, I hope not, Captain."

Mary left the men with their refreshments. "It sure was nice to see you again, Tim. I hope you find your friend."

"Thanks, Mary. I'll give Mum your best."

When the door sealed behind her, Douglas took a sip and pushed his cup aside. "OK, let's hear it, son."

Woodsey called in the local law to ask for their help. Upon realising the missing girl had no water or supplies with her, the officer in charge wasted no time in calling for air support. Within half an hour, two fast, military spec helicopters from Cairo roared overhead and split up to begin a search pattern.

"This is looking serious," Hetfield noted with concern.

Woodsey had enough concern of his own. "Mor, she could be anywhere. The wind really got going last night, wiping out all tracks from yesterday."

"Come on, son. We'll find her."

"I hope so, mate. I really thought we'd have her back by now. We've been at it all day and now we've lost the light."

"Those choppers will be searching with infrared and who knows what else. They'll find her. These local rescue boys the police called in are no slouches, either. Come on, let's join one of their teams and keep busy."

Woodsey nodded silently, following the old man. Simba had been missing for a little over twenty hours. He had to keep reminding himself that their time in the Cretaceous was many years ago, that this was a very different world, but after losing so many people the way they had, any wild place brought it all back to him. This world was full of empty places and, try as he might, the memories resurfaced as the sun dipped in the west.

Woodsey's grasp on Egyptian Arabic included: hello, my name is Woodsey; beach; water; ketchup; and, most crucially, can you direct me to the nearest bar, please? Fortunately, most of the search and rescue people were accustomed to tracking down foreign tourists in difficulty and had at least a smattering of English. The two men soon caught up with them. They were about to beg a ride in one of the four-by-fours that would take them further afield, when the officer in charge hailed them on the run.

"Dr Wood, wait!"

Woodsey stepped away from the vehicle. "Master Sergeant, have you found something?"

The policeman slowed to a stop. "You'd better come with me, sir. Your friend, too."

They fell in behind Master Sergeant Apep Badawi, following him back to his vehicle. "Sirs, one of the helicopters has already found evidence of your friend."

Woodsey and Hetfield exchanged a glance. "Evidence?" the older man asked.

Badawi nodded seriously. "I'm afraid it's bad news, gentlemen."

Woodsey swallowed hard against the bile rising in his throat. "What have you found, Master Sergeant?"

"A leg, sir. It was a few metres above the ground, in a cleft between the rocks. It is no wonder you missed it when you searched the valley floor."

Seeing that his young companion was rapidly becoming overwhelmed, Hetfield asked, "Do we know what happened yet?"

"It looks like an animal attack, sir. We may know more when the police surgeon arrives."

Woodsey held his head in his hands. "Not again. Not again..."

Badawi looked at him askance. "This has happened before?"

"A long time ago, Master Sergeant," Hetfield smoothed over the question. "Back when we were *working* in South America. But like I say, that was a *very* long time ago."

That did the trick. As with most police officers, Badawi had enough to deal with on his own patch without worrying about the rest of the world. "The thing is," he went on to explain, "all the large predators live in or around the Nile. We can't understand what could have done this up in the hills."

"Jackals?" suggested Hetfield.

Badawi mulled the suggestion over. "There are a few about, but they don't usually come near groups of humans – they've learned to avoid us. If they had, you'd have heard them. They're not subtle when they hunt. And then there was the location of the... remains."

Their awkward musings were interrupted by the first helicopter's return. The pilot landed a courteous hundred metres away, so as not to destroy their tents with his downwash. The three ran over to it as the machine powered down. Two men jumped from the rear hatch, carrying something wrapped in a towel. A floodlight activated, illuminating their immediate vicinity as they conversed briefly with Badawi in Arabic. When he turned back to Woodsey and Hetfield, the policeman wore a perplexed frown. "Gentlemen, I'm afraid I will need you to see this. As I have already told you, we have part of a leg. From what we can tell, it belonged to a woman. Perhaps you might recognise the shoe or clothing to help us identify the unfortunate?"

Woodsey swallowed again, but nodded stiffly. One of the men from the chopper unwrapped the bloody towel to reveal a right leg. Woodsey gagged and turned away.

Hetfield patted him on the shoulder. "It's OK, son. Do you recognise the boot?"

Woodsey shook his head.

"The trouser leg?" Hetfield tried again.

The young New Zealander took a deep breath and steeled himself for a second look. "The trousers are the same as the ones Simba was wearing."

"You're sure?" asked Hetfield.

He nodded.

"And yet you did not recognise the boot?" asked Badawi. "It would really help if we knew for sure who the victim was."

"I'm sure," Woodsey confirmed. "At least, I recognise the trouser."

Hetfield still appeared unsure.

"You think I'm wrong?"

"No," the older man said, hesitantly. "It's just that if you didn't recognise the shoe, then..."

Woodsey sighed with exasperation. "A little respect, mate?"

Hetfield blinked with surprise.

Woodsey rolled his eyes. "I never bothered looking at her *shoes*, Mor. But I may've, purely by accident, noticed her legs and pert li'l... y' know, as she walked away. Just once or twice, I mean. Nothing pervy, just admiring God's work—"

"Alright, alright, son. Stop digging." Hetfield threw a fatherly arm around his shoulder. "She was a pretty young thing, I get it.

Master Sergeant, is there any chance she may still be alive? I know it's unlikely with an injury like that, but..."

Badawi could see the hope in the men's eyes and his expression softened. "I think it's unlikely, gentlemen. I'm sorry. And, unfortunately, it leaves us with an even more pressing concern. Clearly, there is a man-eater out there and we must find it. Are all your people in one place back at your camp, Dr Wood?"

"Most are. Some are still out with your search and rescue people."

Badawi stepped closer to the helicopter and spoke with the pilot. Presently, he returned to Hetfield and Woodsey. "I have ordered everyone back here to set up a base camp. The helicopters will continue an aerial search, while we wait for military backup." He spoke to the men who found the leg, again, in Arabic. They shrugged noncommittally, so he turned back to Woodsey.

"Dr Wood, you are a palaeontologist, I understand. Do you have much knowledge of animal, erm... animal..."

"Anatomy?" Woodsey suggested, helpfully.

"Yes, thank you. Animal anatomy."

"Some. Why do you ask? And your English is the dog's gonads, by the way."

"Er... thank you. I wonder if you would take a close look at the bite pattern and tell me what you believe this creature might be?"

Woodsey shrugged. "I'll do my best, Master Sergeant, but I'm not an expert of Egyptian zoology – not from this period, anyway." He took another deep breath and knelt beside the severed leg. Pulling a torch from his pocket, he studied what it helped to think of as 'the sample'. What he saw alarmed him still further.

Instinctively, he stood and looked west, towards the Nile. He could not see the world's longest river through the darkness, but knew it slid by less than a kilometre away, heavy with life-giving nutrients and life-taking reptiles. "Master Sergeant, for what it's worth, I believe this to be the bite of a croc. A real big 'un, too."

Badawi was shaking his head. "This cannot be. The remains were discovered up in the hills. There are no crocodiles up there, Dr Wood. Besides, I have seen wounds inflicted by crocodiles. These teeth marks are too large. Surely, you are mistaken."

Again, Woodsey could only shrug. "'S what it looks like, mate, only..."

Badawi looked at him quizzically. "Go on, Doctor."

Woodsey blew out his cheeks. "It's just that you're right, it's *too* big."

Hetfield turned to him, very slowly. "*How* big?"

"Well, as big as..." Woodsey tailed off. "No, no, no. You don't think...?"

"That our disappearing act today has some bearing on this?" Hetfield completed. "Son, I sure as hell hope not."

Woodsey's nerves were at breaking point, and he snapped, "Look, that's impossible, *OK?* That thing was a hundred million years in the ground."

"I would be grateful if you gentlemen would tell me just what it is you are talking about?" Badawi asked, showing understandable asperity himself now.

Woodsey sighed. "Look, dude, you're not gonna believe this..."

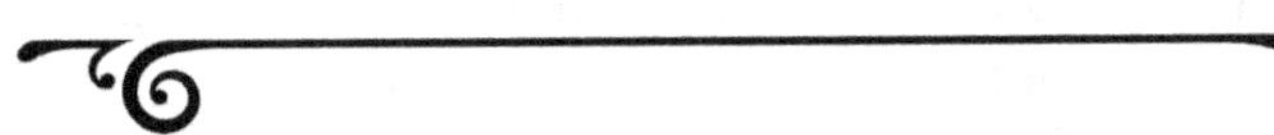

"Ye're telling me the fossilised remains of a fifty-foot dinosaur vanished right in front of your eyes?" asked Douglas. "Had ye been working in the sun without a hat?"

"I wish it were that simple, Cap— James. I was the only one who didn't actually *see* it disappear. Now, if it were just Woodsey, I'd simply think he'd been helping himself to the sauce, but my whole team saw it. Morecombe Hetfield fell into the hole left by the remains he'd just been working on. He said the rock sort of... *healed* itself, flinging him back across the ground. I brought this to you, James, because the only reason I can think of for those remains vanishing into thin air, would be a change in the timeline – more specifically, *someone* changing the timeline."

Douglas stared.

"James?"

The older man sighed deeply. "So she's catching up with us, is she?"

Tim placed his elbows on Douglas' desk and ran his fingers through his untidy hair. When he raised his head, his dark-eyed fatigue seemed to have aged him. "I was hoping against hope you'd have another theory that might explain this, Captain."

Douglas stared bleakly down at his cold tea. "Ah thought... at least, Ah hoped she'd met her maker when that dinosaur attacked."

"You're referring to the Sigilmassasaurus that caught Hiro's brother, Aito, as we left Cretaceous Britain behind at Crater Lake," Tim expanded, recalling the memory. "If Heidi is manipulating time again, what on earth can we do about it?"

"Aye. What indeed?" Douglas held in his secrets one last moment, as was often his way when mulling through difficult facts. "Tim, when Ah resigned my commission, Ah did it for two reasons. Firstly, and most importantly, so that Ah could marry my wife – not that Jill's here that often at the moment, what with the new colonies we're setting up all over the galaxy. The second was that a government job of this type comes with certain perks and inroads to the powers that be. Many of our people have found senior positions – so unique and valuable was our experience." He studied Tim seriously. "Ah know you can be trusted, laddie, but Ah have to warn you that what Ah'm about to say must not leave this room. Understand?"

Tim nodded. "You have my word."

"Thank you. We knew that if Heidi survived whatever trials they suffered in the past, she might yet get up to nae good. Ah made my new superiors aware of the situation and its full ramifications when Ah took this job – that and everything else we'd experienced. When we made our sharp exit from Cretaceous Britain, as you say, she was a spent force with but one capital ship remaining of her fleet, and no wormhole capable vessels. We hoped her people would simply..." He searched for an appropriate analogy, or euphemism at best.

"Expire?" Tim suggested.

Douglas smiled humourlessly. "Good enough. We hoped she would vanish into the rocks of the world's history, as it were, but we planned for something like this, just in case."

Tim leaned forward, all tiredness leaving him.

Douglas leaned forward, too, conspiratorially. "We've built a ship."

"Dr Wood, we no longer believe in mummies' curses, or monsters," Badawi stated scornfully. "Why do you keep looking over there, into the darkness?"

"Because, Master Sergeant, that is where the Nile is. I *so* badly want to be wrong about this, but just in case I'm right, I suggest searching the river for anything – shall we say – out of the ordinary?"

Badawi studied them. "So, both of you were among those people in the news ten years ago – the ones who arrived out of thin air?"

"Yes. Us, my wife, Kelly, and our team leader, Professor Tim Norris," Hetfield expanded. "Our students know about our past, but little of the detail. We tend not to discuss it, except among ourselves. We found, long ago, that comparisons can upset people."

Badawi had a habit of tapping a finger on his cheek when thinking. Eventually, he asked, "You've seen these creatures in real life?"

Hetfield chuckled lightly. "Son, I lived with 'em for nigh on fifty years."

"Don't you think – how can I put this – that your experiences may have led you to leap to such a fantastic rationale?"

Hetfield and Woodsey caught one another's eye. This was old territory. "We didn't imagine it, Master Sergeant," the old man replied, coolly. "It accounted for more than half my life."

"Look," Woodsey reasoned, "if there was anything that big roaming the hills at this moment, surely your aerial search would have turned it up by now. Even if it's just an innocent crocodile, it would be hard to miss."

"I have already told you, Dr Wood, there are no crocodiles in the hills. I have lived here my whole life, and I can assure you—"

"So there's no harm in looking in the river, then, is there?"

Hetfield grinned. "He's got you there, son."

Woodsey pulled out his comm. "Look at these photos. I took them just the day before yesterday. This one clearly shows Mor here working on the Spino's head. Oh..."

Hetfield craned to see. "What is it?"

"I seem to have a nice shot of you leaning over nothing, mate. Holding a really tiny chisel."

"What?" Hetfield snatched the comm to check for himself.

"Nice hair, by the way."

"Woodsey! This is serious. Have you any others?" Hetfield handed back the comm.

Badawi leaned in to see for himself, curiosity piqued. "All of these photos show only your dig team, Doctor."

Woodsey sighed with exasperation. "Well, doesn't that tell you something?"

Badawi looked blank.

"Here, study them more closely. Everyone in these pictures is either holding or working on something – something that is no longer there. Do you think we're *all* crazy? A troupe of palaeontological mime artists touring the deserts of the world to entertain the lizards, perhaps?"

"I never said you were crazy, Dr Wood." Badawi pointed to the comm. "*This* picture does not seem to show anyone holding anything, or working on anything, just two rather attractive young ladies wearing very short shorts."

"What?" Woodsey squinted. "It's in the foreground, dude!"

"What is?"

"Well, nothing now, obviously. Look, that's not important!" He bristled. "There are no *recreational* shots on this device, OK?"

Badawi gave him a smile and a look as old as the missing fossils.

Woodsey squirmed. "There are very *few* recreational shots on this device, OK? Up until two days ago, it was full of photos of fossils being worked on by our people."

Hetfield snapped his fingers. "Got it! Master Sergeant, you must remember the school kids who found the remains sticking out of the cliff over there – back in the spring. That's what brought us down here."

Badawi considered this. "Could you have been digging in the wrong place?"

"Son," Hetfield's patience was stretching, "I know you're only doing your job, and I've never been a policeman, but wasn't it Sherlock Holmes who said 'when you've eliminated everything else, whatever's left must be the truth' – or some such?"

The master sergeant spoke into his comm in his native tongue. "I have asked one of our choppers to leave their planned search pattern and survey the Nile for ten miles in either direction."

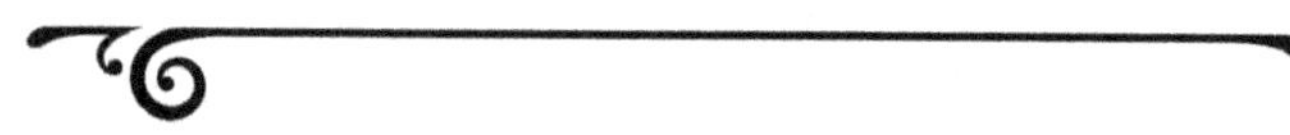

Tim gaped. "Wow. Now *that* is a ship."

Douglas chuckled. "She's the first of a completely new class, originally earmarked to become a ship of the line. But as she's currently

the most advanced vessel in the fleet, Ah nabbed her for our purposes –
should a mission to the past become necessary. It took a little persuasion,
but UNASA saw it ma way in the end."

"What's she called?"

Douglas tugged his ear, a little embarrassed. "She *was* registered
as the UNS *São Paulo.*"

"Was?"

"Aye. Before you say it, Ah know it's meant to be bad luck to
change a ship's name, but then Ah thought... what the hell, and sought
a special dispensation from the UN."

Tim wore the beginnings of a smile. "Go on."

Douglas beamed. "Laddie, say hello to the U-*N*-S *New World.* Is
she no' fine?"

Tim placed his hands together, prayer-like, touching index fingers
to his lips as he shook his head gently. He answered breathily, "She's
perfect." Memories flooded back from the first time he saw the original
USS *New World,* standing at his mother's side all those years ago, not
far from where he stood now.

"And the name?" asked Douglas. "Not too much of an indulgence?"

"Everything we endured, everything we *survived* was only possible
because of the *New World.* She carried us there and brought us most
of the way home, sacrificing herself to save our lives. If we must go
back there, I wouldn't want to travel in anything *but* the *New World.*"

Douglas looked relieved.

"What is it?"

"Ah've just been having this recurring dream about young Mr
Wood going around calling her the *'New' New World.*" He shuddered.
"It'll pass."

Tim laughed. "It's *Doctor* Wood now – turns out that when he
applies himself, he's not as stupid as he looks – but you're right. That's
exactly what he'll do. If I tell him not to, it'll only make things worse,
so we'll just have to shut our ears." His expression turned serious.
"That's if we can justify involving him at all. This situation seems to
be getting more dangerous all the time."

Douglas grunted, noncommittal.

"James?"

"Well, the thing is, we may have to take everyone back with us.
Besides, we all agreed, remember?"

Tim looked at him sharply. "But things were different then – they all have lives, now. Good lives. I don't want to drag my mum back into all this madness."

Douglas held up his hands in a calming gesture. "Believe me, Ah dinnae want that, either, but we may have no choice. If we do nothing, Ah've no doubt Heidi, or one of her cronies, will screw everything up, remaking the world in their own twisted image. What's happened to you in Egypt is proof that something's afoot, and it'll be just the tip of the spear, make no mistake. Of course, if we act, there's no guarantee things will go the way we hope. We could end up with a third timeline – and one much less favourable than this. What Ah'm saying, laddie, is that if we leave our friends behind, we may lose them forever. Now, don't misunderstand me, Ah don't mean that in a selfish sense. Obviously, that would cause us great pain, but Ah would happily shoulder it, if Ah thought their lives would continue on this much-improved course. No. What Ah'm worried aboot, is that we leave them behind and they cease to be."

Tim sagged, deflating. "Yet another paradox." He turned back to the ship. There was a lot to process, but it would have to wait. He changed the subject. "She certainly looks different from the original."

"She's no' had her final coat yet. Her armour's to be covered with a completely non-reflective, heat-resistant polymer. She'll be all but invisible."

"I notice she doesn't carry a Pod under her belly, either?"

"No, Tim. She's in one piece, but her holds and hangars are packed full of equipment for an all-out campaign. *This* ship also has life-support capability for many hundreds of passengers. She was built for one purpose and one purpose only – to save *this* world... although Ah do hate the carpets.

"Look, Ah'm not saying this timeline's perfect. We've lost much that only we few remember, but it's a hell of a lot better than the world we left behind. The population here is completely sustainable, there's plenty for everyone and nature is thriving. Somehow, our crash into 1558 allowed our race to learn from our mistakes. Ah owe it to Mother Sarah and Satnam Patel, and to all the others left behind, to make their sacrifice mean something. Saving this better world, this better timeline would seem about right – would ye no' agree? We left behind a world of fifty billion souls, plus a few thousand on Mars. Here, there are just *two* billion of us on the Earth and another six living among the stars. Ah can only believe that Geoff Lloyd – yes, even Geoff Lloyd – must have done a hell of a job in changing the future for all this to have come to pass, and yet there's virtually nothing written about them. But then, perhaps that's for the best. Who can say? Ours *was* a massive interference. Ah cannae imagine what it cost them, but Ah *can* fight for what they created."

Tim gave him a sideways look. "OK. Save the world – it's easy enough to get behind that, but just *how* is this new vessel to do that?"

"By going back to the Cretaceous and stopping whoever is responsible for mucking around with the timeline."

"And by 'stopping' them, you mean...?"

"Remove them from the game board altogether, if necessary. Though Ah still have hopes for a peaceful solution. We know from the actions of Captain Tobias Meritus, and others, that not all the people back there were bad. We may even find allies.

"As far as we can tell, Heinrich Schultz was killed when Del Bond blew up that ship, along with himself. The last time we saw Heidi, she was running from a dinosaur—"

"The Sigilmassasaurus brevicollis of the Spinosauridae family," Tim enhanced his previous description, absently.

Douglas smiled. "Ah'll bow to yer superior knowledge on that one. My point is, we dinnae really know who's running the show back there, but if we can capture them, and any acolytes they may have convinced, then so be it." His expression hardened. "If not, then Ah intend to wipe them out – *utterly.* Either way, they're going down – no more messing around."

"What about the other people there? As you say, not all were bad – at least, not all the way bad, James. Do you intend to leave them there?"

"Nae, laddie. The new ship is as big as she is because we have orders to bring them back here – all of them. We cannae afford this incursion into our past – never knowing if we'll suddenly disappear from existence or become someone else. This is it, and Ah intend to finish it."

"What if those people don't *want* to come back to the future?"

Douglas sighed. "This *New World* was built with many *secure* quarters, just in case they dinnae come quietly. We're going in with overwhelming force tae save everyone we can and remove them all from that time and place. When Ah leave the Cretaceous for the last time, Ah want tae know this timeline is secure – at least until 1558. That incursion must still happen."

Tim rubbed his eyes, tiredly. "I'm sorry, this is all mind blowing. So, at the end of the day, she's a warship and a prison ship." He turned to the older man, sorrowfully. "When will the violence ever end?"

"Hopefully, this time – but Ah doubt it," Douglas admitted sadly. "The human race has taken a better path in this timeline than we ever did, but people will never be able to leave evil alone."

"Has time really caught us up?"

Douglas placed a fatherly hand on the young man's shoulder. "Old Chronos is no' our enemy, laddie. That moniker belongs to the architects of all this mess, and this time we *will* stop them."

"When we arrived in this world and timeline," Tim began slowly, looking off into the middle distance, "we believed we were completely alone."

"Aye. I remember. Ah thought Ah'd doomed us all..."

0400 hours, Tuesday 1st August 2113, Cheviot Mountain, Northumberland, nine years earlier...
"This time I'm sure, it *is* a Tuesday," Singh announced.

Douglas gaped.

Beckett removed his rain hat and proceeded to batter Singh about the head with it.

"Ouch! Stop. Ow! Stop it."

"Mr Beckett." Douglas prised the historian away from the beleaguered pilot. "Sandy, your delivery really needs work. Can ye tell me *anything* else about this place?"

Singh backed out of Beckett's reach hopelessly, and then an idea struck him.

Douglas noticed and approached. "Sandy?"

"I couldn't find any digital signals – at least, that this device could read – so I'm switching to analogue." The device made a shrill tone, slipping in and out between white noise. Singh switched the audio off, until he had answers. His screen was indeed showing a range of analogue signals. He could make no sense of them, so he increased the gain. "Captain."

They huddled.

"In our timeline, much of the world's electronics are digital, as you know, but we still use – *used* – a surprising array of complementary analogue tech where it was appropriate. I'm getting a lot of readings on the analogue scale. Nothing like what I would have expected in 2113, but..."

"You think this time is, what? Less advanced?"

"Not necessarily, sir. There may be digital signals that work at frequencies we don't use, or it may just be that there's less chatter because there are fewer people. I don't have the equipment here to be sure. It could be anything, sir, but it *is* something. I mean, without completely recalibrating this device..."

"OK. Can we broadcast from your device, on one of the frequencies in use here?"

Singh bit his lip, thoughtfully. "Yes, sir. But what should we say? Hello, earthlings, we come in peace – actually, from just down the road, don't you know?"

"*Up* the road, in fact." Douglas smiled, hope rekindled. "But 'hello' is a good enough start. Perhaps followed by 'we seek assistance'?"

"I'll keep it as simple as possible, sir. Hello. Help. How's that?"

"Sounds like a pop song, maybe two, but it'll do. Carry on, Lieutenant." He turned away to address more than 150 terrified, dripping wet souls. "May Ah have yer attention, people, please. We've identified analogue signals that we believe originate from some form of electronic device or devices. Lieutenant Singh is sending a distress call to anyone who may be listening—"

"Whoa there!" Burnstein interrupted him. "Haven't you done enough damage?"

"If there *are* people here, Mr Burnstein," Douglas replied reasonably – the man had just lost his son, after all, "we will surely need their help."

"And look what happened last time we stuck our heads outdoors, huh? We stumbled right into the middle of Braveheart!"

"Original, or one of the remakes?" Singh asked conversationally while he worked.

"The history wasn't worth a damn in any of them," added Beckett.

"Gentlemen!" Douglas' temper was fraying; it had been a rough night.

"And that was when we still had an indoors to stick our heads outdoors of!" Burnstein shouted again.

"Mr Burnstein—" Douglas tried again.

"Interesting use of a preposition."

"Sandy!" Douglas turned to the crowd. "Mr Burnstein – everyone – we have no choice."

"It's too late now, anyway," shouted Gleeson. "Incoming!"

Douglas turned to follow the Australian's outstretched arm. Sure enough, there were lights in the sky and the unmistakable roar of approaching rocket motors. "Careful what you wish for, Douglas," he muttered to himself. "Everyone step back, off this plateau, let's give these guys room to land – come on, people, please."

"YOU HEARD THE CAPTAIN," The Sarge bellowed above the noise of the machines. "MOVE *IIIT!*"

There were five ships in all. The first was smallish, like a flying limousine, designed more for executive comfort than mountain rescue. The four larger vehicles were all alike. Bearing the unmistakable lines of military craft, they were wide in the belly, resembling Chinook helicopters, but without the rotors.

Baines drew close to Douglas. "I hope we've done the right thing, James. They're bristling with weapons."

"Would we react any differently?"

She shrugged. "Probably not." She turned to face him. "Good luck."

"To all of us."

The larger vessels landed noisily and immediately began disgorging troops, who ran to encircle the bedraggled intruders. Once all their men were in place, the smaller craft landed outside the circle.

A soldier approached from the ranks, insignia picking him out as an officer. He stopped five metres away from the huddling *New Worlders*. "Who's in charge here?"

"English," Baines whispered. "A good sign."

"Speak for yersel'," Douglas spoke out of the corner of his mouth. "Let's just hope Burnstein's Braveheart pop was way off the mark." He stepped forward. "Ah'm Captain Douglas. Ah lead these people. Who are you, sir?"

The officer saluted. "Colonel Brabham, United Nations, sir. Please come with me."

Douglas followed without question, falling in with the other's military bearing and efficient stride. The colonel led him to the smaller craft, just as the side hatch opened with a hydraulic *siss.*

A dark-suited young woman stepped out. In the bright moonlight, Douglas' heart skipped like he had just seen a ghost. *Calm down. It's just the light. Calm down.* The fifty-year-old ship's captain thought he had seen it all after the last few months. He thought he had.

Lights from the military vehicles suddenly lit the whole plateau like a sports arena and Douglas scrutinised the young woman again. "It *is* you. But how can this be?"

She was joined by a man and then another woman, who were now viewing her with a mixture of surprise and suspicion. "I've never met this man before," she explained.

With effort, Douglas tore his gaze from the woman to take in the other – what were they, ambassadors? Seeing their faces clearly now, under the bright lights, he fell to his knees, almost fainting, his voice no more than a husky whisper. "No. It's impossible."

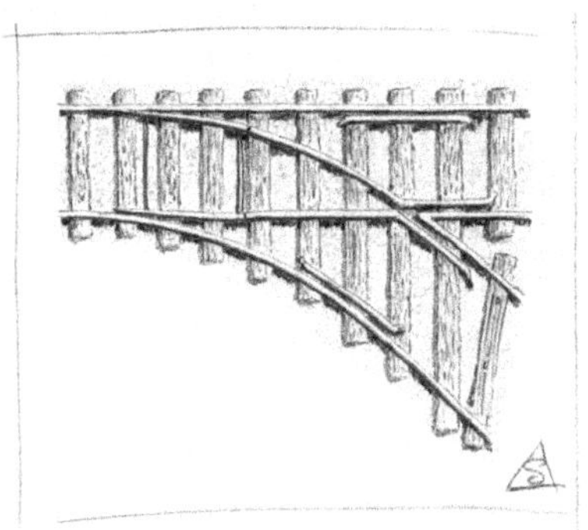

Chapter 2 | The Two Worlds

The explosion was loud, the grenade's effect, variable. There were thirteen Rugops in all, now split into three smaller groups as they executed a perfect pincer movement around the three men on motorcycles.

Lieutenant Devon had bowled his grenade towards the quintet that blocked their way ahead – the way that led back up to their camp and to safety. When Jansen gave him the grenade, he had warned how fleet of foot these creatures were, though it seemed they were also capable of coordinated hunting, more like African wild dogs. Of the five blocking their way, three ran from the bang, one stumbled, regaining its feet groggily, and the last – which happened to be closest to the detonation – appeared to have been stunned. This was also one of the largest, possibly a pack elder, and it was now directly blocking their escape route.

Jansen waited to see the effects of Devon's grenade before throwing his own. He flung it as best he could, left-handed, towards the two remaining animals. The beast that stumbled the first time was already moving away, its manner that of disorientation. As they closed, it became clear that the larger animal *had* been stunned by the first bang, because the second made it fall across their path.

"Oh, that's just great!" Aito shouted, pulling up. He turned to see the other Rugops closing the pincers behind them, staying well away from the giant crocodile still waiting at the river's shore.

"What now? We'll never ride up the walls of this cutting. It's a perfect ambush!"

The loud bangs had at least bred caution among the animals not directly affected. They still approached, but more slowly.

"Guys?" asked Devon tremulously.

"Into the trees," shouted Jansen.

"Are you crazy?" snapped Aito. "We can't ride through there, either."

"We'll have to run, then," Jansen bit back. "It'll be too tight for them to follow."

Aito's response to his suggestion was lost as the high-revving little petrol engine drowned out all further communication. Jansen shot off towards the treeline in a spray of dust and pebbles, dashing right of the downed Rugops, while it lay dazed and struggling to get up. He disappeared into the forest with a rustle of branches and what sounded like rapidly rising and falling scales played on a chainsaw.

Devon and Aito were left looking at one another. "He won't get far," said Aito. "He can't... can he?"

They both turned irresistibly in the saddle as they heard hissing and growling from behind. The pack had regrouped, their fear of the unexpected bangs dissipating with the smoke – they were hungry, and the smell of two-stroke was also losing its cautionary effect. A sudden roar caused the men to spin round again. The downed animal was making a more spirited attempt to get up. Devon gave Aito a look that could not have been more defeatist if he were trapped between two slices of bread, with a large tomato stuffed into his mouth.

Aito shook his head. "Death comes to us all, Lieutenant. Rather than wait, let's take a running kick at him. Come on!"

Revving their bikes, they followed Jansen's route towards the trees. The Rugops, still unable to rise, took a half-hearted snap at them. Aito, as good as his word, kicked out at the monstrous snout as he swerved past. The animal barely registered his boot in the face, the roar that followed them into the trees sounding more affronted than hurt.

They soon came across Jansen's machine, abandoned after becoming wedged between two saplings. "Where is he?" Devon craned around Aito to see further in, when a crashing from behind forced him to drop his own bike and run. He shot through the thick vegetation, hoping it would shroud his presence. He could feel it tearing at his clothes.

Aito took a slightly different route but tracked in roughly the same direction. "Devon? *Devon?* Where are you? I can't see a thing in here!"

A crash followed by a mini tirade gave up Devon's position. Aito vectored towards the swearing, while crashes of still greater magnitude and anger continued in the rear. He reached the lieutenant as Jansen also converged on him from the opposite direction. "Will you two shut the hell up!" he hissed urgently. Shaking his head, he hauled Devon to his feet and limped off in the general direction of their camp, ankle still weak from misadventure, after Heidi had deserted him following their recent robbery of dinosaur eggs. Then he had been running for his life from Deltadromeus; now he was running for his life from Rugops – for a second time. *I need a city break,* he thought, savagely.

The crashing that followed them was augmented by sporadic roars of frustration and even pain from the Rugops pack, a frustration the more aggressive members were clearly happy to spread around. They hunted like dogs, and it seemed they redirected their fear and agitation like reactive dogs, too. Snapping at anything close, even their own.

The three men quickly became entangled, struggling to find passage through the densest growth. Whichever direction they tried, the foliage only grew thicker. "So now what?" Devon asked, not really expecting an answer.

Jansen leaned around him to Aito in the rear. "Have we lost them?"

"Probably. We lost *us,* didn't we?"

"You'd rather go back?"

Aito swatted mosquitoes from his face, his expression thunderous. "Thank you, gentlemen, for inviting me along on this little geology trip of yours. And for warning us about how those things can hunt." His last was directed at Jansen.

"I hadn't seen that behaviour before," the soldier admitted. "I guess it makes sense, though. Heidi has become quite the expert on these creatures since she stole Norris' notes. She told me they're comparatively weak in the jaw, so it makes sense that they would hunt in force. It must have become a learned behaviour over time."

"Like in *our* Africa," suggested Devon, "where smaller canines hunt the same territory as lions that are – individually, at least – vastly superior. Yet the dogs have a higher success rate."

"Exactly. So, you know your animals?"

"I know my hunters." Devon grinned. "I'm a weapons and tactics specialist, remember?"

"Fascinating," Aito concluded with some asperity. "I thought you might be, by the expert way you handled that grenade."

"What? I'm not left-handed, OK?"

Aito violently batted at a scorpion that had fallen onto his shoulder. Shuddering, he rounded on them. "You know, we really must book the same resort again next year. Or maybe we'll try that little place with the snakes, huh?"

"Now we're semi-secure, we could call for help," Devon suggested, hopefully.

"How will they extract us from in here?" Jansen tried to gesture around him, but there wasn't room.

Aito sighed deeply. "Well, this is our lot then, Mr Jansen. We're here and we're stuck here, until those monsters go away, so you may as well tell us your plan for saving the world."

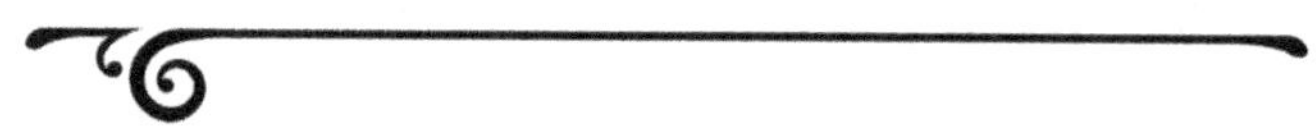

Commander Ally Coleman opened a second channel to her communications officer, asking him to close the encrypted connection from the *Heydrich*. Coleman knew little of Dr Anne Hemmings, other than she was one of the white-coated geniuses that had gotten them all into their current situation. The secretive nature of her call had taken Coleman completely by surprise and begged the question, what should she do with the information now she had it?

Hemmings seemed to be part of a clandestine movement to overthrow the Schultzes. This was understandable, possibly even inevitable, after the way they had conducted themselves. Now Heinrich and Heidi were cut off from their global criminal organisation, their support, though dangerous, was limited. They were as ripe for toppling as they would ever be, however, Coleman knew it was much more than that. There was a deep resentment spreading through their people. Even in Britain, thousands of kilometres away from their leadership, it could be felt. Despite winning an entire planet and all its resources, the Schultzes had plunged everyone headlong into some kind of revenge campaign to disrupt the future. At least, that was how it seemed to her. No wonder everyone had had enough.

Of course, there was always the chance that the call was a setup, to test Coleman's loyalty – Heidi was certainly devious enough to come up with something like that, especially if she was planning some new strategy that required Coleman's help.

She may be testing the water between us, Coleman thought, cautiously, yet somehow it had not felt that way. The fact that Hemmings had dropped Devon's and Jansen's names made it more convincing. Unless she had completely misread them, both men were primarily here to save a tiny group of human beings from the catastrophe unfolding in 2112. As far as she could tell, they believed in developing a long-term survival strategy within this hard-won world – but maybe that was merely the hook to make her betray herself.

She sighed, exasperated. "Damn these people and their games." *"Ma'am?"*

She had forgotten the channel was still open to her command centre on the *Newfoundland*'s bridge. "I wish to meet with all department heads as soon as everyone's back from working the fields. Send them to my suite. Coleman out."

She stood and stretched, gingerly. She had been injured in a recent dinosaur attack. While her people laid a water pipeline deep into the lake, the Sigilmassasaurus – whose territory they were trying to colonise – had followed their shark cage out of the water, flinging it up the beach like a dog toy. They had lost people. Coleman had been among the lucky ones; she was in pain, but her broken ribs were mending.

Dwelling on pains naturally led her to consider one of the people she had just summoned – Dr Brian Alba, her marine and irrigation engineer. Spending an hour with him would doubtless be painful, too. Returning to her viewport, she looked out to see if she could spot the loathsome little toad. Part of her hoped to glimpse him disappearing off into the distance, clutched tightly in the savage claws of a giant pterosaur, but she knew it was just a momentary fancy. Despite their great size, it was unlikely the impressive flying reptiles were strong enough to bear a man's weight aloft. Perhaps if she reduced Alba's rations? She sighed. Never mind.

Great Cheviot Mountain, Northumberland AD2113

"Who is this man, Colonel?" asked the second female delegate, looking down with some concern.

Colonel Brabham stepped forward to help the prone man up. "He gave his name as Captain James Douglas, ma'am."

"What's the matter with him?" asked the male delegate. "Could he be carrying some form of contagion?" Surreptitiously, he took a step behind the two women he had travelled with.

Douglas looked up wretchedly, eventually regaining his feet with the colonel's aid. "*Del Bond?* Is it really *you?*"

The delegate leaned back still further, shock registering clearly on his face. "How can you possibly know that name? I've never made it known anywhere."

Douglas seemed not to hear. He turned to one of the female delegates. "Lieutenant Audrey Jansen, Ah cannae tell ye how happy Ah am to see you alive."

The male delegate now looked at *her* in shock, too. "You know this man?"

Audrey Jansen shook her head in bafflement. "No, Uncle."

The man with the eerie resemblance to Del Bond frowned. "I've told you not to call me that at work." He gave Douglas a penetrating stare. "*If* you will allow me to introduce myself?" He drew himself up, importantly. "I am Minister Lucas Jansen, member of the United Nations Council."

Douglas blinked. "*Not* Del Bond? Ah hadnae foreseen that kind of change, but Ah suppose people could have formed different relationships, made different marriages. It's all a wee bit much to take in."

"You think?"

"But ye recognise the *name* Del Bond?"

Minister Jansen looked shifty. "I did go by that name, once."

"When ye worked undercover?"

"Undercover?" Jansen replied, irascibly. "What are you babbling about, man? It was a pen name I used to publish a novel years ago. It never went anywhere – no accounting for taste!"

Douglas gaped.

"*Lieutenant* Audrey Jansen?" asked the woman, still standing in front of the politician. "But I never joined the military. I work as an assistant for my uncle—"

"Audrey! Will you please use my title, or sir, when we're—"

"Wait!" Douglas held up his hands. "Just a few minutes ago – for me, at least – all three of you were dead. Now you all pop up, having lived entirely different lives, and—"

"So how do you know *me?*" interrupted Special Agent Hemmings.

Douglas turned slowly. Overwhelmed, he wiped a tear from his eye, while he took a breath to calm himself. "Ah once knew a Lieutenant Elizabeth Hemmings – only for a very short time – but she was one of the bravest people Ah've ever had the pleasure to meet. She saved my life, three times over. She provided me with the plans we needed to make it home. She also helped me escape captivity, and protected me from a deadly fall..." His voice faltered, Adam's apple bobbing as he swallowed hard. "Sadly, at the cost of her own life."

Silence, but for the mountain breeze.

"Are you talking about a different timeline?" asked Audrey, eventually.

Douglas nodded.

"So, how did I, that is, how did *Lieutenant* Jansen die?"

Douglas covered his mouth with his hands, sighing deeply as he recalled Arnold Bessel, Lieutenant Audrey Jansen, and the fossilised remains buried for twenty million years under a tyre track in Cretaceous rock. "Lassie, ye'd never believe me."

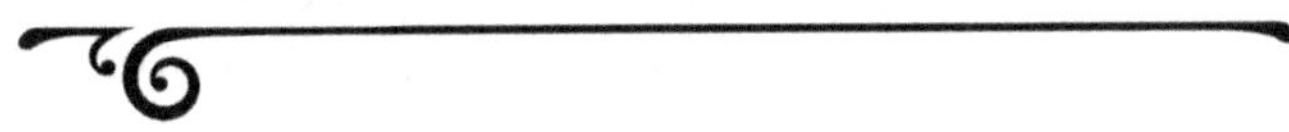

99.2 million years earlier

"Before I tell you my plan, a short history lesson. I used to belong to an organisation known as the Order of the Silver Cross," Benedictus Jansen confessed, feeling a sense of relief to finally be able to shed the load. "As did my uncle and my cousin. You might know them as Del Bond and Lieutenant Audrey Jansen, pilot of the USS *Newfoundland.*"

Devon's jaw dropped. "So there *is* a link. I wondered when Heidi told us about Bond's fake identity. You didn't think it was worth changing your name?"

"What's this?" asked Aito.

Devon explained. "Just after the *New World* vanished into a wormhole across Crater Lake, we had a meeting with Heidi – you were still recovering from your fight with that dinosaur—"

Aito gave an ironic snort. "Fight? All I remember was searing pain from my hand and being flung at that rock face. I don't even remember dropping to the cave floor."

"Yeah, it's a real sad story. We were there," continued Devon.

"Thanks for your concern."

"Yes, yes, but at that meeting, Heidi told us about Del Bond and what he did. That was when she said, 'I doubt that was his real name because he was Dutch' and then followed up with 'Jansen is a Dutch name, isn't it?' She asked Jansen here if he was any relation." Devon whistled with renewed respect. "I cannot *believe* how cool you played it, Ben." He turned back to Aito. "He just shrugged and replied, 'Not that I know of'. Incredible! I totally bought it."

Jansen shrugged again. "When you make your living infiltrating terrorist organisations, it helps to be able to lie. There was no need to change my name because no one knew my uncle's *real* name. Changing it would have only given them a suspicious trail to follow. I'd never previously used my real name on any assignment for the Order, and as this was the motherload – Schultz himself – I knew this would be my last mission."

"You expected to die," Aito stated with grudging respect.

"I thought that was possible – I *expected* to retire! Anyhow, my uncle, whose real name was Lucas Jansen, by the way, not Del Bond, *may* have revealed himself to Heinrich Schultz before the bomb he carried within his body destroyed the *Sabre* – he probably thought it no longer mattered and took the opportunity to rub Schultz's nose in it. Can't say as I blame him, but if he *did,* then the Old Man's survival against all odds may have made things a little trickier for me. Luckily, Heinrich has no way of chasing down information about the Order of the Silver Cross from back here, and Heidi has trusted me ever since the time I busted her out, after her grandfather ordered her imprisonment. Either way, they seem to have let the matter lie, for now, at least." Jansen grinned, shaking his head ruefully. "What's in a name, after all? I tell you, when Douglas' people took the *Last Word* out, and Heinrich got the lowdown, I thought she'd bought it."

"OK. So, what's this 'Silver Cross'?" asked Aito.

"Right. The organisation was formed in 1940, just after the Nazi invasion of the Netherlands – the Netherlands were neutral at the time, too. Not that Hitler, or others like him, ever troubled over little details like that. Back then, most of us were Dutch, or of Dutch descent. After the Second World War, we moved on from resistance work to hunting down Nazi war criminals. Once they were all dealt with, we switched to tracking down anyone propagating or disseminating Nazi sentiments, ideals or race hatred of any kind. Naturally, the Schultzes were people of great interest to us, but Heinrich Schultz was untouchable. At least, he was back in our own time."

"Hang on," Devon interrupted. "I get Heinrich, OK? But why *did* you help save Heidi?"

"Coleman and I realised that surviving the human apocalypse, back in 2112, wouldn't amount to much if we had to live under the regime of a mass-murdering maniac like Heinrich Schultz. Knowing I couldn't get to him before the big kick-off, I, at least, used his organisation to get here – as did others, I don't doubt, just looking to go on living. After that, we decided Heidi was the less dangerous of the two, but also the most likely to take the Old Man down – they're a hell of a family."

"Let me see if I have this right," Devon interrupted again. "You thought Heidi was *less* dangerous?"

Jansen had the grace to show chagrin. "In our defence, we knew she would have to be taken out of the picture, too, if we were to ever live anything approaching normal lives. It's just that she had the access and the temperament to take care of the Old Man."

"But you've been alone with Heidi several times on your away missions since." Devon could not let the point go. "You must have had opportunity to deal with her."

Jansen's feelings toward Heidi Schultz were more complicated than he cared to admit – even to himself. His answer was prosaic, but basically true. "If you're referring to the missions where we were alone – just us and marauding packs of dinosaurs – then, what can I say? I needed the backup. Besides, most of those times were spent running for our lives."

"What about when you slept with her?" Devon pressed.

"I *what?*" Jansen's eyebrows leapt almost off his head.

"You've slept in the same vehicle, I mean. Don't tell me nothing happened."

Jansen stared at Devon as if he were mad. "This is Heidi Schultz we're talking about, remember? You think I'd still be alive if I tried anything like that? Of course, then there's the other small matter – hardly like to mention it, really."

"Go on."

"We were forty miles away through the jungles of Cretaceous Egypt and I'm not a pilot!"

"OK. Just to recap," Aito spoke slowly, working it all out as he went, "Heinrich is back, at least nominally in charge, if living in fear of his granddaughter – whom you thought was less dangerous – and Heidi is now planning a campaign to take over the entire future by rebuilding the Nazi war machine. Did I miss anything?"

"Only that we three are all that stand against them," Devon added, casually, "and we're trapped in a forest unable to move for killer dinosaurs in all directions. Not that we'd have anything to stand against them with, even if we escaped the dinosaurs."

"Coleman will probably help," Jansen suggested hopefully.

Aito placed his head in his hands and made a laugh that turned into a sob. "This would be the Coleman that's thousands of miles away across the Mediterranean and half of Europe – the one without transport?"

"Tethys Ocean. Europe won't coalesce for millions of years."

"I stand corrected." Aito bowed sardonically, almost taking his eye out on a branch. "Ow!"

"She's got a farm and a workforce," Jansen offered in mitigation.

"Forgive me, of course she has. I really don't know what I was worrying about. So, with everything so obviously going in our favour, all that remains is for Jansen to finally tell us his plan for saving the world."

Jansen gave them an enigmatic smile. "It's not quite as bleak as you've made it sound. We do have another ally."

Almost a hundred million years later, a memory stirred within Lucas Jansen – erstwhile philosopher turned heroic triple agent and seeker of Nazi terrorists, now failed author turned diplomat. "What did you say your name was again?"

"Captain James Douglas."

"Hmm, perhaps we should talk in private." He turned away to climb back into his ambassadorial limousine, gesturing for Douglas to follow.

Douglas looked to Colonel Brabham, who shrugged, so he climbed in after the man he could only think of as Del Bond. He found one of several indulgent massage seats within the luxury vehicle and sank into it gratefully. After the freezing bite of the December storm in 1558 and the tumble through a wormhole, only to believe they were completely lost and alone, the sudden comfort in which he now found himself moved him close to tears. The seat heated, warming him through, while pampering his battered muscles.

The hatch slid closed behind them, the diplomat taking a seat opposite. "You wouldn't have had anything to do with the British government about five or six hundred years ago, would you? An insane question, I'll admit, but if you're some kind of time traveller..."

Douglas was suddenly struggling to stay awake. It was a hard thing, but he switched the seat and its pleasures off. "Not the *British* government exactly," he replied warily.

"The Crown, then?"

Douglas gave a small nod. "What do you know, Mr Bo— Jansen?"

"If you really are from another time, Captain, or *timeline* at least, I don't know if you're aware but the British government, that is *our* British government, was dissolved in AD1978, along with every other government. We now govern the planet through a body known as the United Nations."

"We had something similar, but far less developed, and often a little chequered," Douglas admitted.

"Good. OK. Now, each country has its own ministers who sit in the house, very similar to the way representatives sat in the parliaments or senates of the past, but on a larger scale. Our wormhole technology has allowed us to set up colonies on other Earth-like planets throughout the Milky Way. Each planet is also represented in the house – although some of them are now lobbying for independence – which was inevitable, but entirely another story! The reason I'm telling you this, is because you will no doubt be facing a United Nations committee very soon to explain yourselves and everything you know."

Douglas seemed to slump in his seat.

"Don't worry, Captain. We're so used to wormhole travel now that if you have popped into our world via a slightly alternate route, it's unlikely to cause too much of a stir. Before that happens, however, I would have you tell me how you came to be here."

"Mr Jansen, my people have just left a freezing storm and a pressing enemy. Will ye no' get them warm blankets and something tae eat? This conversation might take a wee while."

"Of course." The diplomat toggled a control on the arm of his seat to open a comm channel. "Audrey?"

"*Yes, Uncle. Can I get you anything?*"

He rolled his eyes. "Family. *You* understand." He pressed a button to speak. "I want those people out there given warm blankets and refreshments. Ask the colonel to break out some of the search and rescue provisions, if necessary."

"*Right away, Uncle.*"

He sighed.

Douglas chuckled. "She's very different from the Audrey Jansen Ah knew."

"Yes, well, it's not all her fault. She suffered a complete breakdown a couple of years ago, after her husband died in a sailing accident on his luxury yacht."

Douglas frowned, wondering if lightning may indeed have struck twice – or if not lightning, then Cupid's arrow? "What was his name?"

The minister soured. "Geoff Lloyd. Made a fortune from gambling and then opened his own string of casinos – never met a man with more luck. Everything he touched turned to gold. Well, until the accident, anyway. As I said, he died on his own yacht, strangled by one of the lines. I thought it best not to enquire too deeply into what he was doing, or with whom. Audrey had been through enough."

Douglas rocked, stifling choking sounds.

Minister Lucas Jansen looked at him askance. "Perhaps you're in no good mental state," he offered, kindly.

Douglas roared with laughter; he could hold it in no longer.

"Really, Captain. I couldn't abide the man, but my niece was devastated. She's never been the same."

"Ah'm sorry," Douglas managed between wheezes. "It's just that, hehe, Geoff Lloyd – the luckiest man on Earth! Hahaha! The Geoff Lloyd Ah knew was a little different." He collapsed into another guffaw. It took a full minute before he could stifle his sniggers to try again. "Ah was speaking with him less than an hour ago—"

"He's *alive?*"

"Er, no. Been dead about five hundred years, Ah should think."

"*What?*"

"Ah'm sorry for your Audrey."

A ministerial eyebrow rose in disapproval. "Well, we all deal with grief in different ways."

"If ye think it might help, Ah'd be happy to tell her about him. She was pretty much the centre of his world, actually."

"Really?"

"Oh, aye."

The minister sat forward in his seat. "Perhaps another time. Right now, I need to know how you came to be here."

"Why?" Douglas asked, cautiously.

"Because I think there may be a link between you and my wife's family. Your name is known to them, something to do with Queen Elizabeth I, or something. If I have the tale right, your coming here was foretold."

Douglas wiped his eyes, growing serious once more. "Who's yer wife, Del?"

"Lucas, Minister – Jansen, if you must – but please stop calling me Del Bond!"

"Sorry, Minister."

"I appreciate you're exhausted, but thank you. My wife is descended from an English duke, who may even have been in line to the throne, had he not been illegitimate—"

Douglas roared again, tears streaming down his face this time.

"What now?"

"Oh, Del— Minister, have Ah got a story to tell ye."

"There's been no sign of your dinosaur, Dr Wood," Badawi reported with a 'told you so' expression. The man was as helpful as they could have hoped for, but clearly did not appreciate having his time wasted on flights of fancy. Woodsey half agreed with him, yet there was certainly something strange, even bizarre, going on. Fossils did not just disappear out of the rocks – or people's hands, for that matter.

"Thank you, Master Sergeant. So will you continue your search of the hills?"

"I think we may be better served by waiting until daylight. Unfortunately, it seems there is nothing that can be done for the missing lady and it would only place our people in danger, having them stumble about out there in the dark."

Woodsey nodded. "Understood. Have her family been informed?"

"My office has contacted her local police force. I would imagine they know by now."

Woodsey hung his head. "She had been looking forward to this trip for months. I just can't believe..." He tailed off, thoughts clunking into one another, like trucks on a train. What events could have led to this? Eventually, his memory arrived at its final stop – the last time they saw Heidi. Things had not looked good for her, yet he knew in his marrow she was behind all this. He could feel it, even across such vast tracts of time. It was creepy, his assuredness; almost like being watched.

"One, I want a progress report on your special assignment. You have all the resources you require?" Heidi eyed the balding scientist closely.

One, that is, Dr Reid, for his part wrung his hands – his standard response to her interrogations. He nodded in salute. "Ma'am. We've made some considerable progress with the Germans' help. Some of whom are very clever people, despite being technologically less advanced than ourselves. They learn quickly. Of course, there is also our new, *ahem,* power source."

Heidi nodded slowly. "You refer to tapping the Earth's geothermal power?"

"Indeed, ma'am. Do I assume your trip to 1943 went well?"

"I have your refined neodymium. My contacts in Germany acquired it from California, as you suggested. How long will it be until you are ready for testing?"

"With that material, very soon, ma'am. We're missing just one small component, easily manufactured now. Perhaps even as early as this afternoon? It really is almost finished, ma'am."

"So soon? I may have misjudged you, One. Pull this off successfully and you shall be rewarded."

"May I make a request, ma'am?"

"You may."

"My name is Reid, ma'am. My staff have begun to call me 'One', behind my back. As Dr Hemmings has been incarcerated for some little while, the new people have never met 'Two', and this has led to the suggestion that I may be missing some... some *part* of my anatomy, more usually found as a pair, ma'am. It's eroding discipline."

Heidi laughed and clapped her hands together foppishly. She rose from her seat and rounded her desk to stand before him. "You have done well, Dr Reid. Should you have any issues with discipline among your staff, be sure to tell them that *I* expect optimum performance from them, and if they disrespect you, they are disrespecting me – and they should be *strongly* advised not to do that. Now, take me to your laboratory and show me your device."

Deep in the heart of the *Heydrich,* Reid handed Heidi something that appeared little more than a small gadget attached to a wrist strap. "For your convenience and ease of movement, ma'am. It's pocket-sized, as you can see, but in emergency situations, I thought..."

"Yes, indeed, Dr Reid," she replied, loudly enough for the other three scientists to hear. "An excellent notion. Once again, you impress me. The device is much smaller than I expected."

"The majority of what makes up our ship's so-called wormhole *drive,* is more about power conversion and transference than the actual generation of a wormhole, ma'am. As this device taps its power straight from the planet, it is considerably leaner – as you've observed. Of course, the main difference is our ships can open a wormhole anywhere, whereas the wearer of this device must be on Earth – or at least, a planet similar to Earth."

"Most impressive, Doctor. Now, show me how it works."

Reid nodded. "We'll get straight onto producing the final component with the material you've provided, ma'am. In the meantime, I can show you a simulation. Please, may I offer you a seat?" He snapped his fingers to a subordinate. "Bring refreshments for Dr Schultz."

Heidi accepted, ordered a coffee, and sat in front of the viewscreen to watch Reid's short presentation in rapt silence.

Aito and Devon looked at one another, and then back at Jansen. Devon spoke first. "It's a bit light, Ben. Dare we hope that this plan of yours involves more than a vague notion about preventing Heidi from using the wormhole?"

"Of course," replied Jansen. A loud roar from not far away made them all duck and huddle closer. "Perhaps we should speak more quietly. As you already know, Devon, we asked Dr Anne Hemmings to contact Coleman back at Crater Lake, or, for want of a better description, back in one-day-Britain. She has asked Coleman to run a full inventory on what it would take to get the *Newfoundland* flying again."

"OK," Aito replied, slowly. "Then what?"

"With the help of our new allies from 1943, it should be possible to fix the old gal up – or at least, *patch* her up. There should be no reason why Heidi would wish to block this. The *Newfoundland* is, after all, a very valuable piece of technology."

"More like real estate," Aito muttered darkly.

"Not for long, if Coleman can make her viable again. My plan then involves *moving* the wormhole, using the *Newfoundland*."

Aito and Devon looked at one another again, before looking back to Jansen. This time Aito spoke first. "Move it how?"

"And," Devon chipped in, "how do we move it right from under Heidi's nose? You never told me anything about this, Jansen."

"Never mind her nose," Aito added. "How do we move it from under the *Heydrich*'s guns?"

"Magnetic fields." Jansen delivered his solution with the aplomb of a conjuror.

Aito groaned.

Jansen looked a little put out. "What?"

The Japanese captain pinched the bridge of his nose tiredly. "If we ever get back, maybe we can save that part of the plan for the movie. Have you anything else? Magnetic fields indeed," he spat derisively.

"That wasn't my idea," Jansen complained, bridling at last. "Dr Hemmings thinks it may be possible to contain the wormhole within a powerful magnetic field." He looked to Devon. "Didn't she tell you? It's something to do with the electrical... erm, she did explain it. Look, I'm not a scientist, OK?"

"Must have slipped her mind," Devon replied sourly. "So, after the liberal use of a montage, we now have a working capital ship, and some type of powerful field generator. What comes next? We use a little electrical what's-its-name to *move* the wormhole, did you say? OK, I'll buy that, after suspending all possible disbelief and applying our entire stock of fairy dust. The *Newfoundland,* against all odds, has *not,* in fact, been blown out of the sky and now carries the wormhole beneath her belly – what's our endgame?"

"You guys can be real snide when the mood takes you," Jansen admonished. "*Then,* she takes the wormhole into space, far enough from the Earth to disrupt the power connection."

Devon placed his head in his hands. "But the wormhole is still attached at the other end, in Munich."

"Yes, but with just the one connection the wormhole will no longer be travelling *through* the planet's outer core. Look, the way I understand it, wormholes travel outside our space–time, but when opening and travelling so close to a molten planet core, there can be some cross-dimensional bleed... or something. Anyhow, even if that doesn't work, Dr Hemmings has a plan that may shut the wormhole down from the other end – *if* we can talk someone into doing it. As it happens, we do have a contact with access to the museum where the wormhole currently exits, in Munich."

Devon's eyes narrowed. "Who?"

Jansen looked uncomfortable. "Oh, just a painter I met, when I was there – still to make a name for himself in that world..." He tailed off uncomfortably.

Fortunately, Aito was more concerned with *their* present, and changed the subject. "I have a plan."

They looked at him.

"It's not as cool or as cinematic as Jansen's, but the charm is in its simplicity."

"Go on," prompted Devon.

Aito made sure he had the attention of both before he spoke. "We shoot Heidi... to death."

"I like that plan," Devon seconded. "However..."

It was Aito's turn to prompt. "However?"

Devon sighed deeply. "Perhaps, Jansen, we should compare notes after we speak with Dr Hemmings, in future. As you stated, I told her to contact Coleman and explore the possibility of bringing the *Newfoundland* back to life, but clearly, she has further plans for that asset. You should have told me, Ben."

"I thought you knew."

"Exactly, please refer to my point about comparing notes. However, I'm to blame, too. Obviously, neither of you realise how much of a problem that wormhole represents."

Aito glanced at Jansen, before turning back to Devon. "Almost unlimited personnel and resources from a modern Germany, run by an innocent leadership, ripe for plucking by the Schultzes?" he gabbled.

Devon shook his head, darkly.

Aito groaned. "What else?"

"The wormhole is expanding."

"Are you sure?" asked Jansen and Aito together.

"Deadly sure. And at a rate that's accelerating. And even that's not the worst of it. Dr Hemmings believes that if we do nothing to change the status quo, it will continue to expand until it has used up its power source."

Aito gawked. "The molten core of our *planet?*"

"Yes, but don't worry, everything will be utterly destroyed, and we'll all be dead long before it gets to that stage. From there, it may even create a singularity that devours our solar system... initially."

"*Initially?*" Jansen and Aito spoke in tandem again.

Devon merely shrugged apologetically. In the silence that followed, the crashing of dinosaurs continuing to search for a way through the forest to get to them, was almost comforting – if only to illustrate that there was yet life all around them, for now.

Eventually, Aito continued, "So, to recap, we have to hope that Heidi will supply Coleman with the parts she needs to fix an ancient and utterly ruined spaceship, and that Dr Hemmings can, in secret – and from her prison cell – help Coleman's people build some type of vastly powerful magnetic field generator. Then Coleman can fly here, snatch the wormhole from the ground, avoiding the *Heydrich*'s horrific weaponry, and dispatch it into outer space. Did I miss anything?"

"No," agreed Jansen. "I think that pretty much covers it."

"I have a question – two, actually." Devon held up a hand as if in class. "One, do you think Coleman knows the full extent of this plan, and two, can we still shoot Heidi?"

Chapter 3 | Brave New World

Heidi sniffed the air. It was fresh, far fresher than it had any right to be, given the year. She had made it, alone, into the 22nd century. She grinned, and then realised she was not alone. Not quite.

Thirty minutes and almost a hundred million years earlier
A small but deadly attack ship roared overhead. Jansen, Devon and Aito looked up instinctively, trying to glimpse through the forest canopy as the ground shook beneath their feet. Even their ears seemed to vibrate as they covered them simultaneously.

Once the rocket noise died away, the stillness seemed strange, almost empty.

"They've gone," Devon hissed into the silence. He was right. The constant background noise of large, frustrated animals and breaking timber had stopped, and with its cessation came opportunity. "The bikes!"

They scrambled back through the foliage as quickly as they could, to disentangle their machines. One of them had been found by a Rugops. Sniffing for the three men, the creature had obviously tracked the associated smell of the bikes to this location. Aito's bike would probably never be useful again. "Lift?" he asked Devon, hopefully.

"Let's get clear first. Help me."

They crashed their way back to the treeline. The small valley leading down to the river's shore was empty. Even the vast Sarcosuchus crocodile had vanished from the beach with the passing of the ship.

"You know, the bang of a gun or a grenade startles them," Jansen mused, "but you just don't get the continuous effect that the roar of a ship's rocket motors can produce—"

Devon kick-started his bike, cutting him off. "Can we *go?*" Aito did not need telling twice and immediately jumped on pillion.

"I was only saying." Jansen was left talking to himself as Devon and his passenger shot off in a cloud of dust and carbon monoxide gas. To the south, he heard the alien sound of a sonic boom. "Yep, time to go."

Already fifty kilometres south and still accelerating, Heidi headed for the coordinates Dr Reid had given her. While initially searching for the remains of the isotope that survived within the fossilised remains of a Spinosaurus aegyptiacus, Doctors Reid and Hemmings found 1943 Munich as intended, but a second possible incursion time and location had also presented itself. They knew Ernst Stromer's Egyptian finds would be taken to Germany by 1922; it had been a relatively simple calculation to move forward to 1943 from there, as they could fix the location with absolute certainty. However, while scanning the future for signs of the isotope, the second set of remains appeared in 2122, but rather than in Munich, these were approximately four hundred kilometres south of their position. Somehow, the remains had been uncovered at that time and were visible to their search.

Heidi was keen to test her new handheld device, but flying blindly through time to who knew when would have been beyond foolhardy, so, as they had a relatively safe set of coordinates to explore – exposed, and in the open air – she decided to check them out.

El-Shaikh Ebada, 99,198,017 BC

The river gouged deep, though for the last few seasons it had also grown narrower, the shores to either side drier and less verdant. A female Spinosaurus fished the shallows. Mudbanks led away from the river's western shore. She had witnessed many creatures come to grief there recently, breaking through the dried-up crust to become trapped, only to starve or get sucked under the surface. Danger sense to stay clear warred with the need to feed, her body demanding energy and craving calcium to produce medullary bone.

When a giant fish zipped through the water right in front of her, a spasm, beginning in her tail, travelled through her whole body and she shot forward ballistically through the murky waters. Visibility was low, but the pressure sensitive receptors, connected via foramina to her nasal cavity, meant that she could detect pressure waves caused by movement within the waters – detect them, and strike for the creature that made them.

The fish – Onchopristis numidus[2] – sensed the Spinosaurus, too, and instinctually understood the danger its presence represented. It dashed to the side, hoping to confuse pursuit, but the sensitive snout of the Spinosaurus detected its movement instantly and snapped. Onchopristis would have been no match for such a large predator, even if fully grown, but at a mere five metres – half the length of an adult – it stood no chance at all.

Spinosaurus' jaws closed like a bear trap, yet the speed of Onchopristis jerked its body out of reach, causing the dinosaur to bite deeply into the pectoral fin. Blood haemorrhaged from the wound in great gushes, only driving the predator on to greater excitement. Before its prey could shake itself loose, Spinosaurus surfaced and, with a gargantuan effort, launched the five-metre fish through the air to slap down onto the mudbank.

The dinosaur swam easily to the shore to collect her prize. Lost in a berserk lust, she forgot all about the danger and mounted the bank to slide down the other side. Immediately, her vast weight crashed through the sun-cracked surface to leave her bogged down in a stinking mire. The fish flapped about pathetically in the muck and she snapped at it again, striking true this time – an auto response that killed it instantly. Biting deep into the carcass, she gorged on guts, bones and stinking fish oils.

Immediate desire for flesh sated, her predicament gradually dawned and she began to struggle. Digging through the muck with

---

2   *Onchopristis numidus* was a very long-lived species that survived through most of the Cretaceous Period. It grew massive and looked rather like a sawfish, though its closest living relative may actually be the skate.

webbed claws, Spinosaurus turned back towards the river and began to climb the treacherous bank. Loath to leave such a plentiful carcass behind, she dragged her catch along, too, as she inched forward. The mud bar was much steeper than it had been on the river-facing side and almost completely slick. The more she dug, the more stuck she became, adrenaline of the chase subsiding as lactic acids carried exhaustion through her muscles. Her breathing laboured, she was forced to abandon the Onchopristis cadaver as she battled to reach the top of the bank. Traction was almost non-existent, and toiling under a killing sun only dug her deep into a trench of muck. Stuck fast, she collapsed with exhaustion, and with an equatorial furnace beating on her back and sail, she would have died... should have died.

Heidi throttled back, coming in to hover over some mudbanks at the river's edge. Beneath her an adult Spinosaurus had become trapped. She scanned the creature. "I wonder...? Interesting." Her scans revealed that she had met this animal before, or at least, members of her crew had. There was strong evidence of a strontium-90 and uranium-235 mix in its bloodstream and bone marrow. "*Very* interesting."

Less than twenty metres north was a rocky outcrop, carved away to either side by the river over millennia. It stood as an island; sedimentary stone sheared off to a plateau on its western side. The surface was canted over a little, but not so steeply that it prevented her from landing with care.

The colossal roar of Heidi's thruster rockets sent a spike of terror through the spinosaur's moribund nervous system. A last shot of adrenaline caused it to jump for the river, for its life.

Once on the ground, Heidi lost no time in shutting down so she could step outside quickly. Head tilted to one side, she watched the struggling dinosaur with the morbid curiosity of a small boy, pulling legs off a spider to see what would happen. The animal was obviously exhausted and near death, possibly even from heart failure. The thought struck her that two such creatures dying exactly here was just too much of a coincidence. *This must be the animal that gave us the readings from AD2122,* she reflected.

With her last breaths, one of the most truly awesome creatures ever to have lived made a final effort to free herself, but to no avail.

Heidi held a steel rod against the rock under her feet. A cap exploded, burying the tip several centimetres into the stone, marking this time and place with their unique isotope. The bang made the Spinosaurus jump.

Heidi's eyebrows rose slightly. *Still alive. Impressive. But sadly, not for long – I know the future, after all. See you in a hundred million years, my giant friend.* She activated the device on her wrist. A tingling began in her arm, but was completely sublimated by the shock of seeing a wormhole open right in front of her; the now-familiar haze, while semi-transparent and neither giving nor taking light, reflected, making the river beyond seem to ripple and whirl unnaturally. Unlike the wormhole frozen in place before the bow of a ship, this one continued to move through three dimensions away from her, as if nudged by its leap to life. Powered by the Earth itself, it would never close unless Heidi's wrist device made it do so. She watched it drift eerily towards the edge of the rocky plateau, where she stood transfixed. A thought struck her, as she watched the dying giant through its haze. Her eyes narrowed and, before the wormhole moved out onto the mudbanks beyond her reach, she stepped through.

Heidi sniffed the air. It was fresh, far fresher than it had any right to be, given the year. She had made it, alone, into the 22nd century. She grinned and stepped away from the wormhole at her back. With her strategist's hat on, she noted it was perhaps six or seven metres in diameter – ideal for the passage of vehicular traffic. *"Gut gemacht, Doktor Reid."*

Before her, perhaps some twenty metres away, was a camp. She could see several tents of various sizes, though all the camp's people seemed to be struggling to get into one tent in particular. Heidi was here for reconnaissance only. Wishing to avoid any entanglements with the locals, she stepped quickly away, following the base of a cliff around to the north-east. When she turned to close the wormhole, she jumped – in a most un-Schultzlike manner. The wormhole was drifting after her, almost as though tethered to the device at her wrist.

She had no time to ponder it here, so she moved away at a jog, like a little girl towing a huge transdimensional balloon. The heat caused her to perspire freely, but she could not let up until she was out of sight of the tents. Eventually, she rounded the corner and followed the canyon wall until it opened into a narrow, secluded, sandblasted valley in the rocks. She stopped to rest. The wormhole hung in the air behind her, yet still moving – it was *weird.* However, for Heidi, it was about to get a lot weirder.

Back in *Cretaceous* Egypt, her wormhole had continued its drift towards the dying Spinosaurus aegyptiacus, engulfing the creature just as its mighty heart stopped beating. When it appeared at the other end of the wormhole in AD2122, Heidi screamed in spite of herself.

Her mind raced. How was this possible? The only reason she had coordinates for this time and place was because that creature died exactly where it had, after being shot with her isotope. Yet here it was. Not fossilised. Not buried in stone, and worse yet, not dead either.

It stirred. Snout not two metres from her, iron-hard Heidi almost disgraced herself in wide-eyed panic. Nevertheless, somewhere between bladder and brain an answer presented itself. "Oh, my God. Schrödinger's Spinosaurus! It has to be."

Following on from the popular physics anecdote about Schrödinger's cat – where a hypothetical cat is placed in a box and poisoned, quantum superposition suggesting that at a given time the cat – or the Spinosaurus – was both alive *and* dead. She could only imagine that if the moment of this dual state of life and death occurred as the beast was sucked into her wormhole, it would have... it would have what? Desperately, she wondered, *What the hell is going on?*

Somehow the dinosaur had died at that point, as it was meant to, only to become buried in mud that would become stone, that would become revealed after a rockslide millions of years later. Yet it had also vanished from that point at the exact same moment, thanks to Heidi's wormhole, and being both alive and dead simultaneously, this led her to a horrifying conclusion: if the animal was indeed *dead* in the Cretaceous – as proven by her journey through time, following its remains to this destination – then as it had arrived with her, it must be *alive* in the 22nd century. That quantum instant decreed it so. The odds against everything that entwined them in that exact moment were longer than winning the lottery every single week since the first draw – and with the same numbers, too. Ironic, because Heidi had the sinking feeling that her luck had well and truly run out. That 'it could be her' was no longer in question, but if *she* did not well and truly run out – of the box canyon where she had taken cover – it would be the very last thing she did not do, for Spinosaurus aegyptiacus was waking up to a brave new world, and she had not eaten in a hundred million years.

Making for the western cliff face, Heidi jammed a second steel rod into the stone at its base. Another cap exploded, burying it several centimetres into the rock. She would now be able to track this time and place, too. Her work done, she closed the wormhole down and legged it for her life, fully understanding that Spinosaurus would easily track her scent when fully roused. Other than the dinosaur, she was probably the largest creature for quite some distance, and therefore tempting prey.

When she had flown in to land by the Spinosaurus, all those millions of years ago, she had noticed the dead fish with its guts ripped out. It was comforting to hope that the dinosaur had eaten enough of it to 'take the edge off', but Heidi did not enjoy living in hope. She preferred terms like distance, speed and weapons. Having neither the speed nor a weapon to match the creature, she decided on distance. Quickly discovering a rough trail leading up onto the promontory, Heidi began to climb.

After half an hour's hard march, she stopped to take water from her flask. The gruelling and circuitous route had taken her back almost to where she started, though elevated by some fifty metres. From here she could spy on the camp below.

She lay down, crawling to the edge of the promontory. There were boot prints all around her. It seemed a single person, a man, had been back and forth, searching the area for something. She could not imagine what he had lost or sought, so she took a small telescope from a jacket pocket, closed one eye and looked out over the camp.

Three men and a woman stood away from the busy tent, where the camp dwellers had recently tried to cram in all together. The woman and one of the men looked fairly old, though they gesticulated vigorously enough for all that. Heidi did not recognise them, but the other two...

Her breath caught. She dialled up the zoom on the small device to maximum and looked again. The view through the telescope shook wildly without a tripod, both due to the magnification and her nerves. She gripped it two-handed and gawked. She guessed the two young men were in their mid-twenties, a little older than she remembered, but she definitely recognised the New Zealand boy from her days aboard the *New World*. That had been just a few months ago for her. Most importantly, however, she recognised the third man as her cousin, Tim Norris.

What could she do? Cursing that she had no rifle or long-distance listening equipment, she knew she must wait until dark, and then creep down into the camp. The people below were obviously in a state over something. She would find out what – and then she would really give them something to cry about.

Later that evening, student palaeontologist, Simba, took a shovel from the tool tent, stuffed a loo roll into her jacket and disappeared into the night...

Chapter 4 | Just Like Old Times

[ENCRYPTED MESSAGE – EYES ONLY]

<u>ALERT</u>: YOU ARE HEREBY RECALLED TO *UNASA, CANAVERAL, FLORIDA.*

Dear friends,

As we feared, someone we left behind long ago survived, and has begun manipulating events affecting the here and now. Full disclosure will be made during your induction. In line with our unanimous agreement and ongoing commitment, we must act with despatch.

What you should do now:

1. Tie up any affairs of immediate moment, quickly and quietly. Leave <u>discreetly</u> and proceed to Canaveral Space Port and Airbase by <u>10th November, latest</u>. Avoid travelling in large parties outside your own family groups where possible.

2. Upon arrival at the United Nations building, check in at the entrance foyer stating that you are there for the induction into

Project NW2 c/o Training Director Douglas. UN personnel will verify your identification and show you to special suites where you may make yourselves comfortable, while you wait to be contacted. All meals, and any essentials you require, will be provided.

3. <u>Do not leave your suite until instructed to do so</u>.

4. <u>Do everything possible to avoid media attention</u>.

5. Each of us will be allowed two suitcases. It is recommended that you bring only clothing and personal effects that you will <u>need</u>. Be sure to include comfortable, durable clothing suitable for hiking and outdoor pursuits. All other requirements will be met by the organisers.

This will be hard on us all, but once our task is complete, we will return to continue our lives as we have lived for the last ten years. Going into this, we have huge advantages over last time, both in terms of technology and equipment, not to mention foreknowledge of our destination. Consequently, we expect to return quickly and successfully. It is unfortunate, but we all know the reasons why everyone from *NW* and the *LW* must go.

Together, we can and will put an end to this threat once and for all, allowing us to fully integrate with our new home. I look forward to seeing you all soon,

Training Director James Douglas

[MESSAGE ENDS]

"Encrypt and... *send. *Good." Douglas looked up to a knock at his door. "Come." He leapt to his feet, moving quickly around his desk to greet his friend with a warm double handshake. "You're back! Ah'm so glad you got here before we had to ship out. In truth, Ah dinnae know how Ah can ever begin to thank ye for all ye've done for us."

Douglas' guest was a tall, squarely built, American captain of the space fleet. He pulled Douglas into a friend's embrace. "You can start by breakin' out that Highland scotch I know you've been hoardin'. As of right now, I'm off duty for three whole, sun-kissed days."

Douglas beamed. "Done. Come, sit over here by the window. Three days, you say?"

"Yeah. Some urgent training course my cleaning and maintenance staff have been ordered to take, so I'm grounded."

"Really?"

"Yeah. Couldn't help noticing it says Training Director on your door, James – know anything about it?"

"*Me?* Staff ongoing development schedules are no' really ma department." He chuckled, so obviously guilty as he manoeuvred his visitor to the comfortable chairs that looked out of Canaveral Space Port and Airbase. "Ah'm going to miss this view."

"Not for long, I hope."

Douglas handed his friend a Glencairn glass tumbler with a generous measure of his best scotch in it.

"Ya got any ice?"

Douglas grimaced.

Captain Arnold Bessel laughed heartily. "Still poutin' over mixin' scotch with ice, huh?"

"It ruins the malt," Douglas opined, good-naturedly. "*Americans.* Friends to the end, eh?"

Bessel laughed again and they clinked glasses. "I'll drink to that."

"That, and the last ten years," replied Douglas.

"And a whole lot more to come," countered Bessel.

Douglas took the seat opposite. "Ah wish we didnae have to go. Ah've gotten used to having ye around again."

Bessel smiled. "For me this is the first time around, remember? My old man never served in Scotland. Pity, I hear it's nice this time of year."

Douglas scoffed. "In November? Who's been lying to ye, laddie? Point them out, Ah'll have them fired." His eyes tightened as a little sadness crept into them. "You've been a true friend to me through two lifetimes, now, Arnold. Ah dinnae want tae lose ye again."

Bessel placed his tumbler on the glass coffee table between them. "It's a hell of a story, my friend. I still can't quite believe how I used to be such a hero – tell me again!"

Douglas' smile returned. "Actually, you were no different then, to now. Even when we were at our most desperate, having landed almost a hundred million years in the past with no hope of returning home, Ah knew there'd be one man boneheaded and stubborn enough to come looking for me. Ah'll never forget that, Arnold – in this life or any other. Seems some people are always just who they are. As for others..."

"Must have been hard."

"Aye. But you made it easier. We couldnae have put any of this together without yer help and support for the project. Seriously."

"It wasn't so hard." Bessel took up his glass once more, playing his part down. "Once the brass hats and politicians realised it was their asses that might vanish in a puff of nonexistence, unless we prepared for this eventuality, the money suddenly became a lot more forthcoming."

"Aye. There were times when Ah thought Ah'd be needing that rubber room – the one that comes with the special coat."

Bessel laughed. "I know some of the folks you knew turned out to be different here, but didn't you say that others weren't here at all?"

"Aye, probably most, in fact. Just two billion souls on this Earth and another six in the colonies – we left *fifty* billion just on the Earth. So Ah think it's fair to say, *most* people are no' here. But there's worse – much worse – through a freak of causality, some are now here twice."

"James, I've never asked you this, but knowing what you're about to face, this could be my last chance. Did you ever track yourself down – your *other* self, that is – in this timeline?"

Douglas looked deeply into his glass, swirling the contents. "Aye," he admitted at last. "In the early days, many of us wished to look up either our other selves, as you say, or loved ones we may have lost. It was only natural, especially for the grieving. Ah tracked down... well, *me,* Ah suppose you could say. His history took a different turn from mine – even his family tree is different. Turns out, he's a Scott."

Bessel frowned. "As opposed to?"

Douglas looked slightly confused. Then his expression cleared. "Oh, no. Not a Scot, a *Scott.* His name, in this timeline, is James Scott." He shuddered as if someone had walked over his grave. "It's no' right."

"Which particular part of it?"

"All of it. Take yer pick. After spending time in the sixteenth century borders, Ah dinnae remember the Scott name with kindness, Ah can tell ye. Mind ye, Ah doubt ma own ancestors came out smelling of roses, either. But it's more than that..." He sighed. "Arnold, no one should ever have to see the result of so many different decisions played out differently."

"Nicely phrased."

Douglas chuckled, in spite of himself. "Aye. Well, many of us had similarly uncomfortable experiences. After a wee while, we all agreed to *not* look people up. This was particularly difficult for some of us."

Bessel leaned forward. "How so?"

Douglas took a stiff drink and recharged both glasses. "You remember Tim Norris, the young man who helped us survive the Cretaceous – and the Nazis?"

"You've mentioned him many times, James. I know how important the kid is to you. Did he fall foul of someone here?"

"No' exactly. He lost his parents and adoptive father because of the Schultzes. He never knew his real parents, but he loved his adoptive dad dearly. Dr Ted Norris. Well, it turns out that in *this* timeline, Ted and Patricia never met and he's happily married with a family of his own. Tim wisely, and nobly, decided not to make contact and disrupt the man's life over something he could know nothing about. Tim's friend, Woodsey, had a similarly painful disappointment. His father never married his mother in this world, either, but sadly she died young here, too. Poor Thomas Wood already lost his wife once and has been denied even a chance to try again.

"Added to that, many of us have tried to track down loved ones that were simply never born in this timeline. We've many such stories and none, to my knowledge, has a happy ending. Some things, it seems, should just be left alone. Maybe it's for the best. Ah cannae imagine the wrench for people reunited, only to be torn apart again when we leave. It's probably also fortunate that so many of our own opposite numbers in this world – where they exist at all – have led very different lives. Some do not even share ancestors with us. It's pretty bizarre—"

"Even creepy."

"Aye. However, there are some similarities – you, for instance. You'll never change," he laughed, cradling his glass. "When we arrived that night in Northumberland, and Ah was greeted by three people who had all died heroes' deaths in the first timeline, Ah dinnae mind telling ye, Ah thought Ah was having a breakdown."

"Any theories about why those three should have found you like that?"

Douglas shook his head slowly. "Ah've thought on it, many times over the years. There're some things we're just no' meant to know, but if Ah were to guess, Ah'd say that there are many, many timelines, all twisted together like rope, and Ah believe some people are like zip ties – fixed energies that keep them all bound together to prevent them from fraying." He smiled again. "People like you."

Bessel whistled. "That's pretty heavy duty."

Douglas nodded thoughtfully. "Hmm, but now it's time – nae pun intended – to leave the past behind, Arnold. And to do that, we must stop whoever it is that's doing whatever they're doing. This is a good world – so much better than the broken one we left behind. Even if we wanted to, even if we argued the morality of restoring the original timeline, it would be impossible. What's gone is gone – and there have been colossal losses. But it's ma belief that the people we left behind in 1558 set things in motion so that this altered future, this *kinder* world, would come to be, to *save* humanity – to give us a second chance. And now it's the duty of all who remember them to fight for what they've given us."

"I wish I could come with you, James."

"*Ah* wish ye were coming with us!" Douglas smiled sadly, but raised his glass in salute. "To friendship."

Bessel raised his own tumbler. "Past, present and future."

"Aye. May the last two remain the same."

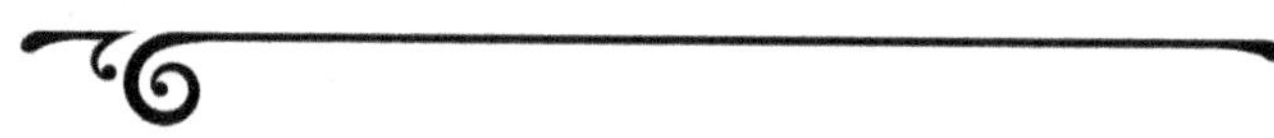

"We know it's here, dude." For once, Tim could tell that Woodsey was in deadly earnest. "Now, I dunno about you, but I reckon that after it..." He swallowed. "After it found poor Simba, it must have retreated to the Nile. Our good constable doesn't believe me – thinks we're influenced by our personal histories and are living in a fantasy world – but I took a jeep and drove south along the east bank for a few miles."

"You found something."

Woodsey nodded seriously. "Half a hippo. They live in more northerly latitudes than they did in our timeline. Master Sergeant Badawi thinks it was just leftovers from the Nile crocs, but..."

"You don't think so?"

Woodsey shrugged. "Crocs do eat dead hippos, but they rarely attack them *before* they're dead – especially not full-grown adults. The hippos are way more dangerous. As you know, it's rare for a croc to even go for a calf, so much do they fear the retribution of the mother or other adults within the herd. This animal has been killed – and yes, the attack does look crocodilian, but dude..."

"Too big?" Tim speculated.

"*Way* too big. A hippo may be crazy dangerous for a Nile croc to take on, but to an adult Spinosaurus aegyptiacus, it would be like a baby rabbit caught by a fox. The Nile is just one big, conveyor-belted buffet for a predator that size. Man-sized fish, like Nile perch, hippos, even crocodiles, as well as anything else that comes to the shore for a drink. There's plenty of suitable food on the menu. The people nearby will be in deadly danger, unless *we* do something."

Tim sat heavily on a packing case and sighed deeply. He had slept badly on the flight back and was exhausted. "You say the police aren't buying our theory?"

Woodsey shook his head. "They don't know what we know, mate – haven't seen what we've seen."

"I know, but what can we do about it? I mean, I'd have brought a bazooka back with me, but what if it had been detected at customs?"

"You're hilarious, you know that?"

"You get what I mean, though."

Woodsey scratched his stubble. "What about asking Captain Douglas?"

"He's got rather a lot on just now. Did you get your recall message?"

"I did, yeah. Listen, we need somebody who'll take us seriously – someone with military clout. So if not him, then who? It's not like I'm asking the guy to paddle over here with an elephant gun and a duck call, dude. I just can't leave these people like this. Even if this crazy mission we're going on is successful, and we make our way back exactly here, we'll have to allow a safety margin for the window of our return, like last time – so we don't end up back here before we left. Anything could happen to these folks in the interim."

Tim considered. "You're right. I'm sorry. If they do send armed forces in, they *will* kill it, though. Have you considered that?"

"Oh, mate. You and your dinosaurs – that is the point, ya know? I just don't think Spino's gonna come quietly, do you?"

"No, but it's a fine creature."

"Always the eco worrier. It's killing people, dude."

"You mean warrior."

"I know what I mean."

"Well, alright, but consider this – what if we could take it back with us?"

That was an unfortunate moment for Woodsey. Taken completely by surprise, he had just opened a can of lager from their chiller box and chosen that instant to take a long, quenching pull. Most of it spilled over his shirt as it came back down his nose. Coughing, he managed, "Get outta my nightmares!"

"*Come again?*" Douglas' distinctly Scottish tones emanated from the small speakers built into Tim's comm, as it sat on the table between him, Woodsey, Marston and Hetfield.

"I think we should take it back with us, sir."

"*Has anyone actually* seen *this creature?*"

"No, but we have found evidence of a huge predator, Captain – bigger than anything here," Woodsey answered.

"Director," Tim muttered.

"What?"

"It's Training Director Douglas, now. Not captain."

"What?"

"*Never mind,*" Douglas interrupted. "*Ah've been recalled to active duty for this mission, anyway, so Captain will do. My point is, if this creature actually exists, it could be anywhere now, and as much as Ah hate to keep using chronological idioms, we're on the clock here.*"

"We have three days, Captain," Tim tried again. "What if we can find it?"

Douglas' sigh travelled through the comm. *"Ye'll be pushing it close, which could upset everything. Ye know we cannae leave without ye. If we dally too long here, someone, back there, might change something so fundamentally that we never get the opportunity to fix things. Ye understand what Ah'm saying. Ye all do. We must go back and put this right. This could well be our last chance."*

Marston nudged her husband. "Tell James about El-Shaikh Ebada," she hissed.

"He can hear you – *you* tell him."

"What's this?" asked Douglas, anxiously.

Marston nudged her husband again, harder.

"Ouch! Alright, alright, I'm telling him! We get you, Captain," Hetfield replied, rubbing a new bruise on his arm. "But the boys are right. If that creature *is* here, as all the evidence suggests, and it decides to take a trip into town, it'll all be on us – *all* of us. As I've just been reminded, the little town of El-Shaikh Ebada is just a mile or so downriver, James. We also know these animals can range over vast territories. The Nile will be like a freeway for a Spinosaurus."

"And what if it swims to a major population centre? Say Cairo?" Marston posited. "Tell him about Cairo, Mor."

Morecombe Hetfield glared at his wife. Still rubbing his arm, he passed her concerns along sardonically, *"Yes,* James, what if it fancies a bit of sightseeing?"

Woodsey cut in before Marston could scold the old man further. "There's a popular Japanese movie franchise that springs irresistibly to mind—"

"Och, OK. Ah get it! So what do you all propose we do?"

"Could the *New World* come here, first?" asked Tim.

"The *New World?*" repeated Woodsey and Hetfield, together.

"Sorry. That was meant to be a surprise. Never mind. But, *could* you bring the ship here, first, Captain? I don't fancy transporting a live Spinosaurus halfway around the world."

"Aye yi yi."

"Captain?"

"Ah'll see what Ah can do. You don't do anything until you hear from me or ma representative. Douglas out."

The ship was sleek and dangerous-looking. It landed within a billowing cloud of sand and mini tornados a hundred metres north of the palaeontologists' camp. As its engines powered down, two figures emerged from the veil of dust and shimmering heat haze. The larger of the pair held up a hand in greeting. "G'day."

"Commander!" Tim greeted enthusiastically. "It's been a while."

"Yeah. I was quite happy to go back to the army, blowing stuff up. Looks like I got me old job back again, though." Gleeson shook hands warmly with Tim, Woodsey, Hetfield and Marston.

"Still handsome, Commander," Marston welcomed him with a hug.

Gleeson shrugged. "One doesn't like to blow one's own trumpet." He grinned. "By the way, folks, this is Special Agent Hemmings. She's here as the UN's representative to oversee our little safari."

Hemmings, now in her late thirties, smiled broadly. "Please, call me Elizabeth."

"We heard all about you from James, Elizabeth," said Marston.

"Well, technically, that wasn't me – I only hope I can live up to that kind of rep."

Marston smiled. Hemmings' job title seemed a loose fit for the woman standing before them. She liked her.

"Special agent, eh?" Woodsey asked, sheepishly. "Is that, like, law enforcement?"

"What have you done?" Tim asked out of the side of his mouth.

"Nothing, nothing. It's just that when we were in the States last, there was that little incident with the vending machine?"

"You said you'd paid for that!" Tim spat.

Woodsey cringed. "More sort of *meant* to. I mean it really was broken – I wasn't stealing from it."

Hemmings laughed. "Don't worry, Dr Wood, we have more serious concerns than a broken vending machine just now. Still, if it eases your conscience, I'd be happy to arrange a payment transfer to the correct department, on your behalf."

"You know all the details of that?" Woodsey was astonished in his guilt.

"We know *everything*," Hemmings replied, seriously. She turned to Tim and winked. "Right, it'll be dark in a few minutes, so let's get down to the business of catching a dinosaur, shall we?"

"OK," Tim took the lead. "How much have you been told?"

"Only that I can't blow it up," Gleeson replied with some annoyance. "So we were hoping *you* had a plan."

Tim's jaw dropped.

"Nah, I'm messin' with ya. We brought some rifles and very heavy-duty tranquillisers. Do you know how big it is?"

Tim smiled ruefully. "We haven't seen it yet – only the damage it's left behind. From what we've seen it must be an animal at least ten metres long. Of course, if it's fully grown, it might be approaching twice that. The local police have searched the area thoroughly – on land. However—"

"However," Woodsey jumped in, "they only gave the river a cursory look-over, 'cause they thought we were off our heads."

Gleeson took them both in, jovially. "*No.*"

Two evenings previously

Having crept into the palaeontologist's camp, Heidi was disappointed to find Tim gone. Listening carefully from the shadows at the periphery, she learned from the students' chatter that he had left for America. If any of them knew why, they were not saying. However, her trip was by no means wasted. Their stories regarding the disappearance of the Spinosaurus remains interested her greatly. As they began turning in for the night, her powerful mind was still struggling with the brain-melting complexity of events. When a girl disappeared out into the night alone and armed only with a shovel, she followed.

The wind was getting up, ideal for hiding their tracks as she closed on her quarry. It was always a good strategy to catch your enemies with their trousers down. However, at that place where metaphor becomes anecdote, even the most villainous of villains are sometimes willing to give it a minute. Heidi waited until the girl had finished her business before she grabbed her from the darkness. Luckily, by that point, the young palaeontologist no longer had the wherewithal to soil herself, though the metaphor about jumping out of her skin was still sound. She screamed.

Heidi clapped a hand about the girl's face, muffling her cry immediately. The wind was blowing away from the camp so it seemed unlikely anyone would have heard. She dragged her struggling charge back towards the gap in the cliffs that led into the hills.

The girl had spirit and bit Heidi's hand. When she released the pressure, shifting grip to secure her victim more thoroughly, the screaming began again. Heidi batted Simba around the head, knocking her sick but not unconscious.

"Be quiet, girl – if you want to live! I have some questions. Answer them truthfully and you may go. Lie, and..." There was something out in the night. Heidi heard it. More than that, she *felt* it. All her hunter's instincts pricked as did the hairs on the back of her neck. What may have caused her reaction required little speculation.

"Get to your feet," she whispered, just loud enough to be heard over gusts that were gaining strength every minute. If her senses and feelings were right, they were upwind; that was bad, especially out in open desert. Worse, Spinosaurus had good hearing, too. It must have heard the scream, even if the gathering sandstorm was scattering their scent.

The sky was clear and the starlight bright. However, the viciously gusting wind whipped the sand up so that visibility on the ground was lousy. Heidi guided them towards the cliffs at the valley's mouth, going with the presumption that large animals preferred open spaces. She was right, but unfortunately, Spinosaurus could not see where it was going, either. The women's first concrete clue that they were not alone was the sneeze, and what a sneeze. Heidi covered one ear, not daring to let her captive go. Bombarded by whipped sand, Spinosaurus' sensitive nostrils made a sound like a bass horn, played uncomfortably, even painfully, close to Heidi's ear. Her mind raced. Far worse than having a horn close to your ear, was having the jaws of a Spinosaurus close to your ear. She fired three shots, almost blindly, at the creature's head to back it off. When Simba screamed again, Heidi was left with but one choice. She lunged across the girl, grabbing her securely on the way. Spinning shotput-style, she flung the student at the monster just three metres away from them, using the angular momentum of her spin to do the work of four Heidis. The girl flew to land on the sand, right under the dinosaur's stinging snout.

The young palaeontologist screamed with impressive wind, which was fortunate for Heidi, and exactly what she had expected. She used the distraction it created to run further into the valley. Once downwind, her movements were masked by the nebulous sandstorm. When the girl's scream ended abruptly, Heidi took it as motivation to distance herself still further from the altercation.

Having viewed the lay of the land earlier that day from up in the hills, she had a rough idea of where she was going. The cliffs to her right became less sheer as she ran east, translating into a steep, craggy embankment. She was close to the box canyon that opened south to where she had entered this time and place.

In theory, her wrist device could open a wormhole from anywhere on Earth, and she would have opened one right where she stood, had the dinosaur caught up with her. However, that would be a further risk, a further unknown. Besides, she fully expected the maelstrom of sand and wind to have deprived the creature of her scent by now, possibly along with all memory that she even existed. She was yet to study the practical intelligence or memory retention of such animals – ironically, there had been no time – but she did know that the wind, while taking *her* scent away, would also inform Spinosaurus about the Nile west of them. After searching the arid hills and valleys all day, it must have been parched – especially after its ordeal before leaving the Cretaceous, where it had technically died of exhaustion.

The thought that the answers to all the dinosaur's most pressing needs lay in the opposite direction reassured her. Presently, she came upon the entrance she was feeling for. The wind subsided as soon as she entered the box canyon, passing the junction by to funnel further down the main valley, east. Illuminated once more by starlight, she walked along the western edge of the valley, eventually stopping right next to the steel rod she had driven into the rock face earlier in the day. Until her wormhole device had been more rigorously tested, it made sense to travel from the known to the known, and she was in no mood to push her luck any further that night.

She shook her head in wonderment, recalling the events that had brought her to that place. Wiping sweat and sand from her face, she pulled back her sleeve to reveal the device. Dr Reid had genuinely impressed her with this latest project. Now she would find out just how good he was; that, or how much trouble she was in.

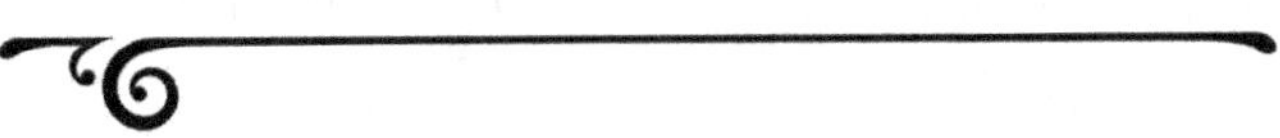

Two evenings later

Master Sergeant Badawi shook hands with Gleeson and Hemmings. "The UN sent you to help us with an animal attack?" he asked suspiciously.

"Well, it's a little more complicated than that, Master Sergeant," Gleeson replied. He glanced at Tim and continued sourly, "Due to reasons I can't go into here, we have to capture the creature alive. I understand you have a couple of helicopters at your disposal?"

"Not indefinitely. I had to let them go, but I may be able to recall them – if I believe there is cause." Badawi gave Gleeson a calculating look. "Just what *is* it we're looking for, Commander?"

Gleeson looked to Tim again and shrugged. "What're we going with? A larger than usual *croc?*"

Before Tim could answer, Badawi's radio crackled to life. "Excuse me, gentlemen, lady." He turned away to acknowledge it, beginning what quickly escalated into a lively conversation.

Hemmings held up a finger, silencing the chatter that arose while they waited. "You speak Arabic?" whispered Gleeson.

Hemmings tilted her hand left and right. "A little." She shushed them and took a few steps away, the better to eavesdrop.

"Sorry," Gleeson mouthed. Slipping quietly back to Tim, he muttered, "This doesn't sound good."

Tim nodded. "We're about to find out."

Badawi broke off the call and ran to his vehicle, rummaging in the back.

Hemmings returned to the men. "There's been a sighting of something – downstream."

"Something?" asked Tim, darkly.

"I only understood a little, but whatever it was came from the Nile. About two hundred klicks north, near Al Khurman. As far as I could tell, there've been some casualties."

"Oh, no." Tim bowed his head.

"Listen, kid, this isn't your fault," Gleeson assured him. "You told 'em, they wouldn't listen. Besides, we don't even know what *it* is yet, so keep it together, OK?"

Tim nodded, taking a shuddering breath. His dreams were constantly haunted by visions of his cousin, coming to claim him and destroy his friends, even after ten years. Although they were yet to discover any proof, suspicions gnawed at his spirit.

Presently, Badawi jogged over to them, now carrying a rifle.

"What have you?" Hemmings greeted brusquely.

The policeman looked unsure where to begin. "We have an animal sighting in Al Khurman. Two teenagers, a boy and a girl, have gone missing. There're some parklands and a playground alongside the Nile, near the western limits of the town. According to the sergeant I spoke with, it's a place young people frequent in the evenings, to—"

"Alright, we get the photograph," interrupted Gleeson. "What happened to them?"

"An older woman on a passing boat said she saw something snatch them from the footpath. She reported it immediately. When local police arrived at the scene there was a little blood, but no other evidence."

They all looked warily at one another.

"What *exactly* did she say had taken them?" Hemmings pressed.

Badawi held out his hands, palms up, baffled. "It was almost dark, Agent. All she could tell the local authorities was that it was big – too big to be an animal. I assume she meant an *ordinary* animal. As you might expect, she and her husband made straight for the nearest jetty, to get off the water."

Gleeson snorted. "At flanking speed, I shouldn't wonder."

"Quite probably, Commander. And who could blame them? The only thing that takes this so far out of the ordinary as to give Dr Wood's theory credence – forgive me – is that the footpath is thirty metres in from the shoreline at that point, and at the top of a five-metre-high embankment. To 'snatch' someone from up there would, quite literally, be a tall order for any crocodile. And we have no other indigenous predators of size that hunt on land and then retreat to the water. People here understand well how dangerous some of the Nile wildlife can be. This must be something new. I have now recalled our helicopters, but as they are currently needed elsewhere, it will be several hours before they arrive."

"Did you say there was blood spatter but *no* other evidence?" Hemmings tried again. "Nothing else at all?"

Badawi reflected. "The local force did find some takeaway food wrappers, so I was told. Apparently, litter is a problem in that area. My contact's belief was that kids just... What?"

His audience exchanged worried glances.

"We'll take our ship, Master Sergeant," Gleeson deflected, "but she's not the sort of craft people expect to see flying low over towns and cities, so you'd better warn everyone ahead. At least we know which way the thing's heading. How the hell did it get so far north in... how long has it been?"

"Two days," supplied Woodsey. "Give or take."

"That's not so remarkable, Commander," Tim stated.

Gleeson sighed, folding his arms. "I'd forgotten about this bit. OK, let's have Tim's fact for the day. Some of us may not be scared enough yet."

"I'm simply saying," Tim countered, "that the Nile's flow, at this time of year, probably averages no more than about four knots – the inundation waters will have mostly subsided, three months after the summer monsoon. Wouldn't you agree, Master Sergeant?"

Badawi nodded, with dubious confidence.

"Anyway, that's about seven, seven and a half kilometres per hour. Now, sadly, most of our time in the Cretaceous was spent cooped up in ships, so we had very little opportunity to study the sleeping habits of dinosaurs—"

"*Ahem,*" Gleeson nudged him back on track.

"OK, hear me out. Birds averagely sleep ten or twelve hours a day, whereas with crocodiles it's more like sixteen, but they nap little and often rather than taking a solid sleep. Our quarry is a dinosaur – a bird, for all intents and purposes – that lives like a crocodile."

"Where are you going with this, dude?" asked Woodsey. "I've already forgotten what it was you were telling us about."

"Look, all I'm saying – *thank you* – is that during the last fifty hours or so, our animal may have been active for easily thirty of them. In the last fifty hours the Nile waters *alone* have flowed from here to Cairo, at seven*ish* kilometres per hour. If our dinosaur swam with the current, it could easily have made it up into the Nile Delta by now. In a way – a very unfortunate way, granted – we may actually have been lucky."

"*Lucky?*" asked Gleeson.

"Yes, Commander. At least it's still within our reach. Imagine trying to look for it out there in twenty thousand square kilometres of delta? Or how about in the Med, hmm?"

"Right. Understood," Badawi cut in. "We must move quickly. Commander, it would take me the entire night to drive there. May I join you aboard your ship?"

"Of course. I think we should alert all the folks down the Nile first, though, mate."

"That's pretty much everyone," Tim stated.

Badawi gave a half-smile. "Professor Norris is correct. My superiors have already been informed and military assistance is on the way to enforce a curfew. The last thing we need is civilians taking an evening stroll along the river. Now, will someone explain to me why we have to take this thing alive?"

Spinosaurs likely had little imagination; if they had, the female swimming down the Nile might have thought she was in heaven. She had completely forgotten about the Cretaceous – this world was hers for the taking.

Since their arrival, she had just watched her third sunset, and after swimming, floating and basking her way downstream with the flow, she was yet to meet a creature that might represent any serious threat to her majesty. This was a world of pygmies. Food was plentiful, the temperature was perfect and there were so many enticing new smells to investigate. Indeed, the further north she travelled, the more there was to engage her.

After her evening meal, strange lights seemed to pop up all over the place, giving her the first pangs of fear in days. Fortunately, the river cut deeply between several islands, moving more quickly through the narrows, and she was able to find security and comfort in its murky depths.

"This is transport vessel UNS Goliath *calling Commander Gleeson – do you copy? Over."*

Captain Douglas had made it clear, to all of them, that the time might come when they must go back to the Cretaceous to clear up the mess they had been forced to leave behind. Gleeson had not been idle during the last ten years. He had undergone a series of intense training courses and become an accomplished pilot in his own right. At the stick of his orbital attack ship, also on loan from the UN, he activated the comm. "Goliath, this is Gleeson. Welcome to Egypt – over."

"*Thank you, Commander. We have a large package for you. Where would you like us to leave it? Over.*"

Gleeson frowned. "*Jill?* Is that you?"

Baines' laughter tinkled through the comm. "*Didn't think I'd let you have* all *the fun, did you?*"

Gleeson grinned. As well as a much larger ship with a storage container for their quarry, Baines also brought another pair of experienced hands to the mission. Things were looking up. He transmitted the landing coordinates supplied by Badawi's people. "See you in a few, Captain. Gleeson out."

"Loving this place you've brought us to," Baines greeted. "It's now," she checked her comm, "2200 hours, and where's the hotel, again?"

Gleeson laughed. "For some reason, the local boys want to keep us away from everyone."

"You don't say?"

Gleeson laughed again. "This is Special Agent Hemmings, who I think you've met."

"Yes, ten years ago and halfway up a mountain. How are you, Elizabeth?"

Hemmings returned Baines' greeting cordially.

"And this," continued Gleeson, "is Master Sergeant Apep Badawi. The first attack happened on his turf and he's now helping us liaise with local authorities."

"Master Sergeant." Baines shook hands.

"Everyone else you already know."

"Don't I just." Baines was now fifty-one, but still a striking mostly-brunette, with a grin forty years younger. "It's lovely to see you all."

"Even me?" Woodsey asked cheekily, moving in for a hug.

"What? The boy who taught Elizabeth I lewd songs? *Especially* you." She gave him a hug and then held him, arms straight. "All grown up, I see. You make me feel old."

"Don't worry, it won't be long before he does something childish to take you right back."

"Tim!" Baines held out her arms enthusiastically. "I knew *you'd* be involved in this somewhere. How's your mom?"

"Please forgive my interruption," Badawi butted in sternly, his words carrying about as much sincerity as if he had just uttered the phrase 'no offence'. "But we have a few problems requiring our attention. Local forces may have been ordered to wait for you to capture this beast, but I must caution you, they will not wait forever."

"You're right, of course, Master Sergeant," Baines allowed. "Are you ready for us to unload the container?"

"We haven't actually located the thing yet," Gleeson cut in. "My ship is a little *unsubtle* for stalking wildlife."

Baines' grin returned. "They didn't give *you* an unsubtle ship, did they? What were they thinking?"

"Oh, I've missed this," he replied good-naturedly, if sarcastically.

Baines laughed. "Don't worry, Commander. The UN also provided us with a little something to help broaden our search." She pulled her comm from a pocket. "Bring them out, please."

"*Yes, Captain,*" replied a disembodied voice.

The rear of the *Goliath* split like a transport plane, throwing a corridor of light out across the desert as a ramp extended. An electric tug towed the first trailer of three almost silently down onto the sands. Atop the trailer was a small, lightweight helicopter with its rotors folded for transport, in line with its small fuselage.

"Each is equipped with an advanced sensor suite," Baines explained, "and they're all-electric. Not exactly silent, but the rotors can easily be mistaken for gusting wind. It's not like we're dealing with a scalpel-sharp intellect here."

"They carry passengers?" asked Woodsey.

Baines turned to him. "They're four-seaters. The pilot and sensor operator-cum-navigator will take up the front pair, naturally, but some of us can travel with them, yes. I assume you have the rifles and tranquillisers?"

Gleeson tapped his pockets. "Oh, no!"

"That's funny," Baines answered, deadpan.

"Can we please take this a little more seriously?" Badawi remonstrated.

Gleeson gave him a half-smile. "Sorry, mate. But you see, for us, this is just like old times."

Spinosaurus dozed in the shallows; just nostrils, located at the top of her head, and her enormous sail above the surface. She drifted slightly, coming to rest on a sand bar at the river's edge. After accidentally taking a branch in the Nile, she had travelled west of the main river, though she continued north. Forced to leave the water altogether in places, she slid back in when it became broad and deep enough to allow her passage. It had been a long night and she had explored far by the time sleep eventually overcame her.

Her catnap was momentarily interrupted by the sounds of something sliding across the sandy shore, followed by a *splosh* as the same something slid into water. She sniffed. An unmistakably crocodilian scent she likened to that of the giant Sarcosuchus imperator with which she shared her home, but they, along with her home, were barely a memory now – not that there had been much sharing. Now she had a new home, the Nile, and the small fry that masqueraded as apex predators here would soon be following her visitor's example – they would leave or die. Her stomach growled after all the exertion, but that would have to take second place to a more pressing need. She dozed.

Badawi placed a holographic map generator on the sand. When it activated, a four-hundred-kilometre section of the Nile sprang to life in three dimensions. "Here is El-Shaikh Ebada, where we started, and this is Al Khurman, where the most recent attack took place." He looked to Woodsey. "Can we assume that the creature will continue north, swimming with the flow?"

The New Zealander shook his head. "No guarantee, mate."

"He's right," Tim agreed. "It's exploring at the moment, carving out a new territory. The Nile gives it everything it could want, so I believe it will stay near the river, but whether it continues north, or decides to consolidate its new territory and turn back, is anyone's guess."

"What about the lake near Faiyum?" Gleeson queried, pointing at the map. "Looks like the perfect environment for our friend. What is that... *Quorun* Lake?"

"Qarun," Badawi clarified. "There are many canals that lead to and from the Nile there, but I believe the monstrosity we seek would easily be spotted, were it to swim along any of those. We would do better to use our airpower in the areas where we have no eyes on the ground."

"Good point," Baines agreed. "Where do you suggest we begin, Master Sergeant?"

Badawi mulled her question over. "If the creature is just as likely to return south, upstream, then we should send at least one helicopter to scan that section of the Nile. The riverbanks north of the attack site become ever more populated the further you travel. I suggest we send one craft to follow the Nile north towards Cairo. The third, we use for an intensive sweep of the area around Al Khurman, in case the beast lingered there – perhaps sleeping off its meal. Does that sound plausible, Professor Norris, Dr Wood?"

"Very sensible," Tim agreed at once.

Woodsey was lost in thought.

"What?" Tim prompted.

"Oh, just wondering why it attacked those kids. The Nile must be an all-you-can-eat. Why would it risk leaving the water for a mere morsel? Sorry, I don't mean that to sound flippant, but it just doesn't make sense."

Tim scratched the three-day growth on his chin. "Woodsey's right. Back in the Cretaceous, we usually came under attack when we trespassed on another creature's patch or happened across them when they were hungry, but if a Spinosaurus can't find a meal in the Nile then there's something wrong. Something must have drawn it out to attack those teenagers."

"Like what?" asked Gleeson.

"I've no idea. Look, I – *we* – will think on it. In the meantime, I recommend we get those helicopters in the air, if they're unpacked."

Banjo was thirsty. While his master had been distracted, *he* had wandered off. Somewhere in the distance, out in the darkness, his master was calling him back, but Banjo was independent. Banjo was stubborn. Banjo was an ass, and like most of his kind, Equius asinus, he was renowned for it[3]. Despite the reins, and the stupid hat that slotted over his ears for the benefit of the smaller tourists, Banjo was his own donkey at heart.

He loved the evenings, loved the coolness they brought. Carrying the two-legs' obnoxious offspring around those pointy buildings in the desert heat was no joke, not when you wore fur every day of your life. So Banjo loved the evenings. He began to trot. Sniffing the breeze, he knew he was drawing near to water. His master had been late with his dinner that evening, which is why he had wandered off in the first place. He had had enough of waiting. What a day. He could still smell the vomit that had cascaded down the side of his noble neck, after one of the gorgons he was forced to transport had become travel-sick all over him – and him such a smooth mover, too. Maybe, if the river was quiet, he might risk a quick wash.

The thought excited him; he was *so* thirsty now. His master never let him approach the river because of the scaly ones. Banjo knew how dangerous they could be, but he was too fast for them. He lapped at the water's edge, greedily.

Something moved out in the darkness. He sniffed the air. It carried a stench that was not good. Banjo whinnied and backed away from the water, his excellent night vision warning him of a shadow that was darker than the rest. When it launched from the water, huge and stinking of carrion, Banjo was already moving. He spun instantly and galloped for his life. No scaly one could possibly keep up with him. He would soon be home with his nose in his dinner bag. It would be alright.

What Banjo did not expect – had no possible experience from which to draw a comparison, in fact – was a scaly one scrambling out of the water and chasing after him, not merely for a few donkey lengths, but for many, *many* donkey lengths, and without tiring.

----

3   It is believed that what appears to us as stubbornness in donkeys is actually a response to danger or threat. When sensing danger, a donkey is likely to freeze while it assesses what to do next (sensible) and will often refuse to move until it has decided (also sensible). This makes it appear stubborn, more so if the rider/handler either misses the danger altogether, or their superior human intelligence fails to realise that a harmless object has alarmed their animal. Of course, from the animal's perspective, it must seem that their human is just being typically reckless. It is easy to see why such situations can become embarrassing, especially when the donkey considers its handler to be an ass.

In his panic, he smashed through a fence and into a crop field. Even the most stubborn of donkeys understood damage like that would mean a most angry master. Fortunately, there was someone on whom he could pin the blame, both for that and for the rest of the fence that had just been flattened behind him – if he got away.

Anyone outside, listening to the sounds of the night, would certainly have been given pause on that evening. Between Banjo's terrified braying and his pursuer's roars of frustration, all to the accompaniment of everything in their path being smashed to pieces, it was small surprise that every bedroom light in the Dahshur suburbs came on, almost simultaneously.

Banjo crashed through another fence, hearing similar if even greater sounds of destruction close on his hooves. The going changed, suddenly. He was on sand. He knew this. He was back in the office. On familiar ground once more, he began to outpace the monster at his back. A terrifying roar followed him. Banjo flattened his ears and ran like hell.

Donkeys are gregarious creatures by nature. All his kind, that he knew, spent their days walking tourists around the Red Pyramid of Pharoah Sneferu. Too terrified to realise that it was, in fact, night, he lowered his head and bolted for the comfort of his own.

Spinosaurus slowed. She had never before encountered prey of this kind, but twenty-five summers of experience told her it was too fast for her to catch. At least, out in the open. She sniffed the air. The smell of the river was behind her, like a lifeline, hidden among myriad alien fragrances, some of which were enticing, others disgusting.

She turned west and sniffed again. Dung. The breeze carried the scent of herbivores. Out there somewhere in the darkness was a meal, maybe several. She drooled hungrily. Although an enthusiastic piscivore, she was happy to eat anyone's flesh.

Sounds of alarm were coming to life behind and all around her, so she made her way out into the desert, following the scent of supper.

"Are you having a giraffe?" Gleeson blurted into the comm. "It's in a town? Where? Dahshur? Where's that?"

"I know it," Badawi called. "Pilot, head due north. Commander, tell our teams to rendezvous with us at these coordinates." He showed Gleeson a map, tapping Dahshur with his finger.

"Thanks. Got it."

Banjo was exhausted, the effects of adrenaline fading as it was absorbed by his system. He almost collapsed as he lay down, panting, his heart banging.

Just two hundred metres east, Spinosaurus sniffed at some dung. With nostrils atop her head, she could not sniff it directly, so she nipped carefully with her front teeth, throwing it back deeper into her mouth. Her senses analysed the aroma as she took another bite. Sniffing the breeze, she continued west into the darkness.

Baines rode the chopper heading north. They were practically at the coordinates Gleeson had communicated when the call came in, but Baines could tell there was already something occupying her fellow passenger. "What is it, Tim?"

"I was just thinking about what Woodsey said earlier, when he questioned why that creature attacked those kids. I thought maybe the smell of their food had simply been too much for it. Anyone who's had a dog drool all over their trousers under the dinner table understands that. Although carnivores *eat* raw food, they *love* our food. But that seems just a bit too simplistic."

"What are you saying?"

"It's just like Woodsey said – and he was right, by the way – the Nile has everything this animal could want. So why risk the unknown? It may have been tantalised by whatever they were eating. It *may* have gone for the meal and eaten the diners by mistake, but..."

"But?"

He frowned, his thoughts nebulous. "I just can't help wondering if it's something deeper than that. Look, when we left the Cretaceous, pretty much all our interaction with dinosaurs had been accidental – Mayor notwithstanding – but who knows what's been happening *since* we left?"

"You think the folks back there may have... what, exactly? Turned the dinosaurs against them?"

He shrugged. "I know that sounds crazy, and maybe it is, but let's rephrase it and ask – what if they did something to get the dinosaur's interest? If you're about to ask what *specifically,* then I'm sorry, I haven't a clue. It's just a feeling."

Baines considered a moment. "Well, assuming she survived the attack she was under when we left, Heidi would be the first to go around shooting and killing things. Doubt many of her buddies were much better, either."

"That's a fair point, Jill, but let's take it one step further, shall we? How the *hell* did that animal get here? What must they have done to make *that* happen?"

Baines fell into silence. After a while she admitted, "You know, with the chase to capture this thing, and with the journey we're about to take – *again* – I hadn't really given that question much headspace."

"We're here, Captain," their pilot interrupted them.

"And we have a contact," said the scanning officer.

Not in all the five millennia since Sneferu met with his surveyor to ask if the plot might not be made perhaps a little larger, had the Dahshur Necropolis witnessed a scene like the one playing out on that evening.

"Does this thing have a spotlight?" Baines demanded.

The pilot responded immediately, and suddenly captured on stage together were a donkey and a vast dinosaur, scrambling one after the other up the roughly sandblasted stones of the Red Pyramid.

"Oh, *donkey.* Why did you have to go up there?" Tim fretted, to no one's benefit.

Banjo was too exhausted for another steeplechase, not that he had bothered to *jump* any of the fences – by the same token, his debut as a steeple*jack* was not exactly going swimmingly, either. His kind had always been more than capable over rugged, mountainous terrain, and so, by the standards of earlier failures and later successes, the comparatively lazy forty-three-degree angle of the shambolic, weather-beaten masonry was not overly challenging for him, but it *was* slow-going. Sand banked unevenly against the stones, and he slipped constantly in his haste to climb, fatigue burning every muscle. Whereas his giant pursuer had only to lift her head to be eight metres up the slope, before her hind legs even left the desert sands.

Fortunately for the errant donkey, the place he chose to climb was covered with wind-blown sand for the first ten metres of the ascent. He had used most of his remaining strength to run up that slope in a hopping, clip-clop fashion. By the time he reached the stones he was tiring quickly, but the stones did make the climb easier under hoof.

On the other claw, the sands around the bottom of the pyramid provided considerably more challenge to a fifteen-ton, semi-aquatic dinosaur. She was happy enough on land, but the quarry was taking her ever further out of her comfort zone. Despite that, the chase had gotten her blood up and she was unwilling to let go, even though the slippery sand was slowing her forward ascent dramatically. She, too, was tiring. Frustrated, she leapt, lunging for her prey, almost catching him.

Banjo honked and squealed as the massive jaws snapped with a nightmarish *clop* right on his tail – literally. He felt a tug on its wire-ended tip and lurched forwards and upwards with all his remaining strength, baldly going where no donkey had gone before. Spinosaurus spat out the furball, while such proximity to certain death provided Banjo with his second wind. Though Master had never allowed him to climb the pyramid, he clattered up the stones well enough on that evening, not stopping until he reached the very top. Tomorrow, he would be in all kinds of trouble, and prising him back down would be a veritable clinic in the use of carrot and stick, but at least that day would now come.

Baines opened the chopper's sliding rear door and aimed one of Gleeson's rifles. She fired the tranquilliser dart. Through the infrared telescopic sights, she saw the dart strike home in the animal's rump. The dinosaur's attention was entirely committed to climbing the slick mountain of sand and it seemed not to notice. She looked to Tim. "How long is this stuff meant to take?"

"I've no idea. I don't even know what's *in* those darts. All I told Captain Douglas was, we *might* have an eight-to-fifteen-ton predatory dinosaur on the loose."

"Great. You know, in some circles, that may have been considered an unusual conversation starter." She sighed. "It's not going down."

Spinosaurus roared at the giant gnat buzzing about overhead.

"Go up! Go up! Stay high!" Baines shouted urgently. "Have you never seen the end of *King Kong?*"

"Which version?"

Baines rolled her eyes. "Pilots."

Tim leaned over to get a better look. "Do you think it's still awake because it's angry? Has a system full of adrenaline, I mean?"

Baines stared at him. "You're asking *me? Don't you know?"

"Not really, Jill. Call me weird, but I make it policy to never anger anyone who's fifty feet long and has a front end made of teeth."

"Should I shoot it again?"

"Ooh," Tim groaned. "*Maybe...?"

"Where?"

"Try the neck."

"Why?"

"I don't know. Because its halfway between the heart and the brain? We want the chemical in its bloodstream, don't we?"

They were shouting at one another now, fear distracting them from what was happening below. Spinosaurus roared again, rearing up to reach skywards. Her jaws snapped shut, just nudging the helicopter's skid.

"*King Kong,* damnit!" Baines hollered.

The pilot did not need telling a third time and they shot up vertically. "I didn't think it could reach that high!"

"Yes, a few people we left behind the last time underestimated these creatures, too!" She leaned out once more, this time aiming for the neck. Another hit. "Oh, come *on!* Seriously?" Frustrated, she turned to find Tim leaning out after her. "What the hell are you doing?" Tim's comm camera was automatically adjusting ISO and shutter speeds to make the most of what little light there was to be had, when the chopper bucked, throwing him into her. Baines shoved him back into his seat. "Fasten your belt," she bellowed over the roar of the rotors. "Are you out of your mind?"

Tim crashed back into his seat, a broad grin spreading across his face. "I captured it in 56K, 3D holotech. This is going to look *great* at my next symposium. 'What Spinosaurus aegyptiacus *really* looked like'. Oh, yeah, this is gonna shut some faces!"

Baines could hardly express her annoyance. "I'm in a flying asylum." She pointed out into the night. "You're watching *this* through a four-inch screen?"

Tim gripped her arm. "Look. It's lying down."

0630 hours, and as Ra began to push the sun once more up into the autumn sky, its rays enlightened a world forever changed. For some, it was as terrifying as it was illuminating – for others, it was a massive headache with associated paperwork.

The man was furious, roaring in Arabic. Somehow, he had slipped past crowd control and was now screaming at anyone who would listen – he did not trouble over whether they understood him or not. Baines managed to extricate herself and palm him off onto Master Sergeant Badawi. Proximity to the Dahshur suburbs had made it all but impossible to keep the situation quiet. The media circus was lost among such a vast sea of onlookers that even the clowns were mere puffins, drifting upon the swell.

Local law enforcement, supported by a couple of military units, had erected a temporary fence to keep everyone back. Though it proved mostly successful, one or two still managed to slip through.

"What was *that* guy's problem?" Gleeson drawled.

Baines shrugged. "I don't know. Something about a donkey, I think."

Gleeson stared.

"Never mind," they said together.

Baines turned to look back at the spectacle of Spinosaurus aegyptiacus, lolled unconscious against Pharaoh Sneferu's tomb. She blew out her cheeks. "James is going to freak. He told us not to attract attention."

Gleeson stroked his stubbled chin thoughtfully. "I dunno. We did stop it from getting to Cairo."

"Barely."

"Is the *Goliath* en route?"

"Yeah. There's no keeping a lid on this now. May as well just load and go. Quickly."

"Still, all this'll do wonders for the tourist trade. Tim told me that thing's name in English is the 'Egyptian spine lizard' – not hard to see why – but to see it draped over a pyramid has gotta be the *most* Egyptian image anyone's ever taken. They should put it on the flag."

"Image taken?" Baines turned back to him, sharply.

"Yeah. Little guy over there with the camera."

"Oh, crap."

From 105 metres – that's 344 feet, plus his own prodigious thirteen hands – Banjo had a truly god's-eye view of the necropolis and desert below. King of the third highest pyramid in Egypt, he watched the events below unfold – events that certainly fell under all three headings of dangerous, threatening and alarming. He could also see his master huffing and puffing up the side of the vast monument, cursing every time he got his breath back. Banjo assessed. There really was only one thing to do. He fell back on the wisdom of his kind. Yes, there would be shouting, but he would not be swayed by that. He was staying put.

Chapter 5 | Sausages

Douglas sat alone in the refectory occupying the ground floor's southern corner, within the UNASA[4] building. After staying up half the night awaiting news from Egypt, he had skipped breakfast at home. Arriving at the office, he found himself ravenous. Munching on a piece of lightly buttered toast, he contemplated his immediate future, while staring balefully at the 'Full English Breakfast' on his plate. Of course, it was nothing of the sort, but they did their best for him, and he appreciated it. Once, he requested fried bread, only to be astounded by the arrival of something that looked more like a dessert, but no, his stare was not for the breakfast, rather it was for all that had been lost – centuries of human endeavour, good and bad, and now they had to risk it all again.

Despite the bright blue sky outside, his thoughts were in darkness. *What if the human world vanishes altogether this time? If it comes to a fight, and Ah fully expect that it might, anything could go wrong – anything could change.*

He stabbed a sausage and inspected it on his fork, contemplating its meaning. For well over half a billion years, from the very birth of complex life in the Cambrian oceans, there had been violence. Almost in the geological blink of an eye, animals went from absorbing nutrients from the seawater around them, to killing one another, and

---

4   United Nations Aeronautics and Space Administration.

that cycle had never stopped, nor even paused since – not even through the most devastating mass extinctions. Douglas was an unashamed omnivore, yet he loved animals and the natural world around him. Loved it all the more, since leaving *his* Canaveral Airbase, a decade ago; a place choked with smog and buried under concrete.

As he studied the morsel – arguably popularised in the west by the Germans[5] in the early 15th century and subsequently formed into links like the one on his fork during the reign of England's King Charles I – it seemed to him that when it came to killing for food, this innocent banger may, latterly, have become the very first totem of guilt, too. Its descendants masqueraded as ham sliced to resemble teddy bears, turkey dinosaurs, and chicken nuggets, but the comically shaped sausage was perhaps man's *first* attempt to put a friendly face to carnivory, by disguising the meat's true identity. He only considered these things because, where they were headed, the creatures had no such scruple, and seeing impossibly huge creatures kill was a lesson in nature he would never forget.

Memories flooded back. Just after they arrived in the Cretaceous, he and a small team had become embroiled and nearly killed during a terrifying Mapusaurus hunting spree. The giant carnivores had burst from the forest to brutalise a young Argentinosaurus huinculensis. Though a mere adolescent, its already vast size meant that the manner of its death had been slow and horribly drawn out. Douglas could still hear its cries through their ship's bulkheads when he closed his eyes.

He replaced the sausage on his plate, feeling a little queasy. Memories warred with sensibilities as another recollection was triggered, this one of his father – another casualty lost to this timeline, like so many others. Neither of his parents now existed as the people he knew, his family tree irrevocably twisted by paradox. Douglas had grown up in Hawick in the Scottish Borders, though his father spoke with the Glaswegian accent of a youth spent in the city. He remembered his words as though it were yesterday.

---

5   Although originally invented 5000 years ago in Sumeria (Iraq), sausages were later used by the Greeks as a way of preserving food without refrigeration and by the 9th century BC were even being sold in theatres, like modern-day hot dogs. Now, from a street vendor in New York to a greasy spoon in the north of England, Douglas could not imagine a world without them.

At six years old, he, like many young children, had found out what meat actually was and where it came from. It had upset him deeply. Of course, he now realised that his family's military standing came with advantages, and he was privileged even to have sampled such delights. Even so, his father had patiently explained that in the modern world there *were* alternatives to eating meat, although in a very real sense it was nature's way for him to do so. "James, ye dinnae have tae eat meat if ye dinnae want tae. Yer mam's been trying tae get me tae give it up for years. But if ye dae eat it, ye should ne'er forget that a creature gave everything so that ye can live and grow strong. Never, ever waste meat, son. It shows disrespect and contempt for life. We dinnae kill for the sake of it, ye ken? We should love and respect our animals for whit they give uz. Ye understand, Jamie?"

Sixty-year-old Douglas smiled and nodded gently at the memory. *Aye, faither.* He felt a tear well at the corner of his eye for all that was and would never be again. He wiped it and ate his bacon, and his sausage, like a good boy.

Lost in a past that, for most, had never happened, he was awakened from his reverie by a minor commotion taking place in the entrance foyer, not ten metres from his table.

A tallish man, with blond hair running to white, was gesticulating and growing ever more agitated with the receptionist. "But I must see him now, *Fräulein.* You do not understand. It is imperative."

Douglas pushed his plate aside, stood and left his table to investigate. The interruption had forced him to leave a grilled tomato and a couple of mushrooms, but he felt sure they would understand; one a fruit, the others fungus, even his mam would not have been able to accuse him of leaving his vegetables.

As he approached, the receptionist recognised him. "Director Douglas, sir."

"What is it, Angie? Can Ah help ye?"

The man in front of the reception desk also turned to face him, irritation turning instantly to relief. "James," he greeted enthusiastically, offering his hand.

"Klaus," Douglas responded, a smile dispelling his earlier mood.

Dr Klaus Fischer was a member of *Factory Pod 4*'s crew, the Pod transported under the original *New World*'s belly in what now felt to Douglas like another life.

Despite his obvious pleasure at seeing Douglas again, Fischer's expression grew serious once more. "I must speak with you, James. It is a delicate matter and most pressing." He looked around. "Is there somewhere private we might go?"

Douglas nodded. "Ma office. Angie, have ye taken a copy of Dr Fischer's identification?"

"Yes, sir."

"Excellent. Can you quickly give him an ID card and book him onto the NW2 programme, please? Once you've arranged his quarters, send the details to ma office."

"Of course, sir."

"Thanks, Angie. Klaus, ye'll need this." He placed the ID card on a strap around Fischer's neck. "Follow me, please. Have ye eaten? They've some nice German sausage, this morning. How about Ah get them to send some up to us?"

"I hate sausages," Aito complained. "Every day, sausages." He replaced the fork onto his plate with the article in question left half-eaten.

"We're being supplied by Germans from 1943," Devon pointed out. "Don't be so ungrateful. If the wormhole had exited in Britain, we'd all be eating cold tins of corned beef."

"I like corned beef," Jansen interjected. "Or they may have given us fish and chips. They weren't rationed during the war. I tried them while I was there, once. Lashings of salt and vinegar, mmm. Don't knock it 'til you've tried it."

Devon shook his head, a gesture of sympathy. "Tragic. Anyway, there hasn't been a war, remember? Not yet, anyway," he added darkly. Turning back to Aito, he forced a grin. "Come on, seriously, what did you expect? McDonalds?"

"Why not?" Aito snapped, irritably.

"Because we're connected to Munich," Jansen explained in a bored voice.

Aito faced him, still hungry and testy. "What could that possibly have to do with anything?"

Jansen shrugged. "Just saying, should have gone to Hamburg."

Devon burst out laughing, spraying their table with semi-chewed Thüringer Rostbratwurst.

"That's not funny," Aito commented sourly.

Wiping bits of banger off his cheek and tunic, Jansen was forced to agree. "It isn't now," he admitted, weakly.

"After our near-death experience yesterday," Aito continued, tetchily, "we're still no closer to a credible strategy for bringing Jansen's hare-brained scheme to fruition and closing that wormhole."

"Hare-brained?"

"I was being kind. Look, let's not get bogged down. We're agreed that closing the wormhole to Germany is our main goal – in fact, if we don't, it might destroy the planet."

Jansen shrugged again, casually. "Well, when you put it like that, I suppose I can let it pass."

"We're still awaiting a response from Commander Coleman," Devon reminded them. "Dr Hemmings told me it's due today, through ordinary channels – nothing to hide."

Aito scratched his cheek thoughtfully. "OK. Assuming Coleman can fix that wreck and build the equipment required to create a magnetic containment field, then fly it all the way here, how's she to snatch the wormhole from right under Heidi's nose?"

Devon held up a hand to calm him. "Shall we see if she can even fix the ship, first? One hurdle at a time, huh?"

"Fair enough, but that could take months. What about if—" Aito's question was interrupted by Devon's comm beeping.

He reached into a pocket, checked the screen and sighed. "Devon." The others could not hear the caller's voice, only Devon's answer. "Of course. Right away, ma'am." He stuffed the device back into his trouser pocket.

"No prizes for guessing who that was," Jansen commented, sourly. "And what did our glorious *Führerin* want?"

"The results of my investigation."

"About?" Aito had to ask, though he already had a sinking feeling.

"About the murder of Sergeant Denholm Haig. The man you killed – *allegedly.*"

Aito shifted uncomfortably in his seat; Devon's words had struck hard. "And what are you going to tell her?"

"That the film was tampered with, and that despite the prima facie evidence against you, I don't believe you're the killer. If she pushes me, I will intimate, without daring to say, that I believe her grandfather to be behind it all. She'll believe that, I think."

"Perhaps, but is that what *you* think?"

Devon studied the Japanese captain and technically his direct superior. "About you?"

Aito nodded once.

Devon's lip twitched. "I don't think I could repeat what I think of you in front of a lady, Captain."

Jansen laughed but stopped abruptly. "Hey, who are you calling a lady?"

"I meant Heid— Oh, never mind."

"Klaus, please take a seat." Douglas gestured. "Can Ah get you something?"

"Thank you, James. Water would be most welcome."

Douglas handed the German microbiologist a glass, also passing him bottled water from a small, glass-fronted refrigerator beside the sofa in his office's sitting area. He took a second for himself, cracked the cap and drank from the bottle. "That breakfast was a wee bit salty. Now, please, tell me how Ah can help ye?"

"I have been working for the UN in Germany for some years now, James. My experiences led me to seek a role within the world of diplomacy, rather than go back to research. They're well ahead of us in the field of microbiology, anyway, and it seemed natural to go home, too. Of course, when I say *home...*"

Douglas gave a half-smile. "Aye, Ah know."

"It seems that, with our unique experiences and skill sets, we have been well received into this world. I have spoken to several of our crew, and many have climbed high in a relatively short time. These people are far more open and accepting than our own, James. More willing to learn, too – I'm a little embarrassed to add."

"They are," Douglas agreed, sadly. "They're well ahead of us in many ways, sociologically, as well as technologically. When we landed here, back in 2113, Del Bond, of all people, explained to me that everything remaining of the *New World* and *Factory Pod 4* had been removed centuries before, to a secure location – a vast hangar in England's Midlands, controlled by the military. So it seems Lieutenants Singh and Nassaki were correct, the mountain *had* slumped. If we'd travelled through a wormhole at the summit, we'd have fallen to our deaths."

That disquieting thought caused both men to reach nervously for their drinks.

"Anyhow, the Midlands became the epicentre for knowledge and technology for the whole world. But in this timeline, rather than 'merely' being the birthplace of the industrial revolution that we remember from our history lessons, by the eighteenth century, that part of the country was spoon-feeding knowledge from the *twenty-second* century to every government on the planet, and within a spirit of cooperation that our timeline simply never saw. Whatever our people did after we left in 1558, they did it well."

"Indeed." Fischer nodded thoughtfully. "It was a truly awful loss to our people when the wormhole cut them off from us – possibly forever. Yet, if they had not remained, I wonder if things would have worked out so well."

Douglas raised his recyclable bottle. "Not the most genteel of toasts, but – to those who remained."

Fischer leaned forward and clunked his glass to it. "To those who remained," he seconded. "So it seems we may also owe our current well-being and positions to their *navigation* of the future, too. That would explain a lot. Now I must tell you what I have discovered, James. You see, working with the German minister's office, and knowing what I know, placed me in a unique position to recognise the importance of a certain piece of historic documentation that crossed my desk. It was all so much ancient history to my minister, which is why it took a while for the file to come to light – or at least, to my attention. And the timing now could not be more critical."

Douglas leaned forward, piqued.

"*They* may not have considered it important, but I *know* it is. James, this is another fixed point – has to be. Easily as important as our brief sojourn in 1558."

"Go on."

"A wormhole was opened almost two hundred years ago. To Germany. Munich, more specifically. It was completely hushed up at the time, remaining classified for decades after that. Only becoming unclassified in 1978 with the unification – the birth of the United Nations single government – and even now, it is not public knowledge."

Douglas was at sea. "A wormhole into *Germany?* From where? And when, exactly?"

"You must understand the remaining evidence is sketchy. Most of it seems to have been destroyed by the people in power at the time. Maybe it was something of a dirty secret? Or perhaps they considered it a near miss. I do not know for sure. What does seem certain is that while the wormhole originated in Egypt – from a time unspecified – in Munich, it was the 8th November 1943."

Douglas swallowed, instantly understanding the ramifications of that time and place. "An attempt to contact the Nazis?" He could not believe it.

Fischer held out his hands, palms up, showing his own frustration. "Not our proudest moment, I know. I can only surmise that if your assumption is correct – as I suspect it might be – then whoever orchestrated it must have had a most explicit agenda."

"To contact... *him?* Klaus, that's almost inconceivable."

"It's certainly audacious. Sound like anyone we used to know? The timing fits perfectly with our own timeline, too."

Douglas leaned forward, head in hands. Then resurfaced quickly. "Hang on, fits with *our* timeline? But surely, anything after 1558 will have been changed? And, seeing this world now, Ah'd have to imagine changed radically."

"Yes, James. *We* know that."

Douglas gave Fischer a sideways look, his mind running to catch up. "Explain."

"I am simply saying that if someone we left in the past had managed to jump forward, then..."

"They wouldnae have known," Douglas completed, automatically. "But surely, if Schultz *had* got her hands on the German people – that is, the German people in *this* timeline's 1943 – she could have potentially corrupted both people and timeline – made a hell of mess."

"And yet, the world seems to have worked out fairly well, I know. It begs more questions than it provides answers, I agree. Unless..."

"Unless?"

"*Unless* someone closed that wormhole before too much harm was done. Closed it forever."

"Ye mean someone from the time in which we left Heidi – some sort of mini rebellion against her, or their leadership, perhaps?"

"*Or...*"

Douglas groaned, seeing the implications. "Tell me ye're no' saying that's item number one on our bucket list when we get back there?"

Fischer sipped his water, saying nothing.

Heidi awaited Devon in the *Heydrich*'s state quarters. She greeted him from an opulent leather swivel chair behind a large desk. "Come in, Lieutenant. I would have your report."

Devon stood before the desk, dread creeping into his heart as he looked around for the Old Man. He had not bargained for being interrogated by both Schultzes and was not sure how he would cope. Fortunately, for now at least, there was no sign of Heinrich. As Heidi had not offered the chair, he thought it best not to take it. "I thought your grandfather was using these quarters, ma'am?"

"He tired of slumming it. I believe he is currently spending a few days in a five-star hotel at the expense of the German people. Apparently there is an opera this evening, and after that he is to be whisked away to a mountain retreat belonging to one of the party leaders." She shrugged, disinterestedly. "He will probably complain about the accommodation there, too, but perhaps his absence is serendipitous for our conversation, yes?"

Devon looked around dubiously.

Heidi smiled coolly. "Do not concern yourself, Lieutenant. I have scrambled all his bugs so that they hear completely different conversations. At the moment..." She glanced at a device on the desk between them. "At the moment, *mein Großvater* is recording a conversation between, let me see, yes, between Dr Reid and his engineers." She placed an earbud next to her ear, listening. "Hmm, fascinating. Apparently, Reid is getting fed up with eating sausages. There seems to be some lively debate."

A thrill of fear shot through Devon. He hoped it did not show. If she was tapping in all over the ship and feeding conversations at random to her grandfather to cover her own movements, they would have to be much more careful. Suddenly, he was even keener than usual to leave her presence, desperate to warn his co-conspirators.

Heidi replaced the earbud next to the device. Her temporary distraction had served to cover Devon's anxiety – at least, he hoped so. He took a deep breath; slowly, so as not to appear overly nervous.

"You may sit, Lieutenant."

"Huh?"

"Lieutenant?"

"Oh, thank you, ma'am." *Dumbass!* Devon screamed inside his head. *Pay attention. You can't help anyone until you get out of here – if you get out of here. Stop acting so damned guilty!* He turned away for a moment, secretly collecting himself, while dragging the proffered chair closer to the desk.

Heidi leaned forward, placing her elbows on the surface between them, scrutinising him keenly over steepled fingers. "Now. Let us get back to your report."

A gentle bell tone emanated from Douglas' desk. He opened a hatch to a small control panel in the arm of his luxurious leather recliner. Still seated across his coffee table from Dr Klaus Fischer, he answered the call from reception while Fischer admired the view from his curved glass viewport. "What is it, Angie?"

"Sir, sorry to disturb your meeting, but I have a young lady here to see you."

"Did she give a name?"

"Miss Burnstein, sir."

Fischer turned to raise a wry eyebrow. He had not heard that name in a while.

"Very well. Same drill as with Dr Fischer. Can you give her a pass, append her to the NW2 programme and assign her quarters, please? When you're done, have her escorted to ma office. Thanks, Angie."

Douglas closed the connection. "Ah wonder what that's about?"

"Would that be Hank's daughter?"

"Aye, Ah assume so."

"Have you had trouble getting Hank to obey the recall?"

"As a matter of fact, no. He went back to live in Texas, so he's one of the closest *New World*ers, anyhow. Ah thought we'd be in for trouble from him, but he's been nice as pie about the whole thing."

Fischer's eyebrow rose again, this time in astonishment.

"Did we get him confused with the Burnstein from this world and leave our Hank back in 1558?"

Douglas chuckled. "Ah can only imagine Hank Burnstein turning the Tudor court into a corporation and tabling a share offer – there'd have been no planet left by 1700. No," he sobered, "the thing is, Ah think losing his laddie hit him harder than many of us would have believed. Perhaps Ol' Captain America is more complex than we originally gave him credit for, eh?"

Fischer nodded thoughtfully. "It must have been a hard thing. Just loss, without even the closure of bereavement. How has Mrs Burnstein coped with the transition?"

"Actually, Ah'm sorry to say Ah've lost touch with many of our number over the years – on a personal level, at least. Maybe we'll find out from Clarrie when she arrives. Ah'm actually more concerned about Lara Miller, just now."

"Jim Miller's wife? What has happened to her?"

"It's more about what she's trying to make happen to me."

Fischer frowned in confusion.

"She's managed to... Look, Ah might be speaking out of turn here, but as you know, none of us have been allowed to marry outside our group. The obvious reason being that should strange anomalies begin to occur, forcing us to travel back in time, then the less we're tied, the less fallout we'll cause and the less we'll suffer. We all agreed that unless we found conclusive proof for the *safety* of this timeline, we would keep interaction of that sort to a minimum."

"I understand. We all consented – so what has she done?"

"She's found herself a rich man – who, in fairness to the mug, probably thinks he's a knight in shining armour. She's been using his resources to declare war on me. At least, mostly me. It's only been a few days since we announced the recall, but she obviously sees me as the figurehead for this whole expedition. Ah also made the mistake, some months ago, of *reminding* her that we're not allowed to marry outside the group. On top of that, Ah had to jog her memory that she was *already* married. Apparently, the suggestion of bigamy – although Ah didnae actually use the word – knocked the lid off the hive and got her new beau's lawyers swarming like bees."

Fischer sat back in astonishment. "She is bringing litigation?"

Douglas surprised him by chuckling gently. "Aye. Ah asked our own Commander Elvis Percival Gleeson for a little help with the legalese."

"Was he able to shed any light?"

"He was succinct, Ah'll give him that. He told me to shoot her."

Fischer laughed.

"That man really hates the law. Anyhow, Mrs Miller is refusing to join us, so Ah'm afraid Ah've had to send a covert security detail to insist. This world is certainly better than the one we left and as she's now – can Ah use the term 'shacked up'? – with one of its wealthier citizens, she sees no reason to leave." He finished his water. "Ah have to admit, sentiment aside, Ah do see her point. Though Ah doubt Jim Miller would have behaved that way. However, the fact remains, we *all* have to do this, for the sake of everyone. If we do nothing, we risk this world vanishing around our ears."

"Has anyone explained that to Mrs Miller?"

Douglas smiled humourlessly. "It's like talking into a stiff breeze. The way dear old Satnam Patel explained it to me – back in the early days, when we first began to worry about damaging the future – the timeline is always splitting and splitting, into infinity. Every single decision made by anyone, or anything, splits it further. Every time more than one course is possible, you get another timeline. So, what does that mean to us? If we go back in time and change things, we risk splitting off onto another timeline, another future. What happens in the one we left behind, we will never know. But if we wish to go back to save *this* timeline, the same events that created it have to play out pretty much exactly, and as we don't know what most of those events should be..."

"We might change something new and end up on yet another timeline?"

Douglas nodded. "Hence, we all have to go. Whatever paradoxes are created around us, they will be lessened if we stay together."

Fischer blew out his cheeks. He was a clever man, but multiple timelines were more than any mortal should have to comprehend.

Douglas' door buzzed, creating a welcome distraction. "Come."

A striking young woman stepped through the doors as they slid open, thanking her escort as they closed behind her. She gave Douglas and Fischer a warm smile and hugged them both in turn. "Thank you for seeing me, Captain."

"It's lovely to see ye, lassie." He sighed, smiling happily. "All grown up now, Ah see. How's yer mum and dad?"

A cloud fluttered across Clarrie Burnstein's sunny demeanour. "Mom's not too bad, thanks. Dad's... well, he's OK, I guess. He's still pottering with online businesses and fixing things, but I don't think his heart's really in it any more."

Douglas nodded sombrely. "He misses your brother."

"Yeah, it hit him pretty hard. Hit all of us, but strangely, Mom made peace with it. You know, understanding that he's out there, somewhere in time, makin' the world a better place and what have you, but Dad..."

"Ah understand, lassie. How can Ah help ye now?"

"I wondered if you might know where in the world my fiancé is hanging out right now? At his request, I went to Egypt and I was told he came here. I came here and I've now been told he's in Egypt!"

Douglas scratched his ear a little sheepishly. "Aye, about that."

"That went down like a cup of cold sick," Tim confided, as he and Woodsey left the tent. The university bus and pickup trucks were parked together at the edge of the camp and Tim directed them towards one of the four-by-fours to use its radio.

"I offered to stay," Woodsey replied with a shrug.

"You know we can't. We've *all* been recalled – there's no choice. I do feel bad about it, though. It's pretty rough leaving in the middle of a dig, but with all this madness, not to mention poor Simba..." He tailed off, shaking his head sadly as they walked.

Woodsey fell unusually silent. Lost in his own concerns, it took Tim a moment to realise. "What is it?"

Woodsey kept a step ahead of his friend, his face away.

"Woodsey?"

"Nothin'."

"Doesn't sound like nothing." Tim caught him up, turning him gently around. He was surprised to see a tear roll down his usually obnoxious best friend's face.

Woodsey naturally wiped it away with irritation.

"Is this about Simba?" Tim asked, softly.

"Nah. It's not about nothin'."

Tim placed an arm around Woodsey's shoulders. "It's not your fault. No one knew she hadn't returned."

"Yeah, but *they* weren't in charge. I should have noticed. I always hate it when you henpeck everybody, telling grown adults what to do and checking up on them all the time. But now..." A tear ran down his cheek into his mouth. He swallowed, licked his lips and wiped his face again.

"I understand, mate," Tim offered, understandingly. "Must be hard to finally face up to the fact that I'm right all the time, and about everything." He grinned.

Woodsey punched him on the shoulder. "Dick!" he snorted, but his usual, near-permanent grin returned. "I'll admit that maybe the Pommy beanpole gets things right *occasionally*."

"No," Tim stated flatly. "You can't go back now. You've admitted I'm always right – case closed."

Woodsey viewed him wryly. "*Right*. Anyhow, all this is not a total loss, dude. *I* saved our bacon, remember? That piece of maxilla with the lower curve of the antorbital fenestra intact? It even had a socket for a tooth. I'm sure there's a big animal out there to be found somewhere."

Tim stopped and studied his friend, amusement now completely replacing the lines of concern on his face. "Carcharodontosaurus saharicus?"

"Pretty sure." Woodsey nodded.

Tim laughed. "Who would have ever expected those words to leave that mouth?"

Woodsey huffed. "I do me best."

Tim clapped him on the shoulder. "Yes, you do. You're certainly not the same lout I met in a bar ten years ago on the way to Mars."

"Hey, steady on, mate."

Tim laughed again. It helped, making him feel better from the inside out. "No, you're a completely different lout!"

"I wish Henry and Rose were here."

Tim stopped laughing but continued to smile. "I think they'd be proud of you."

"Of us," Woodsey corrected.

"Yes," Tim agreed. "I do feel bad for our students, though." He turned back, car door half-open. "At least Dr Brusatte has agreed to bring them back in January – for those who wish to come. He's a fourth-generation palaeontologist, did you know?"

"I didn't." Woodsey gave a heartfelt sigh. "Simba was a tragedy, though, and no mistake. I..."

"Yes," Tim continued for him, "but we caught the creature, and alive, too. So at least it will be *safe* for them to come back, and for the people who live here. We probably saved many lives. And you never know, we might be back with them, yet – it'll probably take 'em several seasons, after all."

Woodsey took a deep breath, in and out, letting it revive him. "I know. I just wish they'd let us see Simba's family. I just wanted to tell them, I mean, you know? Let them know how brilliant she was, how she was always so..." He choked again.

"So good at filling in the paperwork you couldn't be bothered to do, I know." Tim smiled, giving his friend's arm a squeeze. "Why don't we make a deal to come back here with our research students in one year? Maybe we'll even be in time to qualify them?" He offered his hand and Woodsey took it.

"You've got a deal, mate. You know she didn't do *all* my paperwork, right?"

Tim grinned as he reached into their four-by-four to pick up the radio from its dashboard. "This is Professor Norris calling *Goliath*."

After a blast of static, the radio crackled into life. "*Professor, this is* Goliath. *Go ahead, over.*"

"Thank you, *Goliath*. Are we still on for that free lift?"

Almost a hundred million years earlier, Commander Ally Coleman wrinkled her nose. Something was being waved under it. It was unclear whether the thing was being offered or merely wafted. "What is it?"

"It's a *sausage,*" replied Dr Alba, derisively.

"I can see *that!* I'm asking what's in it, Brian?"

"For crying out loud, Commander. You should know better than to ask what's *in* a sausage. Suffice to say that dinosaurs have snouts and anuses, too."

She covered her mouth disgustedly and he laughed.

"Try it. 'S not bad."

"Don't worry, Commander," Dr Bismarck interjected. "It's quality meat harvested from that ankylosaur that was electrocuted crossing our fence a little while back. It tastes rather—"

"Don't tell me, Harry. Let me guess," Coleman interrupted. "Like chicken?"

"I was going to say 'gamey', actually. Please, try some."

Against her better judgement, she took a bite from his fork. She chewed slowly, her expression clearing gradually. "Not bad."

Alba laughed mockingly.

Coleman shot him a filthy glare. "Moving on. You all know why we're here. Can we fix this ship or not?" Her question met with a deafening round of indifference. "Come on, people. *Can we do this?*"

"I'm an engineer, as you know, Commander," Bismarck grabbed the nettle. "I'm not saying it's impossible—"

"I am," Alba cut across.

"I'm not saying it's *impossible,*" Bismarck tried again, "but we'll need a dizzying array of replacement parts. Where will they come from?"

Coleman shrugged. "I've been told not to worry about that. We're to requisition what we need, and they'll send what they can – that's all I know."

"OK," Bismarck agreed thoughtfully, "but then there's the *other* project. What's that all about?"

Coleman fidgeted uncomfortably in her seat at the end of the meeting table. "I'm afraid I can't reveal the full details on that here, Harry."

"And why are our outgoing comms now being monitored?" asked Alba, accusingly.

"We've been told," she hedged, "to keep this work completely confidential. That means no communications whatsoever about the work we're carrying out on this ship or—"

"Or the *other* project," Bismarck completed for her.

"Yes – thank you, Harry," she acceded irritably. "You're still free to contact any friends you may have..." She tailed off, wondering who would possibly want *that* job with regards to Dr Brian Alba. She pushed the thought aside. "Any friends you may have aboard the *Heydrich.* We must simply insist that none of the details about your work on this project leave the base. Now, assuming I have your shopping lists for the *Newfoundland,* can we move on to the other matter?"

"But, Commander," Harry Bismarck tried again, reasonably, "we've been handed a materials list, but not told what the end product is going to be."

"I understand your frustration, Doctors—"

"Big of you," snapped Alba.

"Now understand mine," she rounded on him. "I have orders to tack the materials listed for this second project onto the requisitions for the first, without drawing any undue attention or questions. I'm a soldier, not an engineer or scientist, so I require and *demand – Brian* – your help. So I'll ask again – can we do this?"

They looked at one another and shrugged. Bismarck asked, "Can you at least tell us how long we have to undertake this work? Come on, Ally, throw us a bone."

Coleman sighed, her expression softening. "OK, Harry. As far as I know they haven't put a time limit on this. I doubt we can proceed leisurely, like any time will do." She looked pointedly at Alba. "But we're not being pressured – yet. Keeping it quiet seems to be the order of the day."

The men exchanged looks again, and again, Bismarck spoke first. "OK. We'll give it our best shot. I'm forwarding you a file – here. Based on what you *have* told us, it's the best we've been able to come up with so far. It shows the materials and equipment we'll need, with each delivery including certain *additional* materials that could reasonably be expected to be included around the same time. However, I must warn you, Ally, it will get trickier to hide our purposes down the line, but this is what we'll need to start."

Coleman nodded. "Understood. Thank you, Harry. Doctors." With that she rose to leave.

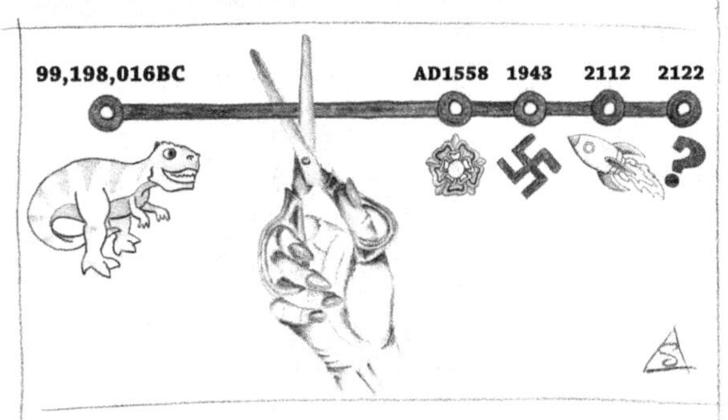

Chapter 6 | Get Me Out of Here, I'm a Temporal Anomaly

"My God, Jill. What have ye done?" Douglas watched in horror as the *Goliath* was unloaded at a secure landing field, away from the main space port.

Baines grinned. "It's true, it's a little bigger than we were originally led to believe, but I'm sure the new ship can handle it. The media are going insane over this. At least we're about to duck out of all that."

Douglas took one last look at the enormous, unconscious spinosaur before turning to stare at his wife as though she were mad. "Ye're right. Clearly, we've got it made!"

Baines laughed and kissed him on the cheek.

"Ye're looking forward to this, aren't ye?" he accused.

"Am I looking forward to getting my still reasonably narrow behind in the captain's chair of possibly the most powerful ship ever built? In *any* timeline? Hmm, let me see..."

"Hey, UNASA put *me* in charge o' this mission, remember?"

She looped an arm through his. "Yes, but James, you're bound to dash off on a vital mission here, or some feat of derring-do there, leaving poor *moi* holding the baby. So what's a girl to do?"

A twinkle of humour came to his eye. "Ye'll forgive me, if ma rash heroism is becoming formulaic."

She smiled, running a finger down his cheek. "Three, no, three and a *half* days' stubble? Is this for the big photo shoot?"

"Too 'action hero', you think?"

"Not at all. Reminds me of those days when we were *always* saving one another's lives." She kissed him again.

"Ah've never stopped. If it were no' for me, ye'd have been crushed under a mountain of dirty laundry and washing-up by now."

"Oh, James. I do believe you become more the modern man with every passing year."

He snorted. "Would ye like to see her?"

Baines' eyes lit up. "Can we?"

After a short ride in one of the electric jeeps that littered the military areas of the space port, Douglas, and Mrs Baines-Douglas, arrived at one of the biggest hangars on the planet. The effect was increased still further by the brilliant white commercial cladding that reflected the worst of the Floridian sun back into the sky.

"Wow. I wish I'd brought my shades."

"Aye, but ye'll be glad of it when we're inside." Douglas jumped out of the jeep and waited for Baines to walk around the vehicle. "Ah'll key ma password and then Ah'm going to have to blindfold ye."

She looked at him. "You're telling me I still don't have clearance?"

"No. Ah just thought it would be more fun." He unfolded something from his pocket. "As the history of this timeline went down rather differently – some might say rather better than our own – Ah had to have this made up especially for ye. No one here really understood its meaning."

Baines examined the motif on a piece of white linen that she was obviously meant to tie about her head. It was emblazoned with iconic red rays shooting out from a red sun at its centre. "Kamikaze?"

"Ah thought it was appropriate, what with yer history of crashing ma ships."

"How thoughtful," she replied stonily, which only made him laugh. "Show me to my chariot, Douglas, before I put you back on washing-up duty."

His eyebrows shot up. "When was Ah ever off it?"

"Honestly, James. The dishwasher does all the work."

"Aye. Ah often see it wandering our home, hollow-eyed, trying to find all the missing plates, cups and utensils, cast thoughtlessly aside to land on any available surface – including the floor – no wait, that would be me!"

Baines laughed and, suitably blindfolded, allowed Douglas to lead her into the hangar. The sun beat down mercilessly, radiating off the building's white-panelled walls, but as they moved inside, it gave way to a wonderful coolness. She allowed him to manoeuvre her into an elevator. "You know I'm trusting you here, right?"

"Dinnae worry, lassie. Ah'll keep you away from the drops at the edge of the gantry."

"*Drops?*"

Douglas laughed as the doors pinged open. "Allow me, Mrs Douglas." He took her arm in his and walked out onto a floor that did indeed clank like a gantry under their footsteps.

"James, if I go over a two-hundred-foot drop here, I'm taking you with me."

"Wouldn't have it any other way, ma love."

She sighed, shaking her head. "You old smoothie. I bet you think you could get me to do almost anything when you talk like that, don't you?"

"Says the fleet captain walking blindfold over a two-hundred-foot drop."

She gave a smitten sigh. "Damn," she added dreamily.

He chuckled, navigating her to a handrail. Carefully removing the blindfold, he asked, "What do you think of her?"

"Oh."

Douglas looked at her askance. "*Oh?*"

The lift doors opened behind them but neither noticed.

"It's just that it looks kinda like, erm... how should I describe this?"

"Kind of like *what,* exactly?" Douglas bristled in defence of his new ship.

"Well, sort of like Thunderbird Two... *ish.*"

"The original or from one of the remakes?" asked a friendly and familiar voice approaching from behind.

Baines hung her head, closing her eyes and smiling. "Pilots."

Douglas turned to greet the newcomer enthusiastically. "Sandy! Good to see ye. How did ye get in here?"

"Captain Bessel brought me to see the ship. He's gone to have a word with the chief engineer. How is Hiro, by the way?"

Douglas pumped Lieutenant-Commander Singh's hand enthusiastically. "He's brilliantly the same as ever, but Ah wouldnae have him any other way."

Singh grinned mischievously. "That's good to hear. It's good to see you, too, sir." He nodded to Baines. "Captain."

Baines put her arm around her now-first officer. "So what do you think of her, Sandy?"

"Magnificent," Singh breathed in awe. "I've been training to fly her for months – in sims, of course, just in case – but no one would show me what she looked like from the outside. It's all been so hush-hush." He whistled. "It seems we pulled it all together just in time, eh, Captains? When do I get to fly her for real?"

Cretaceous Egypt

"Lieutenant Devon assures me that you have been most helpful with his investigation, Two." Heidi enjoyed the sneer on the woman's face as she refused to use her real name. "He was even bold enough to suggest that I release you, so that you may resume your work on bringing the wormhole more fully under our control. Now, can you give me one good reason why I should trust you?"

"You shouldn't."

"An interesting argument. Would you care to elaborate?"

Dr Hemmings merely stared.

"Very well. Would you care to explain why you attempted to strand me in 1943 Germany?"

"I didn't."

Heidi sighed. "Really, Two. I thought we were past the denial and 'I am innocent' stage."

"You misunderstand me – a not unusual occurrence, girl."

Heidi's eyebrow rose with just a touch of amusement. "Then, please, do explain it to me, *Two*."

"It's really very simple. I tried to strand Heinrich in 1943 – I just didn't care that you were there, too. There is a difference."

Heidi studied the older woman carefully. Hemmings was right; there was a difference. Swiftly accepting that point, she moved on to the why. "And the reasons for your actions?"

"Your grandfather ordered the assassination of my daughter, Elizabeth."

Heidi's eyes narrowed. She remembered Lieutenant Elizabeth Hemmings well, from the *Last Word*. She had been killed when Captain Baines used the *New World* to turn their ship over and send it down into a ravine. "I was not aware of this."

Hemmings snorted, unsurprised. "So?"

A muscle twitched in Heidi's jaw, a tell of annoyance. "Why did *mein Großvater* order her removal? Tell me exactly what she had done." She was suspicious now. If Hemmings had been some sort of spy or traitor that might explain a great many things.

"She married the wrong man. Heinrich disapproved. You know how he has always had this obsession with bloodlines, going back to the primitive experiments that passed for science during the time of Professor Eugen Fischer and his ridiculous eugenics. Just because Hitler referenced that fool's research before publishing the Nuremberg Laws of 1935, Heinrich still makes everyone read the subject, despite all its bumbling inaccuracies."

"Who did she marry?"

"That no longer matters. I disapproved of the relationship, naturally, but Heinrich saw it as a betrayal. He had her husband murdered, but not content with that – and possibly fearing reprisal – he placed a contract on Elizabeth's head, too." Hemmings delivered the story with a coldness that belied the fire in her eyes. "Fortunately, the *Last Word* went back in time before she could be found. What happened to my daughter, Heidi? You must know."

"She died in the attack on the *Last Word*. I understand during an escape attempt by Captain James Douglas. Perhaps she was even murdered."

Hemmings had heard that story before, but found it hard to believe. She said nothing, so Heidi broke the silence. "It was regrettable. She seemed competent."

Hemmings' eyebrow rose as her expectations lowered. *High praise. What's she after?*

"During one of our previous conversations," Heidi continued, "you used the phrase '*we* Schultzes'. What did you mean by that?"

Right, Hemmings realised, *she's still digging for information. Let's see how she gets on with this.* "I am your second cousin, once removed."

Heidi's eyes narrowed. "How can that be?"

"Once again, girl, it's quite simple. My great-grandparents were also your great-great-grandparents. I hope I don't have to explain the birds and the bees?"

Her face twisting into a sneer, Heidi replied, "I will elucidate – if we are family, how can it be that I did not know of it?"

Hemmings gave a bored sigh. "You know Heinrich, how he likes to keep everyone in little boxes so that no one else has the whole picture. You came from the 'pure' line, as Heinrich sees it – sired by your great-grandfather. Hence you bear the Schultz name. My family line ran from his sister – my grandmother – for what difference that made."

"Very well, *cousin,*" Heidi replied, sarcastically. "I return to my earlier question. Why should I let you out of this cell?"

"Because, if you ever want to close that wormhole, my girl, you will need my help. Reid may not be a complete fool, but make no mistake, he's no *me* either."

"Of course not. He is not family," Heidi agreed with a hint of flattery.

Hemmings smiled blandly. *Very good, baby Schultz, that's the sort of blind arrogance I can use.*

Heidi returned the smile with one of her own. *If this woman thinks I have accepted her, I can use that to find the others involved in the conspiracy to trap us in 1943. The closer I keep them and the more opportunities I allow them, the sooner they will complete* my *tasks and betray themselves – and the sooner they can be dispensed with.*

"What do you intend to do with *her?*" Hemmings gestured to the drawn-looking woman in the next cell. She still looked ill from the effects of her relatively small dose of cyanide.

Heidi smiled slightly. *Now she seeks to distract me. Her belief that my plan is in fact her own, will only make their demise that much more delicious when the time comes.* She moved to stand before the younger woman's cell. Heidi was still struck by how closely she resembled her fourth-great-aunt. "Oh, I have special plans for the *other* Dr Heidi Schultz. Once she has recovered her strength and her looks, she is going to help me take over the world, is that not so, *Heidi?* Until then, I will just have to see what I can do in your place."

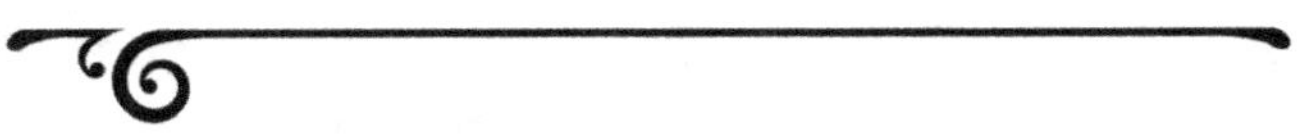

AD2122, space

The UNS *New World* broke orbit and headed for Mars. "Course laid in, Captain, following the same trajectory as ten years ago," Lieutenant-Commander Singh announced enthusiastically from the helm. He turned his perfect white grin on Captains Douglas and Baines. "But not everything is the same. This time, we'll arrive on station 1,800,000 kilometres from Earth in just *nine* hours, sir."

Douglas smiled with satisfaction.

Baines whistled. "That's, hang on... *four times* the maximum speed of the old ship?"

"Correct, Captain. She may be bigger, but she handles like a Right Good Seeing To."

Baines' jaw dropped, but unlike the first time Singh had dropped something like that on him, Douglas had been ready. "That's a sports car, right? Not a two-ton off-roader like the Erotic Violence?"

Singh's grin broadened still further. "Captain, how did you know?"

Douglas tapped his temple and winked. "Ah remember you telling me, at length, about how much money your cousin Bhupati made from that remarkably named SUV. So Ah've been following the automotive press for headline grabbers. The vehicles with the most, shall we say, *edgy* handles? And the most inappropriate celebrity endorsements do indeed lead the market. Your cousin was quite right. Price and reliability seem to have nothing to do with sales. So, as we're planning on returning to this time..." He looked to them both, wiggling his eyebrows in lieu of a drumroll. "Ah bought shares – lots of them – and they're doing quite nicely, too, thank you very much."

Baines turned to him in astonishment. "You sly old fox. You kept *that* little scheme secret."

Douglas surprised her by bursting into laughter.

"What?" she asked, slightly baffled.

"Buying shares is hardly a scheme, Jill. But let's just say," he managed between chuckles, "that Ah didnae want to leave mail lying around our apartment, addressed to me, and bearing the title 'Get yourself a Right Good Seeing To, now!' – Ah've enough trouble with Jim Miller's wife taking me to court without getting the same treatment from ma own!"

Singh laughed raucously. "Good for you, Captain. I bought some, too!"

Baines was both amused and slightly narked as she looked from one to the other. "And you two didn't think to let me in on this opportunity?"

"What?" Douglas could hardly speak. "You want a Right Good Seeing To, now?"

Singh almost fell out of his pilot's seat.

Baines was laughing as well. "Alright, alright. I'll let that one go. I guess I *was* asking for it."

Struggling for breath, Singh replied, "No. That model's not out 'til next year!" Both he and Douglas collapsed again, honestly, if most inappropriately.

Baines held her head in her hands, shaking it slowly, trying not to laugh – she could not let them get away with it, after all. "You know, years ago, Satnam Patel accused me of being an unreconstructed female and a hangover from the mid-twenty-first century – how the pendulum keeps swinging! Just you calm down, boys – crash this one and it's all on you!" The comm beeped for attention. "Thank *God!* Bridge!"

"Captain, this is The Sarge. I'm down in the main hangar, ma'am. We seem to be having a little trouble with the dinosaur."

The bridge crew sobered immediately. "Now I *know* we're going back," Singh commented, bitterly.

Baines nodded agreement. "On my way, Sarge."

Cretaceous Egypt

"I need to make contact with your brother," Dr Heidi Schultz told Dr Heidi Schultz. The woman in the cell glared back at her. They looked so alike, but Heidi knew an uncanny physical resemblance would never fool her fourth-great-aunt's own brother – even if they had become estranged in recent years.

The prisoner stood and walked to the bars. Colour was returning to her cheeks; clearly the antitoxin medication was working, her strength returning. "Why do you need to speak with Hans?" she asked in German.

Heidi also switched to German. "I intend to present him with the opportunity of a lifetime."

The woman in the cell scrutinised Heidi for a moment. "You want him to start a war?"

"Why would you suspect that?"

"Because that is about all he is fit for. You don't know him."

"That is a narrow opinion. From what I have heard about my fourth-great-uncle, he is one of the few within your country to have a secure grip on world events. Your neighbours arm themselves ever more against you, and yet you do nothing."

Confirmation crossed the prisoner's face. "So you *do* want to start a war."

"On the contrary. I intend to prevent one. For a relatively small outlay in finance and lives, I intend to make the world quake in fear of the Fatherland. There will be no extended conflict."

"A first strike." It was not a question. "Because that *always* works out well."

Heidi looked impressed. "You are not so dim as you first appear, it seems. Your world has known peace for many years, but it would take little to upset that balance. You see, mankind's natural state is warfare – they must be ruled with an iron hand, and they will *never* have seen a first strike like this, I can assure you."

Loathing crossed the prisoner's face. "Iron hand or *your* hand?"

"Why not? Who better to rule from behind the throne?"

"You have chosen a puppet? It won't be me. I may have perhaps given myself a little too freely to the finer things in life, but I won't bring my world to war."

Heidi smiled slyly. "No, it will not be you. Have no fear, Aunt. I have chosen my... *puppet,* did you say? Yes, as appropriate an analogy as any."

"My brother?" the prisoner tried again, her concern growing.

"No. There is someone else. A complete unknown, but with *so* much untapped potential. You see, your neighbours arm themselves because they can, because you have always helped them to do so. An incredibly stupid and short-sighted policy, thanks to your Party leaders.

Now they hand-wring and make grand gestures, weakening your country still further. They have gone too far down the road of tolerance and capitulation to make any kind of a stand. I intend to change all that. Your enemies – yes, they are your enemies – are now too strong to be reckoned with, but not for much longer. My people will give you technologies far more advanced than anything your world has yet seen. Proportional and measured response only makes sense on a level playing field. *My* Fatherland will be all powerful and soon the world will either be in our hands or in ruins. We give them the choice, yes?"

"Which technologies?"

"Oh, we have many toys to share with your people, and your people alone. For example, I find it astonishing that you split the atom only to harness it as a power source."

"Your people do not use nuclear power?"

Heidi smiled again, but her blue eyes were windows to a soul of ice. "Of course. But we developed that power primarily as a weapon. Generating electricity was a much later side project."

The prisoner caught her breath. She may have been a doctor of sociology, but everyone in the civilised world knew how badly wrong things could go when nuclear power was placed in the wrong hands.

"Now, how do I contact your brother? Tell me, or I may decide that I have no further use for you... *Aunt.*"

Munich AD1943

Martin Bormann, head of the iNazi Party Chancellery, stood at the end of the negotiating table, hurriedly shipped into the Old Academy Museum and Gallery. Now closed to the public, the Old Academy had become a hive of vehicular and political activity, not to mention intrigue. Joined via a recently constructed tunnel to a nearby industrial park – also now secured – it saw a constant flow of materials to Germany's new Cretaceous factories.

"My fellow Party members," Bormann began. "We have two important guests joining us for today's session. Firstly, we are honoured to welcome Mr Heinrich Schultz. Sir, may we offer you a seat among us?"

An aide pulled out a chair to Bormann's left. The old man took it. Before retiring, the aide poured a little water from a decanter at the table's centre, placing a glass in front of Schultz.

Bormann sat, gesturing for Schultz to address the meeting.

Schultz leaned forward slightly, but did not stand. "Ladies and gentlemen, I sit with you today to bring you a warning. As you are all aware, I have travelled to you from the deep past, though my true place in time was AD2112. Party members, I have seen the future and it is a bleak future indeed for this great nation. Germany will lose itself, lose its uniqueness and its force of will over the next two centuries. It will be crushed by weakness, both from without and from within."

"What proof do you offer of this?" asked Fritz Todt, the Party's Chief of Engineering.

Heinrich's eyes narrowed at the interruption. Bormann introduced Todt and explained that he had recently returned from managing the Cretaceous construction projects to attend that meeting. In the original timeline, Todt was killed in a plane crash, possibly at the order of Hitler himself for arguing against the wisdom of continuing the Russian front. *Once a troublemaker, always a troublemaker,* Heinrich thought, suspiciously. Nevertheless, he needed 1943 Germany's most senior engineer, if he was to complete the manufacturing capability that would enable him to implement his broader plans – for now.

Heinrich waved a hand and one of his own aides stepped forward to place a small holographic device on the table. "I have brought footage from my own timeline, showing the might of the Nazi movement. Forgive the quality – camera technology was less advanced in *my* 1943 than it is now. He played the footage, leaning to whisper into Bormann's ear. Bormann nodded and beckoned his own aide. After another short, whispered conversation, the aide left the room.

He returned a few minutes later with a very nervous-looking artist who bore a black toothbrush moustache. When Adolf Hitler entered the room, he was so astounded by the life-sized hologram of himself standing on the table, gesticulating wildly from the podium, that he tripped and almost fell. Every sentence from his ersatz self was followed by a roar of approval from the vast crowd who stared up at him in adulation, his rock-star status further enhanced by the shocked silence with which his words were received by the gathering around the table.

Heinrich paused the display. "My dear friends, I put it to you that Mr Hitler, who stands beside me here, is a man of hitherto hidden depths."

Coughs and embarrassed chuckles went around the table.

"You do not believe me?" the old man asked, mildly. "Then allow me to take you forward just eighteen years into your future, to 1961, with my next film."

Footage of the lightning construction of the Berlin Wall threw the Party members into a stunned silence. Fritz Todt cleared his throat to speak once more. "If this is all true, how do we know such things will happen in *our* timeline? By your own admission, things are very different here. We are more advanced, less warlike."

Heinrich smiled coolly. "The fate of a weak nation is always guaranteed – only the hour is as yet uncertain."

"We are not weak," Todt argued. "We have lived in peace for well over a century. Why change that now?"

"I am not suggesting that you do," Heinrich countered, smoothly. "Only that you prepare yourselves to *keep* your peace."

Bormann's aide returned and whispered in his ear once more. "Ah, ladies and gentlemen, our second guest has arrived. Please let me introduce a popular figure, well known to us all, I'm sure. Will you join with me to welcome sociology PhD, art critic and internationally renowned philanthropist, Dr Heidi Schultz. Would you care to take a seat, Doctor?"

A second chair was pulled out to Bormann's right. The likeness was spooky, though Heinrich recognised his own granddaughter immediately. Her hair was arranged slightly differently, and he did not recognise the dress, but Heidi he *did* recognise. "Dr Schultz." He nodded a courteous greeting.

She nodded in return but did not speak.

"Dr Schultz is well known for her organisation's good works, and her father, Hans Schultz, had longstanding ties to the Party. Before we make any decisions that affect our nation's future, I wanted to hear all viewpoints. Doctor, you have been brought up to speed with the reason for this meeting?"

"I have, Chancellor Bormann."

Bormann knew that Heidi was not *his* world's Dr Schultz, yet the stranger's uncanny resemblance, as evidenced by his own eyes, nevertheless made him second guess that knowledge.

"Thank you for inviting me to take part in this auspicious meeting. I was shown some of the footage from our parallel time and probable future while I journeyed here. As many of you will know, my brother, and my father's namesake, Colonel Hans Schultz, has long held militant beliefs. Consequently, we have not spoken in some years. Having seen the evidence provided by Mr Heinrich Schultz, I intend to bridge the gap that has grown between myself and my estranged brother, so that we may join in common cause."

A murmur of shocked surprise went round the table of politicians. Dr Heidi Schultz was as well known for her liberal stance as she was for her playgirl lifestyle and had always freely advised others to dig deep into their pockets for this cause or that. Some may have held that it was never any great sacrifice, while her own were full to bursting, but she was beloved by the media, nonetheless – which gave her power. Heinrich merely nodded genteelly, a psychopath's perfect impression of gratitude.

Talks continued well into the evening, with Heinrich providing further selective evidence and submitting it to the assembled Party members as proof of their nation's inevitable downfall. The benefits of the superior technology Schultz offered gift-wrapped were obvious to them all, not to mention the near-infinite natural resources provided by a permanent wormhole to a prehistoric past. However, not all were convinced. Some distrusted the newcomer's motives.

After hours of toing and froing, another session was arranged for two days hence; time for the members to process, advise, and in turn seek advice from, their respective departments.

The *New World*'s cavernous main hangar, so usually filled with the sounds of labour and movement, was unnaturally quiet as Baines entered. Even from a couple of hundred metres away, she could clearly make out the recumbent shape of Spinosaurus aegyptiacus in the far corner. The animal had been placed close to one of the large vehicular airlocks, for ease of release when the time came. From the evidence before her, there seemed to be some disagreement about when that time should be.

She jogged across the hangar to find Dr Natalie Pearson and Dr Dave Flannigan arguing. The steel cage intended to hold the animal showed signs of considerable damage at its rear.

"What happened, guys?" she greeted, slightly puffed.

"Dave shot her," Natalie explained irritably.

Flannigan looked to Baines for support. "It woke up, Captain. Look at the damage it did."

Natalie also turned to face Baines with her hands on hips, though her comment was addressed to Flannigan. "Yes, yes, yes, but its system was already flooded with tranquillisers and now you've given it another dose."

"Well, give it a shot of adrenaline to counter the tranq," Flannigan argued.

"But that might wake her up again! Honestly, what were you even *doing* down here?"

Flannigan rolled his eyes. "Ship's doctor, remember? Someone had a nosebleed – space travel. It happens. Look, it was bustin' up the joint. Have you seen the size of the tail on that thing? People were runnin' and shoutin', I loaded a dart and brought the situation under control."

"There really wasn't time to hang around, Nat. If she'd gotten out..." The Sarge spoke for the first time.

Natalie glared at her husband of three years. "You, stop being reasonable. I'm not in the mood."

Sergeant Jackson grinned, unfazed. "The question is, what are *you* going to do about it?"

"I told you," Flannigan repeated. "Inject it with—"

"Her heartbeat's really slow. What if it doesn't get around her system in time?" Natalie cut him off.

"Inject it straight into the heart..." Flannigan tailed off as realisation dawned.

"Exactly," the zoologist snapped victoriously. "I forgot to ask the UN for a hypodermic javelin. Hope you brought yours! Added to that, we don't know how much to give her. We've no idea how much she weighs." She rounded on Baines. "Captain, I told everyone we needed to make the time to weigh her, and now here we are..."

"Don't suppose my bathroom scales will help?" Baines quipped weakly.

Flannigan opened his mouth to speak.

Baines held up a finger to stop him. "It's so incredibly important to your career that you make no comment about the size of my bathroom scales."

Flannigan grinned. "I *was* going to say, we have truck scales."

"My apologies," Baines replied magnanimously.

"If you're no longer using them."

Her eyes narrowed. "So, we do indeed have the band back together. Wouldn't have missed it."

"Come on, Natalie," Flannigan encouraged. "We're just gonna to have to guess – but guess under."

"Right." Natalie loaded a terrifying needle with something from the locked cupboard built into the containment cage's base. "Here goes."

"Are we going to be able to fix the damage to the rear of the enclosure with the creature still in it?" asked Baines. "How did it break it up, anyhow?"

"Looks like a weak bolt in one of the hinging mechanisms, Captain," The Sarge supplied.

The cage was built onto a structural rolling platform. Roughly Spinosaurus-shaped, the two barred sides hinged up from the edges to close around the animal like a bear trap. The seam where the two sides met had a long slot near its centre that allowed the huge sail on the dinosaur's back to protrude from the cage's top. Intended to wrap snugly around their captive, the enclosure was designed to prevent her from moving, and thus protect her from consequent injury. Spinosaurus spines were fused to the backbone, so any major trauma, such as rolling over, could quite possibly result in a broken back and death.

At the rear, the beast's massively muscular tail lolled out of the cage's side like a baby's arm from a pram. One of the hinges had indeed sheared, allowing the waking creature to damage its enclosure in a fit of understandable panic. The bars around the broken hinge were badly deformed.

"Er, Natalie," Baines called back, along the length of the dinosaur. "I really don't want our friend to wake up again until we have him—"

"Her."

"Until we have *her* off the ship and in a wide-open space. Is that understood?"

"Yes, Captain, of course."

"Natalie, you understand what I'm saying? I mean no matter what, *she* doesn't wake up again until we have her home and safe, yeah?"

"I understand, Captain, but if she wakes after this injection—"

"Then you put her out again."

"But that might kill her."

"Then that's what we'll have to do. Remember the last time we had one of these things running free in the hold? I know you were there when Jack Dorset was killed. Never again – are we clear?"

Natalie deflated. "I understand, Captain."

"Penny for your thoughts?" Tim asked, taking the window seat opposite Woodsey in the ship's reception lounge.

Woodsey gave a half-smile. "Cheapskate. Seems like yesterday, doesn't it?"

"Since you made that indelible impression on Rose?" Tim chuckled. "Yeah, it does. I understand your lobbying for this place to be called the Mud Hole fell on deaf ears, in the end?"

"Yeah." Woodsey shook his head, completely lacking comprehension. "Captain Douglas just wouldn't listen to reason and when I suggested we should call this crate the *New, New World,* he chucked me out of his office."

Tim laughed.

"Seriously," Woodsey continued in earnest. "Must be just nerves, I guess."

"As in, you getting on his? Yeah, you're probably right."

"No, no. He said he was glad to see me, if you must know... well, initially. What are you doing here anyway? I thought you'd be preparing for your marital bliss – or whatever."

"We would have been, but all that has *so* been put on hold by all this. Clarrie's with her mum and dad at the moment. We'll all get together in embarkation later. By the way, weren't you seeing that librarian from uni? The brunette?"

"Yeah, well, you know. We aren't supposed to form serious ties with anyone outside the group, are we?"

Tim's expression softened. "Sorry, mate. Must have been hard. What did you tell her?"

Woodsey looked blank. "Tell her?"

"About us leaving?"

"You think I should have told her?"

"You didn't *tell* her?"

"Erm... well, I thought, you know, with everything. I mean, weren't we supposed to keep all this hush-hush?"

Tim held his head in his hands, but before he regained the patience to speak, he was interrupted by another blast from the past – the unmistakable echo of a dog barking aboard a spaceship. He turned quickly, just in time to grab a pouncing border collie from the air. "Reiver! Hello, boy— *urgh!*"

Tim giggled like a little boy being tickled as he fought to keep the dog's telescopic tongue from his face and mouth. Unsurprisingly, Reiver was quicker, and soaked him with his jumbo bacon rasher.

With so much room in the world for everyone, the collie had also benefited from the advanced healthcare commonplace in their new timeline. Now fourteen, mesenchymal stem cell and sophisticated anti-aging gene therapy allowed him to bound about like a fit seven-year-old, fully in his prime.

Natalie's face was still etched with consternation, but melted at the scene, as Tim batted ineffectually to defend himself from an exuberant display of affection, if dubious hygiene.

"Stop, boy, *stop,*" Tim laughed as he struggled for air.

Natalie began to laugh, too. "Don't worry. He's clean."

"Good," Tim coughed, holding the menace at arm's length.

"Yeah, he's only just given himself a good wash – all over!"

Woodsey burst into raucous laughter as Tim wilted, looking like he wanted to cry.

Natalie put him out of his misery. "I'm messing with you. I meant I showered him this morning."

"Hey, look on the bright side, mate," Woodsey added, trying to keep his face straight. "Now you've just had *your* bath, too. That'll probably do ya 'til next month, won't it?"

Tim helped himself to Woodsey's table napkin and began wiping his face.

"Hey, I need that. I've got a burger on the way."

"Oh, I'm sorry. Would you like it back?" Tim balled the serviette and launched it across the table.

"Dude!" Woodsey jumped to his feet.

"I see you two haven't changed." Natalie smiled at them both.

"Is the Spinosaurus OK, Natalie?" Tim asked with concern.

"For now." She sat next to him and raised a hand for the barman. "The big girl's sleeping, but I'm a little anxious about what we're doing to her pulmonary and nervous systems, with all the shocks and drugs she's been given. I'll be glad when we can let her go."

They sat in contemplation for several heartbeats; all of them on a spaceship, carrying a dinosaur home. Eventually, Tim broke the silence. "In just a few hours we'll be back there. Can't quite believe it."

"Just hope it's not a war zone," Woodsey commented, darkly.

Natalie shrugged. "I'm looking forward to seeing the Cretaceous again. Just hope we don't have to make contact with anyone we don't want to see."

"Well, that is kinda why we're going back, Natalie," Woodsey disabused her. He leaned back as one of the catering staff laid a flat wooden trencher before him. Aboard it, a monster cheeseburger slid, riding a mountainous wave of fries until everything settled. The obligatory greenery, so artfully placed in the kitchen, lay buried. "Wow! *That's* a burger."

"Don't forget to eat your salad," Natalie advised.

"Salad? I kinda think of that like the green borders around a car park, you know? There just to keep your focus on the important bit?"

"No danger of you crashing into a salad," Tim mocked.

Woodsey stopped with the burger two-handed, halfway to his mouth. He affected to look hurt. "I ate an *apple* yesterday."

"No you didn't."

"OK, it was the day before, but it was a whole one... mostly." Several fries continued their perilous journey over the edge, to land on the table. Woodsey was bereft. "Medieval bits o' wood, ping-pong bats, shopping baskets. Why can't these guys just serve food on a plate any more? I'd order another beer, but it would probably arrive in a folded leaf!"

Tim looked through the menu. "Ooh, look. According to the photo, the cheese board comes on a plate."

He and Natalie laughed, each stealing fries from Woodsey's pile as the background music through the PA faded to be replaced by a voice. *"This is Captain Douglas. We're now one hour from our intended jump coordinates. That's one hour, people. Please complete whatever you're doing, secure any belongings, or equipment you may be responsible for, and make your way to our new embarkation lounge in the next thirty minutes. Thank you. Douglas out."*

Tim gestured towards the small hill in front of Woodsey. "Were you anyone else, I'd say you'd struggle to finish that within the hour... if you were anyone else."

"We have the coordinates, sir," Singh announced. He turned to face Captains Douglas and Baines and blew out his cheeks nervously, rallying with a smile.

Douglas also found himself taking a deep breath, unconsciously. "Is everyone ready, Jill?"

"All departments in the green, Captain. Awaiting your command." She turned to her husband with a secret smile. "We're ready when you are."

He exhaled quickly. "Mr Singh, you may engage the wormhole drive when ready."

Singh spun back to his forward position. "Three, two, one, engage."

Douglas could not help offering up a prayer to whoever might be listening. Outwardly, he was an island of calm as he waited, anticipating the usual ripple of distortion across space through the viewport. The last time he, and everyone else aboard the *New World,* awaited the opening of a wormhole in this precise location of space, it proved their final tense moment of normalcy before all hell broke loose. Now, after a ten-year respite, it was set to begin all over again.

"We're here," Singh reported quietly.

Douglas was startled out of his reverie. "What?"

"I said we're here, sir."

"Sorry, Sandy. Ah was, er..." Douglas cleared his throat. "That was very, er..." He floundered again.

"Nondescript?" hazarded Baines.

"It was... *smooth,*" Singh added his voice to the underwhelmed.

"The stars look different. Are ye running calculations, Sandy?"

"Aye, Captain. Set everything up before we entered the wormhole, so we lost no time at all. The computer confirms it, we've arrived at precisely 0800 hours on the 20th April 99,198,016 BC, Patagonia time. Exactly one year and one day after we landed on the planet last time. Obviously, we won't need to waste five days in space this time – hopefully."

Douglas blew out his breath again. "Well, at least we shouldn't meet ourselves, then. Jill, inform the crew we're back in real space. Sandy, set a course for the dark side of the moon. Ah'll be in my meeting room."

"Captain, wait," Singh called him back. "Guess what – it's a Tuesday!"

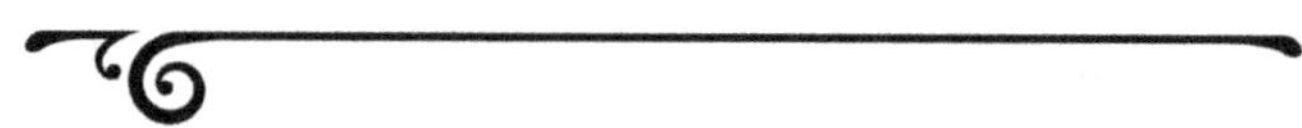

Beck Mawar, like everyone else, was experiencing a serious bout of déjà vu. The last time they travelled back to the Cretaceous, she had had no idea where, or more to the point, when they were going. A few days later, as they began their descent to prehistoric Earth, her turning of the tarot cards had revealed nothing, her spiritual ties to the departed also completely severed by their journey to a time where no human soul yet existed. Unfortunately, Mario and a few other fellow passengers lost their lives during that short voyage back to Earth, either to Heidi Schultz's murderous actions, or to Geoff Lloyd's reckless bombing; but fortunately for Beck's sanity, they had found her.

This time was different. She had begun turning the cards while they were in AD2122 and still connected to the spiritual plane. Last time, the only card she had been able to grasp, amid the chaos of their landing, was Death. A card that more usually meant change; the end of one state or journey and the beginning of another, rather than death in the literal sense. She sighed. Their situation had certainly brought change and no mistake.

This time, as the ship jumped through a wormhole to the past, there was little or no sensation at all – for others. However, for Beck, it was complicated. Physically, there was little to report, but spiritually it was like being disconnected from the Internet, right in the middle of her favourite show.

Her heart fluttered, despite having expected the wrench. She reached out immediately for her lifeline... and he was there – Mario. She smiled as she felt him squeeze her hand. It was not a real feeling, but neither was it all in her mind; rather it was a different level of sensitivity. Blindly, she took a card. She opened her eyes. The Fool. The card itself represented beginnings, innocence, spontaneity, a free spirit – unfortunately, she held it upside down, changing that meaning rather to holding back, recklessness or risk-taking.

She pondered this. Was she holding back? Not ready to take this journey? Were any of them? Or did the card herald the more direct meanings of risk-taking and recklessness? That *felt* more like it, but what choice did they have? If they did nothing, they could lose everything just as easily as if they jumped in with both feet. She straightened and focused on her breathing. If it came to a choice between jumping or being pushed, she preferred to jump, because often it is only when things are in motion that we become aware of them.

What do you think? she thought to Mario.

He smiled, as he did most of the time, always hearty. Never had she met a sunnier shade. In her mind she heard his Italian-accented English strongly. *I wouldn't know. Being dead doesn't give-a you the answers, it just presents you with a new set of questions. But if you want-a my* opinion, *I think you must travel this road – my brother, Georgio, too.* His smile broadened. *I have hope and-a faith in all of you.*

A tear rolled down her cheek. She would have hugged him, but most of the people around her already thought she was mad as a bag of rams. Instead, she took a deep breath and smiled, too.

The door to the meeting room chimed. "Come."

As Baines entered, Douglas was standing with his hands clasped behind his back, admiring the vista of stars through the viewports. She walked casually to stand beside him, running a hand down his spine. "You look tense."

He smiled at her reflection. "Ah wonder why that would be?"

She returned his smile, laying her head on his shoulder. "Remember when we were terrified about finding dinosaurs back there? I've hardly given them a thought this time."

He chuckled gently. "Aye. We've already got two aboard with us, but no, we're a good deal more prepared this time."

"Are we? Really? We don't have a clue what we're going back to, James. And we've so much to lose, this time."

He nodded agreement. "Ah dare say there'll be a few surprises, but we're equipped to deal with them. Ah like our chances." He turned to kiss her.

"And I like you." She smiled up at him.

"*Captains,*" Singh's voice boomed from hidden speakers around the meeting room, making them jump. "*You need to see this.*"

"Ah thought you were going to ask him to lower the volume on that thing?" Douglas rebuked. "He sounds worried."

"I did. It's playing into his Wizard of Oz complex. I'm sure it's nothing."

They stepped out onto the bridge together. Baines' jaw dropped. "I stand corrected," she eventually managed.

20th April 99,198,016 BC, Egypt

Heidi turned away from the viewport in her quarters aboard the *Heydrich*. She had long ago sacrificed the captain's quarters, previously taken by her grandfather, in favour of a standard crew billet – a billet that just happened to have the best view over their construction project and ever-burgeoning complex to the west.

Over the last seven months of development, her grandfather had spent most of his time glad-handing his way around the Party leadership; taking cruises, visiting mountain retreats, attending parties. While Heidi, with the help of the new allies Heinrich's efforts had procured, had built a large array of factories and warehouse units, all surrounded by concrete moats and electric fences to keep the workers safe. The fences were powered by the *Heydrich*'s core and had proven very effective – either killing or sending many of the smaller predators packing. The moat seemed to perturb the larger animals, too, risk of injury keeping them at bay. Occasionally, a patriarch *Carcharodontosaurus saharicus* would walk the perimeter, drooling. It seemed to have taken a particular interest in the human camp and studied the workers like a cat keeping watch over a gerbil cage, just waiting for a mistake. Heidi had heard its stare likened to that of her grandfather. The thought amused her.

The occasional incursion by avian creatures was to be expected, but the only human death had been caused by good old-fashioned human stupidity. The man had been trying to shoo away a giant pterosaur, to prevent it from leaving the most bizarre footprints ever recorded in concrete; a beast that would have had little interest in him otherwise. In return, it snapped with its three-metre beak and the man died. Inevitably, the animal was shot for landing in the wrong place. Heidi smirked, remembering the barbecue thrown by the workers in honour of the dead man. *What a fool. Still, the meat* was *tasty – two lessons learned.*

She was in a good mood. Today marked the successful completion of another stage along their path to conquest: today, their second powerplant would go live, freeing the hastily rigged ship's core from powering the security fences. The first reactor went online five months earlier and was pressed immediately into service supplying power to build the factory complex and security moat.

She nodded contentedly. Soon, the *Heydrich* would be able to move again, freeing up her most powerful single resource. Reports from the *Newfoundland* at Crater Lake were also encouraging. The vast old freight hauler would soon be capable of flight once more. Her decision many months ago to release Dr Hemmings, albeit under guard, seemed to have paid dividends. It had certainly helped the *Newfoundland* project along no end. Splitting her from Dr Reid seemed to have helped his performance, too. She had set him up in one of the new laboratories within the secure campus. Reid and his new German staff were kept segregated from the other workers and from the *Heydrich*'s crew. She would risk no espionage on the special projects they had been tasked with, especially as her suspicions about Hemmings working against her remained. *Yes, segregation is the key this time. Now I understand why* mein Großvater *always keeps everyone ignorant about everyone else... and what they are working on.*

A roar from outside made her turn back to the window. The old Carcharodontosaurus was back. She squinted, leaning forward. The apex predator had dropped a dead Ouranosaurus nigeriensis youngling at its feet. *What is it doing?* she pondered, despite having things to do. *Could that be an offering? Fascinating...*

"*Herr* Jansen," Chief Engineer Fritz Todt called across the compound, tersely.

Jansen sighed. "Chief Engineer, how can I help you?"

"That monster is once again threatening our perimeter!"

Jansen struggled to hide a grin. A couple of weeks ago, Todt had taken a trip outside the defensive perimeter to survey a piece of land earmarked for their next phase of construction. Todt was brilliant by the standards of his age, but not well liked by the people who chafed under his imperious command. Consequently, his arm-flapping flight and near demise at the teeth of Carcharodontosaurus had been as deleterious to his self-regard as it was hilarious to his men.

As Jansen replayed the scene in what he believed to be the privacy of his own mind, Todt appeared to hack his way in, reading the other's thoughts. "*Herr* Jansen, perhaps you would find the continued existence of that monster less amusing had *you* almost been its victim."

"Oh, I've already been there, believe me," the soldier replied with an easy smile. "That particular animal and I go way back. It accidentally saved my life from a pack of Rugops once. Though, in fairness, it was also trying to kill me at the time. I'm sure we'll look back on these little anecdotes and laugh one day, Chief Engineer."

"You may laugh one day, *Herr* Jan—"

"Oh, I'm laughing already, Chief."

Todt soured still further. He had no authority over Jansen but could not tolerate being mocked. "*Herr* Jansen, you have been given control of security for this enclosure. Now, I demand that animal be destroyed!"

"Really? But I think he likes you," Jansen taunted. "Look, he's only doing what he was born to do, Engineer Todt." *And at least he's honest about it,* he added silently. "As you say, it's my job to protect this base's perimeter, not to defend your dignity. That animal is safely outside our electric fences and cannot harm any of our workforce..." He tailed off suddenly, staring. "What's it doing?"

Todt turned too. The dinosaur seemed to be offering a gift.

A look of revelation raised Jansen's features, pulling a smile up after it. "Barbie Friday. Of course!"

"What?" spat Todt, glowering at Jansen like he was an idiot.

"Some of the workers have already begun to prepare this evening's barbecue, out here in the yard. If you ever troubled to mingle or have a beer with your own workforce, you'd know it's like every back yard in Melbourne out here, on a Friday night. There's always plenty of meat to go around – courtesy of the animals that didn't receive the memo about our electric fences – and some of the guys, here, put it to good use. Food's usually pretty tasty, too. Although there are one or two critters that are as nasty dead as they were when they were alive."

Todt was shaking his head, lost between disgust and dismay. "What the hell are you prattling about, man?"

"Look at him!" Jansen snapped, matching actions to words as he spun Todt to take in the scene. "He can smell the cooking – see him drooling? So am I, for that matter, but look, he brought us an *offering*. This is incredible."

Todt was clearly unconvinced.

"Have you never owned a cat?" Jansen tried again.

"I have," Todt admitted, tetchily. "*She* never bargained for biscuits."

"She never caught you a sparrow?" Jansen answered, but he was not really listening. "I'm going to offer him some cooked meat."

Todt's eyes widened – he now knew Jansen to be quite mad. "These monsters are not pets. He will kill you, without question."

"I know that. I'm not going out there. We've barely begun to scratch the surface regarding these creatures' behaviour. Just bear with me, will you? I got an idea." With that, Jansen jogged away to where five workers were preparing the evening's barbecued goodies in advance, before a hungry workforce descended on them. They relied on the smoke and a steel lean-to roof to keep the avians away. Todt watched as the soldier spoke animatedly to one of the chefs before stealing several large cutlets from the flames. He ran to the five-metre-high electric fence and whistled.

He need not have bothered. The Carcharodontosaurus was already bearing down on his position, pacing to and fro as it stooped to find a clear way across the dry concrete moat.

"Don't tease it, you fool!" Todt bellowed from a safe distance.

Jansen tossed a large steak, done to medium-rare perfection, over the fence. The dinosaur caught it with alarming dexterity. Whether it tasted it or not was anybody's guess; the morsel simply vanished. Jansen threw another. Again, it was snatched from the air with a single unerring snap. Once all the meat had disappeared – thrown and caught, first time, every time – Jansen, licking his fingers, retreated to where Todt was still frozen to the spot, a dozen emotions warring within him. Anger, disgust, wonder. Eventually, they cancelled one another out, leaving only his default tetchiness. "Why did you do that?" he demanded. "You only encourage the beast."

"No, the smell of the barbecue does that – every time," Jansen countered. "I'm thinking about training him for sentry duty."

"You're *what?*"

Jansen reached out to take Todt by the elbow. "Come on, hear me out," he requested, reasonably.

"Back away from the vehicle, Jansen," Todt spat imperiously, removing the hand.

Jansen rolled his eyes. "OK, consider this. There're all manner of dangerous creatures out there – you of all people know that, after what happened to you."

Todt's face bridled through a range of expressions, from irritability to embarrassment and back again, before settling at last on grudging acceptance. "And feeding this monster helps how?"

"He won't want to share the bounty with anyone else, will he? Now, I'm not kidding myself that I can befriend an eight-ton predator that doesn't even understand what a human being is."

"Indeed," Todt interrupted, drily. "It is not a spaniel – you can tell by the ears!"

Jansen stared at him. "Was that a joke? Look, obviously this creature can never be domesticated, but I reckon I can still get it to keep coming to a chosen spot at a chosen time – and by doing so it will realise it's on to a good thing and keep the other predators away. He's the biggest carnivore I've seen here. That's how I recognised him, *and* that's why it must *be* him, you see?"

"You think he will frighten the other animals away."

Jansen tilted his head to one side and smiled. "You're an intelligent guy, Fritz. Infinitely more intelligent than these animals around us, wouldn't you say?"

"Naturally."

"And he scared the crap out of you, didn't he? Just think how those guys out there are gonna feel. I reckon they'll stay away, and that'll help when we need to send out survey teams and so on."

"Perhaps," Todt agreed, reluctantly. "Or maybe we have simply swapped many smaller, more manageable hunters for Godzilla."

Jansen was shaking his head. "There are *no* manageable hunters here. But don't you see? You're thinking one-dimensionally. If I can train him to come on demand—"

"You can keep him away from where we are working," Todt completed, catching on. "It's a risky plan, *Herr* Jansen. Are you sure we would not be better off just shooting it?"

"Only if necessary. That beast will keep the others away, I'm sure of it. I've been here long enough now to have a feel for how these guys work. No matter how devastating he may seem, he's just one animal and can only be in one place at any given time. If this works, it will ease the burden on our security forces and make the area safer for everyone."

Todt nodded, accepting Jansen's idea. "Very well, it is worth exploring. However, I cannot wait for a month of Fridays to see if your plan works. I must go out within one week to complete my survey, otherwise our plans will fall behind."

"I'll begin training him every day. If he leaves that dead catch he brought us, I'll start by cooking that up..." He tailed off, scrutinising Todt. "By how much would it set our plans back if your survey could not be completed next week?"

A few minutes later, Jansen met with Aito and Devon.

"Well, if it's not Dinosaur Masterchef," Aito greeted, sarcastically.

"Can't be. He eats like a bird," added Devon.

Jansen blinked. "Word gets around fast. Shut up and listen, I've got a plan."

"Oh, thank God." Aito was full of faux relief as he scratched his arm where his false hand was attached. "Can't tell you how much I've been anticipating this moment over the last seven months."

Jansen soured. "Thanks. Do you want to hear it or not?"

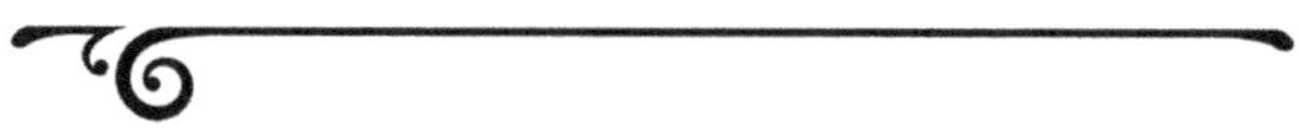

Baines moved to the viewport in a state of wonder. "What...? I can't believe it. Is that...?"

"The moon, yes," Singh replied. "Something must have hit it – *hard.*"

"So that's what happened." Baines was piecing together the evidence of her own eyes with memories from her trip to the moon in 1558 with Queen Elizabeth I. "I knew something had changed, but just put it down to being five, nearly six hundred years too early. Obviously, the changes in the terrain were actually the result of ancient damage from this time. The moon didn't look like this the last time we were here, did it?"

"No, Captain."

"Are you sure, Sandy? We didn't really pay it any mind with everything else we had going wrong. And this effect may not be clear from Earth."

Singh was shaking his head. "No, Captain. When we arrived last time, I ran intensive stellar scans along with full surveys of all local objects, while trying to ascertain our position, remember? There is no way we could have missed this. Whatever has happened here, happened after we left. I'd bet my shares on it."

Baines was about to answer but frowned as he mentioned the potential windfall no one had bothered to tell her about. Instead, she turned back to the viewport. The moon now boasted a delicate set of rings, like a tiny, pale Saturn. That thought prompted a question. "What are these rings made from?"

Singh requested a spectroscopic analysis from the computer. "Basalts and anorthosites – as you might expect. Also reading oxygen, silicon, calcium, thorium, potassium, aluminium, magnesium, titanium and iron. Hmm, this is interesting, though. Very high quantities of H_2O." He looked up from the screen to take in the spectacle with his own eyes. "Ice. Lots of it. All mixed up with the elements and rocks. A comet strike, maybe? I just wonder..." He tailed off.

"Sandy?" Douglas prompted.

Singh flashed a grin. "Just running our new gamma-ray spectrometer, sir. Hmm. Interesting."

"*Sandy!*" Baines and Douglas said together.

He grinned again. "Sorry. I'm reading uranium-235. As Captain Baines is no doubt well aware, as a Luney[6], the moon has plenty of uranium, but to get so much rock to form rings around the sphere – even low-density rings such as these – would have taken one hell of an impact."

A memory snagged at Baines. "Hang on. Didn't Natalie say the blood samples she took from our sleeping beauty in the main hangar showed an unusual uranium-strontium isotope? She suspected the creature must have lived near to a natural, but unusually concentrated, source of radiation. Could there be a link?"

Singh looked sceptical. "How could that be related to the moon, Captain?"

"I've no idea, but clearly some sort of violent event has taken place here, and that dinosaur was displaced by a hundred million years. If I was a betting woman – the sort that might dabble on the stock exchange, if given the heads up by her friends, for example – I'd bet there was a connection."

Douglas shrugged. "Well, it's very interesting, Ah cannae deny it, but we'll have to shelve our questions for now. Lieutenant-Commander Singh, have you placed us in a geosynchronous orbit around the moon?"

"Yes, sir. We should remain permanently on its dark side from Earth's perspective."

"Will that fool their scans?" asked Baines.

Singh spun his seat to face her. "Of course, Captain. You don't know the power of the dark side."

"Don't start that again."

"Thank you, Sandy," Douglas interrupted. "Very well. It's time to launch the SCDs – whenever you're ready." He relished giving that order, the evidence clear on his face as he turned to Baines. "While you were flying missions to colonies all around the galaxy, Hiro and maself were working through a wish list with a group of brilliant UN scientists. You won't believe some of the gear we have this time."

"SCDs?" asked Baines.

---

6   A person born on the lunar sphere. A most unfortunate term and constant niggle for Jill Baines as the first ever 'Luney'.

"Satellite Capture Drones. Think of this as our first strike. What we need, before moving to neutralise any threat Schultz's people may or may not present, is intel. These drones will attack the satellite network they so thoughtfully placed in orbit for us to use. They won't even see our SCDs coming. They're practically invisible to sensors. Once they make contact, they'll give us a clear advantage over the enemy – a cheap and invisible alternative to launching our own net and without the risks of being noticed by enemy assets in orbit."

"Sounds great," Baines allowed. "How do they work?"

"By hijacking their spy satellites. They break into the enemy equipment's casings in such a way that we can take control of them without them even knowing. They will *believe* they have full control, but we'll be able to take over at a moment's notice, and every piece of information their units send out after our insurgence will be copied to us, along with anything stored in memory – also without them knowing. Clever, eh?"

"Ingenious," Baines agreed. "Just one question. How did the UN build the SCDs to take control of units they had never seen and about which they could have no working knowledge?"

Douglas wiggled his eyebrows knowingly.

Baines waited impatiently. "Come *on*. You've given me the first episode. Don't tell me I have to pay to see how it ends."

Douglas laughed. Sobering slightly, he explained, "The plans provided by the late and courageous Lieutenant Elizabeth Hemmings contained more than just wormhole drive schematics. That was our primary concern back then, but there were other technologies explained within the files, too – including Schultz's satellite net. Small memory storage devices were about all we could carry when we left 1558 – those and a change of clothes – but luckily, we were able to bring our entire database, along with the information Elizabeth gave to me. We've been busy – putting our knowledge together with our friends back home in the alternate future." His self-satisfied air slipped slightly; he looked pained. "Sorry Ah couldnae tell ye any of this, lassie. Ah had to toe the line, the work was so important to us."

Baines looked back at him with pride. "It must have been driving you mad."

"Aye." He smiled.

"I just got a curt response from Hiro for asking if the devices were ready," Singh interrupted Douglas' apology. "They're ready and... away, Captain."

Douglas approached the pilot. "Excellent, Sandy. Pass on my regards to engineering. Jill, come and watch this."

They huddled around a monitor, watching the feed from a camera placed in the nose of the missile casement. It shot around the moon, providing an incredible spectacle as it negotiated the tilted ring of stone and ice. On its second orbit it built the terrific speed necessary to slingshot towards Earth.

"Economical, too." Baines noted. "Colour me impressed."

"No gas guzzlers in our new timeline, Captain," Singh quipped. "The device has already tagged all the units in the Schultz net."

On screen, several dozen markers lit up all around the Earth. Singh leaned forward in his seat. "This is the cool bit."

The missile casing split open, releasing a hornet's nest of small robots that shot off in pursuit of individually assigned targets. Singh moved their video to the main viewer, which split immediately into fifty smaller feeds. Each of the tiny SCDs darted and wove, showing myriad views of the planet below.

"Are we recording all this?" asked Douglas. "It'll be a geologist's and palaeontologist's Christmas if we ever get it back to them."

"Yes, sir. I record everything. Sometimes I have to remind even myself that everything I've seen wasn't just a figment of my imagination."

"I hear that," Baines seconded.

Although the little robots moved at unlikely speeds, some of them had to cover tens of thousands of miles to reach their targets. "This might take a little while, Captains," Singh warned them. "They're programmed to strike as one, in case a failed strike from an individual drone should warn the people below that they're under attack. We have about an hour to kill."

Douglas took Baines by the elbow. "Jill, why don't you share what we've learned about the moon with Natalie? See what she thinks about that isotope now we have potentially two pieces to the puzzle?"

"Wilco."

2122 El-Shaikh Ebada, Egypt

Badawi waved as the last palaeontology students drove away. Fallout, after what the press had severally termed the 'DENIAL OVER NILE DINO!', the unimaginative 'NILE DINOSAUR DISASTER!', the ridiculous 'DENIAL OVER DE NILE!', and finally, 'WARMEST NOVEMBER ON RECORD' had left him exhausted – although whoever turned in that last headline would be unlikely to receive a promotion for it. They probably fell over a lot.

With the help of UN personnel and equipment, he had trapped and removed the monstrous threat to the area, but the foothills Professor Norris' students explored for fossils were also popular with walkers and school parties. He could not ignore the possibility of Simba's body being found. Unfortunately, there remained little hope she might be found alive, but he could not just allow tourists or children to stumble across grisly body parts. He must try.

Winter approached, though it was still thirty degrees Celsius in the desert. Taking a long pull of water from his flask, he breathed deeply and set off.

The helicopter crew had discovered the lower leg a quarter of a mile along the main east-west valley into the mountains, so he left his vehicle and set off towards the coordinates they provided. The valley floor was soft with blown sand but not difficult to traverse on foot. He soon arrived at the location where the leg had been spotted, roughly four metres up in the rocks above him. The cleft looked a relatively easy climb, so he scrambled up for a more commanding view.

He took another drink and pulled a pair of field glasses from a case strapped around his neck. He focused them, scanning along the valley. Nothing. It came as no great surprise. Maybe there was nothing to find? A predator of that size could easily have swallowed the poor girl whole. Had the leg not been sheared off just above the knee in the attack, they might well be combing for a missing person still. Badawi shook his head sadly. He would not give up just yet. He had no tracks to follow, after the recent desert winds, but he climbed back down and continued doggedly, deeper into the hills.

A few minutes' trudge across the sands brought him to a gap on his right, in the valley's southern side. It led into a box canyon. Badawi knew the area well and placed himself at the centre of the opening, once more drawing his binoculars from their carrycase. He scanned the short canyon with little hope of discovering anything very much. That was when the sun glinted off something reflective in the western cliffs.

He frowned, staring again with the naked eye. Definitely something shiny; possibly metallic. He looked once more through the field glasses. He was too far away for a clear view. It seemed unlikely that this had anything to do with the missing girl, but the magpie in him could not resist. He set off towards the sparkle in the rock face. Had he come later in the day, a westering sun would have cast the article in the shade, causing him to miss it entirely. Buoyed by this good fortune, he moved quickly.

A short steel rod was indeed sticking out of the canyon wall. He examined it closely. It seemed to have blasted its way into the cliff – he assumed via an inbuilt explosive cap. Though he had no idea what he was looking at, he tried pulling the rod out of the stone.

A brief struggle, with one foot braced against the cliff, left him with nothing to show for it but a wry smile and a sense of chagrin. He had not seriously expected an Arthurian moment, but he was disappointed, nonetheless. All his tools were half a mile away in a police jeep.

He cursed silently and began retracing his steps when a sudden stiff breeze blew around the canyon floor. It lifted sand in mini cyclones, scattering it in all directions – although, he noted sourly, it felt to him like most of it was deposited directly into his eyes. Covering them, he missed his step and almost stumbled. The wind had revealed a largish pothole in the canyon floor.

Badawi waited for the flurry to die down and observed that the pothole he was standing in was not the only one – there was a row of them. Eyes watering, he quickly removed a handkerchief from his pocket, dampening it sparingly from his canteen. Eyes wiped, he thought he might be seeing things.

He had walked this region countless times during his life and was categorically sure the box canyon floor had never contained a line of potholes on any previous visit. He wiped his eyes a second time. "What the...?"

They were not potholes, they were footprints – huge, three-toed footprints. After the events of that week, the sight was not wholly surprising to him. These were obviously the footprints of a dinosaur –

he could only surmise, footprints of *the* dinosaur, but there was a catch. The winds had already erased any signs of that creature. Moreover, these tracks were fossilised in stone. He knew they had not been there before and surely a full team of palaeontologists could hardly have missed them. The wind whipped up behind him once more. He ignored it. "What the hell?" he repeated to himself – or so he thought.

When someone answered, he jumped a foot into the air.

"State your name," a female voice demanded, imperiously.

Badawi turned to find a young and unusually beautiful blond woman holding a gun on him. "I..."

"Out with it!" she demanded.

"Master Sergeant Apep Badawi. Who are you?"

"I am the one with a gun. Drop your sidearm, *now.*"

Her tone brooked no refusal, so he slowly did as ordered. Behind the blonde was a strange shimmer that was hard to describe, more an other-worldly quality to the light. It was several metres across and although he could see through, it was disorienting. He felt that if he stared too long, he may even become travel-sick. "Can you explain these tracks?" he asked her, not knowing what else to say.

Heidi glanced down for a split second only, instantly returning her full attention to the man before her. "Interesting."

"You don't say."

Her lip twisted into a half-smile. "Were you searching for fossils?"

"No. I was searching for a missing girl."

The light of understanding lit Heidi's eyes. "*Really?*"

Badawi nodded. "She was killed – or so we believe – a few nights ago. An animal kill."

"Yes, indeed. I was there."

That gave him pause. He stared. "You saw it *happen?*"

"Why, certainly. And a most fortuitous meeting it was, too. Had I not taken the girl prisoner, the Spinosaurus aegyptiacus may very well have eaten me, instead."

"You *killed* her?" Badawi was incredulous.

"Not exactly. I merely allowed her to die by my hand. The animal did most of the work. Do not trouble yourself so. It would most likely have caught her anyway. She was making the most ridiculous amount of noise."

"So you *threw* her to that monster." It was not a question.

Despite the heat, Heidi's smile chilled him. "More *at* than to – and now I have *you,* Master Sergeant Badawi. So be a good boy. I would hate for anything else to go wrong while you are out here alone. Now, I have questions. How fortunate that I bumped into you."

Badawi swallowed.

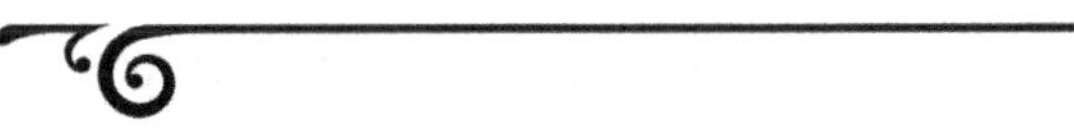

Five high-speed drill bits cut simultaneously through the outer casing. Of a high-carbon-steel-vanadium alloy, they were hollow with sharpened, tungsten tips and helical cutting edges. The four outer bits formed a square about the centre. Once at optimum depth, an ultra-low-temperature foam adhesive shot through the hollow drill shafts to expand within the satellite's case, forming a rapid and permanent bond, while fully utilising the strength of the bits. The centre bit sealed automatically around its outer edges to protect the electronics and optics within from the extreme temperatures of geosynchronous orbit. Each of the Schultzes' forty-two satellites kept relative positions above the Earth at a distance of 35,786 kilometres.

Douglas' Satellite Capture Drones, or SCDs, acted as one, each striking a separate satellite at the same instant. The missile Singh launched contained fifty drones. The remaining eight went into standby mode, awaiting further instructions.

Singh whooped. "Every single one worked first time, Captain. We now have full control of their satellite net! I'm downloading their memories, but otherwise leaving them on station, sir."

"Excellent, Sandy." Douglas clapped the younger man on the shoulder. "Round one to us, eh?"

"Yes, sir!" Singh's enthusiasm was catching, but abruptly dwindled.

"What is it?" Douglas was suddenly wary.

"I've got camera feeds. We have a visual on a ship called the... erm, *Heydrich,* sir."

"Charming."

Singh turned in his seat. "Sir?"

"Ah'm no historian, Sandy, but Ah know that name well enough. Reinhard Tristan Eugen Heydrich, one of the principal architects of the Nazi Holocaust – and even among that brood he was one of, if not actually, the worst. A man of pure evil. Which begs the question, what sort of a creature would name their ship to honour him?"

The muscles bunched in Singh's jaw. "A Schultz kind. I'm afraid there's worse news, Captain. Look at this."

Douglas leaned over the pilot's shoulder. "Tell me those are no' what Ah think they are."

"Tanks, sir, and worse. See here?" He switched to another view of the Nazi complex showing at least a couple of dozen grounded aircraft – more specifically, the orbital assault craft favoured by Heinrich Schultz.

"Oh, my god," Douglas breathed, barely a whisper. "Can we see what they have in those large hangars?"

"Infrared shows several hundred people moving about, sir. From the heat signatures, they appear to be operating heavy machinery."

"What the hell are they up to?"

"This doesn't make sense, sir."

"Go on, Sandy."

"Schultz has, what, a hundred personnel? Half his people defected to us with Captain Meritus. There must be two hundred tanks *alone*, down there – without everything else. Who's going to operate them?"

"More to the point, who are they going to use them on?" Douglas could not help jumping to the obvious conclusion. "They're planning an assault through time. Damnit! Even for Heidi this is audacious. Sandy, get me a comm channel to Dr Klaus Fischer, please."

"Right away, sir." Bare moments passed. "I have him – you're on, Captain."

"Klaus, James Douglas. Ah need you on the bridge immediately, please."

"*On my way, Captain.*"

Singh looked up to Douglas questioningly.

"Fischer has been working with the German Minister's office. He recently found evidence of an incursion to 1943."

Singh frowned. "*Incursion?*"

Douglas sighed. "Aye. A wormhole incursion."

Singh's eyes widened. "1943! Even I know enough history to understand that *that's* about as bad as it gets."

"Aye." Douglas surveyed the large, moated enclosures surrounding the Schultzes' complex. "And Ah thought *we'd* been busy over the last decade. How long has it been for them? Seven months? Ah cannae believe how far they've come."

"If they have a portal between the Cretaceous and Nazi Germany, Captain, they might be able to call on huge resources. And those tanks aren't 1940s, either. They're state-of-the-art, early twenty-second century main battle tanks. Depending on what ordnance they're equipped with, just one of them could potentially level a mid-twentieth century city, while being damned near indestructible to the other side."

The door chimed. "Come," Douglas called.

Dr Klaus Fischer strode quickly onto the bridge. "Mr Singh." He nodded greeting to the pilot. "What have you, Captain?"

Douglas showed him.

Fischer paled. "She's building an army."

"Aye. We need to know everything you know from those secret documents, Klaus. The location of the wormhole, how long it operated, everything. Sandy, get Jill back here. That radioactive isotope the dinosaur carries will have to wait."

"Sir."

"Radioactive... whatever is this, now?" asked Fischer.

Badawi swallowed. The woman before him was obviously psychotic, beauty or no.

"Kick your sidearm over here," Heidi demanded.

Rather than kick the weapon Badawi bent, cautiously, to grab the holster between his thumb and fingertips, and cast it gently at her feet. While stooping he activated the comm in his pocket, setting it to 'black box' mode. Straightening, he deliberately stepped on the edge of a dinosaur footprint and slipped several centimetres down its side, stumbling. He fell forward and cursed, playing his part, while secreting the device just under the sand, from where it began to record and broadcast. Getting clumsily to his feet, he swore again, as if with embarrassment.

Heidi gave him a look of disdain but made no comment. She expected incompetence in others, it was nature's way of putting her in charge. "You have seen the dinosaur, Master Sergeant?"

"I have."

"Where is it now?"

"Gone."

"You have destroyed the animal?"

"No. Some people came here from the UN, in a cargo ship. They captured it and took it with them."

Her eyes narrowed. "Took it where?"

He shrugged. "America, maybe? I was not told."

She scrutinised him a moment longer, weighing the truth of his words. "The people who were camped here – did you meet with them?"

"The palaeontology students? Yes, I spoke with them. It was one of their number that *you* murdered."

"I told you, the animal did the actual killing. I simply created a diversion."

"No, you did much more than that, by your own admission."

Heidi sighed, bored. "Admission? Ah... you are the consummate police officer, yes? Hmm, I bet you are always a hit at parties, too. Now tell me, did you speak with a Timothy Norris?"

"I spoke with a *Professor* Norris."

She raised an eyebrow. "Professor Norris? Good for him. And where is he now?"

"Gone."

"With the dinosaur?"

Badawi nodded.

Heidi considered. "I think I will need you to accompany me, Master Sergeant."

"Where?"

"Through that." She stepped aside, gesturing towards the wormhole.

"Where does it go? Have you come from one of the breakaway colonies?"

She studied him. "I know nothing of these breakaway colonies. No more questions. Come."

Badawi stared at the event horizon with understandable fear and trepidation. "Where does it lead?"

"To exactly here."

He frowned, not understanding.

Heidi laughed lightly. "Not where, Master Sergeant, when. It seems there is much we can learn from one another. I will show you the Earth's past and you will tell me everything I wish to know about its future, yes?"

"Why do you need to take me with you? Surely, I have little value."

"True, but you are now a witness to my incursion. I may wish to open a portal here again in order to move troops and matériel. It seems this is a fixed point."

Troops? Matériel? Who is *this woman?* Badawi wondered, desperately trying to think of a ruse that might allow him to escape her grasp.

She motioned with her trusty nine-millimetre. "Do not worry, you would not understand. Simply obey, or I will shoot you. That is all you *really* need to know."

"When you put it like that," he answered sourly.

"Move."

Badawi stepped through.

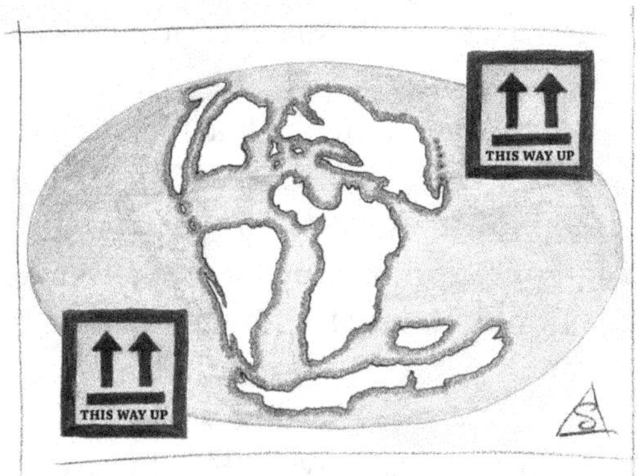

Chapter 7 | Who Would You Kill?

"But there may be a good many civilians down there, Tobias," Douglas argued passionately. "People who've almost certainly been ferried in from a less advanced time than our own to provide a labour force for a maniac. Who knows what they've been told!"

Captain Tobias Meritus sat back, crossing his arms and shaking his head. "James, I have, shall we say, a *unique* perspective into the thinking of our enemy. They will not care who they slaughter or what they destroy as long as they end up on top. *We* have civilians aboard this ship, too – a good many of them!" He threw Douglas' words back at him. "If you recall, I argued strongly against bringing them."

"We all agreed to answer the call, Tobias," Klaus Fischer spoke firmly. "Our reasons for bringing everyone may not make military sense, but may yet be crucial to the outcome of this situation. We are not afraid."

Meritus leaned forward, elbows on the meeting table, his neutral accent slipping to his native Canadian. "Well, I sure as hell am, Klaus. Schultz is a monster and if we play by the rules, we'll die, and so will the future we're working to protect. You understand? There's not a rule or law that Heinrich, or that witch of a granddaughter of his, won't break – not a single one. James, have you seen any schools or hospitals on the ground?"

Douglas blinked. "Not that we can tell."

"Any houses or other signs of civilian occupation?" he pressed.

Douglas could only shrug. "Again, from what we can tell, the buildings are ostensibly factory units and storage facilities—"

"Right," Meritus cut him off. "Well, what you see as civilian workplaces, I see as people creating the machinery of death. For God's sake, we must *act!* They have no idea we're here or that we carry enough munitions to blow them back to the twenty-second century – give up that element of surprise with some well-meaning gesture of fairness and you not only doom all of us, you doom everyone in the future we just left behind, too. A future that was doing pretty well. Whatever the guys we lost in 1558 did, worked. It's a world worth saving – we cannot screw around with this, James."

Douglas brooded.

"I've gotta say, Captain," Gleeson spoke unusually gently, "I think Tobo has a point. We won't get any brownie points from Old Man Schultz for playing fair. He'll just think we're wetter than a dolphin's cozzie[7], and take advantage."

Baines placed a hand on Douglas' arm. "James, if I may."

He looked to her, as if remembering she was still there. "Of course, Jill."

"We need to approach this with cool heads, people. I think both positions are valid. Tobias is correct, in that, if we give any warning, we'll have a full-scale war on our hands with no guarantees we'll win – we don't know what *else* they may have down there." She looked at each of them in turn, to make sure her words sank in. "By the same token, James is also right that we should not just steam in, blowing all hell out of the place and anybody who just happened to have reported for work this morning. Don't get me wrong, I agree they're building the instruments of murder, but if we take drastic action without even knowing what we face, we could wind up destroying the very future we're trying to save."

"I'm not sure I follow you, Jill," Meritus replied more calmly.

"What I mean is, if we drop the hammer on that place while, say, they have an open wormhole, who knows what collateral damage might ensue at the other end?"

"That's a fair point," Meritus agreed, "but let's not sugar-coat this. Nazi Headquarters are at the other end of that wormhole, possibly

---

7   Australian and British slang for a swimming costume.

even the Führer himself. Don't tell me you'd pass up the opportunity to crack that nut."

"Even if it killed thousands of civilians?"

"To save *millions,* yes."

Douglas was shaking his head. "We're forgetting something fundamental here." Everyone looked at him. "The other end of *that* wormhole is not Nazi Germany. The timeline was altered extensively, remember? From 1558 onwards, we're into uncharted territory – who knows what effects that sort of devastation might have on events? The people on the other side of that wormhole are just people – mostly good and enlightened people, to boot, according to the new histories. They might be in the clutches of a scheming autocrat, and it may be that their very innocence is contributing to their undoing, but killing untold hundreds or thousands of them is hardly likely to bring them back into the light."

Meritus let out an exasperated sigh, raking his fingers through his hair. "So what do you propose? We tell them not to accept candy from the bad man?"

"No," Baines stated forcefully. "Firstly, we need to know exactly what is going on down there, before we go blowing it to kingdom come. Our access to the enemy's satellite net is invaluable, but it only tells us so much. We have to get *down* there."

"We have a way." Singh spoke quietly into the sudden silence. "Hiro?"

Chief Nassaki had remained silent during the arguments, his thoughts focused on his brother – whom he suspected was somewhere within the enemy compound on the planet below. He knew that everyone else believed Aito to be dead. The Sigilmassasaurus that tossed him like a ragdoll at the cavern wall, just before they left the Cretaceous last time, left them in no doubt. Kindly, they had suggested he accept the loss – allowing himself to grieve. They had all tried at some point, but he knew they were wrong. He felt it. He knew Aito was alive and if they incinerated that industrial plant below, then he really would lose his brother.

"Hiro?" Singh prompted again.

"We have a spy," the engineer spoke at last.

Tim was beyond gobsmacked. He struggled to speak. "You... you *made* it?" Standing with his best friend and his fiancée, all three stared at a dinosaur. It was something they had done many times over the wild ride that had been their lives, but this time there was a subtle difference. The creature was not alive. They had stood next to dead dinosaurs, too. Some dead for minutes, others for millions of years, but this one had never *been* alive. It was a robot.

Woodsey stepped forward, pointing with both hands. "Whoa. Now *this* is cool."

Tim turned to Hiro. "What animal is it based on?"

Hiro smiled proudly. "Can't you tell me?"

Tim pondered. "Well, it's some form of ornithomimosaur – medium-sized. Maybe Afromimus tenerensis?"

"Very good," Hiro congratulated. "That was the holotype we used for our final modifications – based on your own research and what we now see below."

Tim glowed under praise, always the little boy when around dinosaurs. "But how did you know we had to fit in with North African fauna?"

Hiro shrugged. "Ornio... Ornitho... Erm, these *ostrich-like* dinosaurs seem common enough around the globe and we wanted something fast. Once we took control of the Schultz satellite net, we simply tweaked the colours. Perhaps it's not exact, but it's not as though the dinosaurs will be taking osteo comparison X-rays. Not that it would help anyway. This machine's skeleton is of carbon fibre and bears little resemblance to that of the real Afro... what's-its-name. Most fascinating of all, is—"

"Yes, I like the feathered rough around the neck and along the spine." Tim cut Hiro's technical monologue short as politely as possible. He stroked the plumage, feeling its texture between his fingers. "Very good. Just the thing for keeping the spine warm at night, on the rare occasions when the humid heat of the Egyptian delta relents. It's an excellent job. Especially as – as far as I'm aware – we have no complete fossils of this species, let alone detailed evidence of feathers and so on. I mean, we've been assuming they were feathered for years, especially the smaller, lighter creatures, such as Afromimus – all based on contemporaries, of course. Most fascinating of all, is—"

"We took our best guess." Hiro equally killed Tim's soliloquy before he really got going. "*We* never visited Africa last time we were here, but these small, fast-moving herbivores and omnivores seemed common, as I said. So it stood to reason that the African versions would be similar enough to animals we *had* seen. Wouldn't you agree?"

Tim did, although he winced at the word 'versions'. Hiro made them sound like a similar model from the production line of a competitor. It made sense that there would be many similar or sub-species for practically every animal alive in those times, as there were in every other epoch of complex life, except where mankind or disaster interfered – often consequential events. "Are you saying we've seen these animals on the ground, Chief? From the enemy's satellite images?"

Hiro looked less sure. "We've seen *similarish* animals. We didn't have much to go on before we came – as you stated. We've done what we can with what we have. I think our last-minute changes will work, however. Even if they equate to little more than a new paintjob."

Tim looked into the man-made dinosaur's mouth, checking the teeth. "It's good, Hiro. It's really good." He turned back to the engineer. "Pity it's based on an animal about which we know so little."

Woodsey stepped up to run a hand along its back. "Yeah, it's a crying shame. Did you say it was fast? I like the sound of that!"

"How fast?" asked Clarrie.

Hiro grinned. "Seventy-five kilometres per hour. Of course, that was tracked on asphalt. In the real world—"

"That's too fast," Tim explained.

"The hell it is!" They all turned around to see Captain Meritus enter the storage room from the main hangar. "We don't want anyone catching it, do we? That would let the Velociraptor out of the bag, wouldn't it?"

"Maybe," Tim countered, taking Meritus' hand and shaking it, "but an animal acting abnormally might attract attention."

"No one really knows for sure how fast these creatures are," Hiro countered. "We chose something unthreatening, relatively small and quick enough to get out of trouble."

"You're such a killjoy." Clarrie took Tim's arm, grinning up at him.

Woodsey winked at her. "I heard one student refer to him as po-faced."

"Who said that?" Tim was scandalised.

"Dude, I can't reveal my sources."

Clarrie laughed.

"It looks great, Hiro," Meritus congratulated. "Assuming we don't have all the time in the world, how do we get it down there?"

"We send it down in a dropship, at night, Captain – let it go several miles from the enemy camp. It can run the distance and be there by morning."

"What about the satellite net? They'll see it coming."

"You mean the satellite net we control?" Hiro grinned again. "They'll see a whole lot of empty sky and darkness, Captain, nothing more. I was going to suggest to Captain Douglas that a small detachment of our soldiers go down with it and remain there. We can make sure they stay undetected. It might be useful to have boots on the ground near the enemy complex."

Meritus mulled the idea over. "I agree. I'll run it past James and have a twenty-strong force ready themselves for this evening. Good work, Chief. It's a masterpiece."

"I have to concur," agreed Tim. "Just one thing."

Hiro raised an eyebrow quizzically.

"Before you send it down there, can we switch it on?"

"*Yes!*" Woodsey and Clarrie said in unison.

Hiro looked doubtful. "That may not be such a good idea."

"Why?" Woodsey and Clarrie were joined by Tim this time.

"Because it's programmed to behave like a wild animal and to be skittish around anything unusual, like people. It will try to keep its distance from us." He gave a wry smile. "It is cool, though. It can even poop!"

"No way!" Clarrie burst out, putting a hand to her mouth.

Hiro chuckled. "It can ingest vegetation, taking it down to a storage tank in the gut where acids break down the fibres and eventually it, erm... *evacuates* them."

Woodsey grabbed Tim's arm roughly. "Tell me we can have a crapping robot dinosaur for the faculty!"

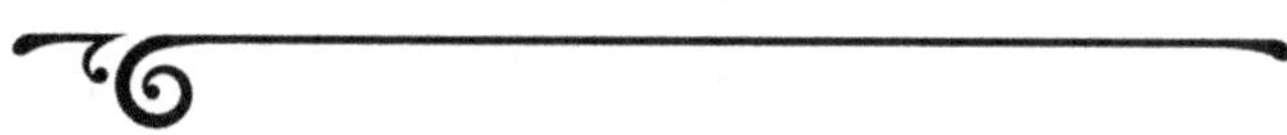

Sergeant Adam Prentice took his seat within one of the *New World*'s purpose-built dropships. He deliberately chose to sit next to their youngest member, Private Mark Radburn. "How are you feeling, lad?"

"Excited, Sarge."

Prentice gave a half-smile. "It'll pass." He eyed the four-metre-long dinosaur cam in their midst with suspicion. "When I joined up, I wasn't much older than you, Mark." He gave a derisive snort. "I joined the army to get better rations, if you can believe it. The grey, slimy enzyme paste we used to eat at home was well depressing, honestly. Now, of course, things are a little different. We're being dropped from a spaceship onto the Earth, a hundred million years in the past, to offer support to a robot dinosaur – so I think I can guess why *you* joined our forces."

Radburn smiled. "I'd be a fool to miss out on all this."

Prentice chuckled. "That's what I thought."

The pilot announced that they were about to leave.

"Here we go, lad. You strapped in?"

"Yes, Sarge."

Despite the young man's bravado, Prentice gave him a confident wink to calm his nerves. A decade earlier, Mark Radburn had been one of the young children who boarded the first *New World* to begin a new life on Mars with his parents. Now, at the age of seventeen, he was a soldier and ready to fight for the life he had made in their alternative timeline. Prentice had some scruple about taking him on this mission, but the young man had begged for the opportunity to see the Cretaceous world for himself. He reminded him a little of the younger Tim Norris – all wide-eyed wonder and idealism.

"*Hope you're all buckled up, back there,*" the pilot's enthusiastic voice boomed from the comm speakers in the rear of their little ship. "*We're going down!*"

Prentice rolled his eyes. *Pilots.*

Badawi thought he was seeing double; the smack about the head from the butt of Heidi's pistol grip gave some credence to his belief. In the cell next to him was yet another stunning blonde. When he turned to check if Heidi was still behind him, he gawked, his foggy mind trying to understand what he was seeing. "You?" was all he could manage.

"We'll speak in the morning, when you have regained your senses. If you had any to begin with." With that, Heidi locked the cell and marched out of the *Heydrich*'s brig.

"What the hell?" he mumbled, blearily.

"Who are you?" asked the woman in the next cell.

Badawi rubbed his head, blinked hard and took a deep breath while he collected his wits. He introduced himself honestly before asking the same question of her.

"I am Dr Heidi Schultz."

He slumped onto his cell's bunk. "This is a nightmare – or a delusion. I am imagining things, obviously."

"No you're not, Master Sergeant."

"Call me Apep."

"You're not imagining things, Apep. I am *that* Dr Heidi Schultz's great-great-great-great-grandaunt. At least that is what I have been told."

Head in his hands, he looked up sharply. "So I have been drugged, too. Are you part of my torture?"

His fellow prisoner wore a grey, all-in-one jumpsuit. Elasticated at the waist, it did not entirely hide her femininity. With one hand on her hip, she slipped right into an S-curve like a catwalk natural, appraising him. "Most men would not consider being locked up with me exactly *torture*. Unless you refer to the bars between us?" she taunted.

"Forgive me," Badawi apologised chivalrously. "Of course, I didn't mean..."

She smiled mischievously. "No, forgive me. I've been locked up here for about seven months, now. Alone, for most of it. I have to take what small amusements I can get. Why are you here and where did you come from?"

Badawi told her.

"Interesting," she mused, after he had finished speaking. "Not so long ago I would have thought that story most strange."

"May I ask where you are from, Doctor? Do I note a German cadence to your English?"

"You have a good ear, Apep, for someone also speaking a second language, I suspect. I am from Munich."

He listened politely.

"In 1943."

He gaped, spluttering disbelief in his native Egyptian Arabic.

"What was that, Apep?"

"Sorry. Just something about stopping the world and letting me off!"

She laughed lightly, approaching the bars. "I have been locked up in here for a long time and am most keen to leave. So now there are two of us, and we each know who the other is, the next question, I think you will agree, is how might we escape?"

A man's hand reached down into the sands of Egypt to retrieve an abandoned comm unit. It was still broadcasting an SOS beacon. The policeman blew any remaining grains from its surface and opened out its screen. He noted the device was still recording, too. He pressed [stop] and then [play].

After rewinding the recording several hours, it suddenly became far more interesting. He recognised Apep Badawi's voice instantly, but the other's was that of a stranger; a woman, he believed. She sounded European, though he could not be sure. His command of the English language was less advanced than Badawi's, but when she began talking of wormholes and the moving of troops and matériel to this location, his eyes widened – he understood enough. He also understood that his colleague had vanished and was clearly in trouble. Striding back to his jeep, he pulled the radio from the dashboard and placed a call.

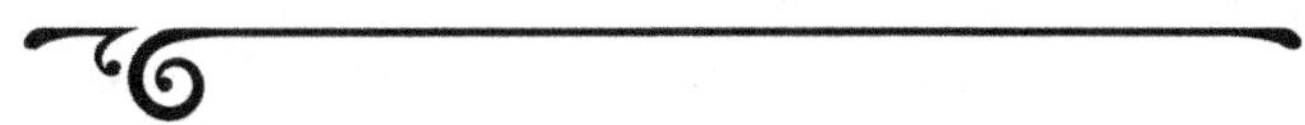

Their 'eyes' on the ground were guided by artificial intelligence programmed with a specific mission. Even so, Douglas still thought it wise to keep a round-the-clock watch on the broadcast footage they received from their faux Afromimus. He wished to avoid any situations that might lead to the asset being lost or destroyed – or spotted. To that end, he enlisted Tim and Woodsey to advise on how best to employ their 'dino spy' without attracting attention.

The robotic Afromimus ran quickly. Beautifully balanced and surefooted, its eyes recorded the night-time Cretaceous plains in infrared. Under the bright, waxing gibbous moon, high in a clear sky, the pictures were sharp but eerily pale. Other animals moved around it in the unnatural light, going about their nightly business. Some were huge; sauropods feeding on treetops at the edges of forests. Tim pointed out a family group of Paralititan stromeri, their long, giraffe-like necks stripping tough leaves and stems from high branches, even in the dead of night – so insatiable was their need to feed.

"I wish we could study their sleep cycles," Tim muttered wistfully. "On such a poor diet we know they spend their lives eating, but even *they* must require rest."

"I know what you mean, mate. How long do they sleep? What position do they like to sleep in? What do they dream about? That type of thing."

"Erm... yeah. Sort of."

"It's just a shame this thing was built for war. What a great piece of kit. Moving constantly at this speed without tiring is just incredible. How far has it travelled already?"

Tim checked the readouts and whistled. "We've covered four kilometres in five minutes."

"*We?*" Woodsey was grinning.

Tim snorted. "Alright, *it*. But that's an average of forty-eight kilometres per hour, over all kinds of rough terrain. You were right about one thing, though."

"Yeah?"

"Yeah. We have *got* to get one of these for the faculty!"

Woodsey laughed, then stopped suddenly. "Whoa! Look at *that*."

367,000 kilometres away, from the safety of the dark side of the moon and during its perigee[8], the young men watched events down on the planet unravel. It felt like a television show set during the Earth's deep past. They had seen many such, over the years, and had to keep reminding themselves that this show was the real thing. Their roving camera, still moving at speed through low-lying fern, crested a rise in the plain. The slope down the other side was steeper,

---

8   Perigee is the closest point of an object's orbit around the Earth or a planet. The moon's perigee occurs when it is closest to Earth – approximately 363,300 kilometres distance. Its apogee occurs when the moon is furthest away – approximately 405,500 kilometres.

and for just an instant, they were blessed with a perfect view over a sleeping herd of Ouranosaurus nigeriensis – mid-sized herbivorous dinosaurs of the clade Hadrosauriformes and closely related to the 'duck-billed' dinosaurs. Tim noted that they slept on their bellies for they, like the mighty Spinosaurus aegyptiacus with whom they shared their world, sported great sails along the length of their backs and tails. Skin stretched taut across the long spines; spines that formed part of the creatures' vertebrae. Also like Spinosaurus, a seven-metre-long animal weighing two or three tons might easily snap those spines, should it roll onto its back, probably causing irreparable spinal injury or even death.

Many hundreds of the magnificent beasts slept in the ghoulish twilight of night vision, while several dozen rotated a permanent watch. Crouched on the ground with their sails in the air, they reminded Tim of a vast, marauding pack of Dimetrodon; a famous genus of sail-backed predators from the Permian Period – already lost to the Earth 180 million years before this herd of ouranosaurs explored its surface. Although Tim's and Woodsey's view was fleeting, they noted that every time an animal lay down to rest, another got up to keep vigil. It was the most remarkable division of labour with neither command nor concurrence necessary.

"They're as much a product of programming as our friend down there," Tim marvelled.

"Hmm." Woodsey stroked his chin. "I've been thinking about that."

Tim glanced at him. "What?"

"I think he needs a name – something a bit more than 'eyes and ears' or whatever the code number was that Hiro reeled off."

Tim chuckled. "Go on, let's hear it."

"Remember when Rose told us about what we now understand was an Ekrixinatosaurus? She named it Custard, to make it seem friendlier, remember?"

"She named it Custard to make it less terrifying because she thought she was about to die. It *had* been hunting them through the jungle all day before it finally caught up with them."

"Yeah, well, whatever. I just thought that – for Rose – we should name this guy Rhubarb."

"Oh, for the love of..." Tim tailed off, putting a hand over his eyes.

"So what would you call him, genius?"

"Actually, I was thinking Afauxmimus. A-faux, instead of *Afro*mimus, get it?"

Woodsey sighed, shaking his head sadly. "Rubbish."

"And Rhubarb isn't?"

"Look, no one will—"

"Right. Fine." Tim cut him off. "For Rose, then. Rhubarb it is."

"Really? Not too lowbrow for you?"

"Really. Now look at..." Tim sighed, "*Rhubarb* making his way through the herd. They're not responding to him at all."

"*Him?*"

"Well, you're the one naming him Rhubarb – seemed a bit heartless to continue calling him 'it' after that."

"Might be a girl," Woodsey chuntered under his breath.

"Honestly, everything's about sex with you, isn't it?"

"Mate, it's a remote control dinosaur – keep your mind on the job."

"What? You, you—"

"Picture's pretty good, considering the speed it's running," Woodsey continued, leaving Tim blustering. "I expected it to feel more like a handheld camera, you know – more shaky."

Recovering, Tim had to confess that Woodsey was right. The picture was excellent. "It must be something to do with its— *his* eyes being the cameras. Our eyes don't feel particularly shaky when we run, do they? Not like something you'd hold in your hand... What?"

"*You* run?"

"Woodsey!"

"How's our latest creation doing, laddies?"

They turned to see Captain Douglas standing in the doorway to the small control room, and both spoke together.

"It's incredible."

"He's called Rhubarb."

"Come and see, Captain," Tim beckoned. "We're seeing the Cretaceous at night in a way we never thought possible. It's just amazing. It would be so dangerous for us to go out there like this, I..."

"He's lost for words, Captain," Woodsey finished for him, grinning. "What's really cool is that the other animals seem to be ignoring our friend down there."

"It's probably because *our* dinosaur doesn't smell like... well, *anything* to them – anything of interest or to be feared, at least," Tim added.

Douglas pulled up a seat behind and between the younger men. He nodded thoughtfully as he leaned on the backs of their chairs. "That's good news. Hiro hoped it might prove so. Poor wee lad is still out there in harm's way, though. Pretty scary."

"He's getting closer to the enemy now, Captain," Woodsey noted as he checked the distance readout. "Less than a kilometre and we should get a look at their camp."

"I wouldn't call it a camp," Tim corrected. "It's huge. Frightening – how much they've built in such a short time, I mean. It's like an entire industrial estate spanning dozens of acres."

"Aye," Douglas concurred. "Frightening is exactly the right word."

They watched the landscape slip by under Rhubarb's feet for a while. It was mesmerising.

"We could use an interval," Woodsey spoke into the silence. "Get some girls selling ice creams or popcorn – or ice creams *and* popcorn."

"Girls *again.*"

"Dude, you're practically a married man – you should get your mind off such things."

"I..." Tim sputtered.

Douglas laughed, putting an arm around each of them. "Well, as it happens, Ah already have the needs of my men well in hand—"

The door slid open behind them, interrupting him and revealing Mary Hutchins with her trolley of delights. "Mary!" Woodsey called out, jumping to his feet. "Thank God you came with us." He gave Mary a bear hug, making her giggle. "Now, please tell me you have popcorn!"

Rhubarb approached the enemy alone.

Colonel Hans Schultz knocked on the door. No answer. He knocked again. Nothing. Impatiently, he banged harder.

"Stop beating my door down, I am coming!" The door's timbers failed to muffle the agitation in the voice. Eventually, it was opened by the Party's Chief Engineer, Fritz Todt, still tucking his shirt into his trousers. "Have you no patience, man? Come in."

"I am here *exactly* at the time you stated," the uniformed soldier replied stiffly.

"Well? Have you never just, you know... had to *go?*"

The colonel raised an eyebrow, coolly.

"It's this damned IBS," Todt complained. "And you kicking my door down hardly helps. Look, never mind, take a seat. Drink?" He poured them both a whisky and took the second wingback leather chair in front of the fireplace, opposite his visitor. The colonel looked around a very traditional home, with lots of paintings, dark wood and stone. He did not doubt that technology lurked within its walls and voids, but the fireplace was real. However, it was June in 1944 Munich, so it was not lit. Seven months had passed since the opening of the wormhole in November of '43, and huge volumes of manpower and material had been transferred back and forth in that time.

"Hans, I asked you here to talk about... the *project.*"

Hans Schultz took the smallest sip of his whisky. "I am yet to receive a visit from my illustrious sister, after being recalled halfway around the world."

"Yes, well, I am sure you can understand the importance and urgency of this situation. It is about that I wish to speak with you. Hans, I am becoming very concerned about our direction in all this. As for the involvement of that tiresome little man—"

"Which tiresome little man?"

"Hitler. Apparently, in some parallel timeline, he was a great leader – according to your sister."

"I've seen the footage – he acted like a maniac."

Todt cradled his glass thoughtfully. "Perhaps. Perhaps not. He was probably insane – doubtless a natural response to wielding almost absolute power, but he was not just the ranting demonic figure at the podium we have seen. Heidi has a recording of his real voice. She played it to the senior Party members to help convince us that he might be useful. It was apparently recorded secretly by a Finnish sound engineer named Thor Damen. He worked for the Finnish broadcaster Yleisradio, or YLE. He does in this timeline, too – I looked him up. It seems some things are the same here as there, whereas others are wildly different. Damen had been assigned to record the official proceedings in honour of Field Marshal Carl Gustaf Emil Mannerheim's seventy-fifth birthday. This was almost exactly two years ago in June of '42. Apparently, Thor Damen recorded the first eleven minutes of Hitler and Mannerheim's private conversation – without Hitler's knowledge – during what they called the Second World War. When you hear that voice..." Todt shivered. "It is like hearing a ghost, but so reasonable and so rich. He tells tremendous lies during that short recording, apparently. Yet he does so, so judiciously – almost conversationally. That man is far more dangerous than we ever gave him credit for, and Heidi is giving him – on the surface, at least – more and more power. To a painter!"

Schultz leaned forward in his seat. "I know Mannerheim, or at least, I have met him. He is running for the Finnish presidency, I believe. A good man, despite being a politician."

"Hmm. Your sister and *her* grandfather seem to remember him less favourably. And all the while, I believe Heidi is actually goading Hitler's insanity, like that's the quality she wants from him."

"What? Slow down. Never mind Hitler for a moment. My grandfather – that is, *our* grandfather – is dead."

"Ah, yes. About that. You may also have wondered about the remarkable new politics your sister has been endorsing, including some fairly high-profile appearances alongside her puppet, it has to be said."

"What new politics? What are you talking about? She has always been politically infantile. That is why we have not spoken in years. I certainly have better things to do than listen to her idiotic prattle, or the pathetic hot air and nonsense from her ridiculous lip-service friends."

Todt puffed out his cheeks. "Well, if you have not heard, then I suggest you start to listen, because hot air or not, the wind seems to have changed. Heidi, and her creature, are turning ever more towards xenophobia and hatred."

"*What?*" Schultz almost laughed. "Heidi 'open our borders and give everything away as long as it does not cost me anything' Schultz?"

"I am afraid so. We have had no major wars in almost two hundred years, but mark my words, Hans, war is coming. It is also the main reason I called you here. I know you have always believed that Germany's political stance has been too weak, that we lack the foresight, or indeed the backbone, to defend ourselves. And that, conversely, is why it must be you."

"Why what must be me? Speak plainly."

"Why it must be you who saves us. Hans, I have always judged you to be, first and foremost, a man of honour. You may find this hard to believe—"

"Try me."

"Dr Heidi Schultz is not your sister. She is your great-great-great-great-granddaughter and will be born in the year 2086."

Colonel Hans Schultz placed his glass on the arm of his chair and missed. It caught the Persian rug's edge only to smash on the flagstones, but he hardly noticed.

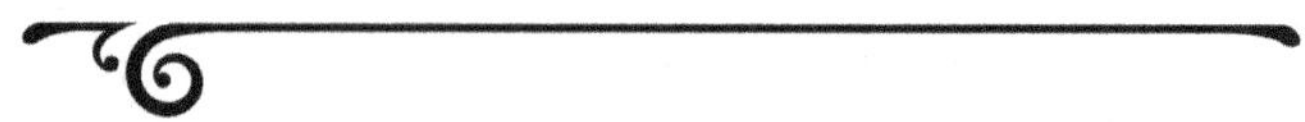

Sergeant Adam Prentice moved to the dropship's co-pilot seat, also watching the video feed from their robotic spy. The man-made Afromimus stood just over a metre tall, so the perspective was a little lower than a man's eye level. Combined with such speed of movement, the visual gave the constant feeling of falling forward. Prentice rubbed his eyes; he was beginning to feel a little travel-sick. However, this was not the moment to bow out. The little machine was closing on the enemy plant.

Intricate and immensely costly sensors scanned the terrain ahead, far in advance. Much of the complex was built on top of a bluff commanding the local area with views over the river, just east, and the plains to the west, with delta and coast to the north. As their spy ran up the wooded bank that led up the escarpment from the river's shore – avoiding what appeared to be a well-travelled vehicular road – it popped out of the treeline to find its way blocked by a moat. Some of the moat was constructed from concrete, whereas other stretches seemed to have been hewn from the living rock. It extended as far as the cameras could see in both directions. Still in fully remote reconnaissance mode, the little machine set off west, walking more casually now, mimicking the behaviour of a real animal, stopping to graze here and there.

Prentice smiled to himself. *Go, Chief Nassaki, and whoever else worked on this thing, for that matter,* he thought proudly. It went without saying that it would be under the watchful eye of the enemy's surveillance equipment, but he felt confident that it would be of little interest to them. They most certainly would not be expecting an attack from the *New World,* but they would be extremely wary of the local wildlife. Their spy had not merely been programmed to mimic animal behaviour; it was also designed to exhibit the life signs, temperatures, and so on, of a small but active dinosaur. Many of its characteristics were borrowed from an extensive study of Mayor, who still lived with Dr Natalie Pearson[9].

Prentice began to laugh.

"What is it, Sarge?" young Radburn asked, popping his head into the cockpit to see.

Prentice turned to the young man, grinning. "Our little friend has just taken a dump."

Suddenly, there were voices. He spun back to the console immediately, increasing the gain.

"*Todt is going to finish surveying the next plot tomorrow.*" The voice was a man's, possibly American, but with a recurring Northern European cadence.

Another male voice replied. "*I understand that, Jansen. I just don't see what we can do about it. Look, we've been through all this, round and round again.*"

"*That's why we need to try something different,*" the first man pressed. "*I suggest we capture him.*"

Silence. Eventually, the second man answered again. "*I stand corrected. That's a completely new and completely* insane *approach!*"

"*No, hear me out. Heidi is distracted right now. She's got that whitecoat, what's his name? The bald guy?*"

"*Reid?*"

"*Yeah, Reid, working on something big, really big, and I think it's nearing completion. And as for what's she playing at in 1940s Munich – who the hell knows? But she* is *distracted. That means the whole day-to-day is falling ever more into Todt's remit. If we—*"

"*What? Take him out?*" Another silence. "*Well? Come on, Jansen, out with it.*"

"*Not exactly, Devon. What if he could be turned?*"

"*Are you serious?*"

"*No. Well, yes, but think about it.*"

---

9 The irony of building a spying robotic dinosaur to mimic an animal already named 'mimus', and from the Ornithomimosauria clade that were named initially for their mimicking of birds, no less, was not lost on her. However, other scientists working on the project refused her suggestions to call their creation either *Dinomimus*, or *Spynosaurus*, in case that led to confusion. Although the species name of *Afromimus batterisnotincludii* was kept, though it is usually dropped for simplicity.

The man named Devon was clearly trying to keep his voice down as he replied frustratedly, *"I've thought about it, and I don't know what scares me more, the plan, or the fact that you think it's a good one!"*

"I didn't say it was a good one, Devon. Look, I've been to the 1943 Munich of this timeline—"

"It's 1944 there now."

"Whatever. I've seen it and it's a good world. Heidi and Grandpa Fruit Basket want to turn it back into the mess we left behind, just so they can end up on top, clutching everyone's lives in their fists. We have complete control of this primitive world, Devon, and it's beautiful. Mission accomplished – we won, but that's not enough for the Schultzes, is it? No, they need a slave race at their feet – they're insane."

Devon sighed. *"I'm not arguing any of those points, Jansen. I'm simply saying that if Todt doesn't see it our way, we will be revealed and when that happens, we lose any chance we had to effect change."*

"Of course, but taking Todt may at least stall their plans – slow them down."

"How?"

"Because, if Todt doesn't see it our way, they're going to be looking for a new head for this little project – literally!"

"You'd go that far?"

"Well, I suppose we could just let him report everything back to Heidi... of course I'd go that far! Look, we can't stay out here, we don't know who might be listening. Are you in?"

Prentice could hardly believe his ears, but there was nothing he could do about it. His orders were to respect a full comms blackout. Any message from the planet's surface not originating from within the enemy complex might ring alarm bells, regardless of whether or not it could be decrypted. Their dinocam had been programmed to piggyback on signals to and from the Schultz satellite net specifically to avoid detection, and with the exception of Rhubarb, dinosaurs were not known for their affinity with digital technology. He shook his head slowly. "I hope they're paying attention up there."

Tim and Douglas looked as though they had been slapped across the face. They were joined by former NASASEC operative and police detective, Rick Drummond. Even Woodsey had stopped munching his popcorn. As things turned more serious, Tim confiscated the pack to stop him from rustling.

Rick Drummond had easily secured a position within Douglas' department some years ago, his expertise ideal to help the United Nations guard against a looming separatist threat among the off-world colonies. Though the young palaeontologists had watched diligently over their new asset, the Afromimus spy drone was now in position outside the enemy stronghold, and Douglas required a different skill set.

"Ah cannae believe what Ah'm hearing."

"We hoped we *might* find help among the people we left behind, Captain," Drummond reminded him.

"Aye, but what do we do with that information now we have it?"

"I suggest," Woodsey cut in, "that we move our assets on the ground in closer, to make sure those two men succeed... I mean, should they need backup, or whatever."

Tim and Douglas looked at one another, giving Woodsey the opportunity to steal back the popcorn. "I'm just saying," he added, munching again.

Drummond gave a wry smile. "Seems they grew up devious, Captain. I think the kid's right."

Douglas stroked his chin while he mulled it over.

"You think 'the general' here might be on to something?" Tim asked, slightly incredulous.

Reaching a decision, Douglas stood. "This needs careful planning – they're armed to the teeth down there so we cannae reveal ourselves. No' yet. At least we seem to have allies in the enemy camp. Like you say, Rick, it's as much as we could have hoped for, and Ah was right to hold back our attack until we knew more." He made to leave.

Drummond raised a hand to stop him. "But how will you get a message down to the dropship without breaking the comms blackout, Captain?"

"I know what I'd do," Woodsey spoke again around a mouthful of popcorn, cheeks bulging to make room for his words.

They all turned for a second time, to hear the wisdom.

"Speak, oh great oracle." Tim genuflected sarcastically.

The New Zealander belched loudly. "Not all o' those little satellite catchers were needed, were they? They're still out there, inert. 'S what Hiro told me, anyway, while you were drooling over the toy dinosaur."

"*Toy?*"

"Yeah. Hiro said they could be reactivated and even sent down to the planet to operate as spycams in case anything happened to Rhubarb – for as long as their limited fuel lasts, anyway."

"Rhubarb?" asked Drummond.

"He's right." Douglas grinned, ignoring the question. "And we can make sure the entire Schultz satellite net is looking the other way while we do it. That'll be much safer than sending a message, even a coded one. We must remain invisible. Good work, laddie." He tousled Woodsey's untidy hair.

"Steady on, bloke. M'style doesn't look like this all on its own, ya know?"

Douglas strode out, laughing.

"What's with him?" Woodsey asked, bemused.

"He doesn't want to kill all those people down there – or any of them, if he can help it." Drummond elucidated. "This development may just have offered him another way."

Shocking explanation complete, chief engineer for the Party, Fritz Todt, collected up the broken glass onto a tray and poured Colonel Hans Schultz another whisky – a large one. "So you see the problem, Colonel."

Hans remained in silent thought, trying to get the facts as they understood them straight in his head before he answered. "I'm not sure I do, Fritz. What *I* see are about a dozen *partial* problems – none of which seem to have solutions."

Glasses recharged, Todt sat heavily with a sigh. "A fair assessment. The way I see it, the German people are at a crossroads. Many believe we have become weak, even reticent to defend ourselves. Of course, until now, there has been no clear path to change – when along came Heinrich and Heidi Schultz from the future, peddling tales of glory and power, offering technologies well beyond our own. They tell us that, for the paltry cost of just a few unspecified *examples,* we can place our nation centre stage in a world where all would fear us and do our bidding."

"Intoxicating, I'm sure," Hans replied with complete sobriety. "And my sister? My *real* sister? I'm sure she was suitably 'outraged' by all this and making lots of noise that would save her the pesky effort of actually doing anything about it. What has happened to her?"

"She is being held prisoner."

Hans was taken by surprise, but rallied quickly via the power of scorn. "I dare say she would have been useless in any event."

"Maybe, maybe not."

"How so?"

"Your fourth-great-granddaughter is pretending to *be* your sister, calling on the influence of her friends and associates – swinging them to her cause."

"That bunch of fools!" Hans spat derisively. "What use would they be if she wants to put Germany on a war footing? They're pathetic."

Todt sighed. "Hans, you have been too long a soldier. The power of the types with whom your sister associates, lies in being seen and heard *saying* the right things – or what is fashionably held to be so. They don't believe any of it, it simply curries favour, or mass appeal, at least. A sweeping statement, perhaps, and for the one or two good apples in the barrel, I reserve an apology, but it is largely true. They are full of s—"

"Self-indulgence?"

"Close enough. However, my point is this – your sister has always been a trend setter and people are already beginning to follow. It is almost a *brand* thing. If we could bring her back, it might just set the cat amongst the pigeons. At least it would stop Heidi recruiting such weak and greedy individuals to her cause. Imbeciles they may be, but they wield great wealth and an astonishing level of influence. It might just blow the lid off the whole affair, and if we are to stand any chance of carrying out such a mission, it would only be with your help."

Hans grimaced like a man who, upon biting into a biscuit, finds a grinning Jack Russell on its wrapper and the name 'Little Chap' emblazoned over a stylised bone across the top. Revulsion for the idea carried into his voice. "You want *me* to save *her?* After she stole our father's fortune and cut me out of her life?"

Todt realised his mistake and immediately changed tack. "She is imprisoned aboard the Schultzes' warship."

"My..." Hans sought an adequate description, "*relations* have a *warship?*"

Todt nodded seriously. "But not like any kind of warship you might be imagining. It is a spacegoing vessel carrying a terrible arsenal – I understand it is also capable of travelling through wormholes across the galaxy and even through time itself."

Hans blew out his cheeks in alarm. "And they are offering these godlike powers to our government? Do you have any *good* news?"

Todt shrugged. "Apparently, its wormhole drive is out of commission, but I do know that some of our finest physicists have been recruited to work on something special. Something about which even I have been left in the dark. I suspect it may have something to do with that aspect of the ship. At least, I hope so."

"You *hope* so?"

"Indeed. If not, then it would mean that Heidi is up to something even more dangerous or nefarious."

"Do I assume this ship is the heart of their power?"

"Maybe. I know they also have assets elsewhere on prehistoric Earth. There has been talk of other ships, far larger and perhaps even more dangerous than the one we have been allowed to see. I do not know their locations or their condition. They may have suffered some considerable losses before Heidi arrived in our time. It seems that on a world of less than four hundred souls, she nevertheless managed to start a fully-fledged intercontinental war – she is some kind of woman!

"The warship I know of is located right at the mouth of the wormhole, on the other side. Any form of direct attack would be incinerated before it even fully rematerialised in the Cretaceous."

Hans digested that for a moment. Eventually, he changed the subject. "Have you seen or spoken to my sister in the many months of her incarceration?"

Todt shook his head. "No one has seen her. At least no one from our side. By the way, there is something else you should know, too. They call their ship the *Heydrich*."

Hans stood abruptly. "That *Schweinhund!* What has he to do with this?"

"Nothing, as far as I know, Hans. However..."

The colonel sat slowly, but leaned forward on the edge of his seat. "However?"

"According to the film and documentary evidence shown to us, he had quite the illustrious career – Heinrich Schultz's words. That was in the alternative timeline, of course. Apparently, he was one of the principal architects behind 'the greatest cleansing operation in history' – again, Heinrich's words."

"Why does that not surprise me? So what actually happened?"

"The vilest genocide imaginable. At least, that is what I believe. We have been given little more than the high-minded ideals of their cause, naturally, but it does not take a great deal of scrutiny to see behind the slogans, and there you find the murder of innocents – *millions* of them. From what I have been able to read between the lines of their rhetoric, the whole truth is horrific. Their censorship of these facts and events is disturbing, though thankfully, not impenetrable – at least, not for anyone wishing to look. From what I observed of my colleagues in the cabinet, I may be alone in that wish. Although..." He trailed off thoughtfully.

"What is it? You think we may have allies?"

"Sadly, no. It simply occurred to me that if I saw through the rhetoric, then surely others did, too. Just maybe, the old man, Heinrich Schultz, *wants* them to suspect."

Colonel Schultz gave a little shudder at the use of his family name in such context. "Why would he want that? You believe he is insane?"

"No. At least, not in the way that you mean – far from it. I suspect that he simply enjoys the idea of our government *knowing* that it is about to commit evil. Corrupting innocents amounts to little more than brainwashing, and can be undone. No... I think he enjoys their suspicion that what they are about to do is wrong, yet knowing they are too greedy to stop themselves. It's like a sick game and it certainly would not surprise me. I find it hard to believe that such a tactician would leave any loose ends unless he wanted them to be found. Of course, once our government commits, there will be no way to back down without admitting that they knowingly did whatever they arc about to do. He will have them tied into his scheme neatly. It is quite diabolical.

"Of course, we have no access to the entirety of the proffered information, other than through Heinrich Schultz himself. It is not as though we might slip into a parallel timeline to take a look around, but I believe he is spoon-feeding only that which he wishes us to know, with just a few trimmings – he has them bedazzled. I must confess that I, too, was taken in by their offer – at first."

"What changed?"

"Just little points that did not quite add up. There is something about the Old Man himself, too. As I said, something sickly. I know his health is failing, though he tries to hide it, but that is not my meaning. Psychologically, there is just something. Heidi is simpler. She is psychotic. I have observed her closely in the Cretaceous and have no doubts about this. Heinrich is cooler, more level-headed and yet, hmm... let me see, how to explain this... Heinrich is like Hell's salesman – he draws you in, though you know it to be wrong."

"If you suspect that, why have you not called him out on it?"

"Because, Hans, the Party cabinet don't want to upset what they perceive as a meal ticket to world domination. Many of our leaders preach peace because they fear war on a level playing field, possibly even on the back foot. Take away that level playing field and... well, you know some of them, Bormann, Himmler and the rest. What do you think they will do? Heinrich and his granddaughter have offered them, at a stroke, power enough to significantly unbalance the whole world order, but in our favour. We would likely be unstoppable and, if self-interest were all that mattered, crazy not to take them up on it."

"Bormann and Himmler are not soldiers," Hans bit back scornfully. "They're clerks."

"Does that matter?" Disgust crossed Todt's face. "They are eating out of Schultz's hands. Were I to speak out, I would be but a lonely voice on the wind, and they would certainly have me removed, possibly even from the world."

"You think so?"

"Let us just say that Cretaceous Egypt is a phenomenally dangerous place, Hans. If they even suspected my misgivings about 'the project', I would soon be food for one of the terrifying reptiles that dominated there before Heidi began to replace them with monsters of her own."

"If they are so powerful and have such a hold over much of our leadership, then what do you suggest we do about it?"

"That is the rub, Hans. Firstly, *should* we do anything about it? The threat from our neighbours, whom we have fed with technology and wealth for many years, is real and grows daily. I believe they wait only for the right opportunity to strike."

"What right opportunity?"

"That's just it, we have no way of knowing. It might be another swathing cut in our military budget, a recession, perhaps just another social trend that takes our media by storm and makes us appear – in their eyes, at least – soft or pathetic. Ripe for the taking. Heinrich Schultz may *actually* be offering salvation. So if we refuse, or destroy his help, taking the moral high ground could doom our nation and whole way of life. How foolish might we feel should *that* come to pass?"

"Ironic," Hans agreed sourly.

"You do not yet realise the full tapestry of their plans, my friend. In a rare moment of geniality, Heidi – not your sister, the other one – told me that it was their programme for saving humanity that began all this. They came up with a strategy to go back in time and rebuild the human race – or should I say, the bit of it they deemed worthy. They succeeded, though it did not entirely go as planned. They set up a human colony on a pristine world, theirs for the taking. Leaving behind another world choked and overpopulated, dying. The future would be rewritten, everyone gone, all sins washed clean. It seems that God has a sense of humour."

"How so?"

"Because, invariably, doing the right thing gets you killed. Heidi's enemies from the future fought to stop them carrying out their full scheme, in order to secure a dying future – one might say, *no* future. I wonder who will be around to laugh at the final punchline?"

Hans linked his fingers and sat back in his comfortable leather armchair, still listening keenly. "I sense a 'but' about to enter the conversation."

Todt wrung his hands, nervously. "Well, a *perhaps,* at least."

"Go on, Fritz."

"Perhaps it is still better to die with honour than to hide under the devil's wing? Perhaps it always was? *Perhaps* fighting evil is enough and after that, whatever will be, will be? I do not know, but it is how I feel."

Hans considered Todt's words. "I am no philosopher, but it is clear that this situation is far more dangerous than I realised. My first instinct, as a soldier, is to take the weapons the Old Man is offering and hold them in reserve, for defensive purposes only. However, soldiers rarely decide policy when it comes to waging war, Fritz. We just get to die in them – usually when the government glove puppets run out of lies and can no longer cover up their cover-ups. We are but the engineers to our ministerial architects. They sell themselves on a painting of the future, then wheel *us* in, with orders to make it stand up in the real world."

"That's harsh. I *am* the cabinet's chief engineer, you know."

"And here you are, worrying about how we can possibly make this work in the real world – need I say more? What you have revealed to me today requires our most careful consideration, with eyes open and without political agenda."

"Yes," Todt agreed with a sigh. "And I confess that, alone, I've been thinking in circles, getting nowhere."

"Is that why you came to me?"

"Partially. I also believe we need to rescue your sister."

Hans gave a snort of derision. "You know my sister and I cannot abide one another."

"Yes, I have no doubt she would leave you to rot, too, but would you do the same to her? Let me explain. Should we act against the *future* Schultzes, I believe our only salvation will be to terminate that wormhole and destroy their ability to open another. However, to answer your question, I came to you *because* I know of your long-held beliefs that our leadership is weak. With what is happening now, I can no longer argue that point. Our lack of moral fortitude is depressing to behold. Although, I still have hopes that when all this is exposed in the Bundestag, it will meet stiff opposition. I know you believe in a strong Germany, therefore..." Todt leaned forward in his seat, too. "Hans, I risk my very life by entrusting you with this information and by being so candid with my thoughts. Our government may stumble, but our people do not deserve to be dragged into a terrible war that will leave us vilified for generations to come.

"Now, you may be the sort of officer who would welcome such an overwhelming martial advantage, should it fall into your lap. Your familial ties alone would secure your welcome into the Schultz fold – you *are* their direct ancestor, after all. For myself, I believe that, should any give in to that temptation, it would only result in your relations being left on top, the ones holding *all* the power.

"However, prophecies of doom aside, I believe you to be honourable, yes, but more than that, a man of good sense. Making our nation stronger, perhaps impregnable, does have its appeal, no? But plunging our world into a war such as we have never seen, merely to leave people who should not even *be* here in charge, feels very wrong to me, as I am now hoping it will to you. The cost to us, to our nation, to all humanity, will be higher than we can imagine if we follow down that road. Yes, just speaking these thoughts aloud with you here has helped me to order them. I have at long last made up my mind. I feel it. I know it. We should reject what the Schultzes offer. Our world should continue along its natural path, and our people write their own futures, without external interference – for better or worse. Then there is the other matter."

Hans looked at him sideways. "Continue."

"Well, the truth is, you may be the only person in the world who *can* stand against them."

"Me? Fritz, from what you have described, I fail to see what force I could possibly bring to bear that could overwhelm such powerful adversaries."

"In that you are mistaken, my friend. You are familiar with the grandfather paradox?"

Hans straightened, his face registering shock. "You refer to my children's children's children?"

Todt chuckled humourlessly. "Give or take a 'children', yes."

"But my future relations are already here. Surely their own timeline is broken, no longer relevant. They must already be on a divergent path, albeit an earlier one..." He tailed off, massaging his temple to clear his thoughts.

Todt chuckled again. "Hmm, quite the mind-bender, yes? But you have placed your finger firmly on the nub of the matter, my compliments. And you may well be right, of course. The paradox *has* already happened, but I'd be willing to bet that Heinrich will most certainly not wish to tempt fate by destroying you. That may just be one roll of the dice too many for him. Hans, you are married, I understand?"

The soldier nodded affirmative.

"But as yet you have no children?"

"Correct."

"How prescient of you. If you'll take my advice, you will leave any plans in that regard well enough alone, for now."

"What does that have to do with... *ah.*"

"Exactly. Should you have a son, a male Schultz heir to continue the name, Heinrich, or Heidi – *especially* Heidi – might decide it is in their best interests to revoke your VIP status. Permanently."

"You make a compelling argument, Fritz."

Todt stood and walked to the fireplace, glass in hand. He turned, leaning an arm upon the mantel. "So now I must ask you, Hans, was my faith in you well placed? Will you be tempted, or will you become our very own Aragorn?"

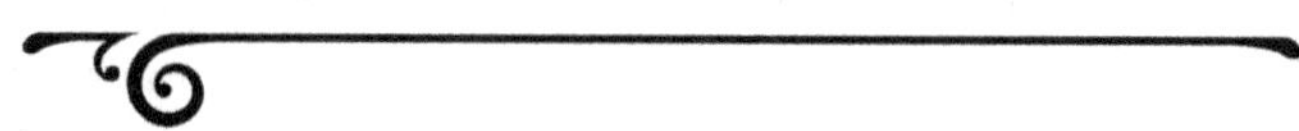

"Perhaps you were planted in here with me as a trap?" Badawi postulated, his foggy mind finally starting to clear.

His fellow prisoner wrapped delicate fingers around the bars of her cell and made to shake them. "Oops, too late."

"There are traps within traps, miss," he replied, tetchily. "That was quite a story you told me, after all."

"And you think I would have imparted such a tale were it not the truth? Hardly believable, was it? That is, unless you happen to be imprisoned aboard a spaceship from the future while surrounded by dinosaurs?"

"Terrifyingly, you have a point."

She smiled. It made Badawi uneasy. The last thing he needed was base distraction right now, whether it was her intention or not. He knew nothing about this woman, other than her crazy story – but then his own begged a certain disbelief suspension. "It seems we have little choice but to trust one another," he confessed at last, although in the privacy of his own mind he added, *for now.*

"Good." She smiled again, warmly. "I have been thinking on the problem for a long time."

"You have a plan?"

"Indeed, but it is a... I believe the term is *two-hander?*"

Badawi looked around suspiciously, certain they were being observed by hidden devices. He stood and moved to the bars between their cells to whisper. "Perhaps we should speak more quietly."

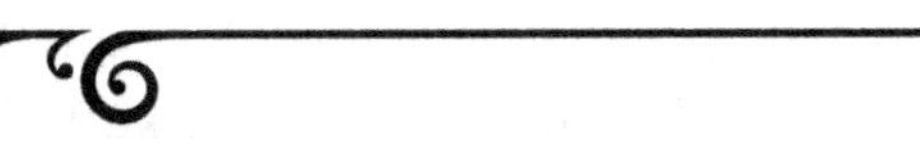

"I think it's Captain Douglas, Sarge," Private Radburn blustered as he burst into the dropship's cockpit.

Sergeant Adam Prentice turned to see the young man holding a small, black sphere. "That's one of our satellite crackers," he stated.

"*Adam, this is Douglas,*" the device began to speak. There was no two-way communication; it merely delivered a message and a set of coordinates – coordinates Prentice had already noted from the spy drone's feed as he watched it.

As the message finished, he stood. "Alright, lads and lasses. I want two guards, everyone else hit the sack. We change the guard in two hours and move out at 0400." A moment's pause. "Well, get to it!" Prentice bellowed. "You lot can't even lie down without me losing a boot up your backsides! Move it – or you'll *all* be on guard duty!"

His threat rang like an end-of-class bell, and a heavy-booted shuffle ensued immediately as the troops followed his order.

One hour later, Prentice awoke. He listened. Nothing. He considered turning over and trying to get back to sleep but knew it would be impossible. Something had stirred him to full wakefulness, some sixth sense, there was no *way* he was going back to sleep.

He slipped from his sleeping bag and quickly laced his boots. Grabbing a rifle, he moved silently to the rear hatch, which doubled as a ramp for paratroopers to jump, or as a point of egress for small vehicles. He reached for the controls to lower it. Within atmosphere there would be no alarms or fuss, but once again some instinct warned him against doing so. Set within the ramp was a smaller hatch that, at a crouch, would allow passage for a single person. He unlocked it and stepped through into the night.

Closing it softly behind him, he hissed, "Walker? Engel?" Neither guard answered.

Cloud covered the moon; the darkness, absolute. Prentice could only rely on his other senses. There was a smell. Elephants were extinct in the world in which he had grown. A decade in the alternative timeline had given him opportunity to collect on a childhood desire to see them ranging across their natural habitat. This smell was very reminiscent. He was no naturalist, but it seemed likely there were large herbivores close by.

OK. Could be worse, he thought, trying to bolster his courage as he stumbled through the pitch of night on Planet Dinosaur. He felt his way around the starboard side of their ship. "Walker? Engel?" he tried again.

A deep rumble vibrated from the ground up through his boots. The sound that caused it was on the limits of human hearing, so low it was perceived, rather than heard. He strained his eyes to make out anything among the inky blackness all around. Unsure whether he saw or imagined the movement right before him, his training and reactions took over well ahead of his brain, forcing him to dive. Prentice hit the ground and rolled as a stupefying *boom* came from just over his head. The dropship jumped and skidded to port, as the night awoke around him to a bass cacophony of rumbling bellows and the thuds of immensely heavy footfalls.

"Sarge?" A voice cut through the ensuing chaos.

"Engel?"

"Over here!"

Prentice scrambled towards the voice and what little comfort it offered. Before he realised what was happening, he pitched forward into a hole, his shock-driven tirade serving the region's dinosaurs with their first helping of Anglo-Saxon invective. "What the—"

"Footprint!" Engel's voice sounded every bit as rattled as Prentice's own. "You've fallen into a footprint. Stay down!" Corporal Heinz Engel[10] had not furthered his rank over the last decade, deciding instead to leave the military altogether, until their recall. Now he was remembering just why he had made that decision.

Another boom. They were surrounded, their ship taking another hit. Obviously, whatever the animals were, they were distressed, probably because they had bumped into something very alien in the darkness. Prentice could not see a thing. "What the hell are they, Corp?"

"Something big!"

Both men screamed as something else 'big' slid across the top of their hole.

---

10 *See Author's Notes.

"We're under the ship!" Engel shouted. The footprint in which they hid was roughly circular and a metre in diameter, perhaps slightly more in depth, forcing them to hunker down together. "We're lucky the ground was so soft here." He knew his commentary was more to keep terror at bay than to reveal anything Prentice had not worked out for himself.

"Why didn't you answer me, when I called?" Prentice demanded.

"I was standing right underneath one of those things. I didn't think it was a good idea to call out!"

Another boom and the ship above them skidded again, filling what little space remained to them with further mud. They could not hear anything through the ship's armoured bulkheads, though they imagined the shouting and cursing from within.

"We'd better dig our way out of here fast, lad," Prentice cried, fighting panic. "Because if the geniuses upstairs decide to fire up those engines to get 'emselves to safety, they'll turn us into pork scratchings!"

Above them, among all the hullabaloo, they distinctly heard a *tick, tick,* heralding the warming up of electrical coils as part of the engine's start-up cycle. They both looked up, irresistibly drawn towards their doom. As it turned out, their shared Germanic heritage supplied them with just the words to sum up their predicament. Although, technically, 'oh' is more exclamation than language, the second word was full-on Saxon.

The comm buzzed for attention on the *New World*'s bridge. "Bridge," Singh answered brightly. "Yes, he's here. Please stand by. Captain?"

"Yes?" replied Baines and Douglas together.

A twinkle of amusement showed in the pilot's eyes. "That never gets old. Captain *Douglas,* I have a call for you from Dr Pearson, sir."

"Put her on open channel, Sandy. Natalie, what can Ah do for ye?"

"Captain, she's beginning to wake up. Can we take her down yet?"

Douglas winced; he had been so wrapped up with the fake dinosaur he had temporarily forgotten about the real one. "Can ye knock her out again, Natalie? We cannae risk sending another ship down at this time. It might blow everything for Adam's team, and he's got enough to worry about as it is."

"I'm afraid I can't, Captain. If I tranquillise her again, I'm worried it might damage her heart, even kill her. When I heard we were sending a ship down, I hoped—"

"Sorry, lassie. Maybe if ma wife had bagged a couple of beavers or a red squirrel, we might have been able to oblige, but releasing a fully grown Spinosaurus back into the wild would be a wee bit tricky under stealth conditions. Can ye no' just keep her torpid?"

"Doesn't sound like I have much choice. I can't keep her like that for long, though, Captain. We took this responsibility on. Now we're going to have to make it right."

"Understood. Do what ye can, Doctor. Douglas out." He turned to Baines. "That new pet you picked out for us on your travels, Jill – how can Ah ever thank ye?"

"Don't blame me. You told Tim he could try to save it." She leaned close. "You're such a softie really, James."

He frowned sternly at her, punctuating his words in three monosyllabic stabs. "No. More. Pets."

"Captain," Singh called across the bridge. "I have Dr Pearson again."

Douglas slumped. "On speaker. Natalie, go ahead."

"Captain, she's really coming round. I think a combination of fear and adrenaline from finding herself trapped is getting her all fired up. It's understandable, I—" Whatever Natalie was about to relay next was completely drowned by a colossal *roar* in the background.

"Could she try feeding it something?" Baines offered, hopefully.

Douglas' eyes narrowed. "Dinnae tempt me."

He reached the main hangar as quickly as the intra-ship transport could carry him, only to find a ring of armed personnel already surrounding the dinosaur's cage. Stepping from the elevator-style car, he got the distinct impression that if the dinosaur *fully* returned to the land of the living, she would empty it of life. "Oh, *crap!*" he swore, picking up the pace.

He arrived on the run at the zoologist's side, slightly puffed. "Natalie, how are we doing?"

Before she could answer, a bellow of anger escaped the giant's throat. Reiver reacted instantly to his mistress' danger. Running at the apex predator, he barked and snarled aggressively, reaching through the bars in a frenzy, just feet away from the monstrous snout. *"Reiver!"* Natalie screamed hoarsely, leaping to follow her beloved pet. Douglas expected the move and snatched her from the air. "Get back here!" he ordered, roughly.

"John!" she shouted.

It took Douglas a moment to realise who she was calling for, then he remembered that The Sarge, now Natalie's husband, had actually been born John Jackson. The career soldier was already in motion, grabbing the little hero suffering with acute scale awareness deficiency by his collar. He flung him roughly away from the jaws of oblivion. "GET OUT OF IT, YOU BLADDY STUPID ANIMAL!" he hollered as only The Sarge could. Even the dinosaur stopped struggling to stare at him. Douglas had never heard anyone with a louder voice; truly The Sarge was a man who had found his calling. Reiver stayed back, as he was told, but continued to bark and jump about, making the most vehement if bantam threats when the Spinosaurus lifted its head. The bars of its cage groaned with the unmistakable sounds of imminent structural failure.

"The cage is breaking," Natalie wailed.

"Ah can see that, lassie. Where did we buy the damned thing? The 'Everything Under a Tenner' shop?"

"It was built in a hurry."

"Oh, aye, Ah can see that as well!" Douglas let her go and asked the nearest soldier for his rifle. Based on their original Heath-Riflesons, these new weapons packed both electrical and traditional ordnance. Douglas dialled up its stunning capacity to fifteen tons on the small screen built into the stock and fired at the dinosaur's head.

The head dropped, biting down on a lolling tongue. Blood spilled everywhere, causing Reiver to renew his barking. Natalie ran to the cage's control panel, urgently checking on the spinosaur's vitals.

Douglas walked casually towards her, rifle hanging low in one hand. "Is it alive?"

"Yes, sir. For now. But she's really been through the wringer."

"*She's* been through the— Ye know what, never mind." He turned away, then turned back. "Ah used to transport freight to Mars, ye know. Aye, just boxes – a few people. Never any trouble with boxes. Boxes never eat *anyone!*"

Natalie stared at him in astonishment, then she heard the lapping. "Reiver? Oh, *no.* Stop it!"

Reiver was lapping at the puddle of dinosaur blood pooling on Douglas' hitherto spotless hangar floor. He handed the rifle to Jackson. "Sarge, it's a madhouse."

The Sarge gave a half-smile. "Good shot, sir. And thanks for saving my wife from herself."

Douglas patted his old friend affectionately on the arm as Reiver whined in the background – a commentary on wastefulness, as an automatic cleaning machine moved in to mop up the mess. "Yep. We're living in a madhouse," he chuntered as he walked away.

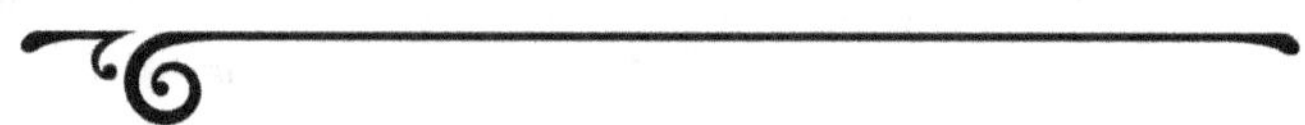

Prentice and Engel were almost deafened by the booms and bangs just centimetres above their heads, but that was nothing to the noise that would come when the rocket motors fired up. Prentice switched on his rifle's torch. Concealing his position hardly mattered now. He was buried alive and about to burn to death. He could only hope they would be evaporated, instantly. Another boom. More mud slid into their footprint foxhole.

"Aaaargh!" they shouted together. It seemed the thing to do, but then there was fresh air. The ship had been knocked back the other way. They looked at one another in the madly flashing torchlight. "Jump for it!" Prentice screamed at the top of his lungs.

They jumped, slipped, kicked and scrambled their way out of the hole. Trying to help one another actually made things worse. Poor timing hampered them like a three-legged race. Eventually, they slithered over the mucky top onto marshy but firmer ground. There was a distinct advantage in not weighing fifty tons when crossing soft soil. On the downside, they were surrounded by creatures that *did* weigh up to fifty tons, and it seemed they all had a mind to panic.

Their wildly darting lights hinted at a menagerie of huge bodies, heads so far in the air they could not even be seen, tails flicking and slashing like demonic tentacles.

"Run!" cried Prentice.

"Where?"

"*Any* bloody where!"

About the only thing going for them was that their people had had the sense to stay inside the ship. Prentice looked around enviously at its armoured bulk. The panicked herd batted it this way and that, making it impossible for the two men outside to get back in. "Where's Walker?"

"I don't know," Engel replied solemnly.

"Why are they going so crazy? The animals never used to bother overmuch with our equipment before—" A visceral roar split the air, making both men cover their ears. Dread crawled through their flesh. They snapped back-to-back with rifles, torches and hackles up. Having witnessed the vast titanosaurs of the plains continuing to eat, even during the dead of night, a second realisation thrust itself upon them – maybe their predators worked the night shift, too.

"We are really in trouble," Engel spoke through gritted teeth to stop them from chattering.

Another boom sent their ship rocking as it spun into them, luckily with minimal force, yet easily enough to send the men sprawling. It had been caught by the last sauropod dinosaur to pass them.

Prentice dared hope they might yet survive and offered up a prayer of thanks to the people who made their new vehicles dino-safe. While in the process of raising himself from the muddy ground onto all fours, something warm and slick fell onto the back of his neck. It was horrible and stank like the gutter through an abattoir floor. He was about to cry out in disgust when Engel snapped a hand around his wrist urgently.

They looked up, and up again. Directly above them was what could only be described as a dinosaur's chin. The animal was not looking at them, but straight ahead into the night. They could hear its huge nostrils sniffing the air, following the herd of Paralititan with its senses. The two men turned slowly to look at one another, a that look begged the question *why aren't we dead?*

Prentice honestly could not imagine how this night could possibly get any worse – which only left him cursing his own lack of imagination, because in the darkness they could now hear other movements, too. The predator standing over them, with its head four metres in the air, was not alone. Now he felt *certain* things could not get any worse.

When the rear hatch of their ship opened and a voice called, "Sarge?" he almost swore.

If he had, it would have been the *last* Anglo-Saxon invective the region's dinosaurs ever heard. He just about managed to bite his lip, praying for the young man behind them to realise their peril and shut up.

Once again, he was disappointed. He heard other voices and the distinct sound of the dropship's ramp lowering. Prentice was fit to burst. There was absolutely nothing he could do to help the situation. Any movement, any *sound* on his part, would not only get Engel and himself killed, but might even unleash the very destruction he feared. Space–time took a breather, though he clearly heard the clockwork of doom being wound in his mind. Any second now, the machinery of the universe would start up again and *their* time would be well and truly up.

"Sarge?" the query came through the darkness again.

Oh, no. Not the lad. Prentice recognised Private Mark Radburn's voice. His rifle was at least three metres away, after their fall. Engel's was closer, but still out of reach. Besides, he had no way of communicating his thoughts to the corporal. He was aware that after crawling from a mucky hole in the ground, they must have looked like mud men – though the passage of many terrified titanosaurs had left them wearing more than just mud. When assessing their situation, Prentice never bothered to add that to his bad news column, deducing that it was the only reason they were still alive. Keeping still and hiding under a veneer of manure remained their only hope. Later, there would be cringing and frantic washing, perhaps even vomiting. He could live with that, as long as there was a later, as long as they lived at all.

The dinosaur above his head leaned forward and down. From the ambient light thrown behind them, Prentice guessed the young soldier was lit up like a close encounter. He squeezed his eyes tight shut, willing Radburn back inside. Could he not see the giant killer just metres out into the darkness? Obviously, he could not; blinded by the light from the ship.

The tension in Prentice's muscles was becoming painful as he fought to remain rock steady. He could feel Engel shaking, too. Something had to give, any second. He knew it. The dinosaur was obviously wondering what their ship might be. It had worried the much larger sauropods, after all. Although, now he came to think about it, perhaps it had been the scent of the carnivores that sent them running – inasmuch as a fifty-ton animal could run, while keeping at least three monolithic legs on the ground at any one time.

The monster above them sniffed again, head bobbing slightly, obviously confused by so many new and strange stimuli. It reminded Prentice of the time he had been trapped up a tree in Patagonia with Jim Miller, ten years ago for him personally. A vast Tyrannotitan, unofficially named Matilda, had fallen asleep on her feet, right next to them in the darkness. That time, the smoke, from which she had been running, masked their presence. It was the most bizarre incident of his entire life – aside from being dumped a hundred million years in the past. *Why do I always get the weird ones?* he raged in agonised silence.

The ship's open ramp was oriented almost ninety degrees away from them, its light spilling all behind. "Sarge?"

Oh, for crying out loud! Prentice nudged Engel to gain his attention. They could just about see one another in the light thrown across the ground by their rifle-mounted torches. Engel nodded and they leapt for their weapons.

Badawi was kicked awake. He slipped from his bunk and sprawled head-first across the cell floor. Scrambling back to a sitting position, he wiped some drool from his black goatee, while trying and failing to get his also-black hair to sit down. It was not his best look, he felt sure, but any embarrassment quickly evaporated when his eyes came into focus on the muzzle of a pistol.

"It is time for answers," Heidi stated simply.

Still groggy, he felt a surge of fear, too. "W-what do you wish to know?"

"Tell me what you know of my cousin."

"Your cousin?"

"Timothy Norris."

"He is your *cousin?*"

"Yes."

"Professor Norris is your cousin?"

Heidi rolled her eyes. "Yes, I believe we have established that, Master Sergeant. Clearly, there was no need for Poirot while you were policing the Nile. Now, tell me what you know of him."

"Nothing. Other than he oversaw a palaeontological dig near El-Shaikh Ebada. He helped me track down the dinosaur *you* let loose in my country," he added accusingly.

"The Spinosaurus aegyptiacus, yes. Just how *did* you capture it?"

"The UN sent personnel and equipment. A cargo ship and air support, along with some powerful tranquillisers." He shrugged. "We also had the help of a donkey."

"A donkey?"

"Called Banjo."

Heidi frowned. "A donkey called *Banjo?*"

"I believe we have established that, miss."

Her eyes narrowed. "You may call me *Doctor* Schultz."

Among other things, Badawi thought in the privacy of his own mind.

She seemed to read the insolence in his eyes, and struck him with her pistol grip.

"*Ow!*"

"What happened to the animal?"

"The donkey?"

She raised her hand again.

"The dinosaur, of course," he added quickly. "It was taken away by a Captain Baines—"

"*Baines?*" She spat the name furiously.

His eyebrow rose ironically. "Yes, I believe—"

Heidi raised the gun to strike him again.

"—that was her name," he finished, with just a hint of indolence.

The other Dr Heidi Schultz giggled. Despite the months spent in her cell, she had only met her fourth-great-grandniece a handful of times and hardly knew her. When Heidi turned and fired a round into her cell, with no regard for the outcome, she felt she knew her a little better. She screamed as the bullet hit one of the bars and ricocheted. Badawi jumped back to bump his already sore head against the wall. "Are you mad?" he yelled.

While her ancestor tucked her knees into her chest, head buried in a pillow, sobbing, Heidi turned back to Badawi with a sneer. "Not yet. This is merely impatience. What happens next is up to you."

Badawi stared wild-eyed, suddenly terrified for his life.

"Now tell me, Master Sergeant. Why did they capture the animal alive?"

He took a deep, steadying breath. "That was Professor Norris' idea. He thought they might be able to..." He tailed off, realising that whatever the UN's plans were for that creature, sharing them with this psychopath might be a bad idea.

"Able to what, Master Sergeant?" She added weight to her question by pulling back the hammer on her nine-millimetre; it would now take only the merest pressure to fire.

Badawi swallowed nervously. "I believe they took the creature to America, Doctor."

Heidi saw the lie in his eyes. "That was not your first answer, Master Sergeant. Do not attempt deflection. I will know all *you* know of this, otherwise I will empty your mind all across the wall behind you. Do we understand one another?"

He nodded. They certainly did. "The young professor thought they might be able to get the dinosaur home."

Heidi studied him, weighing the truth of his words. "And what did you understand him to mean by home?"

He held his hands out, palms up. "I assumed he meant wherever those creatures came from. He told me that he and some of his friends were among the people who appeared out of nowhere, ten years ago. Somewhere in England, if I remember correctly."

Interest piqued, Heidi clicked the hammer back down and pulled up the cell's single seat. Still holding the gun on Badawi, she asked, "I would know more of this."

Badawi told what little he knew or could remember of those events. It was all ten years in the past for him, so he hoped there would be no harm.

"They have lived in your world for *ten* years?" Heidi asked, at last.

He nodded nervously.

Her mind raced to comprehend. Only seven months had gone by in the Cretaceous, so clearly, they had set their return for one year after their first arrival in Patagonia; the question was, why? To avoid the risk of meeting themselves, perhaps? That seemed sensible, but she knew that the actions of Douglas' crew after leaving Cretaceous Britain had somehow changed the future timeline. Seeing 1940s Munich with her own eyes, it was unassailable, but perhaps the *new* Munich was also a clue? The people living in Douglas' altered timeline 1940s were obviously more advanced by at least a century, technologically; perhaps more, sociologically. At least, some of them were. Now she had absolute proof that the *New World*'s crew had spent at least a decade back in the 22nd century, or rather an altered version thereof – altered almost certainly meaning *enhanced*. If so, it must surely follow that they had access to very advanced, very powerful technology – in all likelihood, sixty or seventy years ahead of her own due to the changes in the timeline.

"Doctor?" Badawi asked into the strained silence.

Heidi ignored him, her mind whirling with new information and theories. If Tim had a plan to bring the Spinosaurus back to its own time, that could only mean that Douglas was up to something. Would he really risk coming back here? If so, there could be but one reason – to destroy her. Perhaps her incursion into 2122 with the dinosaur had triggered a response? She had learned the hard way that when push came to shove, Douglas was not as soft as he so often appeared, despite his penchant for following the rules; and should Baines be involved, the scenario might be even worse. Heidi well remembered the impregnability of her position aboard the *Last Word* battleship – or so it had appeared – and knew first-hand that where Baines was concerned, *push* often came to a knee in the groin.

Heidi had been building her forces, but they suddenly seemed inadequate to counter whatever her enemies might have brought from a raid into the future. Reaching a decision, she stood, knocking over the chair. Without another word, she strode from Badawi's cell and left the brig.

Picking up the chair, Badawi asked the other Heidi, "Is she always like that?"

She got up from her bunk and approached him, hesitantly. "I-I don't really know her."

Badawi felt his jaw where Heidi had hit him, moving it gingerly from side to side. "Well, she was very rude to me."

His fellow inmate smiled, though she was obviously still shaken. "If I ever get out of here, I will have a few choice words for my brother about how he brings up his children – when he has them."

Badawi stared. "What did you say? Get out of here...?" he repeated thoughtfully. Moving quickly, he stepped to the cell door and slid it open. He turned excitedly. "She closed the cell door but forgot to secure it. I *knew* I hadn't heard the clunk of the locking mechanism."

His co-prisoner was less enthusiastic. "Good for you."

He stepped out of the cell. "I'll come back for you. I promise."

She stepped to the bars. "You saw how she reacted to a mere cross word – how do you think she will be when she finds you gone?"

Badawi frowned. "What are you saying?"

"Simply that you had better come back for me quickly."

"We've taken only the most subtle control of the satellites thus far, James," Baines explained when Douglas returned to the bridge. "Nothing that would be noticed. So the information gathering has slowed dramatically."

"Aye, we dinnae want to tip our hand just yet. What have you found from what we have?" Douglas loved her smile lines, often commenting that she was aging backwards – always the right approach, the way he saw it. However, she was not smiling now.

"James, they've opened a wormhole."

"Aye. Klaus suspected as much. They'll be toing and froing to 1940s Munich – at least, that's the theory."

"It's more than that. The wormhole seems to be *permanently* open."

He stared, astonished. "Is that possible?"

"No," Singh chipped in, uninvited. "Not by any means *we* understand."

"And yet the evidence would seem to disagree," Douglas countered.

The pilot shook his head in bewilderment. "I can't account for it, sir. The power requirements for a prolonged connection are beyond anything we could produce."

Douglas stroked the stubble on his chin as he thought about it. "But our tech is far more advanced than anything Schultz has, isn't it?"

"Yes, sir. The only thing, short of a collapsed star, that could power it is..."

"Go on," Baines prompted. "No matter how bad it is, Sandy, we'd better know it."

"Yes, Captain. The only thing I can think of, is that they have somehow tapped the power of our planet to... oh, no."

"Sandy?"

"Captains, as we found out from our own crash in 1558, opening a wormhole while down on the planet is a really bad idea. We had no choice, but if I'm right, Heidi may have chosen to open a wormhole from their location to Munich direct. I'm just calculating the straight-line route from Egypt to Munich. Or should I say, the secant line, because it cuts through the planet's outer core. My God, if she's tapped the core directly, the wormhole could... could... I don't know what it could," he floundered.

"We all know she's tapped," Baines answered sourly. "But what does this mean?"

Singh spun his seat to face them. "If the wormhole has cut through the planet's core, it would stand to reason that the only way it could remain open for this long was because it was using the geothermal energy along its route. That could mean major instability for the planet going forward and..."

"And?" Baines prompted.

"*And,* if I'm right, the wormhole might stay open indefinitely."

"So that's how she's pulled so much gear through in such a short time," Douglas mused.

"It's far worse than that, sir," Singh continued. "The physics is well above my paygrade, I'll admit. I wish Satnam were here, but from what I *do* understand, a wormhole powered this way, with so great a power source, would continue to expand."

Into the silence that followed, Baines tentatively asked, "Just how much *expansion* are we talking about, here?"

Singh kneaded his brow against the headache he was developing. "In theory? It could expand until it swallows the Earth."

"Now Ah know she survived," Douglas spoke bitterly, banging a fist on the arm of his chair.

Baines turned to her husband. "You mean Heidi?"

"Aye. No one else would try anything so... so *insane!* Not content with reinventing the human race and changing all our history, now she's risking the very planet itself. The arrogance!" He glared at the main viewscreen showing a satellite image of the enemy complex.

Baines stood and took a few steps closer to the image, which clearly showed the *Heydrich* at the centre of a spider's web of industry. "Hmm," she mused.

"What are you thinking, Captain?" asked Singh.

"I'm just wondering how much of that monster we can kill if we simply cut off its head."

Douglas rose and moved to stand beside her. "Ah know who Ah'd kill, given half the chance."

Baines' brow furrowed with concern; it was not like him to talk that way. "Are you OK, James?"

"No. Ah'm not."

Baines turned back towards the enlarged image of the *Heydrich* once more. She knew her husband – he was fair-minded, tolerant and just. Far less volatile than she. Yet she hardly recognised the silent, clench-jawed figure beside her. If Heidi *was* still alive down there, she suspected that Flight Officer Schultz, formerly of the USS *New World,* might soon regret she was ever born.

Chapter 8 | Who Would You Save?

Just after midnight, Cretaceous Egypt

Prentice snatched his rifle from the ground as he rolled onto his back. Firing powerful stun bolts up into the dinosaur's belly, he continued the roll out from under the massive beast. Engel clearly had the same idea and dove out from under the animal's other side – also firing. Both men wondered which way it would fall. As it happened, the young adult Carcharodontosaurus saharicus dropped straight down, hitting the ground with an unpleasant crack, chin first.

It was unconscious before it landed, having taken several shots to its softer underbelly. Prentice breathed a sigh of relief, pleasantly surprised that neither of them had been crushed during such a desperate action.

Engel picked himself up, unconsciously wiping muck from his uniform, when a deafening roar split the night. Whatever had made it was close. Still in shock from the last few minutes, his legs turned to water. He slipped. In his nervousness, all dexterity deserted him and despite a scramble to regain his footing, he went down on something slick. It made no sense; he had landed where bedrock peeked through the soil. His footing should have been guaranteed. Slithering back onto all fours, the reason became apparent when his own erratic torchlight fell across a face. It was Walker; his rictus grin that of a dead man. Looking down under his own belly, Engel could see why. Walker's remains were spread wide and thinly over the exposed stone, just the head and lower legs remaining more or less intact. He must have fallen and been stepped on by one of the vast Paralititan sauropods, squashing him to a jam.

Engel gagged, but another monstrous roar soon fortified him to find his feet. He got up and spun around, desperately searching for the threat in the darkness, when his wildly strobing torchlight fell across another face, only this one was alive. He had heard of long faces, but at two metres, Carcharodontosaurus was not playing fair.

Engel screamed.

Before he could turn his rifle on the demonic visage, the massive head split wide to *roar* expansively. The grand gesture was intended to terrify him, and it worked, though it also sideswiped him, sending him flailing in one direction, while his weapon sailed off in another.

"We need help out here!" Prentice hollered at the top of his lungs. He ran at the side of the dinosaur he and Engel had brought down with their stun bolts and half jumped, half climbed over its back, to get a clear view of Engel's situation. In the horror-film light of flashing torches, he saw what remained of Walker, as an even larger carcharodontosaur flung his comrade through the air. He aimed and squeezed the trigger, but as he did so, the unconscious animal beneath him jerked spasmodically. His shot went harmlessly up into the sky, while he was pitched forward, falling heavily to the soil, now on the opposite side of the massive creature. The wind was knocked from his chest and a wave of nausea swept over him. Had he fallen further from the beast, he too would have landed on bedrock and broken a collarbone or even his neck. As it was, he lay temporarily immobilised. All around him, the night was filled with sounds of the hunter's siblings as they scratched at the earth and bellowed at things they did not understand.

The animal that had tossed Engel so casually now had Prentice in its sights. He would have screamed, but he simply did not have the breath. He scrabbled around in the muck for his rifle. He could see the light, but it was out of reach.

In the end, there was only the foetal position – never planned, nor ever any kind of a plan, just basic instinct. Prentice curled up and waited for death.

"You leave him alone!" someone shouted – more than that, someone fired. The stun bolt hit the giant in the snout, backing it off instantly, as it shook its head to clear it. The bolt was followed by the cracks of live rounds from automatic weaponry, fired into the air. Prentice adjusted his arms to see what was happening. He caught sporadic muzzle flash in the darkness along with a roar – this time, that of a young man, running into peril to save his friend and mentor. The words, if there were any, were unintelligible, but the Carcharodontosaurus backed off. Dazed and alarmed by so many new sounds and smells, it turned and ran into the night, the rest of the pack following in their alpha's wake. Only the unconscious animal remained.

Prentice got shakily to his feet, retrieved his rifle and walked, with as much dignity as he could muster, towards his teenaged saviour. "Private Radburn."

"Sarge? Is that you?"

For the first time, Prentice considered his appearance. Covered in mud, blood and faeces, he must have looked like something dug out from a bog. "Aye, it's me, Mark. Thank you. You saved my life." He patted the young man on the shoulder, then looked at his hand and winced. "Sorry, lad."

Suddenly, Prentice was surrounded by his own troops. "Find Corporal Engel. He's over there." He waved vaguely into the night.

"We'll find him, Sarge."

He grabbed Walker's rifle and dog tags before making his way back to the ship.

Within moments Engel was carried up the rear boarding ramp, unconscious.

"Lock us down, Mark," Prentice ordered, gently. "That thing out there will wake up soon enough."

The detachment's medic checked Engel over and then brought him round. Prentice kneeled by his side. "Heinz? You OK, lad?"

Engel was helped into a sitting position. He held his head groggily. "Adam, I want to move. This neighbourhood's gone to the dog— *dinosaurs!*"

Prentice chuckled. "Aye, the gangs are gettin' a bit much, that I'll grant you."

Regaining his full senses, Engel suddenly looked concerned. "Sarge, did I imagine it, or was there gun fire out there?"

"You didn't imagine it, lad. Some rounds were loosed into the air, to scare t'animals away."

"Do you think they might have been heard?"

Prentice shrugged uncomfortably. "We'll find out soon enough. I'll bet you a month's pay the lads saved our lives, though."

Engel rubbed his aching head. "They're *paying* you for this? No one told *me*."

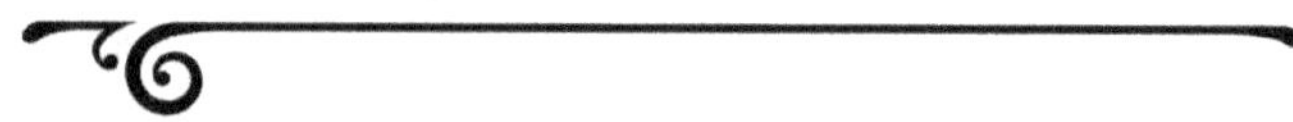

Local ship-time aboard the *Heydrich* was 0513 hours. Having left his comm behind in 2122, Badawi could not say with any accuracy how that correlated to his own body clock, but he guessed it was close, and would explain how Heidi had taken him so completely by surprise when she kicked him awake – no doubt a deliberate interrogation tactic. Most of the crew were still in their bunks. If he were to stand any chance of escaping, now was the time. He stuffed his pillows under the blanket provided and closed the cell door behind him so that, superficially at least, it appeared locked to any casual observer, with the prisoner asleep inside. He hoped to be away before anyone checked the back-footage.

The brig was located in the lower decks, so he found his way easily to the main cargo hold aft. The space was full of smaller vehicles, spare parts and equipment. It resembled a flying hardware store. Badawi smiled.

He could hear movement and the hammering of metal on metal coming from the hold's far end. Someone was working the night shift. He hid behind a tracked personnel carrier, sneaking a look around the corner. Two men were removing a wheel from a smaller vehicle – one that looked as though it had lived a hard life. The front wing was also hanging off and bore what looked terrifyingly like bite marks. Badawi shook his head with anxiety and no small measure of disbelief. Turning back, he took a route around the rear of the APC and spotted what he needed against the wall of the hold – a short length of tow chain and a long, steel crowbar with a high-strength oval shaft.

He removed his jacket and wrapped the chain within it to muffle any clinking. Grabbing the bar, he checked no one had seen him, and made his way back to the connecting corridor that led fore, to the brig.

The incarcerated Dr Heidi Schultz lay on her bunk, facing the wall. Badawi felt suddenly sorry for her, trapped and alone – completely within the power of a psychopath. She seemed to have given up, probably believing that she would never see him again, but Badawi did not roll that way. He stepped back into his still-open cell. The vertical front bars of each were cross-braced with lateral supports at three points along their length. The reinforcement made them immensely strong and completely resistant to bending by any human means. However, the bars *between* the cells were not braced. They were still far too strong to bend by hand, but with clever use of leverage, Badawi hoped to make a gap wide enough for the slender woman to escape. She would only escape into his cell, but as that was now unlocked, he anticipated a quick getaway. He would worry about *where* they would get away to, once they were out.

"Heidi," he called softly. She seemed to have drifted back to sleep. "Heidi!" he hissed a little louder.

She rolled over and woke with a start. "You came back."

"Of course." He grinned. "Do you have a middle name? This is getting confusing."

She smiled, still softened with sleep. "My friends used to call me H."

Unpacking the short chain from his jacket, Badawi wrapped it around the bars, selecting the first and fourth in line as he faced them. "Aitch? Oh, H, right, I see. H it is, then." He fed the large bar through the links at each end of the chain and twisted until it drew up tight. Grasping the bar at each end, he twisted further. Gradually, with much grunt and struggle, the bars at the end of the set of four began to bend towards one another. As he tightened the chain, the work became harder, until he had to feed the bar out, using its full length for maximum mechanical advantage. Eventually, the bars bent to touch the next in line. Badawi selected the four bars immediately to the left of the ones he had already deformed and repeated the operation. Soon, the bars in the middle were bent as far away from one another as the space allowed. Most importantly, there was room for the woman's head to pass. She was lithe as a dancer, so he had no doubt she would be able to slip through. "Come," he offered, urgently.

She held the bars while passing her head through at the widest point in the bend, straightening up as she went, and skewing her shoulders, she reached her arms forward for help. Badawi took her hands and pulled. She caught – in a couple of places – fortunately, those were places soft enough to squeeze through and she was free.

She thanked him a little uncomfortably, while rubbing her bruised bits and adjusting her costume. "And now?"

"Now, we get out of here."

"Good plan," she agreed, "and probably better than my idea of trying to pickpocket the guard's security card while I distracted him."

Badawi was sweating freely after his exertion, but the smile she gave him raised his temperature still further. "Erm, perhaps we should..." He gestured towards the open door, awkwardly.

Once outside the brig, Badawi noticed the corridor lighting had automatically brightened to a daylight setting. He knew the corridors would soon be buzzing as people began their day. "Do you know the way out?" he whispered.

She shook her head. "My lovely fourth-great-grandniece poisoned me and forced me through a wormhole. I am still hazy on what followed."

Badawi looked appalled. "Come." He took her hand, and they ran for the main hangar. They slowed just before entering, allowing a cursory check. Badawi pulled his head quickly back into the corridor. "Still just the two men working on a broken-down four-by-four. We may be in luck." Since his last brief visit to the hangar, there had been a development. The vehicle they had been working on now had all its wheels and the damaged wing removed to reveal the chassis. Of greater importance was the hangar's main boarding ramp, which had been lowered. He doubted it was necessary, but nevertheless placed a finger to his lips.

H nodded and they slipped into the cavernous space. Badawi led them to hide behind the tracked vehicle again. They watched as one of the mechanics got behind the wheel of the partially repaired truck and started its diesel engine. The other guided the driver out of the repair bay to back down the *Heydrich*'s side-opening ramp. An unhealthy grinding sound caused the driver to stop at the bottom, with front wheels still on the steel plates of the ship. Handbrake on, he jumped out of the cab and both men were soon on their backs under the vehicle, looking up at its underside and bickering about what might be wrong and whose fault it was.

"This is our chance," Badawi whispered. "Are you ready?"

She nodded. Once again, he took her hand, and they ran as quietly as they could across the deck plates to the exit. Once on the ramp, Badawi jumped off the side, down onto the sand and out of the mechanics' field of view. He turned quickly, gesturing for H to do the same. She jumped. He caught her. She looked up into his eyes, and in keeping with the traditions of romantic fiction throughout the ages, they shared an intense, smouldering moment, lost in one another's arms like the world around them had no meaning. He may well have kissed her, but fortunately, this is not one of those tales, and what the world around them lacked in meaning, it made up for in meanness. Any romantic urges gave way to copper's instinct in Badawi, waking him to their danger; little perspicacity was required to realise that if they stayed where they were much longer, he would soon find himself a *dead* copper, holding a gorgeous blond heroine – also dead. So they ran away together, and at just after six in the morning, not even into the sunset, either[11].

"Find them!" Heidi hissed, waspishly.

"Yes, ma'am." Lieutenant Devon saluted and left her as quickly as his legs would carry him. Once outside Heidi's quarters in the corridor, he turned towards security and commed Captain Aito Nassaki as he walked. "Aito? Devon. The prisoners have escaped. Yes, both of them. Heidi wants me to track them down. I know we have plans, that's why I'm telling you. What...? No, of course not. What do you think I should have done? Told her to catch them herself? You'll just have to manage without me – I know how hard that will be, but you'll have to try. At least you'll have Jansen. What? Oh, har har. Very funny. You're a funny man. Devon out."

He cursed silently. This was the last thing they needed; their plan was desperate enough as it was without being derailed by a pointless jailbreak. Where the hell did those imbeciles think they could go? Just as he was about to step into security, he bumped into Dr Anne Hemmings. "Anne. We have a problem."

---

11   Due to limitations of the written medium, readers are asked to imagine a moving musical score at this point, to mitigate the sun's wantonly anticlimactic sense of timing.

She listened to his quick explanation, nodding thoughtfully. "Maybe it's for the best."

"How so?"

"If things don't go as planned for Nassaki and Jansen, at least you will still be free to act. If their plan goes very wrong, I fail to see what you could do anyway. No, this is for the best."

Devon turned to leave.

"Wait. I've received a communication from the *Newfoundland* this morning. She's almost ready to fly."

"Excellent." Devon warmed to the news. "And the other project?"

"Almost complete, too. And no eyebrows raised... yet."

"Great. I'd better get going, Anne. Keep me posted, yeah?"

"You, too."

"Ah, come in, ma'am," Dr Reid greeted Heidi, offering her a seat in his lab. "Thank you for coming."

"You wished to see me, One?"

He gave her a long-suffering look.

"My apologies. You wished to see me, Dr Reid," she amended, looking anything but contrite.

"Yes, ma'am. Look at this list of materials." He handed her a tablet, pointing at the list about halfway down its length. "These items in particular raised an eyebrow or two."

"What do you believe this means?"

He shrugged. "That they are up to something?"

She looked up from the list. "Can you be more specific?"

"I'm sorry, no, ma'am. I couldn't begin to guess what they're making, but these materials are not for repairs to that ship. *That* I can tell you."

"Have you queried this?"

"Not yet. Brought it to you first, in case it was something you'd already sanctioned."

Heidi brooded a moment. "Very well. Make the query. In my name. I wish to know exactly what it is they are up to."

"It may be harmless, ma'am. They are trying to build a new colony and develop the land for agriculture."

"If that is the case, they will have nothing to fear, will they?"

"No, ma'am." *If only that were true,* he added in the privacy of his own mind.

"If there is nothing else?" Heidi made to stand.

"Actually, there is, ma'am."

She sat again. "I'm listening."

"I've discovered a strange signal, ma'am. Being broadcast from this campus – or very near to it."

She leaned forward in her seat. "What sort of signal?"

"Again, I must apologise. All I can say for sure is that it's encrypted and is being bounced off a couple of our satellites. As we're the only human beings on this world, aside from Commander Coleman's contingent thousands of kilometres away in Britain, and as the signal seems to originate from here, I can only guess that it's being transmitted by the Germans, ma'am."

"Why would they need to send messages to our satellite net?"

"Not messages, ma'am. Whatever it is seems to be a continuous feed. Perhaps they've managed to hack our system and are using our own equipment to spy on us? I can only hypothesise."

"What benefit could they derive from that?"

"Perhaps they don't fully trust us, ma'am. We *are* asking them to commit their entire country's resources into our hands, are we not?"

Heidi chewed the point over. "Plausible. Stupid, but plausible. They risk queering our deal. Unless..."

"Ma'am?"

"Unless we are *not* the only people on this Earth."

Reid took a moment to mull the possibility over. "You think we're being spied on?"

"Perhaps."

"But by whom? I mean, who could the feed possibly be relaying information to? There won't be a foreign, man-made satellite in orbit for almost a hundred million years."

"A ship," she stated flatly. "A ship in orbit."

"But, surely, ma'am, our satellite net would have detected any such encroachment into our space?"

"Not necessarily. I have reason to believe that Douglas' people are planning a second incursion into this time. They will have vastly superior technology compared with their last sojourn in the Cretaceous, and they will be coming for us."

Reid swallowed nervously. "How do you know this?"

"The prisoner—"

"Who escaped?"

Her eyes narrowed. "Yes. Fortunately, I was able to interrogate him first. Douglas' rabble have spent the last ten years in the 2122 of the new, more advanced timeline. The timeline that followed on from the 1940s we, ourselves, have witnessed. Damn the man, he has caused all these temporal disruptions."

Reid nearly choked at that, just about managing to turn it into a politic clearing of the throat.

"Who knows what knowledge and equipment they may have," she continued, looking away absently. "If only I could find the exact time of the divergence and stop them! From the history I have picked up in Munich, the knowledge of mankind seems to have undergone a quantum leap in the late sixteenth century. Perhaps I should look into it."

"But, ma'am, that might destroy everything we've built here. I cannot even begin to imagine the paradox we might cause if we continue tinkering in this way. May I suggest we focus on dealing with the problem in front of us? Hopefully, we can put things right from here—"

"*Hopefully?*" Heidi cut him off. "We are *way* past hopefully, Doctor. I must go."

"Actually, ma'am, there is one more thing."

For a second time, she sat back down. "Go on."

"I thought it was nothing, probably just a weather system or some such, but after speaking with yourself, well... perhaps it was more than that.

"I fell asleep at my desk last night. When I awoke, it was late, so I decided to take the couch in my office here in the complex. Anyway, I couldn't get back to sleep, so I went for a stroll outside to get some air when, in the distance, I heard something resembling thunder. Though now I come to consider it, it sounded rather light, rather *tinny* for thunder, perhaps. It was far off, and at the time I thought little of it, but as you've raised the possibility of others invading this time, I fancy it just may have been weapons fire."

"What time was this?"

"Just after twelve? Certainly not much later."

Heidi brought her hands together, prayerlike, to her lips – a mannerism inherited from her grandfather. "We must accelerate our plans. How close to completion is the new satellite?"

"Very. A few days. No more. All the devices are already loaded. We just have a few modifications to make to the guidance system before we assemble the outer case, then she'll be ready to fly."

"Very good, Doctor. How many devices does the satellite carry?"

"Three hundred, ma'am."

Heidi actually smiled. "Excellent. That should level the playing field, as the idiom goes. Your work has been exemplary these last months, Doctor. I should have separated you from Dr Hemmings long ago. And our orbital attack craft, how many are ready to deploy?"

"To *deploy*," he considered, "I believe five, maybe six. We've been using them to make deliveries to Commander Coleman in Britain, but I've not been hands-on with that project, as you know. We have twenty-four in all – two squadrons – almost finished. Plus the bespoke ship you requested with long-range fuel capacity and basic accommodation. That one is practically ready, too."

"Along with its special ordnance?"

He nodded soberly.

"Excellent. Very well, Doctor. Launch every one of them that is fit for orbital flight – excluding my own, of course – and make sure they are all fully armed."

"Of course, ma'am, but what are they looking for?"

"I suspect they will find a ship, either in very high orbit or perhaps..."

"Ma'am?"

"Perhaps in some other way hidden from us," she replied thoughtfully. "We may be dealing with technology that is beyond us, so we must take the initiative and strike first, and with stealth. And, Dr Reid, tell the pilots to strike hard! They are to destroy anything they find up there that is not us – do you understand?"

"But again, ma'am, wouldn't our satellite net have warned us of a ship in orbit?"

Heidi stood, ready to leave, but turned back. "Dr Reid, we must assume that our surveillance net has been compromised. We must further assume that Douglas has eyes on us and is here to destroy us. We must also be more vigilant with regards to our German workforce. Doctor, trust no one. Now, carry out my orders. Tell Commander Coleman I will expect an answer today regarding those rogue materials. Good day."

Todt looked through the eyepiece of his Electronic Distance Measurement theodolite. He gestured to a woman holding an optical prism staff. "Left. A little more – stop!" He checked the reading on his Total Station's flatscreen and frowned. "What is this?" He looked to where the woman was standing 153.457 metres away – at least, that was the last measurement the machine had recorded. He looked through the small telescope again and rolled his eyes. "You have stepped into a dip!"

"What?" the young woman called back.

Their voices were drowned by the launch of five orbital attack ships. Each circled above the complex until they were all in the air. From there, they moved into an arrowhead formation and with a blistering crackle of distorted sound, shot near vertically upwards, heading for space. Multiple sonic booms were transmitted through the air to the ground below.

Todt covered his ears, crossly. He was already annoyed. Denied access to the Schultz satellite network, he was forced to use older equipment for measuring distances and angles. Back in Germany, he would have used surveying kit with Global Positioning System capability and carried out the work alone. The EDM system required an assistant to carry a prism staff about the site and place ranging rods at his temporary benchmarks. At least, he had requested one helpful assistant. It must have amused someone to send what Todt considered to be three imbeciles from the office, instead. He waited for the rocket noise to abate, cursing the day he left pure engineering behind to work with government. Once he could hear himself think, he cupped his hands to continue shouting at the help. "You've stepped into a hollow! It's a small anomaly – no good to me. Step out of it!"

He made a gesture to move right. "No, my right! I cannot get a reading for the height of collimation if the laser is firing over the top!" He sighed. "God help us."

"You should try using a radio," said a voice right by his ear.

"What the—" Todt crashed into his tripod, almost spilling the EDM's expensive optics and electronics to the ground. "What are *you* doing here, Jansen? You scared the hell out of me! Oh, damn! Now look what you have done. My tripod has moved in relation to the peg." He pointed to a red plastic peg in the ground. "I will have to set up all over again and take new benchmarks. *Dummkopf!*"

"Ooh, that does sound frustrating," Jansen replied casually.

"Working with the fools I have here, you have no idea! And she is by far the brightest of the three. The other two only want to look at their comms all day. Just look at them. That one can't even place the ranging rods upright. *Oi! Straighten it up!*" He shook his head disgustedly, his engineering sensibilities making him almost vibrate with agitation. "*Bananenbieger[12]!*" he bellowed.

Jansen frowned. "But there's no internet here."

"I know! They download it at home to scroll through it at work. Welcome to the twentieth century!"

Jansen chuckled. "All that by the 1940s, incredible. Now that's what I call progress." He placed a hand on the irate engineer's shoulder. "Don't worry, Fritz, it gets a lot worse, believe me. Anyway, I'm here to talk to you about this project. Along with my colleague, that is."

Todt looked around. "Colleague? Have you an invisible friend, Jansen? That would explain a great deal about you."

Jansen chuckled again. "Always so courteous, Fritz. That's what everyone says about you."

"Do they?"

"No. Ah, here he comes."

Captain Aito Nassaki approached them. He, too, was visibly annoyed about something, though he attempted to walk with nonchalance. The effect was a sort of irate sidle.

Jansen's face split ear to ear. "Nice of you to join us. Where's Devon?"

"He's been otherwise detained," Aito replied brusquely. "Heidi's prisoners have escaped."

"Escaped?" Todt was clearly surprised, edgy, even. "Dr Schultz, too?"

---

12   Amusing German slang often used to describe a person with no concentration span or direction in life, or perhaps engaged in something pointless. Literal meaning – banana bender. It's a curvy job, but someone's got to do it.

Aito nodded. "If you mean the liberal 1940s version, yes. The 2112 version with the psychotic updates is still with us."

"Oh, good," Todt replied, deadpan. He could sense a shifting in the wind and began to wonder what these two could possibly want with him. His mind raced. If Dr Schultz got herself killed, how would they possibly offset all the damage her persona, in the form of her fourth-great-grandniece, was wreaking in Munich. Despite competing thoughts, the question that emerged from his mouth was more prosaic. "Where could they possibly hope to go? They will be shot on sight if they approach the wormhole." He and her brother, Hans, had planned everything so meticulously, and now this. He placed his head in his hands.

"What is it?" asked Jansen.

"Nothing. What can I do for you gentlemen?"

"We need a little chat about the future of this programme, or should I say the future of Germany," Aito led directly. "We believe—"

His words were cut off abruptly by a cataclysmic explosion. The three men cried out in shocked unison, completely drowned out by a second explosion. The Schultz campus had expanded so rapidly that, at the extreme boundary of the new plot, they were now half a kilometre away from the commotion. Todt spun his theodolite round and looked through its telescope. "Oh, my God."

"What is it?" Jansen demanded urgently. "What's happened?"

"I would not know where to begin." Todt spoke as if in a dream.

Aito snatched the theodolite, pulling the tripod onto two legs as he brought it near his eye. Out of the boarding ramp of the *Heydrich* rolled one of their brand-new Tiger XII tanks. Behind it, the ship's cargo hold was an inferno.

Chapter 9 | Mons Huygens

"Bladdy night duty," Gleeson complained. He lifted a suspiciously light coffee mug to his lips, frowned, and peered dolefully into its empty depths. "Bladdy 'ell." Levering himself from the captain's chair, after a very long night, he walked to the small galley, off the bridge. Without even stepping into the room, he could already see that the coffee percolator was also dry. "Oh, bladdy *hell*. Did *I* drink all that? And now I'm talking to myself. Great." Alone on the *New World*'s bridge, he checked the ship's chronometer. "Still, they'll be here in a few. All enthusiastic and well rested. Hmm... Gleeson, you're *still* talking to yourself, mate. Bladdy 'ell."

As a fully qualified pilot these days, Commander Gleeson had fallen – or perhaps been tripped – into taking the graveyard shift. He could not remember the last time boredom had settled on him so completely. So bad was it, that he had even caught up with his paperwork. "How that man loves forcing us to produce reports."

By 'that man', he meant Captain Douglas, and by 'reports', he included anything remotely administerial. Gleeson only owned a chair in case someone dropped by. He viewed desks as the instruments of slavery. "If something doesn't happen soon, I'm gonna go crazy." A proximity alarm beeped urgently. "Baggar! I didn't mean it!" he informed the cosmos, but it was too late.

He ran over to the pilot's station. The Schultzes' satellite net had picked up a small group of objects entering Earth orbit from the planet below. He examined the feed, zooming in on the craft. Five identical Schultz-style attack ships, flying in an arrowhead formation. His eyes narrowed. *They can't see us. They don't even know we're here, so what are they up to?* Opening a second window at Singh's usual station, he called up the feed from their Afromimus – the tiny, dinosaur-shaped spy drone, a quarter of a million miles away. There was a short delay, which was only to be expected. What he eventually saw came as a surprise. "Ooh, seems someone else is blowing stuff up." He refocused on the attack ships. They were leaving high orbit and heading straight for the moon.

A big red button sat just to the left of Singh's station, within easy reach. It had been tempting him all night. "Hmm, what to do? Ah, what the hell." He pushed it.

Sirens went off all over the ship, along with the repeated message: *All hands to battle stations! All hands to battle stations!*

"That oughta get 'em outta bed." He opened a connection to security and Captain Tobias Meritus. "Tobo? We have incoming. Five bandits – repeat, *five* bandits. ETA in... give me a second here..." He queried the computer. The enemy craft were flying at astonishing speed – more than 60,000 miles per hour. He made a quick calculation. "Oh."

"Oh? Oh, what? What's happening, Commander?"

"Er... ETA in three hours, forty-eight minutes. Sorry, Tobo. Bit of a scaling miscalculation. Still, better too prepared than not at all, eh? Ready fighter screen for launch at 1100 hours – over." He closed the channel and winced.

Douglas burst onto the bridge with a napkin still tucked into his collar. "Commander, what's happening?" he demanded.

"Incoming, Captain. Five enemy attack craft. They're a little further away than I first thought. Sorry, mate."

Douglas looked at the relative positions and made his own calculation. "No need, laddie. Ah'd rather we were too prepared than not at all."

"That's what I just said to Tobo. Not sure he agreed, mind you."

"Perhaps we could switch off the red alert for a wee while, though, eh?" Douglas answered with a glint in his eye as he removed the napkin. "Well done, Commander. Running aboot ma ship dressed like this reminds the crew to make allowances for ma age! Was the evening quiet otherwise?"

"As the grave, Captain. However, this morning—"

"Aye?"

"Looks like all hell's breaking loose down there. This just in. Look at the feed from our little dinocam. Everything happened at once."

Douglas' eyebrows shot up as he watched the recorded explosions within the *Heydrich*. At that moment, Baines and Singh shot onto the bridge. "What's happening?" they asked in unison.

"It's alright." Douglas waved them down. "We have guests, but they're no' due for hours. Jill, Sandy, look at this." He directed them to the footage from the planet below.

"Nothing to do with Sergeant Prentice's squad, is it?" Singh asked.

"With the radio blackout in place, there's no way to be sure, but Ah doubt he'd take it upon himself to launch a full-blown attack, Sandy – at least, no' without a damned good reason."

"You think something else is going on, James?" Baines forced a sausage sandwich into his hands, hastily constructed from remnants of a breakfast abandoned during the brief red alert.

Douglas shrugged, biting into it without taking his eyes from the screen. He chewed twice and then looked down at what he was eating. Out of the corner of a full mouth, he asked, "Sausage? Again?"

"You told me you like sausage. Reminds you of your dad, you said."

"Ah dinnae wish to be reminded of him every morning." It was an age-old conversation between man and wife, one that went back to when Eve – bored with apples – decided to have a go at cooking something. After some sod ruined her garden, Adam found himself eating serpent for dinner – a lot. Yet, untold millennia later, and even allowing for the changing roles within relationships, the conversation remained very much the same. Douglas felt the temperature in his immediate vicinity begin to drop. He looked up to see his wife standing straight as a gibbet, with arms crossed and a hanging judge expression. He swallowed and took another bite. "This is really good," he spoke around another mouthful of food. "Very thoughtful, lassie. Thank ye."

Baines drummed her fingers on her arm. "You'd better show me this footage again."

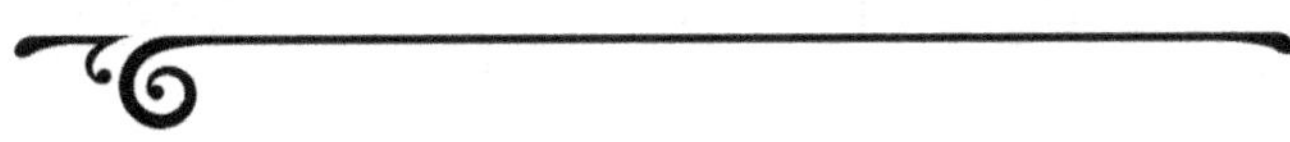

"Déjà vu," Aito stated dumbly.

"And there goes the last of the Dawn Fleet," Jansen added.

"What the devil are you talking about?" Todt demanded, anxiously.

Aito shook his head. "Nothing."

"Perhaps she's not totalled?" Jansen suggested.

"Perhaps not, but I doubt she'll be flying any time soon. And what about the wormhole?"

"You think it may have failed?" Todt interjected again, extremely concerned now.

"Oh, man!" cried Jansen, suddenly anxious himself. "I think you might have more to worry about than wormholes, Fritz. *Run!*"

Todt's survey team had driven the half-kilometre to the proposed site for their next phase of construction. It would have been a chore to drag their equipment all that way under the murderous Cretaceous sun, even so early in the morning, but the real reason they drove was for the protection the armoured personnel carrier afforded. *"Run!"* He forwarded Jansen's warning on to his unenthusiastic work crew at the top of his voice.

The young woman was already moving, confirming his suspicions that she was the brains of the bunch – and talking of bunches, the banana benders were only just waking to what was happening. Todt and the girl, along with Jansen and Aito, soon leapt into the back of the vehicle, chests heaving.

With bovine slowness, the young men still outside dropped most of their equipment – though not their comms, naturally – abandoned their benchmarks and set off in a dead panic.

A large family group of small, swift-running dinosaurs sprinted across their path, fleeing in terror for their lives after the explosions. Some species of ornithomimosaur; they were not especially dangerous if left alone, but fear could turn even the most placid creatures savage.

The two men collided with them and were mown down. Covering their heads, they at least had the sense to wait until most of the group had passed before trying to get back up.

Todt unconsciously placed a hand to his mouth as he watched in horror. The pair regained their feet, but one of them staggered, requiring help from the other, who still clutched a red and white ranging rod in his other hand. He flailed it about unthinkingly, to aid his balance as he helped his companion along. Todt made to run from the safety of their vehicle, intent on assisting the young men in any way he could, regardless of how they irritated him.

Jansen grabbed him by the arm and yanked him back inside.

"What are you doing?" Todt demanded furiously, but Jansen was not looking at him. Irresistibly, Todt followed the other's line of sight to its shocking conclusion. "Oh, my God."

Behind the rapidly departing ornithomimosaurs came another animal, also fleeing the booms and the smoke. Though it moved more slowly than the smaller dinosaurs, it thundered across the open ground with a terrible inevitability that was far more alarming.

"Look out!" Todt screamed.

Jansen passed him to Aito. "Don't let either of them step outside."

Aito nodded understanding and pulled both Todt and the young woman away from the open hatch.

Jansen jumped through to the front compartment and started up the vehicle's powerful diesel engine. "Hang on to something," he bellowed over his shoulder. Without waiting for acknowledgment, he selected drive and pushed both levers forward. The tracked vehicle lurched off the mark, throwing dry soil up in the air from its tracks. He heard the people in the back spill across the passenger seats but spared no time to worry about that. He threw the APC into a hard right until the two young men were directly in front of him. They were still a hundred metres out. He did a rough calculation in his head. The massive Carcharodontosaurus he had been training to come for morsels of cooked meat was bearing down on them, no more than fifty metres behind, but travelling at half the speed.

"Damn. This is gonna be *really* close. Hang on!" He maxed the throttle, but the ground was extremely rough. Although the young men were running, one of them was clearly hurt after being knocked to the ground in the stampede. With the best will in the world, Jansen knew he could not possibly beat the dinosaur to them. The likelihood was that they would arrive simultaneously.

The Carcharodontosaurus continually adjusted its route to coincide with theirs. Jansen could actually plot the deviation in the creature's progress as they closed. He had to buy some time – just a few seconds would do. Their vehicle had no weapons, so he blasted the horn.

The dinosaur slowed a moment, raising its head higher for a better view of its surroundings. Sensing no further threat, it picked up its stride once more. Obviously determined to leave the smoke and noise behind, its superb eyesight was nevertheless drawn irresistibly to what it saw as a red and white crest being flicked about by one of its prey. Still carrying a ranging rod and dragging his injured workmate behind him, the young man's gait was somewhere between a skip and gambol, his colleague barely able to keep his legs under him.

Jansen pulled the right lever back slightly, reducing the power fed to its right-hand track. The vehicle veered right. The manoeuvre, though slight, still cost him some of their forward momentum, losing any benefit granted by the predator's brief slowdown. His hopes for cutting the dinosaur off before it reached the desperate runners faded altogether. He simply did not have the speed over such rugged terrain. Just a second or two's delay in the APC's arrival would be all the dinosaur needed to make a kill. "Any brilliant ideas, anyone?" he called into the rear compartment. "We're not going to make it!"

Aito lurched his way forward, hanging on to various handles and grips, like a man trying to leave a night bus slaloming through an obstacle course of parked cars at three in the morning with a drunk at the wheel. "I've got an idea!" He flew through the air as the words left his lips, the vehicle having jumped over an exceptionally large bump in the ground. *"Ouch!"* He cracked his head against the bulkhead, releasing a stream of bi-lingual bad language as he rubbed his brow. Eventually, he reached a short ladder, climbing to the vehicle's upper hatch. He pulled himself up and popped open the lid. Using the augmented strength of his artificial hand, he held on tightly to a handrail while removing his sidearm from its holster with the other. He emptied the clip at the colossus running towards them, while Jansen continued to blast the horn. Flat out, the APC was now bucking like a bronco in a ground quake. Aito managed to hang on, but with everything and everyone in motion, he had no idea if any of his shots found their mark. He could only hope the gunshots might back the dinosaur down and was indeed rewarded with a momentary stall.

Jansen took stock, anxiously. Lives were at stake, but he could see no way of heading the creature off before it reached Todt's companions. Their vehicles were alien to this world, but the animals were becoming used to them – as yet having no reason to fear them. If they all collided together, he might sideswipe the behemoth, but the men would die anyway. He reached a decision. To avoid running them down himself, he spun the vehicle into a full about-turn. With less than ten metres to the open rear hatch directly before them, he prayed they would have enough time to dive for the safety of its interior, while he himself hung on the horn.

The injured man stumbled and fell again, causing his companion to go down a couple of metres further on. Todt sprang from the hatch on the run. After just half a dozen strides, he reached the first, helping him to his feet. They both turned to reach for the third man. He lay in the dust, reaching out pathetically for help as tears streamed down his face. Todt tensed to move again when the man disappeared under a huge, three-toed foot. Talons at the end of each dug deep into the ground and the body, as the animal shifted its weight to turn on them. Stooping, it leered, jaws opening wide almost casually. The stink of its breath alone almost floored the petrified humans under its hypnotic gaze. When it roared, the force of the sound hit them like a physical blow, sending them sprawling onto their backs.

"Jansen, back up!" Aito screamed as he ran back to the rear of their vehicle. "Do it *now!*"

As the machine roared and began to move, Aito stumbled against the frame of the hatch, almost falling through and under the tracks to be crushed himself. Barely managing to shoulder past the aperture, he slapped another clip into his pistol as he fell into one of the side passenger seats. Grasping for another handrail, he pulled himself to his feet and pointed his gun at the giant, grinning face to fire again and again.

The dinosaur backed off, snapping its jaws like a bear after a miscalculation with a beehive. It turned and ran, tail flicking furiously in its wake as it gathered speed to escape the smoke now billowing across the plain towards them.

Todt stared balefully down at the corpse, while holding the man he had saved to his chest, allowing him to sob gently. He understood the lad's need. Closing his eyes, he hung his head, too.

"Fighter screen deployed, Captain." The voice over the comm was that of Captain Meritus. *"According to my instruments, two enemy*

craft have split right, following the prograde motion of the moon to come at us from behind. The remaining three have split left, to come at us in a retrograde orbit."

Douglas looked to Singh, who nodded confirmation. "We can confirm your observations, Captain Meritus. Be sure to give our visitors a warm welcome. Oh, and Tobias..."

"*Yes, James?*"

"Safety of our pilots is of principal concern, but if it's at all possible, a few prisoners would provide us with some much-needed intel."

"*Understood, Captain. Let's see if we can't bag you a couple.*"

"Aye. Good luck, Captain."

"*Same.*"

In a low geosynchronous orbit around the moon, the *New World* stayed on its dark side, and inside the new ice rings. She followed the prograde motion of Earth's only natural satellite as they both orbited the planet in a counterclockwise direction.

Heidi's small force came on fast. Their own satellite net had precluded the possibility of any unknown ships in orbit. Despite her warning that they should not trust information from those satellites implicitly, it made sense that anyone wishing to hide a ship near Earth would use the moon as cover.

They flew in tight formation out into the black unknown. As they rounded the moon, the pilots lost the benefit of sunlight and relied solely on their instruments to scan the terrain ahead. Following an equatorial flightpath, the computers took their craft to a minimum safe altitude of 12,000 metres, thus avoiding the Selenean summit, located along the north-eastern rim of the Engel'gardt crater at approximately 10,786 metres. With just a three-degree slope, the vast body of rock may not have been classified as a mountain, but that would be of small consolation to a pilot crashing into it. The moon's horizon was no more than 2.4 kilometres away from an observer on the surface. At their cruising height, the view ahead was improved, but still gave little advance warning when factoring in the speeds at which they travelled.

From 100,000 metres above the surface, Meritus' two squadrons of single-seat orbital fighters saw them first and dove to intercept.

By the time Schultz's people realised they were under attack from above, their pilots were granted mere seconds to react. The two small groups scattered as missiles rained down on the lunar surface. Hopelessly outnumbered, they regrouped into two wing pairs following a leader and made for the light.

The rearmost pair came under fire almost immediately and began jinking and turning in a desperate attempt to shake their pursuit. The left wingman vanished in a ball of superheated atmosphere, instantly freezing to nothing more than fragments encased in ice. The survivor poured on all the power his ship could muster to catch up with his leader. Once back in formation they split again into two wing pairs.

Meritus' pilots hounded them with withering fire, attempting to funnel them into a killing zone. The attackers were now fleeing for their lives. Against all expectation, hopelessly outnumbered and outclassed, they knew their only slim chance of survival lay in dangerous low flying through the moon's mountain ranges. Once snarled up in the valleys of razor-sharp rocks, their pursuit's superior speed would be all but useless.

They soon reverted to the light side of the moon and came upon the Montes Apenninus; a rugged mountain range spanning hundreds of kilometres across the northern hemisphere, named after the Apennine Mountains in Italy. They headed instinctively for the tallest peak of Mons Huygens. Just topping 5,500 metres, the vast mountain was surrounded by innumerous tall and craggy peaks, each dropping to deep valleys and lethal gullies.

Meritus watched one enemy wing pair tilt to port. They approached Mons Huygens at perilously low altitude, skimming lesser peaks and dropping, often blind, into the ravines that followed. He had to admire their courage, even if it was born of desperation. He understood their tactics, too. In their position, he might have done the same, but that did not mean he would follow them into oblivion. Lieutenant-Commander Sandip Singh had named the *New World*'s fighter squadrons Red Squadron and Gold Squadron – Meritus had no idea why. He had drawn command of Red Squadron and now ordered his dozen to higher altitude. *"Red Squadron, split into wing pairs and search the mountains from on high. Think eagle, rather than wolf. If you spot a contact, call it in and we'll flush them out. Don't get snarled up down in those valleys unless you have absolutely no choice. That's what they want. If you get chance to disable them, take it. Captain Douglas wants prisoners if we can get them – but no unnecessary risks! Red Leader out.*"

He and his wingman rose to a safe elevation, a thousand metres above the highest peaks, where they trained their crafts' extensive sensor suites upon the valleys below. They soon found a lone contact – the enemy had been forced to split up completely. Such close quarters through the gullies and ravines left no room for coordinated flying. Meritus' laser targeting system painted the enemy vessel for all friendly ships, while he and his wingman dropped like stones, powerful rocket motors drastically augmenting the moon's weak gravity to bring them, almost instantly, to within a few hundred metres. Both fighters fired and both hit.

The enemy vessel took the impacts surprisingly well, sacrificial armour saving the ship underneath. *Tough little bird,* Meritus thought to himself as pieces of plated hull flew in all directions from the impact. He pulled back on his stick and climbed vertically out of the deadly canyons. As he and his wingman left the mountains behind, a missile crossed between them, narrowly missing both ships. "Where did that come from?"

"*Down in the rocks, sir. Can't locate the source.*"

"One of them must be hiding. Perhaps there's a cave? You sneaky little—"

"*Sir, the missile's coming back – must be a heat-seeker, or a smartbomb.*"

"Or it has artificial intelligence," agreed Meritus. "I'm firing decoys."

Both pilots jinked wildly, instinctively turning away from one another to reduce their profile and the chances of collision. The missile took the bait and exploded. A second explosion from the surface also caught Meritus' attention. "This is Red Leader. Call signs – everyone!"

Twenty-four men and women called in. Meritus heaved a sigh of relief.

"*Maybe we hit our target harder than we thought, Leader,*" his wingman suggested. The words had barely left his lips when a blinding explosion took his ship. Meritus spiralled away from the blast. "Two? Come in? *TWO!*" He made a tight loop, trying to make sense of what had just happened, when he spotted the flash of rocket thrusters from the corner of his eye. "Two?"

"I'm alright, sir. Saw it a second before impact and managed to eject."

Meritus slumped with relief. "Their rockets must be using some breed of stealth tech. They only register if you're really on it. I'll have a word with Chief Nassaki when we get back – see if he can't improve our odds. *New World,* this is Red Leader. We have a pilot extra-vehicular – repeat, we have a pilot EV. Sending coordinates. Request immediate evac from the conflict zone – over."

"Copy that, Red Leader." Singh looked over his shoulder to Baines. "He got a little cooked, but he's OK." He had always wanted to say that. "Captain, are you sure we can't go with Rogue?"

Baines frowned with disapproval. "Please inform Captain Meritus a dropship is on the way for his EV pilot. We already went through this, Sandy, when they refused your suggestion to call this ship the *Executor.* The powers that be thought it had a negative connotation."

"For second choice, I also suggested *Home One.*"

"Yes, you did, but Captain Douglas had other plans. You only got away with Red and Gold Squadrons because they'd never watched the movies."

"Yes, ma'am," he replied dejectedly.

A decade of incarceration had left former Lieutenant Richard Weber with an education in microelectronics equal to any university syllabus in the world. Criminals often mockingly referred to prison as 'university' – he had taken it literally. Since his failed attempt to break Heinrich Schultz out of the USS *New World*'s brig ten years ago, by taking hostages in Dr Flannigan's hastily rigged field hospital, he had occupied one prison cell or another until they finally made it back to AD2122. Despite being summarily dumped into a military prison immediately after that, the people from the new timeline saw him only as a minor threat. Learning from his own stupidity and incompetence, he quickly came to grips with the rules of the new game he had been forced to play – good behaviour went a long way with those people.

Now in his mid-thirties, he had spent most of the last eight years in what equated to little more than a low-security 'gentlemen's prison'.

He would have been released long ago had it not been for the perpetual veto of Training Director Douglas, who refused to believe in his reformation. Weber clenched his fists, then relaxed them. Of course, Douglas had been right. Weber had been trained under Heinrich's personal youth regime – he would never waver from the cause. Although, it seemed that only Douglas and he himself now believed that.

The UNS *New World* was a brand-new ship and was fully loaded with some very impressive technology, but being a new ship, she was riddled with snagging faults, too. He suspected they had launched before they were truly ready. When they came to remove him from his prison cell, he surmised that something had forced the situation – perhaps the Schultzes were attempting to reach across time to save him? He was adamant they would never leave a true believer such as he to his fate, were it avoidable. He had been assured of that throughout each day of his education, his *indoctrination*. The Schultz empire was the light and the rest of the world represented only darkness, weakness and decline.

He also knew that something big was going on right now. He had heard the red alert warning a few hours ago, followed by the more recent roar as many fighters launched from the squadron bays on each side of the ship. He had the full schematic layout of their vessel – stolen from the main computer. He would never have been given access to such information, but during his 'university days' he had built an exquisitely advanced decryption device, running software of his own creation. No one knew he had it. It fitted into the heel of a shoe – another trick picked up from his ingenious master – and ran wirelessly.

Weber could leave his quarters whenever he liked, his door's locking mechanism but a minor formality. When ready, he would bypass it in seconds. He just needed to pick the best moment for maximum effect. Somewhere, down on the planet, was his family. He found the thought intoxicating, wondering what rewards his triumphant return might garner him. Sitting in his quarters' armchair, with the lights turned down low, he considered. Perhaps it was time for a brief reconnaissance and then... well, then he would have to see.

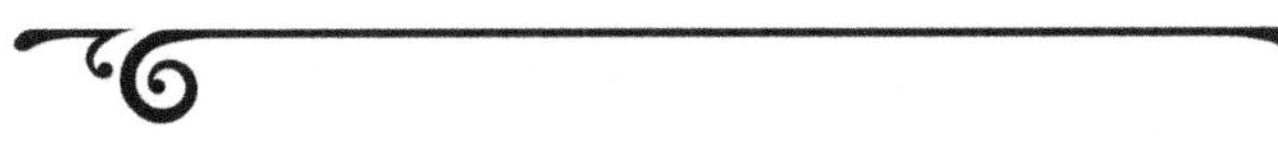

"Where are you taking us?" asked Dr Heidi Schultz, sociology PhD and art critic.

"The hell away from here!" Badawi bit back harshly. He had driven tracked vehicles during his career, but had never before stolen a tank, let alone used one in anger. His nerves were jangling – it had been quite the morning so far, and the sun was far from passing the yardarm[13].

The tank rocked on its tracks as it pushed through steel-mesh compound gates like they were made of paper. Badawi heard a decidedly feminine squeak from the rear as his passenger bumped her head. From there, he had a twenty-metre run-up, through what the Germans called 'the airlock'. Basically, a long cage that allowed two vehicles at a time into the complex – a failsafe against unwanted guests, specifically extraordinarily wild animals, as they remained within the confines of a high-voltage enclosure. At its end was a heavy, vehicle-rated, hydraulic drawbridge, long enough to bridge the concrete moat. Badawi had no idea how to activate the drawbridge, even if such a thing were possible from inside his stolen tank, so he rammed it, full tilt.

The boom as they connected shook his teeth, but the twenty-ton drawbridge had little choice but to follow the laws of physics when a tank pushing seventy tons hit it at forty kilometres per hour. It smashed down across the moat, allowing them to cross.

Badawi knew they had taken the opposition completely by surprise, but was willing to bet there would be an army of ready volunteers waiting to jump into the battle group of tanks they had just left behind – not counting the aircraft they had seen during their run through the complex, and whatever else Heidi had at her disposal. Nothing would surprise him. She was obviously a very angry young woman – she would be furious now. "We had better find a place to hide."

------

13 A traditional nautical saying. In northern latitudes the sun would usually show above the foreyard of a ship by 1100 hours – about the time of the forenoon 'stand-easy', when officers would pop below decks for their first drink of the day. The euphemism survives as a quaint English idiom, meaning it's just about late enough to justify breaking out the booze!

"In a tank?"

"At the moment, I am thinking that is better than *not* being in a tank, no?"

She grunted in semi-agreement. "Well, can you at least warn me before you perform any further stunts? What is next? Are you going to jump us over a line of motorcycles?"

"You think you can do better?"

"Did you have to blow up their ship like that? They will wish to *kill* us now."

"What did you think Heidi would have done to us if we hadn't? Just had us *lightly* killed?

"Apep, you are not pleasant to be around when you are cross."

"Cross? I'm terrified!" He stole a look behind. "How are you holding up?"

She tilted her head to one side and gave him the catlike stare of the unimpressed.

"I think these things usually need about three or four men to operate them," he tried, changing the subject.

"Three or four *men?*" came her cool reply.

"I don't suppose you have ever fired a tank?" He grinned sheepishly. "Silly question, forgive me. Actually, it was surprisingly easy."

"Apep, my work with machinery usually begins and ends with using a pair of scissors to cut a ribbon that opens a gallery or a supermarket somewhere."

"Are you saying you are useless?"

She glowered. "I am *saying* I am *very* good with scissors!"

The man with his back to her took the hint. "I'm sorry. I'm panicking – oh, my God!" The tank squealed to halt. Not expecting the sudden emergency stop, H was thrown forward to land at Badawi's feet, among the controls.

"What the hell are you doing? I thought you could drive this thing!" When no salty reply came back, she looked up from the vehicle floor to see what was wrong. "What is it?"

"A d-d-d—"

"Dune?"

"D-d-d—"

"Delta? Drop? A sudden drop – is that it?"

Badawi seemed to have lost the power of speech altogether.

"Out with it, man!" she demanded angrily. "Doughnuts? Dirigibles? Disco? Whatever is the matter?"

"Dinosaurs!" he blurted at last.

She attempted to get up and slipped again. "Can you get me out of this hole?" she screeched at him.

Dumbly, he helped her up to view the monitors that surrounded the driver's seat on three sides.

"Ooh..." she murmured softly.

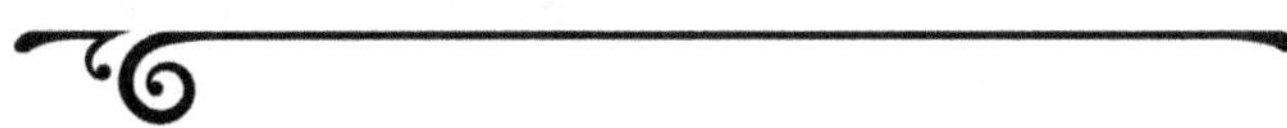

Meritus saw a rocket trail flash out from the side of a cliff. He smiled to himself. "Gotcha." His computer-aided sights zoomed in on a cave mouth approximately a thousand metres from Mons Huygens' summit, facing south. The craggy nature of rocks never touched by rainfall threw hard shadows in the direct sunlight. Had he not noticed the rocket trail, he would never have found it. He aimed just above the opening and launched a pair of his most powerful missiles.

Dropping from their mountings under his wings, the missiles shot forward, leaving Meritus behind. Almost immediately, an explosion bloomed from the side of the mountain and the cave mouth collapsed. He noted the coordinates and sent a message to the *New World.* They would send combat engineers to search for survivors and salvage once the battle had ended.

His comm burst to life. *"Red Leader, this is Gold Leader."*

"Go ahead, Gold Leader."

"Two bogies have taken to flying in and out of the moon's orbital rings. Some of the ice blocks are bigger than houses."

"We're clear down on the surface, Gold Leader. Do you require assistance?"

"Yes, Red Leader. We've lost six birds already."

Meritus frowned. "And their pilots?"

"All ejected safely and awaiting a rescue craft, thankfully. These guys are crazy. The leader of the pair flies like a son of a bitch. Never seen anything like it."

"Understood. Red Squadron is on its way. Let's see if we can't corral them."

As good as his word, Meritus took his squadron up into high orbit and towards the rings recently left behind after Heidi's forced comet collision.

He quickly understood Gold Leader's problem. Without even intending it, he found himself drawn in after the extraordinary enemy pilots, right into the ring of ice boulders. Gold had been right about the pair's leader, too. He had never seen such skilful flying and almost came to grief when the enormous shards of an ice boulder, shot to pieces by his quarry, suddenly filled his viewscreen. He doubted he would ever know just how he threaded his craft through the eye of that needle, to survive. Luck had certainly been on his side, whereas the enemy pilot displayed a oneness with his machine that eclipsed mere talent, and against terrible odds. The wing pair blew another couple of spinning bodies of ice and rock to a thousand smaller and even more dangerous pieces, cutting a pathway for their escape. Meritus' craft had to take a wide arc to remain clear of the debris, giving Schultz's remaining ships their opportunity to run.

Meritus wondered at that. They must have already judged the *New World*'s more advanced craft to be faster and superior. They would catch them long before they made it to safety. Indeed, the only reason the enemy were still flying was down to the extraordinary skill of the men or women at their controls, but rather than run for home, they broke for the dark side of the moon instead – and then he saw it. "*New World,* you have incoming. We're in pursuit but are unlikely to catch up before they reach you. They have a couple of real devils at the stick. Watch yourselves."

"Understood, Red Leader," replied Singh. "We have them on our instruments, Captain."

Douglas sighed. "Damn. Jill, bring our weapons online. Looks like we're going to have to shoot them down."

"Are we giving up on prisoners?" she asked.

"Doesn't look like they're about to give us much choice. Ah'll no' let them blow holes in ma new ship! Trouble is, the weapons we have on board, here, will annihilate a small vessel like those incoming." He rubbed his stubble in thought. "Sandy, how far away are they?"

"Sixty seconds – closing fast, sir."

"Let's see if we can depth charge them."

"James?" Baines queried.

"Set our missiles to detonate twenty metres from their targets. The blast force might disable them. Only if that fails, shoot to kill on the second salvo," he added, regretfully.

The enemy craft approached to within ten kilometres of the *New World* when their sky bloomed into superheated gas and light. The rattle of shrapnel hit their hulls like machine gun fire and the rearmost craft suffered explosive engine failure. Unresponsive, it was suddenly on ballistic course out into the solar system. The leader continued at full throttle, launching all six of his remaining missiles at the *New World*.

"Firing decoys," Baines called across the bridge. "Although the phrase 'barn door' comes irresistibly to mind. Brace for impacts."

Four of the enemy missiles followed the decoys, but the last two continued along their original flightpath to slam into the portside fighter bay's massive airlock hatch. The hatch had been closed after Gold Squadron's launch, protecting the ship from worse injury, though the hatch itself and parts of the airlock were severely damaged.

The whole ship, more than half a kilometre in length, shook with the aftershock.

"Damage report!" Douglas demanded against the blare of warning klaxons.

Baines checked their systems and queried all departments. Meanwhile, Singh called out, "Captain, enemy attack ship seems to have stalled."

"Heavy damage to port fighter bay. No casualties. We're venting atmosphere. Repair crews en route," Baines rattled off her report. "Shall I fire on the enemy vessel, Captain?"

"Wait a second, Jill. Sandy, is he dead in the water?"

"Yes, sir. We didn't hit him, though. It seems his ship malfunctioned."

"Is this a fox trick? Theories?"

Singh spun his seat to face Douglas. "We saw at least two dozen of those ships on the ground, sir. Yet they only sent five against us, so perhaps the others are incomplete. If that's the case, then the five we engaged may have been rushed into combat service. The dead vessel seemed to experience engine failure on its attack run. Maybe the pilot pushed it too hard? If it's a trick, it's a bad one, sir. We have him under our guns and he's going nowhere."

Douglas nodded. "Sounds plausible. We're no' fully ready after ten years. What they've accomplished in just seven months is hugely impressive. They must have been working at a hell of a pace, so it would nae surprise anybody if their ships had a few flaws. Can we bring that vessel aboard?"

"I can manoeuvre us around to bring it into the main hangar, sir."

"OK. Let's hold that in reserve. Commander Gleeson, open a channel to that ship."

Gleeson activated the comm on a longwave, short distance frequency. "Enemy attack craft. This is the UNS *New World*. We have you bang to rights – will you stand down?"

"*New World, wir geben auf.*"

"Come again?"

"He surrenders," Baines elucidated. She opened an internal comm channel. "Dr Klaus Fischer to the main hangar immediately, please. Dr Fischer to the main hangar." She closed the channel. "Looks like we're going to need a reliable interpreter, gents. I wonder who that guy is?"

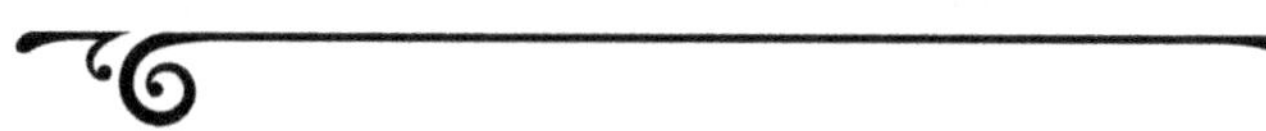

A young man of twenty-two years clicked his heels in salute. He wore the uniform of a *Leutnant,* the lowest rank of Lieutenant in the German *Luftwaffe*. "I am *Leutnant* Erich Hartmann, sir." He spoke with heavily accented English.

"We intercepted some of your radio chatter," replied Meritus. "Your pilots called you *Bubi*. Is that your call sign, *Leutnant?*"

The young man frowned slightly, so Fischer translated into German. His expression cleared as he turned back to Meritus. "A nickname, sir. It means 'the kid'." In German, he asked Fischer if Meritus had been the pilot who followed him through the exploded ice debris.

Meritus, who had a tolerable command of the German language, replied for himself. "I was."

The young man bowed. "You fly well, sir. And I thank you for your rescue of my, er... *gestrandet Piloten.*"

"Stranded pilots," Fischer supplied the translation.

"I understood, Doctor, thank you." He turned back to Hartmann. "I was lucky. You, on the other hand, fly like no one I've ever seen. Had your ship not developed problems, I doubt we'd have taken you – not alive, at least. Please excuse us a moment, *Leutnant.*" Meritus took Douglas aside. "My God, James, I think I know who this man is – or at least who he was in our timeline – and I bet you do, too. You were a fighter jock in your younger days, weren't you?"

"Aye, long time ago. Who do you think he is?"

"Erich Alfred Hartmann was the most decorated and revered fighter pilot in our history. He was also none other than the fourth-great-granduncle of my friend Captain Aurick Hartmann of the *Sabre.*"

Douglas' eyes widened in surprise. "Of course, now I remember the name. He was awarded the Knight's Cross of the Iron Cross with Oak Leaves, Swords *and* Diamonds in 1944 for 301 aerial victories. In fighter command, we all knew his name and reputation. He won Germany's highest military decoration at the time. You say he's an ancestor of the Hartmann you knew?"

"Aurick was immensely proud of that fact, James. If you recall, he was murdered by Captain Emilia Franke who used to command the *Heydrich* – the ship that seems to have caught fire down on the planet."

"Ah remember. She tried to pin his murder on ye, did she no'? And was later killed by Del Bond in the destruction of the *Sabre.*"

"So we believe. James, this is remarkable."

Douglas scratched his chin as he scrutinised the young German officer they had just captured. "Aye, Ah cannae deny that. It certainly gives my 'fixed point' theory wings, too."

"What's that?"

"Oh, nothing really. Ah wish Satnam Patel were here to explain things better. It's just an idea Ah had, that some things in history, along with some people, are unchanging. Ah believe ma friend Captain Arnold Bessel to be one. Perhaps this young fellow is another, and also destined to be exactly who he is, whatever the timeline. As Ah recall, he was incarcerated by the Russians after the Second World War for war crimes to which he would never admit."

"That's right. The Chief Military Prosecutor in Moscow acquitted Hartmann of all historical charges against him in Russian law, after the dissolution of the Soviet Union. The government agency even went so far as to *admit* that he had been wrongly convicted – hard to believe,

I know, but that was during Moscow's brief brush with democracy. James, many of us joined Schultz's armada because we saw it as the only way to save at least some of the human race. Aurick Hartmann was a good man. Maybe this young officer is, too."

"That remains to be seen. He did try to destroy us, Tobias."

"Very true, but I wonder if he knows why?"

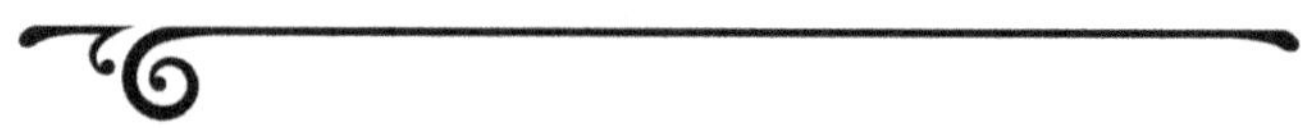

Jansen drove the APC over the lowered drawbridge and was met by soldiers at the ruined gates. He popped the vehicle's top hatch and called down to them. "I have Chief Engineer Todt and the surviving members of his survey team on board. Let us pass."

"Sir, before you do," one of the men replied, "can you pull the drawbridge back up? We're exposed, sir. The animals won't be spooked for long, especially when the smoke's cleared and they smell dead bodies, sir."

"Good point." Jansen exited the vehicle via the rear hatch and opened a storage locker in its outer hull. He pulled a set of chains from the holdout and passed them to the guards. They hooked them through hoops bolted into the girders that formed the drawbridge's sides. They connected the other end to a hitch on the APC's rear.

The soldiers ran alongside the vehicle to get clear. "Pull!" their leader hollered.

Jansen restarted the engine, selected drive, and pulled forward gently. As he felt the chains grow taut, he poured on the power. The tracks skipped and skidded, while the drawbridge hopped a couple of times, but remained resolutely down, its hinging mechanism deformed from the earlier impact.

Jansen popped the hatch again. "She's not heavy enough. I can't get enough traction to put the power down. Get someone to bring one of those tanks over."

Two men ran to oblige and soon returned with a massive new Tiger XII main battle tank. Despite the trundle of its immense weight, its electric motors were almost silent. It was a terrifying machine – a realisation not lost on Jansen, as it squared up right before him and his lightly armoured personnel carrier. Troops on the ground linked the tank to Jansen's APC with heavy chains. Without warning, the larger war machine began to reverse, pulling Jansen and the drawbridge with it. He quickly threw his vehicle into drive to regain some control, along with a little dignity, as the APC was dragged from the caged gateway, pulling the drawbridge back up behind it. As both vehicles came to a stop, he jumped out of the hatch. "Corporal, get some engineers to work on those hydraulics, right away."

"Yes, sir."

"Jansen! What the hell is going on?"

He recognised that voice, though it had not spoken to him directly in months. "Dr Schultz," he greeted unemotionally.

Heidi stormed towards him, seemingly speechless as she gestured towards the flaming *Heydrich* and their heavily damaged gateway. "Why is there no fire suppression?"

"I don't know, perhaps the soundwave extinguishing equipment was hit in the attack?" he replied coldly. "I can't hear it, can you? It will obviously take them time to bring all that under control by traditional means. I was rescuing Chief Engineer Todt from the dinosaurs while it happened – where were *you* while our compound was under attack?"

Heidi's eyes narrowed. "I was in a meeting with our senior scientist. I left Lieutenant Devon in charge of apprehending the escaped prisoners. Were they responsible for this?"

Jansen stared dolefully into the flames belching from the *Heydrich*'s main hangar. "I don't know, but if Devon was in there..."

"Never mind that now."

Jansen noted her callousness but pushed it aside – there was a crisis to deal with. "The guards on the gate said a tank was stolen. That would explain the destruction. Should we send a battle group to run them down?"

Heidi pondered for a second only. "No. That does not matter now. We need our forces here. This situation has only reinforced my decision to accelerate our plans."

"And what plans would those be, ma'am? Ever since you abandoned me, after we stole those dinosaur eggs, I've been left out of the loop."

She scrutinised him. "I did not abandon you, Ben."

"The hell you didn't!" he replied emotionally and hating himself for it.

"I looked for you, but had only limited time before the embryos within the eggs we stole lost viability. I sent rescue as soon as we picked up your SOS."

"While *you* were already in Munich," he accused.

"Of course. Had you been lost, I would not have allowed your sacrifice to be in vain."

"Noble," he stated, his voice raw from months of suppressed bitterness. He gestured at the debris around them. "So what do you suggest we do about all this?"

"We clear up the mess and continue to work. We are very close to our goals. I will not allow Douglas' fools to interfere again—"

"Douglas?" he interrupted. "What does he have to do with this?"

"We have engaged military craft in orbit around the moon. Who else would it be?"

Jansen's jaw dropped. "When did this happen?"

"Surely, you saw our ships lift off, earlier? None have returned and we have lost contact. Douglas must have come armed, for we sent our very best pilots – including Erich Hartmann. They should easily have dealt with such a rabble."

"Any relative of Captain Aurick Hartmann?" he asked, not expecting a serious answer.

"Yes."

Again, Jansen was agog. "Small world, erm... *worlds.*"

"Indeed. Unfortunately, we are not yet ready to leave this one. We must hold this position for the next three days – two, at least – in order for One, that is, Dr Reid, to finish his work. Do you understand? *Whatever* the cost."

Jansen nodded. He understood alright. That cost would be high, but as always, neither Heidi nor her grandfather would be the ones who had to meet it. "Have we lost our link with Munich?"

"*Nein.* It would take an explosion great enough to rip this very continent apart to break *that* connection, Ben. Do not worry."

"I'll try not to." He kept his tone level. *She is completely insane. Devon was right, we should just shoot her.* He looked to the smoke billowing from the ship. At least the main conflagration seemed to be out at last. *I hope he's still alive.*

"Ben."

Jansen turned at the use of his name, surprised to find Heidi still standing close to him. Her face showed indecision. Eventually, she simply said, "Be ready to leave soon."

"Leave? To go where?"

"I will return." With that, she strode away, leaving him baffled and with conflicting emotions.

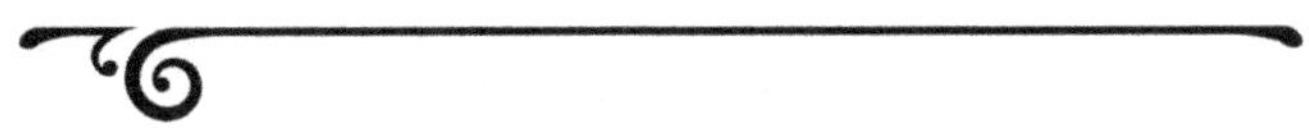

Douglas mused over Meritus' question. "Very well, you can give him and the other pilot the back-story. Let me know how they respond. Assign them temporary accommodation, too – secure quarters, naturally, but treat them well." He blew out his cheeks. "Somehow, we'll have to figure out a way to get them home. Ah dinnae want to take them with us unless there's absolutely no choice. They belong in the 1940s, with their families."

"Of course, James. I'll get right on it—" Meritus broke off as they found themselves in sudden, complete blackness. A moment later, emergency lighting sprang to life, leaving everyone looking around, confused. "What just happened?"

Douglas shook his head and pulled out his comm. "Ah dinnae have the vaguest. Looks like internal communications are down, too." He switched his device to radio. "Bridge? This is Douglas – report."

"*We've lost main power – everything!*" Baines answered. "*Sandy is on a radio call with Hiro. They're trying to work out what's going on. James, we've got it covered up here. Suggest you go to main engineering.*"

"On ma way – Douglas out." He pointed to the enemy pilots. "Tobias, keep them secure. Ah'll be in touch when Ah know anything."

Hiro was very upset. He and Georgio were screaming a mixed bag of encouragement, commiserations and reprimands at one another, all across main engineering. "It's-a not-a my fault! I told you our security was under par. You said – and I quote – there would be no one there to understand this coding, not the Schultzes, not the dinosaurs, not anyone – you said!"

"This has nothing to do with security. It's a power issue. Don't blame yourself."

Georgio almost burst. "Blame *myself?*"

"Yes. We've been in tight spots before. You've always come through for me."

"Well, now you come to mention it, I did learn from the best – hey, just a minute. This is not-a my fault!"

"Will someone tell me what the hell has happened to ma ship!" Douglas bellowed from the entrance.

"A fault with main power, sir."

"We've been hacked, sir."

Douglas looked from one to the other. "Which is it, gentlemen?"

"It's not clear, Captain," Hiro reported, a little more calmly. "What is clear, however, is that our orbit is decaying."

Douglas leaned back in a gesture of total disbelief. "No, no, no. Ye see, Ah've already seen this movie. Tell me we're no' about to crash – again."

His comm beeped to life with a call from the bridge. "*James, we're losing altitude.*"

"I know, Jill. Dinnae crash ma ship!"

"*No, sir! Should I get out and paddle?*"

Douglas rounded on his chief engineer. "Hiro! What can we do about this?"

"Hang on a minute, all of you. Let me think. OK. We *are* losing altitude due to gravity – no surprise – but the moon's gravity is weak. It will have completed a half-spin – and subsequently half-orbit around the Earth by the time we... erm."

"Ah dinnae want tae hear the word crash, Chief."

"Right... er, well, we'll be on the daylight side of the moon when... I mean, our orbit will have slowed without motorised control and adjustment."

Douglas placed a hand over his eyes. "We'll be over the daylight side of the moon when what, Chief?"

"You said you didn't want to know, sir."

"Hiro!"

"Don't worry, Captain," Georgio came to his friend's rescue. "We have twelve hours before we... before we'll be in any trouble."

Douglas groaned. "We havenae even paid for this thing yet. The paint's no' dry!"

"I'm sure it's a security issue, sir," Georgio tried again. "Look at this."

The three men grouped around his station. "This is the new operating system," the Italian continued. "Now, look here."

Hiro leaned forward. "Why is the code hidden?"

"Exactly."

"Exactly what?" asked Douglas. "Ah can see the code."

"No, you can't," Hiro replied thoughtfully. "At least, you can only see some of it. Where is—"

"I know," Georgio cut him off. "And look what's missing from the—"

"They've been removed!" Hiro pre-empted, becoming more rattled. "And all of the—"

"All gone, I know—"

"Gentlemen!" Douglas felt the need to interrupt. "Will someone tell me what's happened to ma ship?"

"We've been hacked, sir," they replied together.

"Finally, consensus. Now what do ye suggest we do about it?"

The engineers looked at one another. "The safety protocol?" suggested Georgio, doubtfully.

Hiro shook his head. "Whoever did this will simply do it again, and we'll have tipped our hand."

"What's the safety protocol?" asked Douglas.

Hiro took a breath. "Captain, if you remember the last time we were about to crash into a planet—"

"Oh, aye, funnily enough, it's all coming back tae me. Go on, Chief."

"Well, the reason we were in so much trouble was because our ship, the old *New World,* couldn't fly or even function due to a small program that kept hijacking our navigational controls."

"Ah remember it well. Our only recourse was to reset the whole operating system to factory settings. But she was a much older vessel with who knew how many fixes and adaptions – this bird's all new. Surely we can reset her without too much loss?"

"Indeed, Captain. That's not the problem."

"So what *is* the problem?"

"I've programmed a secret safety protocol into this ship's OS, where it backs up every single change automatically and can revert to any point in the past, thereafter. I didn't ever want to lose my system and have to rely on factory settings again. Georgio and I are the only ones who knew about this protocol. We didn't even let the people at UNASA know what we were working on."

"So we can put everything back," Douglas tried again. "That's good, yes?"

Hiro and Georgio looked at one another.

"*Laddies,*" Douglas' temper was fraying.

"Yes, sir. It's good," replied Hiro.

"But you haven't told him what's bad," muttered Georgio.

"I'm getting to it! What's bad, sir, is that whoever did this might simply do it again. And if we bring our safety protocol into effect—"

"They might sabotage that, too," Douglas completed, catching up. He ran his fingers through his hair in frustration. "So we're crashing again. This time *with* a fully operational OS that we cannae use. Fantastic. Do ye have any good news?"

"We're going to crash on the moon, rather than Earth?" Hiro suggested hopefully.

"That's the *good* news?"

"At least we won't risk burning up in the atmosphere, this time, Captain," Georgio tried to help his friend out again.

"And at one-sixth gravity, there should be far less damage," added Hiro.

"Good. That's good," Douglas replied pleasantly. "Just one small point. Hardly like to mention it really."

"Sir?"

"We cannae live on the moon!"

"Which is why," Hiro rallied as inspiration struck, "we must find the saboteur before that happens, sir."

Douglas stared at him. Without answering, he opened a channel to the bridge. "Jill, start putting together a list of anyone on board who might like to see us crash into the moon. One name springs to my mind. While you get on with that, ask Sandy to check for any unauthorised computer access anywhere on the ship. And when he's done *that,* tell him we might need a soft place to... land gently, like a leaf on a pond. Did he no' mention an almost flat basin left behind by a lava lake? Somewhere near Mons Huygens, Ah think?"

"*In the Imbrium Basin. Yes, James, I know it.*"

"Very well, everyone," Douglas continued. "Keep this quiet. We're just having a few technical difficulties with the new systems, OK? And remember, people, Heidi must know we're here now, so we need to get this sorted quickly, before she sends another attack wave at us."

"*Do you think she can?*" asked Baines.

"She's Heidi. Who knows what she can do?"

"*OK. What are we going to do?*"

"Aye, about that – Ah've got an idea."

Chapter 10 | Time Bomb

After the night from hell, Sergeant Adam Prentice, Corporal Heinz Engel and their troops were in poor condition to enter a potential warzone. After cleaning themselves up, they had sealed the hatches and attempted to rest. Prentice slept badly, his mind fixating on what he knew must come next.

With the morning sun came the grisly duty of collecting what remained of Private Walker. It had simply been too dangerous to attempt in the dark and with a hunting pack of apex predators in the area. As the youngest, Private Mark Radburn felt the need to keep a stiff upper lip most keenly, though his was a shocking introduction to the perils of service.

"You alright, lad?" Prentice asked kindly, interrupting his gloom.

"Yes, Sarge." The young man's voice stuttered slightly, as though his breath were being taken away. He watched as stoically as he could, while the body bag was zip-sealed and carried onto their ship.

"You did well, son. Really. That thing would have killed me last night, if you hadn't shown up when you did." The stunned Carcharodontosaurus was nowhere to be found by morning. Prentice naturally assumed the effects of the stun blasts had worn off. "Now I need you to do an important job for me. I want you to check the ship's camera logs to find out how long the dinosaur stayed down. That's crucial info."

Pride lit the young soldier's face, driving away some of the pain. "Yes, Sarge."

Prentice smiled, though his eyes still bore sadness. "Aye, lad. Come on. You look at that, while I see what our little spy recorded overnight."

"Will we be in trouble for not making it to the enemy camp this morning, Sarge?"

"No, Mark. Sometimes in the field things just happen that are beyond your control. Captain Douglas will know something kept us back, but we can't break radio silence until ordered to do so. *So*, until we receive further instructions, we'll watch, we'll pay attention, and we'll look for opportunities. Got it?"

"Yes, Sarge."

"We're almost ready for a live test, Commander." Dr Bismarck gave Commander Ally Coleman a walk around the new device. It had taken them months, working in secret.

"It's big," Coleman stated, wryly. "What do we call it, the wormhole catcher?"

Bismarck chuckled politely. "Yes, I like that."

"And how are repairs to the *Newfoundland* coming?"

"Again, almost there. If we'd been allowed to call on the expertise of our friends aboard the *Heydrich* it would have gone quicker. We've struggled at times with things outside our fields, but hey, we did our best."

"Yes, you did, Harry. Thank you. I'm impressed. Perhaps now I can get Dr Hemmings to trust us with her whole plan."

"Hmm," Bismarck grunted noncommittally.

"Harry?"

"Oh, I was just wondering whether we really want to know." He smiled disarmingly, but she could tell his point was sincere. If truth be told, she felt the same.

"I can't believe Heidi has left us alone all these months. She must be up to something big, if she—" A beep from her comm interrupted them. "Coleman."

"Commander, we have a ship incoming. It's one of ours, a small orbital attack craft. The IFF is good, but its serial number isn't recognised by our systems. Could be a new ship, ma'am."

Coleman and Bismarck shared a glance. Coleman muted the comm. "Speak of the devil..." She reactivated the channel. "Must be. OK, Lieutenant, assign them a landing berth in the south compound. I'll go and greet them. Send an armed guard to join me there, just in case – Coleman out."

Bismarck raised an eyebrow. "What do you think this will be?"

"I don't know, but cover this up – all of it – with a tarp, or something. We can't risk any stories getting back. Talking of stories, do we have one to cover our extra requisitions, yet?"

After ordering his people to cover their work and power everything down, he looked suddenly uncomfortable.

"Harry?"

"Short answer, yes."

"And the long answer?"

"Yes, we have a *crap* story to cover the extra requisitions."

She snorted softly. "Needs must when the devil drives – or *flies* to your farm. I'll need you to come with me. Most importantly, don't forget, we know nothing of the wormhole to 1940s Munich. If Heidi finds out Hemmings told us, we'll all... well, actually I don't know what she'll do."

"Got it. No problem, Ally."

"I know *you've* got it, Harry. Just make sure that idiot, Brian Alba, gets it, too. Or believe you me, he certainly will get it!"

Bismarck chuckled again. "After you, Commander."

They shielded their eyes against the sand blown by the little craft's landing thrusters. Eventually, the engines died, the noise abated, and the dust devils dissolved, falling back to Earth. A hatch opened in the side of the ship and Coleman's heart sank a little further.

She stepped forward to offer an erect military salute and greeting, nonetheless. "Dr Schultz, welcome. It's been a while. You remember Dr Harry Bismarck?"

"Commander. Doctor," Heidi greeted in return, glancing around at the farmlands that now climbed up from the beach all the way into the foothills. "I can see you have been busy – fields all sown for the next season. I commend your industry."

"Thank you, ma'am. We were surprised when you didn't send the *Heydrich* to collect your share of last year's crop. Is all well in Egypt?"

"Well enough," Heidi lied. "We have found other sources for our food and additional requirements. I assume you made adequate provision to store your surplus?"

"We did, ma'am."

"Good. Very good. In fact, one of the things I wish to know *involves* your requirements and surpluses, Commander."

"Doctor?" Coleman played dumb. It was unlikely to fool anyone, but she would be damned if she would *give* anything away.

"You have consistently ordered certain materials in quantities well outside the remit of your repairs to the *Newfoundland*. Such materials as copper. Despite the antiquated nature of NASA's core computers, most of the high-performance data networking for these ships nevertheless uses optical fibre connections. I understand you've even ordered significant quantities of tetrafluoroethane. Now, what in the world could you possibly want with that? Please explain."

"Commander, if I may," Bismarck dove heroically into the fray. "We have a requirement for large scale refrigeration, Doctor. A need that became ever more pressing when you failed to collect your half of the harvest. I'm sure you understand."

"*Are* you?" Heidi spoke slowly as she scrutinised him, weighing the truth of his words.

"Indeed, ma'am," he continued, beginning to feel uncomfortable under the Schultz stare. "We're using the copper for piping and the Tetrafluoroethane as coolant gas. Simple."

"Really. So if I were to inspect your stores, I would find evidence of this, Dr Bismarck?"

"You would, ma'am. Although it's in the very early stages as we've been focused on fulfilling your orders to fix the ship."

She eyed him, catlike, once more. "If what you say is correct and your refrigeration system remains incomplete, how have you stored all the surplus crops so diligently?"

"By vacuum sealing, ma'am. Not a long-term solution, I'm sure you'll agree."

Heidi merely stared.

"Erm, perhaps," he conceded. "The power consumption is high to remove air from part of the Rescue Pod's storage facilities, and it places added stresses on a structure that has already taken several beatings. Were it not designed for space, we might not have been able to save as much as we have. You see, it would have been ideal for us to simply bury certain harvested crops, such as the grain the *New World* people planted before they left. Once in the ground, the outer layers would have rotted down, using up the oxygen present, thus sealing the rest and preserving it, but unfortunately, we couldn't do that."

"Why not?" Heidi challenged. "Such storage techniques have been used successfully since the Bronze Age. I know I took the best and the brightest with me aboard *Heydrich,* but surely you could have managed that?"

Slighted, Bismarck struggled to keep the annoyance from his face. "Yes, ma'am, but the, erm... *birds* are rather bigger here, and they have a remarkable facility for digging with those vast beaks."

She eyed him sideways. "Very well, continue."

"Well, that's pretty much it, ma'am. By next season, we should have our refrigeration system in place as we're almost finished with the repairs you ordered to the ship, like I said. We had some considerable trouble with the damaged thrusters. In fact, we rebuilt one of them from scratch. And as for the lower of the four main rocket engines, that was a right ba— erm... bad job, ma'am."

In his nervousness, he was beginning to ramble, and Coleman was tempted, *so* tempted, to order her guards to simply gun Heidi down. That would end all their problems – perhaps everyone's problems – but firstly, she was not absolutely sure they would obey, which would only result in her own death instead; and secondly, she had a duty to her people, to give them the best possible chance to live and build a home in this place. If they removed Heidi, they might expect an overwhelming attack from the Heydrich to follow on swift wings. Bismarck had stuck his neck out bravely but was beginning to quail under scrutiny. Before he tripped himself up, she had to do something to deflect Heidi's questions. "We do have a small confession, ma'am."

Heidi released Bismarck from her gaze to focus on Coleman. "Oh? Do tell."

"We added the extras to our requisitions surreptitiously because we didn't want to see half the crop go to waste – just in case we needed them. There are so many unknowns in this new and dangerous world and we were unsure..." She tailed off theatrically.

"Unsure of what, Commander?"

"Unsure whether you would have complied with our requisitions for a non-military project like crop storage. We were concerned about food shortages all round, you see? For *all* our people."

Heidi clapped her hands foppishly, releasing a short bark of laughter. "Relax, Commander, Dr Bismarck. You seem to have exceeded all expectation. I can see I did well to leave Crater Lake Base in your hands, Commander. Excellent. Now, on to the second reason for my visit. I wish to know the exact coordinates, including altitude, for the *New World*'s last known location before they entered their wormhole last autumn. I remember they flew across the lake, but I was rather busy evading a predatory dinosaur at the time."

"Sigilmassasaurus," Coleman and Bismarck stated together.

Heidi raised an amused eyebrow. "You have seen it since."

"Yes," they answered in tandem once more, and with equal bitterness.

Heidi smiled. "Do I infer from your reaction, and from the awkward way you are holding yourself, Commander, that there will be some interesting tales to come from the farm? You have been injured, yes? I look forward to hearing them, but another time perhaps. Commander, the coordinates, please. I must move quickly now."

Twenty minutes later, Coleman and Bismarck stood in one of the *Newfoundland*'s observation lounges looking northeast, over Crater Lake. "Well done, Harry," Coleman congratulated. "You were great."

"I was full of it! I hope things go to plan now. I'd hate to have to explain myself next season."

Coleman laughed. "How are we really using all that copper and coolant gas?"

"We're building a machine that creates a massive magnetic field. Passing electricity through copper coils is the quickest, dirtiest, easiest way of achieving that. If we went for a more modern, high-tech approach, that would really have raised some eyebrows over there – the very thing you wished to avoid, if I remember correctly."

"True. And the gas?"

"We're simply using it as a shielding gas, to protect the welds within the machine's delicate interior from the corrosive effects of oxygen, nitrogen and hydrogen in the atmosphere – improving the purity and quality of the weld. Again, relatively low tech and just about plausible for building a massive fridge."

"Simply, you say? Well, for now at least, you've certainly saved our bacon."

"*Oh,* don't do it."

"Do what?"

"Use the 'b' word. Everything here tastes like chicken – even the damned crocodiles! What I wouldn't give for a few slices of pig."

"There's always fish..."

"What? With no potatoes for chips?"

"We have potatoes."

Bismarck pulled a face. "Not good ones. I've got someone working on it, to improve the genetics of next year's yield. Most of the seed stocks aboard the *New World* left with them. We only have what we have," he added regretfully.

Coleman smiled and then pointed out across the lake. "Look. There she goes."

Bismarck squinted. "What the hell is she up to?"

"I don't know. She's barely moving. Those must be the coordinates she was after. How odd. Do you think she— *Whoa!*"

Heidi's orbital attack craft vanished into nothingness, leaving them gawking.

An old man placed the reins loosely in the hands of a stable boy, who led his stallion away to be made comfortable for the night. He expected a welcome party and sure enough, a man in his sixties, another in his late forties and a woman in her mid-forties were indeed making their way across the hangar towards him. He made to close the gap between them, when they suddenly vanished behind the bow of a vessel. They all cried out in alarm.

The lorry was old. An eight-wheeled, thirty-two-ton beast. Having seen much service both in prehistoric Patagonia and 16th century Britain, its paint was worn – where it remained at all – particularly around the load areas, where its high-sided tipper back began to crumple, seemingly without cause. Soon, the whole vehicle was being shoved across the scuffed and scarred hangar floor, squeaking and screeching in its displacement.

Conversely, the ship that appeared in its space was brand new, and as she had not yet returned home, was technically still on her maiden voyage. She would make many subsequent journeys, but none would ever take her home. The prow of the small orbital attack craft kept on shoving into the lorry's side until she was fully revealed; a warship, built for toughness and durability. The collision was more shunt than crash, and it proceeded with surreal slowness – an effect exacerbated by the ship's appearance out of thin air.

Now entire, the portal that birthed the vessel twisted the light around itself with an eldritch shimmer and was gone.

The old man stared in disbelief. Stumbling forward, he muttered, "Douglas?"

A hatch opened with a hiss and his jaw dropped. He could not have been more wrong. His old eyes narrowed. "*Heidi.*" Her name left his possession like a curse, but there she was – young and beautiful as ever.

Six hours earlier, Egypt
"Dr Reid, I must speak with you immediately."

The scientist looked up in surprise. "Dr Schultz. I didn't expect to see you again today, given our situation."

"I understand how busy you are, but I need one of our orbital attack ships, right now," she demanded.

He blinked. "I'm sure we could make one available, ma'am, though they've not been tested in vacuum yet. Hence, we sent only the five up earlier—"

"That does not concern me. I need to fly to Britain. Can one be made ready to get me that far?"

"Certainly, ma'am. What equipment will you need, if any?"

"I will need some of the special ordnance from the ship you are building for me. Just one will do."

Reid's eyebrows shot up in astonishment. "You're going to destroy our base at Crater Lake?"

"*Nein.* Nothing like that. Douglas is here and has superior technology from the future. I do not know the full extent of his plans, but must assume he wishes to destroy all we have built here. And his latest incursion into the Cretaceous may be just the tip of the spear. Were he to bring reinforcements from 2122, it would be difficult to see how we could possibly stand against them. I intend to take that option away from him."

"Might I ask how, ma'am?"

She smiled coolly. "Let us just say that I have seen the future, and it is far more advanced than I can allow."

"But, ma'am, if you change the future, well... what about our situation here? We might lose our connection to Munich."

"I do not believe that likely, Doctor. My actions will simply restore the timeline. We will still receive the help we require from 1944. *We* are the brains, after all – the Germans are merely our resource. Besides, with my fourth-great-grandaunt in the wind, and only those fools out there to catch her, our current plans in Munich may be in danger of going awry anyway."

"Isn't your grandfather still there?" Reid was wringing his hands and beginning to perspire. He had barely gotten used to the new order of things and now Heidi was talking about shaking up the bottle all over again.

"He is," she replied simply. "And so he shall remain, whatever the outcome. Make my ship ready, Doctor. I wish to leave for Britain within the hour."

"Why Britain?" Reid asked, perplexed, and before he could think better of it.

"Just get my ship ready and all will be well." With that, she strode out of his office. Once outside, she found an open space away from the buildings and any trafficways. Taking a metal rod from her vest pocket, she held it perpendicular to a slab of bedrock. A small explosive cap fired its tip into the stone. Her route home secured, she went to collect a few provisions.

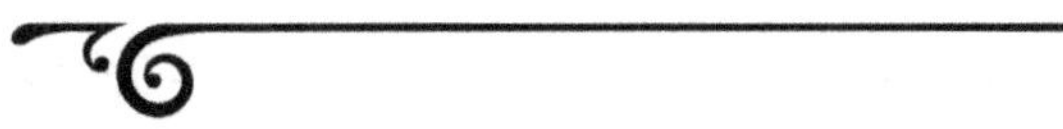

Six hours later, Great Cheviot Mountain, Britain
Heidi stepped from the ship's hatch to look the old man up and down. She frowned, uncertain. "Geoffrey Lloyd?"

He closed his gaping mouth and nodded, dumbly.

"I see you have lost your hair."

He bridled; he had always been good at that. "I'm eighty-three, young lady!"

She sneered. "Are you wearing *tights?*"

He opened his mouth to remonstrate, but could only mumble something about the style of the times.

"And the doublet with slashed sleeves – not to mention the bejewelled codpiece – you wear *those* too, to appear fashionable?" She gave a girlish laugh.

"Well, I can hardly pop along to the Elizabethan court in a pair of khaki shorts and a baseball cap, can I?" Lloyd recovered himself and his usual asperity.

Heidi had not expected to be entertained by her short visit to the future, but she continued to laugh until another two men appeared from around the aft end of her ship. The elder pulled a pistol from a holster at the hip. "Heidi Schultz!" Major Ford White also could not believe his eyes.

"No way," muttered Henry Burnstein, skidding to a halt, his mind pinwheeling, too.

"What's going on?" asked a female voice with a Surrey accent. A woman in her mid-forties squeezed between the prow of the little ship and the shunted lorry.

Heidi spun on her heel, quick as sight, to grab the newcomer around the neck, a nine-millimetre pistol appearing in her hand like an illusionist's trick. "Rose Miller, I presume? Still beautiful. The years have been kind."

"With my mother gone, there were a lot more beauty products to go round," Rose quipped, thinking quickly. Looking to create a diversion, she gambled Heidi needed her as a hostage and so risked elbowing her in the ribs.

As Rose made to pull away, Heidi exhaled with the blow and tightened her grip still further. "Do not try that again, young lady—"

"I'm forty-six!"

"Why does everyone seem to believe I would care to know their age? Now be silent, or I will spread your pretty little brains all over the side of my shiny new ship. You may remember, Major White, that I had no compunction about using one of my own men to make a similar demonstration in this very hangar, just last year."

White swallowed. "That was thirty years ago – for us, at least – but I certainly remember it like it was last year. What do you want?"

"Firstly, drop your weapon to the deck – or I will be forced to drop my hostage to the deck."

Henry and White shared a glance. "OK. You got it," White answered, placing his weapon carefully, near his feet.

"Nice try, Major, and I love the holster, by the way – very 'cowboy'. Now, kick the weapon over here. I would hate for you to stumble and accidentally pick it back up. That would necessitate your death, also."

White muttered under his breath, but did as instructed.

Heidi bent to pick up the second gun, almost strangling Rose as she did so. She secreted White's weapon within her jacket and returned the muzzle of her own to Rose's temple. "Now we have that out of the way, open the hangar doors."

The three men looked at one another in surprise. Lloyd spoke first. "Just where do you think you're going to go out there? What are you up to, Heidi?"

"Let us just say, I am here to clear up a mess."

"And you're going to leave your ship, everything, here with us?" asked White, dubiously.

"I am." A thought struck Heidi. It would make no difference, given her plans, but she was in the mood for sport. "In fact, I also have another gift for you. I did not require lunch in the end, so please do help yourselves to my turkey salad sandwiches. It may amuse you to learn that, though they have travelled almost a hundred million years, they were freshly prepared only this morning... in the kitchens of the Brown House, Nazi Main Headquarters, Munich, 1944." It was a lie, but it elicited the desired response. She smiled cruelly, while the men gawked stupidly. Hope seemed to die in the major's eyes as he processed her meaning. It was delicious, but she wanted to make sure they all understood the depths of their failure. "If you know your history, you will realise that this was some nine months *after* the Allied bombing."

"Why did the Allies want to bomb your sandwiches?" Rose asked through gritted teeth as she tried to relieve the pressure about her neck.

Heidi glanced at her with disdain bordering on disgust before returning her attention to Lloyd. "The bombing never took place, the Allies mounting no serious threat. Your efforts have changed the future forever, and for the better. My compliments." She offered an abbreviated bow, then gestured sharply with her pistol. "The hangar door – *now!*"

"Alright, I'm on it," Henry placated. "Just, please, don't hurt her. OK?"

"You care for this one?" Heidi asked, mildly interested. "I always thought you would end up with my cousin, Rose Miller. However, I suppose living more than five centuries apart would place a strain on *any* relationship."

"Actually, it's Rose Burnstein, but *you* can call me *Mrs* Burnstein – married by Archbishop Matthew Parker himself, in fact." Rose was still hoping to distract her captor. "You see, it's all about *knowing* the right people, rather than killing them!"

"Your cousin?" Lloyd blurted, his suspicious mind finally catching up. "What are you talking about, Heidi?"

"Tim Norris. He is my first cousin. I am sorry." Heidi looked nothing of the sort. "Did my dear cousin not tell any of you? And you, *Mrs* Burnstein – you did not tell anyone, either?"

"Some of us knew," White admitted. "So if you think you can lay any bombshells on us, you can't."

Heidi smiled again, this time secretively, as the huge hangar doors began to part behind her. "Of course. Never mind. I will just leave you with the sandwiches then, Major. Enjoy the goodness. Fresh from the *Reich.*"

White glowered, tormented by how they might have failed to make the future right.

"The girl comes with me." Matching action to words, Heidi backed towards the opening hatch. Cold, fresh air filled their metal-ceramic enclosure. "It appears to be a crisp evening. Clean and new. This is good. An auspicious beginning for the next stage of my journey."

She stepped outside into a cutting through the hill. The trackway had obviously been paved long ago with local flagstone, well weathered. The three men followed as Heidi dragged Rose up the gentle slope. The sky opened out before them as they neared the opening, already black in the east, fading to a deep blue in the west. The sun had barely set, leaving a brilliance of stars in its wake, and under them a dusting of early snow twinkled on the highest hilltops. "A very scenic home you have made for yourselves, here, gentlemen. I am almost sorry to leave it, but things to do, places to be – you understand.”

“Stand and be recognised!” a man bellowed roughly from behind her, in a thick Scottish accent.

“Stand down, Billy,” Lloyd called out. “’Tis but I, John.”

Heidi stared at Geoff Lloyd in astonishment. “John?”

“A story for another time, Heidi, don’t you think? Now, how do you see this ending? My friend and colleague, Captain Billy Maxwell and his men, here, have their muskets trained on you.”

“It is very simple, *John*. You will all turn your backs, or I will kill the gir— woman. Understand?” She pressed the muzzle hard into Rose’s temple, making her cry out.

“Don’t hurt her!” Henry made to move forward, but Major White grabbed his arm.

“Your wife will be quite safe *if* you do as I say – safe for a little while, at least. Now, turn around, gentlemen. *All* of you.”

“Henry...” Rose pleaded with her husband.

Henry swallowed nervously, but turned his back as ordered.

“Turn your backs, gentlemen,” Lloyd called out for the guards’ benefit – a mix of English and Scots. Once everyone had complied, he turned himself. “OK, Heidi, we’ve all turned around. What party trick do you have planned for us next...? Heidi?”

He spun round to find Rose on the ground, seemingly unconscious. “She’s gone! Billy, search the hills – she can’t have got far. Tell your men to search in pairs and have a care. That woman is the most dangerous creature under God’s great sky. If they see her – shoot her!”

“Aye, sir.” Billy touched his cap and bellowed at his men to comb the heather.

“Rose!” Henry darted forward, but Rose was already coming round – and she woke up angry.

“That bitch! She clubbed me.”

“Where is she?” snapped Lloyd, spinning around, searching the darkness, anxiously.

No one had any answers, and within minutes Billy Maxwell’s guards returned, also empty-handed.

“What the hell is going on here?” Lloyd growled.

“Nothing good,” replied White. “No way that... that *woman* just dropped by to deliver a sandwich. Not to mention she left her ship behind.”

"Her ship..." Lloyd repeated, thoughtfully.

White caught on immediately. "She said Rose would be quite safe – for a *while*. Everyone, quick!"

Rose got crossly to her feet and ran after him, with Henry after her.

"Wait for me," Lloyd shouted after them all. "I'm eighty-three, you know!"

"We *know*, Geoff. Get a shake on!" White roared over his shoulder, already at full tilt.

Presently, they arrived back at Heidi's crashed ship. White jumped straight in through the hatch and pulled up short. "Oh, my God." He stuck his head back outside in time to see Geoff Lloyd puff and chuff his way over to them.

"I'm an old man," he complained.

White eyed him coldly. "Yeah, I guess these pesky terrorist reunions must take their toll at your age."

"I'm eighty-*three*," Lloyd wheezed.

"Never mind all that," White snapped. "Come and see what your old buddy has left us."

"Turkey sandwiches?"

"Geoff, will you get your head on straight? Get over here." White beckoned Lloyd inside the little ship.

"What is it she's..." Lloyd tailed off. "Oh, crap."

"What is it?" asked Rose and Henry, together.

White paled almost to his namesake. "It's a bomb."

On the 8th of August AD1588, Queen Elizabeth I made her famous speech at Tilbury. The English were braced for invasion, awaiting the now-famously powerful Spanish Armada. Almost thirty years after her accession to the throne of England, Elizabeth's rule was still threatened by the great Catholic powers of Europe – specifically Phillip II of Spain and the Duke of Parma, Alessandro Farnese, an Italian nobleman in service to Spain. Her words were destined to echo down the centuries, carrying with them a universal meaning and statement of defiance, long after the world should have paid heed.

"I know I have the body of a weak and feeble woman; but I have the heart and stomach of a king – and of a King of England too, and think foul scorn that Parma or Spain, or any prince of Europe, should dare to invade the borders of my realm."

1730 hours, 5th November AD1588, West of the Isle of Mull, Scotland
The eight-hundred-ton galleon, *San Juan de Sicilia,* sailed through high seas under the overall command of Diego Tellez Enríquez, but captained by Luka Ivanov Kinkovic. She followed a course west of Scotland and Ireland, out into the relative safety of the North Atlantic, but unbeknownst to her crew of sixty-two sailors and somewhere between four and five times as many soldiers, the Gulf Stream pushed her ever northwards and east, back towards the Scottish coast.

Over the past months, she and her sister ships in the Armada had been harried and savaged by man, and the elements, to the point where many of the remaining ships were held together only by cables, reinforcing their hulls. The Armada's cause was lost long ago. Now all their crews prayed for was a safe return home.

Almost a fortnight ago, the *San Juan de Sicilia*'s squadron had become scattered by poor weather. Alone, she sailed into what her senior officers believed to be safe harbour in Tobermory Bay. In exchange for essential supplies, Enríquez hired out his soldiers' bloody services to a local chieftain, Lachlan MacLean of Duart, to deal soundly with his neighbours. Unfortunately, one of the merchants offering reprovision turned out to be an agent of England's Sir Francis Walsingham – principal secretary to Queen Elizabeth I and popularly known as her 'spymaster'.

Now, two weeks later, and in deadly danger of betrayal to the English, the *San Juan de Sicilia* was forced back to sea. Once more alone in a night of gales, she was surrounded by walls of water on all sides, but far worse than those, for her hardened seamen, were the omens.

A bright light streaked across the night sky at tremendous speed, moving southeast to northwest. High above the *San Juan de Sicilia,* the unnatural light show was accompanied by such a terrific roar that the men below quaked in fear of the devil himself.

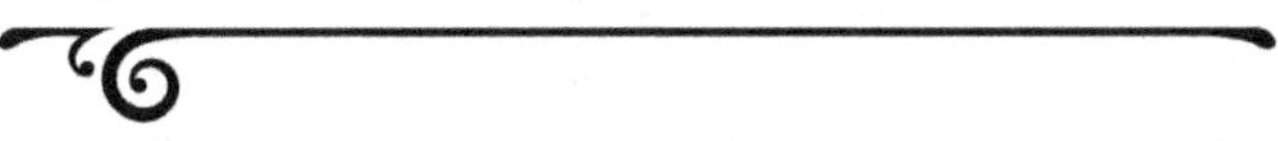

Thirty minutes earlier, Great Cheviot Mountain

Lloyd shoved his way past White in his usual brusque manner. "That's not just any bomb," he added, anxiously. "It's a tactical bloody nuke!"

"Can you disarm it?" asked Rose.

"I... I... I don't know," he admitted.

He looked to White, who could only shrug his shoulders, too. "I've no experience with nuclear ordnance. You're the engineer, Geoff."

Lloyd gently lifted the guard covering the bomb's controls. "Looks like we have thirty-five minutes, give or take, to make our minds up."

"How much damage could a bomb like this do?" Rose asked again.

Lloyd shook his head, uncertain. "I can't say exactly, but as I said, it's a small, tactical device – a city killer, rather than a weapon designed to bring down a country. Unless you happened to live in Luxembourg." He smiled weakly.

Rose did not return it. "So, if you can't deactivate it—"

"I didn't say I couldn't," Lloyd interrupted. "It's just that, if I try..."

"You might blow us all to hell," Henry completed for him.

Lloyd shook his head regretfully. "I wouldn't even give our chances as fifty-fifty. I'm sorry."

"Well, the solution is obvious, then," Rose stated.

"What did you have in mind?" asked White.

"This ship looks in good order," Rose noted. "The crash wasn't serious. We should fly it away. Well away. This vessel appears to be almost identical to the one Captain Meritus' people left us, so I assume flying it won't be a problem?"

White looked to Lloyd. "She's right. In half an hour we could easily reach a safe distance."

"Are you suggesting a suicide mission?" Lloyd stared at him in disbelief.

"Better than letting it take everybody, including the future," White answered stoically.

"If young Heidi is to be believed, the future is a bust anyway," Lloyd argued.

"What do you mean?" asked Henry.

The old man sighed, not taking his eyes from the bomb. "Weren't you listening? She said her turkey sandwiches were made in Nazi Headquarters. If Hitler's regime still comes to pass, then it must follow that we fail to change the future – at least, fail to change it enough to make a difference."

"In fact," White corrected him, "she said that the Allies never got it together, so it seems we may have made things even worse."

There was a rustling from behind them. "Hmm," said Henry. "This is good."

Lloyd spun round. "What the hell are you doing?"

Henry had his mouth full. "Iceberg and mayo. My God, I'd forgotten."

"Are you out of your mind?" Lloyd exploded.

"Are you kidding? This might be my last meal. Wanna try some?"

Lloyd's furious expression slipped a little. "Good, is it?"

"Are we going to stand around here all night eating turkey sandwiches?" Rose shouted at them. "As for a suicide mission, what a silly idea, Major, honestly."

White looked put out.

"Why don't you just take it out – I don't know – over the Atlantic, or up into space, and throw it from the hatch?"

White considered that. "Could we move it, Geoff?"

"Hmm?"

A look of annoyance flashed across White's face. "Will you two leave the sandwiches, already! Could we move this thing?"

"It'll be heavy," Lloyd replied around a mouthful of turkey and mayo.

"Surely the four of us could do it?" Rose tried again.

"Perhaps," Lloyd allowed. "We couldn't take it into orbit, though."

"No?" White queried.

Lloyd shook his head. "These ships only have two compartments, the two-man cockpit and the load bay, for matériel or personnel. If we vent atmosphere from the load bay, how are we to throw the thing out?"

"We could get suited up?" suggested White. "Low gravity would help, too, surely?"

"Yes, it would, if we had that sort of time, Major. It would take us at least half an hour just to get our spacesuits on! No. The Atlantic it is. Everyone, better get strapped in."

"Right." White stepped quickly towards the cockpit. "Geoff, with me. You've got more flight experience than any of us."

"But I'm eighty-three."

"*We know, Geoff,*" they all answered as one.

"You're also the only one of us who was trained by NASA." White tapped his wrist in mime. "Tick tock! I'll explain to the council what's happened, and what we're up to, en route. *Come on,* Geoff!"

Thirty minutes later, West of the Isle of Mull, Scotland

Several miles out to sea, the orbital attack ship streaked high above the towering seas, cruising at 30,000 feet. "It's calm enough up here, but the weather below is pretty rough," White stated from the co-pilot's seat.

"It's about to get a lot rougher," Lloyd quipped.

"Is this going to be a problem?" asked Rose from the rear.

"A bigger problem than our suicide?" Lloyd lashed out again, on a roll. "Of course it will cause problems. When was the last time you heard the words 'nuclear weapon explosion – that'll be good for the environment'?"

"Tetchy," Rose shot back.

"What's going to happen," Lloyd continued, "is we'll drop the bomb and the atmosphere around the explosion will be immediately vaporised."

"Couldn't we drop it in the sea?" asked Rose.

"This isn't a barrel of nuclear waste, young lady."

"I'm forty-six," Rose retorted.

Henry turned in his seat. "Seriously?"

Rose soured. "Never mind. Go on, Geoff."

"If we drop this into the sea it will kill everything living in the local waters for tens of miles at least, not to mention sending a tidal wave towards western Scotland and Northern Ireland. Not good."

"At least by detonating in the air, we should avoid much of the collateral damage. We are fortunate that there is a strong north-westerly this evening, so the wind should mitigate the explosive force and help disperse the radiation, driving it out into the Atlantic. This is only a small bomb – by the standards of nuclear ordnance, anyway – so it's our best bet."

"Just one thing," White noted. "We know from the Scottish court that many vessels have been sighted off the coast of Scotland.

Remnants of the Spanish Armada. There could be eighty or ninety ships down there, somewhere."

Lloyd turned and glared at White as though he were mad. "You think we should sacrifice ourselves instead? And possibly the entire future of our race, if we stop guiding the court? We've seen what the future holds, left untended, remember?"

"I thought you said the future was a bust?"

Lloyd reached across the cockpit and pulled White roughly towards him by his tunic. "The Schultzes *lie,*" he snarled. "As for the Armada, if they get caught up in this, may it serve as a reminder to anyone who decides to invade another sovereign nation by force! Now, are you going to toss that thing, or shall we continue this discussion to the accompaniment of the harp?"

White had to concede. "You make a strong case. Henry! Rose! Give me a hand, will ya?"

Between the three of them, they managed to manhandle the bomb to the side hatch while Lloyd dove to 14,000 feet to avoid explosive decompression when they opened the hatch. Their orbital attack ship streaked high above the *San Juan de Sicilia,* terrifying her crew, though no one aboard even saw the galleon below them.

Holding the small combat ship as steady as he could, Lloyd was suddenly fighting high winds and brutal driving sleet at the lower altitude. "This is as good as it gets," he called through from the cockpit. "Ford?"

"Yeah?"

"From this height above sea level, it will fall for approximately sixty seconds—"

"Approximately?"

"What do you want from me?"

"OK. Sixty seconds, check. Anything else?"

"Yes. You will need at least twenty seconds to close the hatch and strap yourselves in. Otherwise, our acceleration might smear the lot of you across the bulkheads – I don't intend to hang around. We will then need at least another fifteen seconds to reach a safe distance at maximum acceleration."

"So what are you telling us?" White called back.

"What's it say on the timer?" Lloyd asked.

"One minute, thirty-seven seconds."

"Are you all wearing safety harnesses, strapped to the ceiling rails?" Lloyd asked again.

"Yes," they all called back.

"Right. Open the hatch and hang on tight. We can't release the bomb until the countdown reaches forty-two seconds, or it might land in the ocean. You will then have two seconds – that's *two* seconds – to chuck the thing out. After that, close the hatch immediately, strap into your seats and call out the *second* you're done – are we clear?"

"Clear."

White hit the open stud. A blast of wind and ice cut into their faces and hands, freezing them as the ship bucked, its aerodynamics seriously compromised by the open hatch in the crosswind. He watched the timer count down to fifty and began to call out, "Forty-nine, Forty-eight..." At forty-two, all three gave the bomb a huge heave and it fell into the night, buffeting wildly in the storm.

White wasted no time in closing the hatch. "Get strapped in," he barked. Within the twenty seconds allotted, they were all soaked but seated, strapped in and seriously keen to leave. "Geoff – punch it!"

G-forces blackened the edges of their vision as the little ship leapt forward with terrific acceleration. A further seventeen seconds out over the Atlantic and night became day as mankind witnessed its first ever artificial nuclear explosion.

The mushroom cloud filled their rear cameras. As the atmosphere ignited, it sent a shockwave in all directions from the epicentre, while leaving a sudden vacuum in its wake and an unprecedented low-pressure zone. Nature abhorred the vacuum and got stuck in immediately to solve the problem. Air rushed in from every point of the compass, as well as from above and below, at incredible speeds, bringing with it all the ferocity of a ten-thousand-year storm.

Lloyd took their little ship in a vast loop, hundreds of miles south, to avoid the blast and its radiation. He nodded with satisfaction. "The wind seems to be driving the worst effects out into the Atlantic as we hoped."

White unbuckled his harness to join the old man in the cockpit. "So...? We did it?"

"Looks like," Lloyd agreed reluctantly, suddenly less sure of himself.

White sensed his change in mood and subsequent uncertainty as he buckled himself once more into the co-pilot's seat. "What is it?"

Lloyd glanced at him and shook his head. "What the full effects of this will be, only history will tell."

History recorded a brief, blinding flash, bright as daylight off the northwest coast of Scotland on the evening of 5th November 1588. Many vessels and their mariners were lost in the raging seas that followed. Some were smashed off the coasts of Scotland and Ireland, while others were never heard from again.

Just west of the Isle of Mull, Scotland, the *San Juan de Sicilia* was in the trough of a large wave when the firestorm struck her, side on. The wall of water to starboard shielded her hull, though its surface fizzed and boiled, while the searing nuclear heat of the explosion tore across her top decks, incinerating everything and everyone. Her masts and sails turned instantly to ash, the violence of the blast wave scattering them over miles of ocean in seconds, while tongues of superheated wind reached below decks to find her powder magazine. Still mostly full, after the Armada's failure to successfully engage English vessels, the ensuing explosion was terrific, yet all but lost amid the hellfire in the sky.

With the sad loss of all aboard, what remained of her hull passed into the enduring silence beneath the waves to tantalise and confound future generations of treasure hunters, maritime archaeologists, and even royalty, down the ages.

"What is this place and why have ye brought us hither?"

"It is known as Dun Altabrug from the old tongue – a fortified structure dating back to the Iron Age."

"Back tae tha wha'?"

Robin Rotmütze rolled his dead black eyes in their deep sockets. "All you need know for now, is that these ancient rings of stone have power. Surely, you remember the demise of your living body within the circle at Ninestane Rig?"

Sir William de Soulis no longer had a body, merely an enduring spirit filled with malice and driven by spite and a lust for revenge. If he had, he would have shuddered. "And we're here because?"

"We are here, William, to witness the future. I felt one of my old crewmates appear aboard the intruder's ship. She was lost to me, millions of years ago – you wouldn't understand. But once I felt her presence in this time, I knew we would have entertainment. Call it a distraction while we recoup our strength. Although…" Rotmütze looked warily around the tiny island jutting out into Loch Altabrug, connected to its northern shore by a short boulder causeway. The ten-metre diameter, circular drystone structure on which they stood was barely above sea level; a low-lying strip of land to the west all that separated it from a raging Atlantic – and Rotmütze knew only too well that they had not seen anything yet.

The fear of that place, generated by those without and those who had lived within, had left the stones charged, energising them for millennia. Had *he* a body, he would have breathed deeply of it. "Not long now, William. However, the land is very low lying here. We should retreat to the hills behind us. Perhaps Beinn Mhòr would be appropriate. At more than two thousand feet, we should have a better and less troubling view of the wave from there."

De Soulis turned in alarm. "*Wave?*"

The night was dark and stormy. An even deeper, denser darkness whirled around them, vanishing the world to leave them shrouded. In moments, they found themselves at the top of Beinn Mhòr without the pesky need for several hours' hiking. "You see, William, there are some advantages to being dead."

De Soulis could not smile; he barely had the knack when he was alive, and he certainly had no intention of doing so while he felt imperilled. Beinn Mhòr was the highest mountain on the island of South Uist in the Outer Hebrides of Scotland and from its peak, Rotmütze smiled for both of them. "Do you understand any of the ancient tongue, William?"

"Aye. Some."

"Beinn Mhòr – what does it mean?"

"Big Mountain."

Rotmütze laughed. "Of course it does. Ah. It begins."

To the west, miles out across a wild ocean, a white light divided the darkness like a small sun.

Again, had De Soulis a body, he might have jumped out of it. His was a twisted soul, but none valued self-preservation more highly. What he was seeing was the end. He was unsure whether he feared it, or enduring *after* it, the most. Suddenly, he was looking down an eternity where everyone and everything he had ever known was gone.

Rotmütze continued to laugh heartily. "Feel the power, William. There's more of this to come, I promise you – *so* much more..."

Chapter 11 | Duck the Fan

Tim wore a frown of concern. "Is she OK, Natalie? I'm starting to wonder, now, if trying to get her back might not be proving crueller than... well, you know."

Natalie nodded sadly. "Her pulse is steady, but it's growing weaker."

They stood in dismay before the sleeping giant in the *New World*'s main hangar; their captive for some days now. Natalie reached through the bars to stroke the warm, scaly skin. "I'm sorry, girl."

As if in answer, Spinosaurus gave a belly growl. Natalie removed her arm from the cage sharply. "A reflex, right? A dream, perhaps?"

In response, Tim appeared to back away, whilst trying not to move.

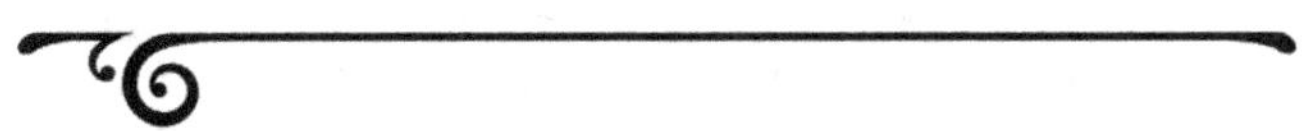

Douglas was back on his bridge. Unfortunately, any sense of power or control was illusionary as his ship continued its decaying orbit around the moon. "We've had nearly twelve hours to work on this now, so here's the plan. Hiro and Georgio will bring main power back and restore our full operating system. However, they will *only* do this when we're in position over the Mare Imbrium within the Imbrium Basin. And when Ah say over, Ah mean we'll be less than a hundred metres above the surface. Hopefully this willnae give our saboteur time to take down our systems again before we've landed."

"Imbrium Basin?" Singh queried. "That would be the big flat bit, am I right?"

"Aye, but let's no' get overly technical."

"I remember playing on the basin's surface when I was a girl," Baines chipped in, wistfully. "I took my first driving lesson in a moon buggy there."

"Well, dinnae worry. We'll no' be crashing this time. Will we, Sandy?"

"I never *said* I crashed."

"Sorry, lassie. Ah thought that was where you were going with that story."

Baines scowled at him. "Will they be able to bring all systems online in time, before we..." She faltered.

"Crash?" Douglas suggested, sweetly. "The way Ah see it, either we'll have full control and we'll land – *safely,* Sandy – and after that we'll get down to finding out just what the hell caused all this, or..."

"Or?"

"Or we make a new crater."

"Wonderful."

"Aye, but as a token of ma trust, Ah'll be leaving ye in charge of the bridge while Ah go to help Hiro and Georgie."

Baines brightened. "You *do* trust us."

"Aye." Douglas winked at his wife, remembering her extraordinary piloting of an escape pod in a dogfight over Cretaceous Patagonia, against a vastly superior war craft. "If the two of ye cannae handle this, there's naebody who can. And it's about time we were about it. Bring her home, safely, Captain Baines, Lieutenant-Commander Singh."

"Yes, sir," Singh replied from the pilot's station.

Douglas took a surreptitious last look around his bridge. "Captain Baines, the bridge is yours. Good luck."

"To all of us, sir," Singh answered as he spun back to his lifeless controls.

Baines grabbed Douglas and kissed him. "Be careful, James." She watched him stride purposefully from the bridge. "Sandy, we really must bring her home safely."

"With the power back online, should be straightforward, Captain."

"Yes. It should, but if we get it wrong, there'll be a bit more than a prang on the garage door to explain away."

Cretaceous Egypt, 1250 hours, local time
Sergeant Prentice maintained his vigil via their dinosaur spycam. He watched Heidi place something on the ground in an open area, just inside the electric fences. Zooming in, he could make out a small, metallic rod or bar, but was otherwise at a loss. Soon afterward, he saw her head across the compound to a vast, open-sided, portal frame building. Underneath its protective roof were several of the Schultz-style orbital attack craft. He could only surmise that the structure was built to shield the vehicles from large avians – though what damage the lightweight animals might cause them, he could not guess. The tanks needed no such protection and, with there being no one else in the world to see them, the enemy saw no reason to hide them or keep them secret, either.

One of the ships was tugged out from under cover and he watched Heidi board. Just minutes later, she took off. What happened next was hard to comprehend. Hardly any time had passed when Heidi stepped out of nothingness, right where she had fired the steel rod into the ground. "What the hell?" he muttered. "What happened to her ship?"

The shimmer in the air behind her could only be that of a wormhole. He had stepped through one himself, along with well over a hundred colleagues, on that sleety, stormy mountainside in the far north of England and recognised it all too well.

Cretaceous Egypt, 1255 hours, local time
"Dr Reid," Heidi greeted peremptorily as she strode once more into his office.

He looked up again, this time in shock. "How did...? But you...?"

"Have been there and back again, Doctor. Your device works perfectly. I left you just a few minutes ago, but am in fact seven hours older, having journeyed thousands of kilometres to spend a little time at Crater Lake before traversing millions of years to visit the quaint English countryside of AD1588."

The balding scientist got to his feet, knocking over his coffee cup. "Damn! Er... were you successful, ma'am?"

"A trip through the wormhole should establish that, but I fully expect our device to have fulfilled its purpose. Any attempt to disarm it would have set it off, yes? That was how you designed them to *my* specification?"

"Indeed, ma'am. So you believe that, through the wormhole, is actually 1943 – that is, *our* 1943 – the one we left behind in our original timeline?"

"I expect so. However, should that not be the case, we must prepare for the worst, *Herr Doktor.* It is time to begin our withdrawal. Time to place our operation in Chapter 11, so to speak, yes? You have heard of Chapter 11, Doctor?"

He nodded. "A form of bankruptcy whereby the debtor's business is reorganised while they remain in control, without need to liquidate assets."

"*Jawohl!* Very good, Doctor. It may be time to wrap up our organisation here, but we must certainly retain our assets for the next campaign."

"And our German workforce, ma'am?"

"Them, we do *not* need."

Reid's brow furrowed in confusion. "I believe Chapter 11 was meant as an honourable solution allowing continued trading to offset debts, ma'am. I'm not sure how, erm..." He stalled under the sudden and shocking cold of her scrutiny.

"Pedantic, Doctor. Chapter *12,* then."

"Enable financially distressed family farmers and fishermen to propose and carry out a plan to repay all or part of their debts, ma'am?"

Heidi's eyebrows shot up, genuinely surprised.

"My father was an accountant," he explained sheepishly.

Her expression soured. "Yes, I should have seen that. Very well. Let's call it Chapter 11.1, then, shall we?"

He opened his mouth to illuminate her with regards to 'scope and coverage', pedantry warring with his survival instinct. His face was a mask of agonised discomfort as he managed, "I'm sure Chapter 11.1 describes our circumstances exactly, ma'am."

A beeping from his computer distracted them, possibly even saving Reid from being shot. "What is that?" asked Heidi.

"Ma'am, there's widespread damage throughout the *Heydrich*'s systems after the attack, so I tapped into our satellite net from here. Your concerns about Douglas, and possibly a ship from the future, forced me to consider a reboot. After restarting the system, I set it to search for anything abnormal. The net located our Crater Lake base a little while ago. It also spotted your..."

"My what, Dr Reid?" she asked, icily.

"My God. Look at this." He spun his monitor around to show her images of an orbital attack craft flying across the Tethys Ocean towards the island chain that would one day become Great Britain. "That's you. Now. In real time! Whatever *that* is nowadays." His face was alight with wonder, his voice breathless. "And yet, here you stand..."

Heidi was far more impressed and certainly more rattled by that realisation than she let on. She was here, but also *there,* flying across the ocean as they spoke. "An amusing paradox, I will grant you. However, we have more pressing—"

"What's this?" he interrupted.

Heidi bent close again. The view had switched to a different satellite – one that seemed to have found something of interest just ten klicks south of their position. "That does not look like one of our ships."

"No, indeed, ma'am." He zoomed in close, painting the vessel as a target. "I don't recognise its configuration."

"Douglas," Heidi spat.

"Oh, what's this?" Reid muttered, clearly intrigued. "They're sending a coded signal, ma'am. Maybe we'll be able to crack it later."

"Perhaps. However, right now, it is time to prove that we no longer need our German friends, Doctor."

"Ma'am?"

She smiled wolfishly. "Let us test our automated battle group."

A fire of excitement lit Reid's eyes. "Yes, *ma'am.*"

Cretaceous Egypt, 1304 hours, local time

The realisation that Heidi not only had wormhole technology, but *personal* wormhole technology – seemingly with the ability to travel through space and perhaps even time, at will – hit Prentice like an unexpected tax bill. He struggled with indecision for several crucial minutes. On the one hand, orders were orders, but no, this was a game-changer and far too important to keep to himself. Eventually, he opened a channel to the *New World,* but received only static in response.

He turned to the pilot, who shrugged helplessly.

"What day is this?" Prentice asked.

"In *this* timeline? Who knows, Sarge, why?"

"It's probably a Tuesday. Too far from last weekend, yet with no hope in sight. Nowt good ever came of a Tuesday. That signal may have been noticed, lad. So better get us out of here and set course for t'moon. Quick as ye like."

"Er... Sarge. Something's wrong."

"What is it?"

"*Incoming!*" the pilot shouted as shells began landing all around them, tearing the ground and the silence to shreds.

The mixed greys of the moon filled Singh's monitors. "We're cutting this really close, Hiro," he fretted across an open channel. "We're now sub one hundred metres! Hiro? *Hiro?*"

"More would be accomplished with less panic, Sandy." Hiro launched into a complicated discourse where he described, in detail, how many complex and convoluted tasks he was undertaking at once to bring everything back online.

Singh felt the need to interrupt. "Hiro! You can tell me the whole story later. Please don't ruin the end for me – no, seriously, don't ruin the end for me!"

The Mare Imbrium, within the Imbrium Basin, was created by a massive impact during the Late Heavy Bombardment[14], the better part of four billion years before the Cretaceous Period. The collision released so much energy that the moon rock was instantly melted into a lava lake, filling many previous craters to leave a smooth surface. Once cooled, it left behind an almost perfectly flat plain, roughly circular and more than 1,100 kilometres across. The *New World* was so close to it now, that Singh felt he was in danger of scratching the paintwork. Over the last four billion years, innumerous smaller

---

14   The Late Heavy Bombardment (also known as the lunar cataclysm) occurred 4.1 to 3.8 billion years ago during the Neohadean and Eoarchean Eras on Earth. A period where large numbers of asteroids collided with the early planets in our inner solar system, possibly drawn by their increased gravity. While generally accepted, the theory is as yet unproved. Singh paid that theory little mind, however, focused as he was on the impending much *later* heavy bombardment, as the UNS *New World* plummeted towards the moon's surface.

impacts had pockmarked the once pristine surface, making the perfect flats they saw from a distance anything but, when viewed up close – way too close, as far as Singh was concerned.

"*Hiro!*" As he shouted his desperation into the comm, everything came back to life all around him. No longer were they just another ballistic body, flying through the heavens. He was once again in control of more than half a kilometre of coherent metals, polymers and ceramics. "Yes!" he hissed triumphantly.

Lack of atmosphere and low gravity helped him bring the ship to a stop in less than thirty seconds. Hovering at an altitude of just fifty metres, Singh deployed the landing gear and lowered it to gently kiss the surface of the moon. The *New World*'s immense weight settled on four vast hydraulic legs that easily soaked up the unevenness of her landing site.

"Are we down?" Baines risked, finally.

Singh spun his pilot's seat nonchalantly. "Yes. No problem, Captain. I wasn't concerned, were you?"

She raised a wry eyebrow. "Who, me? Hiro, is Captain Douglas down there with you?"

"*No, Captain. Was he meant to be?*"

Baines and Singh looked at one another, equally surprised.

Singh opened a channel. "Captain Douglas, this is the bridge. Come in, please. Captain Douglas?"

Baines stood. "Something's wrong."

Cretaceous Egypt, 1305 hours, local time

"Something's *wrong?*" Prentice cried in disbelief. "It's a bit more than that, lad. Get us *out* of here! Strap in, everybody. We're going for another ride!"

"Let's hope she'll still fly after being kicked around by those dinosaurs last night, Sarge," the pilot fretted as he began an emergency start-up cycle.

"Don't give me that," Prentice hollered while strapping himself into the co-pilot's seat. "Just make it go!"

Rockets fired and their dropship began to lift. Just three metres above the ground, a shell caught it a glancing blow to starboard.

A bone-rattling *boom* shook them, mostly generated by the explosion from where the shell struck the earth, right beneath the ship, flinging it to port. The pilot used its energy to increase their rate of climb. "That was close, Sarge."

"Aye! It hit my side, tha knows!" The Yorkshireman retreated into the dialect he had known as a child. "Are we in one piece?"

"I think so, just a little scorched. Where to now?"

"Take us home, lad, to the *New World.*"

"About that, Sarge. I may have been premature when I said we were OK."

The ship began to shake violently. At several hundred metres, Prentice gave his pilot a look of pure, unadulterated panic. Fighting with the controls, the pilot was too busy to elucidate, so Prentice pushed, "Are we going to crash?"

"No. I just don't think we can fly."

Prentice's look of panic skipped several levels, passing alarm, dread and horror, to stand on stone-cold inevitability. "If we can't make space, then head for the enemy camp."

The pilot nodded and poured all the engine's remaining power into making the ship jump forward. Almost ballistically, they travelled north. He toggled the microphone at his throat. "When we arrive, our landing won't be pretty. Everyone, brace yourselves!"

Prentice seconded the order to his troops to reinforce that they should strap in. They covered the ten kilometres to the enemy enclosure in just forty seconds, spending most of the last kilometre decelerating. As they approached, they saw what looked like the parking lot outside a car factory, only this particular factory turned out tanks – many of which seemed to be firing in their direction. Fortunately, tank command's telemetry was lagging behind, and their elevation – to reach a target they believed was still ten kilometres south – sent their shells whistling well over the little dropship.

"How did they know we were there?" the pilot asked, anxiously.

Prentice allowed the battle calm to flow through his mind and quickly arrived at a hypothesis. "The *New World.* Whatever happened up there, our side have either lost power or..." He could not bring himself to complete that line of thought. "If they've lost power, they've lost control of t'satellite net, an' all. Allowing our enemies to see what's really out here – including us. Take us down near their capital ship. If it's on fire, we may be able to take advantage of—" Before he could finish explaining his plan, a shell hit their port rocket motor. The explosion within the ship was deafening and sent them spiralling into an erratic corkscrew down towards the ground.

Tanks were now on the move all over the Schultz base. Many were firing high into the air towards something in the south. Todt appealed to Aito and Jansen through the smoke and the deafening booms. "I must get these young people home and damn their orders, gentlemen. Will you help me?"

Aito and Jansen shared a look. "Alright," Jansen agreed for them both. "Follow me. And stay low – all of you!"

He took them a circuitous route around the rear of a factory building, out of the *Heydrich*'s field of vision.

"Have you heard anything from your people in the large ship?" asked Todt.

Jansen shook his head but otherwise said nothing, concentrating on their route ahead.

"You have friends on board?" Todt tried again.

"We hope so," Aito answered for them. "I'm curious, Engineer Todt, why do you never refer to my ship as the *Heydrich?*"

"*Your* ship?" Todt seemed surprised.

"I am still her acting captain. Now, will you answer my question?"

"I know Reinhard Heydrich."

It was Aito's turn to show surprise. "*Really?* And?"

"And he is a dick!"

Jansen held up a hand for them to stop at the factory's northwest corner. He risked a quick peek, pulling his head back immediately as he flattened against the factory wall. The others followed his lead as another tank rumbled by to take up a position in the north of their enclosure. They covered their ears, but mercifully, it was not firing.

He popped his head around the corner again. "Let's go."

They jogged across a concrete courtyard between the three large space-framed buildings that were the first port of call for all their supplies from Germany. They were getting close to the wormhole. The buildings were separated from the *Heydrich* by a large thoroughfare, where several German lorries were parked in a line.

Jansen caught Aito's eye and smiled.

Aito nodded, turning to Todt and his surveyors. "We must run to the first lorry and then the next and the next. We'll hop our way along until we're parallel with the *Heydrich*'s bow – that's the front, the pointy end. We'll run one at a time to avoid notice. Look, it's..." he glanced at his comm, "1306 hours. We're not expecting another delivery from Germany for almost an hour, so we should have plenty of time, and with so much going on, we'll be able to—" His words were drowned by a huge crash and boom that reverberated through the ground like an earthquake.

"James!" Baines called again, the stress in her voice plain.

"*Jill?*" replied a mild voice with an unmistakably Scottish cadence.

"James! You scared the hell out of me – us – where are you?"

"*Ah took a little side track on the way to engineering. I didnae say anything because Ah knew ye'd disapprove and Ah needed ye focused on landing us safely.*"

Baines frowned, perplexed now. "What do you mean?"

"*Meet me on deck eight, corridor five – and bring The Sarge, Jonesy and Rick Drummond with ye. Douglas out.*"

"Well, that was enigmatic."

"Inscrutable, even," added Singh.

As ordered, Baines arrived at deck eight, corridor five. She was not surprised to find The Sarge and Jonesy already there and chatting quite relaxedly with her husband.

"What's all this about, then, gentlemen?"

Douglas was about to answer when he spotted former NASASEC officer and Detroit detective, Rick Drummond. "Rick, thanks for coming. Please, follow me."

Baines was left out in the corridor with Jones. "I'm sorry, am I invisible? *You* can see me, can't you, Dewi?"

Jones walked straight past her, to follow the other men.

Baines straightened. "Charming."

He turned and gave her a wink.

She snorted and followed the giant Welshman into what she suddenly realised were secure quarters assigned to Richard Weber, a former lieutenant in the Schultz regime. That became obvious almost at once, when she saw his body on the floor – apparently dead. "Whoa. What happened?"

"That's what Ah'd like to know, Jill. Ah'll get Dave Flannigan to deal with the body in a wee while, but Ah wanted the crime scene thoroughly inspected before anything's moved."

"Rick?" They all turned to the sound of a woman's voice from the corridor.

"In here, Patricia," Drummond called.

"Rick? Oh, my..." Dr Patricia Norris stepped into the apartment, pulling up short when she saw the body.

"Yeah, I hear you, Trish, but I need a full forensic sweep of these quarters, please."

A sadness registered in Douglas' eyes. The last time he had instructed Rick Drummond to work a crime scene, it had been with the assistance of Dr Wright, the DNA specialist – just one of many left behind in 1558. *Ah wish we had them with us now,* he thought wistfully, though he had total faith in Dr Patricia Norris to help Drummond find any signs of foul play.

"How did you know this had happened?" Baines broke into his thoughts.

"Ah know everyone thought Ah was crazy, keeping such close tabs on Weber and refusing all his requests for parole, but it wasnae a vendetta. Ah just never believed in his rehabilitation. He was one of Schultz's true believers – there's no coming back from that kind of indoctrination. Anyhow, Ah knew he'd spent the last ten years learning everything there was to know about micro-electronics. Ah tried to prevent it, but the people from our new timeline place great store in educational rehabilitation, so they wouldnae withhold learning in any form he requested. It's one of their basic tenets. Knowing that, it wasnae much of a stretch to conclude that if there was anyone who could crash us, and would want to crash us – *again* – and be perfectly willing to sacrifice himself to the cause into the bargain, it would be Richard Weber.

"It was a last-minute decision, but Ah decided that it might be better use of ma time to prevent him from making us crash, rather than trying to help Hiro prevent us from crashing – Ah hope that makes sense? Looks like Ah may have been right."

"How so?" asked Baines.

"We didnae crash, did we? And clearly there's something fishy going on here. My suspicions were initially aroused by the body on the floor. That of a young man in perfect health—"

"Aside from being dead," she finished for him.

"You found him like this, Captain?" Drummond interrupted them.

"Aye. Ah checked for a pulse immediately, but didnae find one."

Drummond nodded, mulling over the situation as he took in the room. "No obvious signs of a struggle. A glass of water on the coffee table nearby. Looks like he took a drink from it before he fell, but he had time to replace it carefully onto a coaster, so I doubt there's poison involved. Still, we'll check the contents to be sure. I'd like to get Dr Flannigan to inspect the body now, Captain. And carry out a post-mortem straight after that, if possible, please."

"Of course, Rick. Jill, would ye get Dave Flannigan on to this right away, please?" Douglas' comm beeped. "Douglas."

"Captain, Hiro. I need to see you in engineering urgently, please."

"On ma way, Chief." He turned to Baines. "What now, Ah wonder? Can you take care of things here, please, Jill? Hopefully, Hiro has found out what happened to ma ship."

Cretaceous Egypt, 1306 hours, local time

"What's happened to the ship?" Prentice bellowed the question. Everyone's ears were ringing and muffled after the explosion.

"We were hit, Sarge. I've barely got any control. Trying to level her as best I can – we're going in. Five seconds, brace for impact!"

As good as his word, the pilot fought the dropship to a near-level descent so that, when she struck the ground, she skipped twice before ploughing a deep furrow. The second skip carried them fortuitously over the concrete moat and through the electric fence in a shower of sparks and whiplashing steel. The ship insulated her passengers from harm and the sand slowed them, exactly as their pilot had hoped, but a collision with a large boulder, just beneath the surface, crumpled the portside bow and flipped them over to roll again and again. They crashed at such speed that their rolling gambol took them all the way to the *Heydrich,* where their journey ended with a very final *clang.*

When Prentice came round, he could only guess at how long he had been unconscious. The chaos of running and screaming all around them, seemed to be the same running and screaming that was taking place before he blacked out, so it must only have been seconds. He unbuckled his harness and immediately fell headfirst. Automatically he raised his arms – or lowered them, depending on perspective – to protect his head. The ship was upside down.

Grunting and struggling to right himself, he opened his mouth to ask the pilot if he was hurt. However, once his eyes registered the situation, he realised there was no need. The brave man, whose skilful crash landing had saved Prentice's life, had lost his own. Collision with the hidden boulder just below the surface had also crushed the pilot. Prentice felt sick to his stomach. One of Captain Meritus' men; he had not known him well, but he had died saving them. He snatched the dog tags from the torso, trying not to look at the crushed head of his courageous comrade in arms.

Staggering and nauseous, he stumbled into the rear compartment to check on his men. That was when machine gun fire began rattling and pinging off their outer hull.

Douglas strode into engineering to find Hiro and Georgio still bickering. "Déjà vu, gentlemen. Ah hope ye've figured out what happened now?"

"No, sir," replied Hiro.

"Yes, sir," replied Georgio, simultaneously.

Douglas blinked. "Which is it?"

"You tell the captain your *theory,* Georgie, while I go and see if I can find out what really happened." Hiro left them and began opening service hatches, taking readings and muttering to himself.

Douglas raised an eyebrow, questioningly.

"Sir, come with me." Georgio led Douglas into the chief's office, closing the door behind them. "Captain, I'm worried about Hiro."

"How so?"

"I believe that he's... Look, sir, you know Hiro's my best friend in the whole world, so I choose my words carefully."

"Ah understand. Go on."

"He's really off his game. He's been wrong more often than he's been right so far on this mission. It's just not like him. We all have off days, but I'm-a really getting concerned now, Captain."

Douglas frowned. This was bad news – the worst. "What do you think is wrong, Georgie?"

"I think it's his brother, sir. Being back here... well, he just hasn't let it go. We all saw Aito get killed by that dinosaur—"

"We dinnae actually know whether it *killed* Aito, Georgie."

Georgio pulled a face. "I suppose not, but it seems pretty likely. Hiro, on the other hand, won't hear a word of it. He's convinced his brother's down there in that camp – reckons he has footage."

"Footage?"

"Look at this, sir." Georgio called up a section of captured video from the Afromimus drone before they lost contact. "See those three men talking together next to that theodolite? I don't recognise the two Caucasians facing the camera, but Hiro has convinced himself that the man with his back to us is Aito."

Douglas shrugged. "Not much to go on. He's roughly the same build as Hiro, which is how Ah remember Aito, but without seeing his face..."

"Look closely, sir. What do you notice about the man's hands?"

Douglas frowned, tapping the zoom. He looked up in surprise. "They seem to be odd. Ah mean, each is a different colour."

"That's Hiro's evidence. Some of our people witnessed Aito losing his hand during the attack in the cave, immediately before we left the Cretaceous last time. It would stand to reason – at least, Hiro's current reason – that if the Schultzes carried 'spare parts' they would be white, yes?"

"Ah see. An intriguing theory, Georgie."

"It's wishful thinking, sir."

Douglas studied the engineer. "You disapprove of Hiro retaining some hope for his brother?"

"No, sir. Of course not. I just believe it's interfering with his duties."

"You mean he's upset."

"No. Yes. Well, maybe. I think it's more to do with our purpose here, sir."

"Explain?"

"I don't wish to speak out of turn, Captain, but we came here armed for war. I believe that you will explore any and every possible avenue to end this without bloodshed, but it's not much of a stretch to work out what you'll be forced to do if all peaceful options fail."

Douglas' frown deepened. "Ah hope it willnae come to that, Georgie."

"I know you do, sir. We all do. But we also know we can't just leave and let Heidi continue doing whatever it is she's doing. When push comes to shove, you might have to destroy that base down there on the planet. And that, I believe, is at the bottom of Hiro's problem, sir."

Douglas looked sceptical. "You think he's trying to sabotage our efforts?"

"Not exactly, sir. I could never believe that Hiro would consciously raise a hand against you, sir. Not in any way. Rank aside, Captain, we've become family over the years – all of us."

Douglas smiled sadly. "Aye, laddie. We have that. So you're suggesting that while Hiro would never consciously hinder our efforts to make the world safe, his subconscious might have different ideas?"

Georgio nodded. "It's an idea that's been growing in my mind, sir. I don't think Hiro is even aware of it. I believe his subconscious fears of losing his brother again – possibly even at our hands – are affecting his actions."

Douglas blew out his cheeks. "The only psychologist among our crew died of a heart attack last year. We no longer have anyone with that sort of expertise – at least, not enough to make a determination."

"I know, sir, but there is some good news – and in a way, it's related."

A little hope returned to Douglas' eyes. "Go on, Georgie."

"The *New World* is fixed, and she's ready to go, Captain."

"That's great news. But the chief believes..."

"Exactly, sir. He's chasing ghosts. Someone shut our entire operating system down – engines, the lot! But we designed a workaround for that, after the last time, Captain. The entire system is mirrored in four separate, redundant systems. We can reinitialise whenever we want to, in under a minute. Now, while I agree we need to find whoever shut us down, the ship is fine, sir. We left the restart until the last second to prevent further interference before we could put down safely, knowing that Sandip's skill would be more than up to the task. We were never in any real danger, sir. Not this time. The last time Heidi destroyed our operating system, forcing us to reboot from factory settings, left an indelible impression on the chief, Captain. He made sure it couldn't happen again."

Douglas looked through the office's window, out over the engineering bay to where Hiro, one of his closest friends of many years, was talking to himself. Douglas cast that thought aside. Hiro was probably talking to the ship – he had always done that. Yet he could not quite shake the feeling that Chief Nassaki seemed somehow more fragile.

Nurse Justin Smyth unzipped the body bag, peeling it away from Richard Weber's recently vacated cadaver. He began to loosen the collar in order to undress the corpse, when its arm jumped – culminating in a backfist under Smyth's nose.

"Justin? *Justin?* Come on, kid. Snap out of it."

"Happy birthday," Smyth muttered groggily. "No. I'm not going..."

Flannigan laughed. "Let me sit you up. Feel up to telling me what happened? And where's Weber's body? Did you fall on the way to the cold store?"

"Wha'? Dave? That you?"

Smyth was clearly struggling and now Flannigan could see why. As well as a bloody nose, which Flannigan attributed to the fall, he also had some blood on the back of his head. "Whoa, kid. You're banged up front and back..." He frowned. "Now, how did that happen? Let's get you under a scanner. Weber's post-mortem will have to wait—"

"Never a truer word spoken, Doctor."

Flannigan jumped round. "What the—"

Weber stepped from behind a storage locker with a pistol trained.

The *New World*'s chief medical officer deflated. "Some type of new drug, huh? Something that drastically slows the metabolism and heart rate? Something you had smuggled into prison and knew we wouldn't recognise? How am I doin' so far?"

Weber treated Flannigan and Smyth to a condescending smile before changing the subject. "I really must thank Captain Douglas for putting weapons in so many key locations this time around – including sickbay. Makes you wonder what he was expecting, doesn't it? Still, I doubt he was expecting my return from the dead."

Flannigan scowled. "You son of a... We shoulda left you behind the first time."

Cretaceous Egypt, 1307 hours, local time
"Corporal Engel!" Prentice barked at the top of his voice to counter the deafening gunfire hammering their hull. "Get the men ready for evac!"

Engel had blood running down the side of his head where it had struck the bulkhead in the crash. His wild-eyed glare made him look crazed, but he believed Prentice's order crazier still. "You cannot be serious," he yelled back.

"Heinz," Prentice tried again. "They're moving tanks in – tanks! I've seen 'em, through what's left of t'windscreen. If we don't make a run for it, right now, we'll stand no chance at all."

Engel nodded, understanding at last the awful choices left open to them.

Of the twenty troops, only nine still lived after the crash, including Prentice and Engel. Prentice looked around desperately. "Radburn? *Radburn?*"

"Here, Sarge." Movement from the floor, which used to be the ship's ceiling, betrayed their youngest member. He was struggling to unbury himself from beneath several backpacks.

Prentice reached down and pulled him to his feet. "Good lad." He ruffled his hair affectionately. After taking the young man under his wing, it would have been like losing a son. "Now, find your helmet. We've got to go."

The rear hatch was twisted and failed to open wide enough to allow them passage, so they opened the smaller hatch within it. Bullets whistled past them from the right as they flung it wide. Engel gave Prentice a look that clearly said 'this is suicide', though he said nothing.

Prentice gave him a pat on the arm. "I'll go first, lad."

"Good luck, Sarge."

They shook hands. "Radburn, with me. Keep on my left – *go!*"

Prentice ran, shielding his teenaged protégé as best he could while they ran for their lives. Engel gave them a three count and began sending the surviving men and women after them, finally leaving the hatch himself. Bullets whizzed in all directions, pinging off their ship and the much larger hull of the *Heydrich*. Three tanks approached their position, all firing. Now he could see around him, Engel understood that they were refraining from using their cannon *because* of the *Heydrich*. "Keep close to the big ship!" he roared over the machine gun fire. It was all he could do to keep them safe from the tanks' heavier weapons, but it was a forlorn hope.

Prentice was spun round as a bullet nicked his arm. It was a graze, but the force had been incredible. He struggled back to his feet when a helping hand pulled him up by the back of his flak jacket. "Thanks, lad."

Radburn's proud smile changed instantly to agony as his leg was taken from under him. He screamed as he hit the ground.

Dry throated, Prentice cried, "NO!"

Manhandling the teenager over his shoulder, he ran in the only direction open to him – up the *Heydrich*'s boarding ramp and into her main hangar. Once inside, he swerved immediately left, to hide them from enemy fire. The ship's hangar was a mess of twisted hull and smoke damage. Ahead, he saw a heavy-duty hatch, partially open, and ran for it. He hit the release, but the hydraulics were battle damaged. He squeezed inside as carefully as he could with his delicate cargo. Come what may, it could be no more dangerous than what he left behind.

All hell seemed to be breaking loose aft of the *Heydrich*. "This is our chance. Go, go, go!" Jansen snapped. Keeping low, he followed just a few seconds after Todt's female surveyor. She was either tiring or suffering from shock, because he caught her easily and pulled her in, to hide behind the first lorry. He peered round her, trying to ascertain what was happening just two hundred metres south of them. It looked like a crashed ship, but not one of theirs. That gave him pause. *What the hell is going on?* He beckoned for Todt to make his run.

Using the parked lorries as cover, they made their way quickly to the *Heydrich.* The tanks were no longer firing their heavy guns, but several surrounded the crashed ship and were pulverising it with machine gun fire instead. "I pity the poor souls in that broken hull," he said, shaking his head sadly. "Wonder who they are? Aito, do you recognise that ship?"

"Hard to tell, the state she's in. Doesn't appear to be of Schultz design, though."

They heard the screams of men and women under fire and exchanged a meaningful glance. There was absolutely nothing they could do but get the young surveyors out of there. "Mankind is too sick to continue," muttered Aito, darkly. "Maybe we should fix that."

"What's that?" asked Jansen.

Aito shook his head. "Nothing. What now?"

Jansen looked around to Todt. "Can you get them the rest of the way? The wormhole is open and just behind those barricades. The vehicular entrance this side is sealed off. You'll have to sneak under the ship and approach from the south. With everything that's happening over there, you'll never get a better chance than this."

"We could wait," Todt postulated.

Jansen shrugged. "We don't know who these guys are. Presumably they didn't just drop in to say hi. What if their mission is to close the wormhole?"

"You are right." Todt nodded in salute. "Thank you. Both of you."

Taking each of the young surveyors by an arm, he ran under the prow of the *Heydrich.* The sunlight was so bright, just after noon, that they almost disappeared once they were under the great ship's shadow.

Prentice opened a hatch on the right. The corridor he had chosen ran forward, along the ship's port side. He expected the hatch to open into a large room or perhaps another corridor leading into the heart of the ship. What he actually found was a long, narrow plant room. It was filled with bank after bank of NeuralNet 5 supercomputers. *The brains of the ship,* he thought. Sealing the hatch behind them, he carefully placed Private Radburn in a swivel chair before the nearest bank, facing the door. He was extremely pale, bleeding profusely from a leg wound. A fifty-calibre bullet had made a terrible mess of the young man's thigh and had clearly nicked the femoral artery. "You'll be OK, lad. Mark?" He slapped the young man's face. "Mark?"

"Here, Sarge."

Prentice's breath caught. The young man always answered with those words. Suddenly, he seemed even younger. Forcing himself to breathe deeply, Prentice pulled a cord from a pocket within his jacket. Wrapping it around the injured leg, he pulled it tight and fastened the tourniquet. Radburn cried out.

"I'm sorry, lad." Prentice struggled to find his voice, his heart breaking.

"Sarge." For a moment, Radburn was lucid again. "Sarge, you have to go."

"No! I'll bloody well carry you out of here on my back before I—"

"Sarge," his voice was weaker this time. "This place – it looks important."

Prentice took a second glance around. "Aye, 'appen it is."

Radburn raised a bloody hand holding a grenade. He smiled exhaustedly. "This would stop them, wouldn't it, Sarge?"

"That it would, but we're not there yet, lad. I'm going to get you out of here. I promise."

"Training with you, Sarge, and the lads, it's been the best time of my life."

"There'll be plenty more good times, son. Plenty..." Tears were streaming down Prentice's face, forcing him to turn away. He batted at them angrily. He owed it to Radburn to keep a clear head.

While he wiped his eyes, the young private picked up a carton from the floor and flung it at the door release. The hatch sissed open, causing Prentice to jump back to his feet and turn around, rifle up. Cautiously, he stepped closer to the hatch and looked each way, up and down the corridor.

Radburn was close to losing consciousness. He could feel the darkness reaching for him. "You're the best friend I've ever had,

Sarge. Been like a father to me. Thank you, for everything you've taught me." With that, he pushed the chair away from the computers. It travelled on its castors, and he kicked out savagely with his good leg, fetching Prentice a boot in the rear that launched him through the hatch. Radburn threw himself towards the closing stud and slumped to the deck as the hatch closed between them.

"What the—" Prentice got back to his feet, furiously, only to see the hatch closing behind him. He reached for the opening stud, but before he got to it, a concussive thud shook the deck plates under his boots – a grenade detonation in an enclosed space. All power aboard the ship died instantly, leaving him in almost complete darkness. "NO!" He clawed at the sealed hatch and its lifeless controls. "Mark? *Mark?* Radburn!" He slumped against the doors, defeated. "Why? Why would you do that?"

Of course, he knew the answer. Private Mark Radburn may have been just seventeen, but he had worked out that the only way for his friend to escape this ship alive would be by leaving him behind, and he knew his sergeant would never do that, not while there was any chance at all – and probably not even then.

Prentice sobbed. "I would have carried you, lad. I would."

Todt and his young surveyors kept low, as ordered, and ran for the massive portside landing strut; one of a pair that supported the prow of the *Heydrich*. They hid. Voices came from behind the solid timber barricade that shielded the wormhole from the outside world. Heidi ordered its construction originally to protect the wormhole, and any travellers, from the dinosaurs. However, it now served as a security faucet, allowing the Schultzes to operate a border control of sorts.

The vehicle entrance was indeed closed to them, as Jansen had warned. The pedestrian gate was on the opposite side of the ship from where they hid. Todt was about to order a quick sprint under her hull to the starboard landing strut, when barked orders from inside the barricade froze him in place.

Eager, the female surveyor took a step forward anyway, but he held her back. She looked at him in surprise. Todt merely placed a finger to his lips and shook his head. The landing struts were large enough to easily hide any one of them from view. He knew hiding three of them there was a big ask and could only hope the fog of war would provide distraction, if not actual cover.

Three men, heavily armed, burst from a movable section of the barricade to run aft along the *Heydrich*'s starboard side. Todt watched them go and then heard weapons fire as they joined the altercation. "Now!" he hissed to his wards.

They ran under the ship, heading straight for the open barricade. Focused on the combat ahead, the armed men had forgotten to pull it closed behind them. Todt and the surveyors ran north along a corridor, also timber, with a solid roof of railway-sleeper-sized balks. At the end of their ten-metre dash, they popped out into a large enclosure and before them was the wormhole. Unfortunately, it was still guarded.

Todt skidded to a halt as three of Schultz's security officers raised their rifles towards him. "Gentlemen, lady," Todt greeted them courteously, vainly attempting to collect himself. "I must travel back to Munich immediately."

"No one leaves," the female guard stated. "We are under attack from terrorists."

Todt straightened. "Do you know who I am, young lady?"

The guard smiled indolently. "I know who you are, Engineer Todt. No exceptions."

"But my survey team have been injured—"

"They look fit enough to me," she interrupted him.

"One of them is dead!" he spat furiously.

"Perhaps he or she was one of the anarchists? Perhaps they got what they deserved?"

"What *is* this, a comedy routine parodying our security forces?" Todt was a brilliant engineer. Consequently, he had a predilection for seeing stupidity everywhere; an arrogance that often worked against him. This was one of those times.

"Take them!" the female guard barked.

"*What?* On what charge?" he blustered.

"That may be determined once you have been interrogated. Take them to a secure area."

The male surveyor, survivor of the Carcharodontosaurus attack, made a break for the wormhole. One of the guards fired at his back.

The young man fell, but fell *through* the wormhole. "We'll pick him up later. If he survived," the woman in charge stated unemotionally.

The female surveyor began to scream; she could take no more. One of the soldiers hit her about the face with the butt of his rifle. She went down, spitting blood and coughing.

"How dare you lay hands on my staff!" Todt was outraged. He had always disliked the Schultz security people. The old man and his granddaughter seemed to favour bullies and sycophants in equal measure, but they had been allies – a necessary evil. No more. He reached out to help the injured girl and was knocked to the ground for his trouble by the second male guard.

His young surveying assistant tried to get up on her own, but the man who hit her grabbed her by the hair and threw her down once more. "Terrorist scum!" he snarled, while he set about kicking her, brutally and repeatedly, as she curled into a ball on the ground, screaming for him to stop.

Todt cried out in wordless horror, only to see the same guard turn in his direction. The man grinned evilly, then his expression slackened, and he fell forward. The headshot had taken him side-on, removing the back third of his skull. His face remained unblemished – all the better for Hell's gatekeeper to recognise him and streamline his journey straight to the fire.

The surviving guards turned immediately to face the new threat. The second male went down instantly, his chest torn to bloody ruin by the newcomer's automatic weapons fire. From the ground, Todt saw the female guard raise her weapon to fire and scissor-kicked her legs from under her. She squeezed the trigger on impulse, tracing a savage line across the enclosure's timber wall, but that was to be her last act of violence. A single, economical shot took her under the chin, blowing the top of her head away. She lay still.

The lone man who had burst into the enclosure, in time to save Todt, looked like a vision from Hell himself. Angry bruising and dried blood covered half his face, his uniform was torn in a dozen places, and he was caked with blood, dust and all manner of nameless filth.

Whatever he had been through, it had been bad. Todt lay still, taking the man's measure, not daring to get up. Once it became obvious to everyone that they were alone – temporarily, at least – Todt risked asking, "Who are you?"

"Corporal Heinz Engel, and you?"

"Fritz Todt – Chief Engineer to the Party."

"Get up. Help the girl," Engel ordered. He studied Todt a moment. "You probably saved my life when you tripped that guard."

Todt glanced around ironically. "It seemed like the right thing to do at the time. Who are you, Corporal? I know your name, but who *are* you, really?"

"We're on a mission from the future to stop the Schultzes eradicating everyone from the timeline. Any incursion into Nazi Germany must be stopped."

"*Nazi* Germany?"

Todt's puzzlement seemed genuine, making Engel tilt his head slightly as he scrutinised the engineer. Shouting from behind them made him turn.

Todt seized the initiative. "Do you know where they came from? The Schultzes, I mean?"

"Yes," Engel replied without taking his eyes from the corridor.

"Then come with me, Corporal Engel. Please do not think that I exaggerate when I say, Germany needs you."

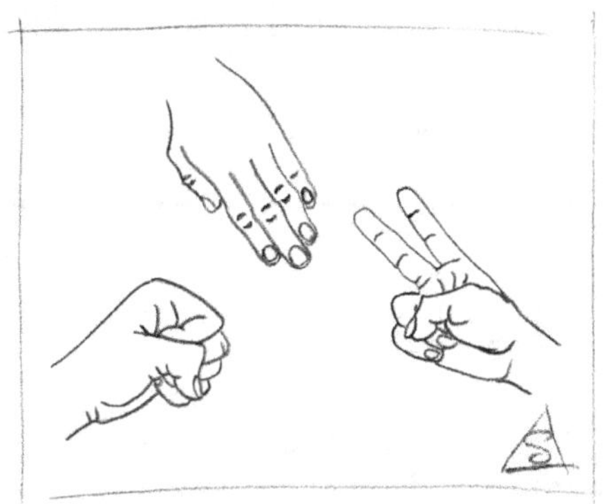

Chapter 12 | The Joining of Hands

"Dr Reid." Heidi burst into his office for the third time in less than an hour. "We must launch the satellite now. You said it was ready, yes?"

Having a psychotic boss who popped up repeatedly out of the blue, even when it was not possible to do so, was opening the door to a grotesque new horizon for Reid. He answered cautiously, "I said *almost*, ma'am. We're still to test the guidance systems—"

"Do you have any reason to believe they will not work?"

"Well, no, but..."

"Excellent. As for my ship – the one you have been building for me especially – I will need it also. Make everything ready, and Reid?"

"Yes, ma'am?"

"Hurry!"

"But, ma'am, again, it's not been tested."

"Then there is no time like the present, is there?"

"Most of my staff have been called to the *Heydrich,* now the firefight's over, ma'am."

"Recall them. I expect an attack on this base imminently. I therefore order you to make my ship and satellite ready for action even more imminently, Dr Reid. You will also need to pack a bag. You are coming with me."

The lab coat until so recently known as 'One' gulped. "I-I... ma'am?"

Heidi let out an exasperated sigh. "Is it not obvious that the plan of *mein Großvater* is failing. Now it is our turn – you and me. We have the technology and the precise levers required to remake this world into whatever we wish. It is time to use them. Recall your people. I have a special task for you, and you alone. No one must discover what you are about until we are gone from this place. Now, listen carefully."

"What are they?" H stooped over the driver's seat within the tank, speaking quietly, as though they might be overheard. The creatures before them were small to mid-sized theropod carnivorous dinosaurs. The pack of Rugops had been scavenging the area for months. Occasionally, they killed. More often, they used their numbers to scare away other predators from any carcasses they came across; beating a hasty retreat when larger carnivores passed through. It was a strategy that worked well for them.

"You're asking *me?*" Badawi replied frantically. "This may technically be Egypt, but we had nothing like those things in the Nile! What I would not give for an innocent crocodile."

"I wish you hadn't said that."

He tore his gaze away from the forward viewscreen to see her transfixed on his left-hand monitor. With a sinking feeling, he turned his head to follow. In a way, his prayers had been answered. He screamed in a most unmanly fashion. H hardly noticed – she was too busy screaming herself as they stared into the maw of the biggest crocodile they, or anyone else, had ever seen. As the vast, two-metre-long jaws snapped closed with promise – they were way beyond threat – Badawi could now see there were several others, right behind the giant, and he was not the only one to take note.

The dozen or so Rugops were all on their feet, bellowing rage as the bask of Sarcosuchus imperator moved inexorably up the beach from the river to take over their place in the sun. Despite their show of defiance, the Rugops had no choice but to move on, giving ground as slowly as they dared, salvaging whatever dignity they could. Their full and unequivocal retreat soon cleared the way, and Badawi gunned the tank's powerful electric motors. The steel behemoth leapt forward, leaving the snapping and snarling giants behind.

"They could not harm us in here, could they?"

Badawi dared a glance at her. "Miss Schultz—"

"Doctor."

"*Doctor* Schultz—"

"Call me H."

Badawi sighed. "*H,* I do not believe they could break into this machine, but that is not to say they could not cripple it. If they damaged one of the tracks, for example, we would be left as sitting ducks."

"So where are you taking us?"

"To hide in the forest, as per my original plan. Perhaps we could find our way back, under cover of darkness." Without waiting for a reply, he steered hard right, straight into the forest. As they smashed aside smaller trees around the periphery, the creaking and snapping of sapwood was horrifying from within the steel hull. Slightly muffled, it sounded as though they were driving across a bed of broken bones. Booms from beneath betrayed tree stumps, too stubborn to break, instead uprooted and rolled as the tank's immense weight carried them along.

"Does this thing have a rear-view mirror?" she asked.

"Erm... maybe. Yes, here." Badawi's forward monitor split to show the rear view alongside the view ahead.

"Hmm. You know, I think someone might spot where we turned off," she noted cautiously.

Badawi turned hard left, essentially hiding them from any observers back at the turning. "Better?"

"But now *we* cannot see out."

He stared at her. "You must be a nightmare to work for. How do you get tradesmen?"

"I pay very well." She frowned. "And what do you mean by that?"

"Nothing. Let us get to know our tank. It might become important very soon."

"Have you noticed the bullets in the racks have different colours, Apep?"

"Bullets?"

"The big ones."

"Shells. The big ones are called shel— never mind, show me what you've found."

"Look. These are all bullet-coloured, but there are also these four blue ones and one bright red one."

He stared at them. All the shells were racked and ready for the automated loading system, which was good for him, but it also prevented him from handling them or trying to read anything printed on their casings. He had been fortunate in that the tank seemed geared towards fully automatic running. It had made it easy to steal and to use its weapons – clearly Heidi had not expected thieves a hundred million years before man. However, there must also be a control somewhere that offered the *other* shells into the breach of the main gun, too. "I think we should make it our priority to find out how these are fired."

"The blue ones?"

"All of them."

"Pretty colour. I *looove* cornflower."

Badawi could feel a headache coming on. "All that matters is that we don't fire one of these by accident, and call me reactionary, but I think the red one we should especially avoid."

Hank Burnstein Snr swore and sucked his knuckles. He sat at the Burnsteins' kitchen table within their quarters aboard the UNS *New World,* surrounded by the scattered components of their new coffee machine.

Chelsea Burnstein bustled in with an armful of laundry, humming. "What's wrong, honey?"

"This damned piece 'o junk! It never gets the temperature right."

And never will again, looking at this mess, she thought uncharitably. "Honey, you're not an engineer. Why don't you get someone—"

"I've learned to do and fix things for myself the last few years, since we lost everything," he interrupted her, still glaring at the jumble of spare parts.

Her expression softened to a smile, *Yes, you have, dear, but you've absolutely no aptitude for it at all.* Chelsea knew that when Hank referred to 'losing everything' he actually meant their son, Henry. It saddened her that while Henry had been with them, Hank had seemed only to care for his wealth and his business empire. The final acceptance that they would never see Henry again in this life had left Burnstein Snr a broken, yet somehow better man. Chelsea could only ponder the effects of loss – at times a double-edged sword, yet it always stabbed to the heart.

Rather than leaving everything to their army of servants, they now made shift for themselves, like regular people. She would never recover from losing Henry to the past, but in other respects, this new life suited her better.

She had effectively been auctioned off to Hank by her family as a young woman; a family who hoped to climb up the coattails of her suffering, but then, ten years ago, everything had changed. It now seemed proven that Henry and Rose, along with a few others, had made a huge difference to the world, changing the future for the better in innumerable ways. The pride she felt, just knowing that, swelled within her. It allowed her to continue. Her husband was a more complicated case. He blamed himself for losing their son. Although he could never have foreseen the course their lives aboard the old *New World* would take, it had been his money and ambition that got them into all this. So now he spent his time trying to fix things.

Chelsea sighed, running her fingers through his greying hair. "Never mind, honey. Try to relax. Why don't I make us both a nice cup of coff— Oh."

Their door chimed, covering her embarrassment. "Coming." She unlocked the door. It slid aside with the gentle hiss of hydraulics to reveal their daughter. "Come in, honey. I thought you were with Tim?"

"He's with his *other* women," Clarrie greeted sourly, striding into the Burnstein quarters to flop heavily onto the sofa. "Where's Dad?"

Chelsea nodded towards the kitchen. "He's, erm... fixing the coffee machine."

"It's broken already?"

"*Well...*" she answered uncertainly, and then brightened. "Would you care for some tea?"

"Fine," was Clarrie's lacklustre reply.

"Will Tim be along soon?"

"Who knows?"

Chelsea sat next to her daughter and took her hand, stroking it with her thumb. "Is everything alright, sweetie?"

Clarrie sighed. "I guess. It's just that, with the wedding postponed because of this crazy trip, I just thought he'd at least spend a little more time with me."

Chelsea smiled warmly. "And these 'other women', are they the problem?"

"He always loves spending time with Dr Natalie Pearson." She pouted. "I really wish I didn't like her so much."

Chelsea laughed. "And the *other* woman?"

"That honking great dinosaur he brought home. Honestly, most men come back from work with a stray dog, or a cat that suckered them out of their lunch pail – not my Timmy!"

"Darling, Tim will always be inseparable from his dinosaurs. You've always known that. They're always on his mind and in his soul, but only *you* have his heart."

Clarrie pulled a face. "Seriously, Ma, is that kinda 'one out of three ain't bad' speech meant to make me feel better – the blushing bride *not* to be?"

Chelsea pulled her daughter into a hug. "No, that's a 'you got the only bit that matters' kinda speech. Without the rest of it, he wouldn't be Tim. And you'll get your big day after all this, honey. I promise."

Clarrie tried not to smile. "Stop being so wise, Mother – it makes you seem old!"

The door chimed again. Chelsea gave her daughter a final squeeze before leaving the sofa to answer it. "Tim, come in. We were just talking about you."

"Hello, Mrs B. Is Clarr—"

"Yes, I am, and *you're* late!" a voice shot from the sofa.

"I was just about to make some tea, dear. Would you care for a cup?"

Tim gave Chelsea a conspiratorial wink. "That would be lovely. Thanks. Would you mind bringing it *to* me, please? I'll be just over there, you see? In the doghouse."

Chelsea wandered back into the kitchen, chuckling to herself.

Tim was about to explain, but it occurred to him that he was not yet sure what it was that he had done wrong. He decided it would be wisest to find out before offering excuses that might easily open another avenue of attack – he could always save those excuses for next time, or for when he was surer of his ground. Instead, he lit up his best smile and said, "Hello, sweetheart. Missed you."

"Huh! I'm surprised you even noticed I was gone with your, your *Brontosaurus*..."

Tim had not really expected his charming 'hello' to work. It was but an opening gambit – little more than a sacrificial pawn. Clarrie's response had been more telling, however, throwing just a crack of sunlight across the trouble in his path. Way forward partially lit, he should have been able to avoid it, perhaps even step past it into the sunshine, but his teacher's instinct kicked in before he could think better of it and he corrected her. "You mean Spinosaurus aegyptiacus." After a faux pas of such magnitude, he should have kept his head down from there onwards and grovelled. Especially as he was simply not dressed for the Arctic coolness already spreading towards him across the sofa. Having nothing whatsoever to do with the environmental system, the encroaching winter was all set to squeeze his early daffodils by the bulbs, when he was unexpectedly saved by the bell.

"Wouldn't you just know it, everyone's coming to see us today, it seems," Chelsea muttered happily as she bustled through the apartment's open plan lounge to the door for a third time. "Hello?"

"Step back!" The gunman shoved her further into their quarters and closed the hatch behind him. "I'm here to wait for *Herr* Norris— Oh, I see he is already here. How serendipitous. Remember me, boy? Richard Weber, at your service."

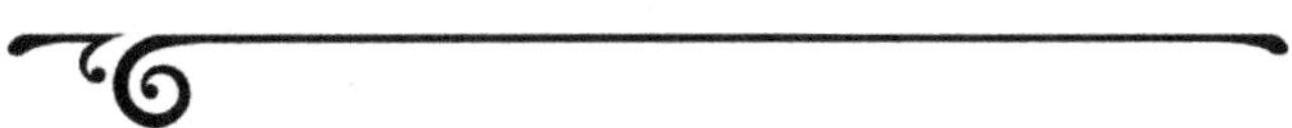

Prentice knew he could not remain where he was. The shooting outside had stopped, so either his people had escaped, or they had been taken captive. He would not allow himself to ponder the third choice at that moment. He tried the hatch once more – the one that separated him from Private Radburn. It seemed the ship had gone into total lockdown when the computers died, so he made his way along the corridor towards the bow of the ship. The hatch at the end was also sealed. From behind it, he could hear shouts and the sounds of tools and levers being employed. He jogged back the way he came. Fortunately, the hatch had failed to fully close behind them when he carried Radburn into the ship, explosion damage having twisted it so that it could no longer seal. The gap was just wide enough for him to squeeze through. Blinking in the sudden daylight, he waited for his sight to adjust before going further. As soon as he could see, he ran towards the main hatch and the outside world.

Upon reaching the exit, he literally bumped into two men coming the other way and raised his rifle instinctively. "Get out of my way or die," he ordered gruffly, barely recognising his own hoarse voice. "Choose!" Blackened from smoke, covered in blood and dust, and worse, he must have looked like a subterranean monster blinking its way into the light, because both men recoiled.

Armed with pistols, only one had a weapon in his hand. "Who are you?" he asked.

Prentice raised his rifle to shoulder height and pushed them back. "You were out there shooting at my men?" he demanded.

"No, we weren't," the smaller of the two replied, raising his hands in surrender.

Prentice studied him for the first time. "Don't I know you?"

"I'm Captain Aito Nassaki," he replied. "And you are?"

"Nassaki... of course. So you *did* survive. No one believed it possible – except your brother, of course."

"Hiro? He's with you?"

"Does it look like he's with me?"

"I mean, he's here, in this time?"

Prentice levelled his rifle once more. "You can come with me, *Captain* Nassaki. Turn around and move."

"I don't think so." Jansen lifted his own weapon. "Who *are* you, Sergeant?" He noted Prentice's stripes, just visible below the filth. "And more importantly, how the hell did you get here?"

"I am sorry, sir. We received a message through the wormhole to arrest anyone who stepped through – no exceptions," the young soldier stated uncomfortably.

Todt rolled his eyes. "Again!"

"Again, sir?"

"Where's your commanding officer?" Todt barked, rattled and annoyed. He did not have time for this. The guards had disarmed Engel immediately as they rematerialised in 1940s Munich. The corporal looked like he had crawled through the seven hells on his belly, but gave up his weapons without comment. Todt was not sure whether

Engel trusted him instinctively, or simply felt that he had nothing left to fight for. That would soon change, when the truth came out.

A young officer appeared. "Lieutenant Sonne, sir. I'm sorry, but we have orders to detain you."

"Do you know who I am?"

"Yes, sir. You're the people who stepped through the wormhole after we were ordered to detain anyone who came through, sir."

"Stand down, Lieutenant." Another man appeared from the next chamber within the Old Academy Museum.

Todt turned. "Colonel Schultz, thank God."

Schultz placed a hand on the younger officer's shoulder. "I'll take them into my custody, Gunther."

"Yes, sir."

Todt nodded his gratitude. "Colonel Hans Schultz, meet Corporal Heinz Engel. The Corporal has a great deal to tell us. We must—"

"You will *all* be coming to a secure location with me," Schultz interrupted. "Come."

As they moved out, Engel leaned in close to Todt. "Do I assume our situation has not improved?"

Todt glanced at him with concern but had no answer.

UNS *New World* approached the Earth. Once they had power restored, Hiro immediately took back control of the satellite net to make sure it was looking the other way.

"What's our play, James?" asked Baines.

"Get to within striking distance and hold our position, until we can find out more about what transpired down there. Ah'm very worried about Adam's unit."

"Sergeant Prentice? Are we sure it was the dropship under his command that we saw crash?"

"There was so much going on, our wee dinocam was jostled about as much as all the real animals. The footage we received was shaky, but Ah cannae imagine who else it could have been."

"But why would he have ordered them to dive straight into the enemy camp?"

"Ah cannae answer that until we talk with the man. Either he had a damned good reason or no choice. If you look closely at the film, the ship left a trail of smoke before she even hit the ground – so Ah'm guessing the latter."

"Sir, the satellite feeds are showing a lot of movement on the ground," Singh interrupted. "They have close to two hundred tanks, more than half of them on the move and taking up positions all around their compound."

"Getting ready for an attack," Baines assumed. "The crashed ship *must* have been ours to set the cat among the pigeons to this degree."

"Maybe, Captain."

"What? You have some doubt, Sandy?"

Singh turned in his seat to face her. "It's just that the positions the tanks are taking up are... *strange*."

Douglas approached him. "What have you?"

"Look, sir, ma'am, rather than defensive, their movements are more—"

"Like they're laying siege," Baines completed. She frowned in confusion. "But why would they..." Her expression cleared. "Oh, I've got a bad feeling about this."

"Timothy Norris – or should I say, Timothy Schultz?" Weber spoke to Tim while leering at his fiancée's legs.

"No, you shouldn't." Tim stood, covering Clarrie instinctively from Weber's pistol. "My name is Tim Norris, but *you* can call me Professor Norris. Oh, I remember you, Weber. The imbecile that tried to free my..." He could not finish.

"Your *grandfather,* yes. You have no sense of the honour you hold, bearing his name, do you, boy?"

"*Honour?* I'd spit, but I'd hate to soil my future in-laws' carpet."

"You would marry into these commoners when you could be royalty? You are a fool, *Herr* Norris, but either way, I shall return you to the Old Man, or Dr Heidi Schultz. They can decide what is best to do with you while determining what my reward shall be."

Tim laughed bitterly. "You're the fool, Weber. There won't be any reward. They'll just use you up and discard you when it suits – it's what they do."

"It is honour enough just to serve Heinrich Schultz's cause – *that* is what you will never understand."

"On that at least, we can agree. They're evil and insane – what the hell would I want with them? And you're a complete wantwit for believing they assign any value to your service, or your life, for that matter."

Weber's jaw clenched in anger. "I need you, but this, this *family* you care so much about, I do not need." He fired at Chelsea Burnstein without warning. The pistol was in electric rather than ordnance mode, but the shot was a killing blast.

She hit the floor spasming, making gagging sounds. Clarrie screamed, kneeling beside her mother, tears of fury streaming down her face. "I'll kill you for this," she cried, voice breaking.

Tim also knelt beside Chelsea, checking for a pulse. The heartbeat was erratic, and she began to choke on her own tongue as she foamed at the mouth. "Let me call a doctor!" Tim bellowed. He pulled a marker pen from his pocket and used it to flatten the woman's tongue, forcing an airway.

Weber's face twisted with glee. "I have been waiting many years for this. You took the Schultz gift and spat it back in the Old Man's face, while your *friends* took everything from me." He hedged around them, with his back to the kitchen door. "Now it is I who will take a senior post by their side, and they will be generous."

Tim could see that ten years' incarceration, with nothing but electronics manuals for company, had clearly taken its toll. Now in his mid-thirties, the bright-eyed zeal Weber wore as a younger man showed the cracks of fragility.

"I always knew it had to be you, Norris. Douglas looks on you as a son. He will not allow anything to happen to you – vowed as much, years ago. I will get him to drop us off down on the planet, and we shall—"

Tim never found out the full extent of Weber's intentions, because at that moment, Hank Burnstein burst into the room from behind the gunman with the chassis of a coffee-maker in his hands. It trailed a cable to a power point, and Burnstein jabbed the mild steel frame hard into the back of Weber's head, switching it on. The bang and puff of acrid electrical smoke was like a school physics experiment gone wrong, but it sent both men flying – Burnstein back into the kitchen and Weber sprawling across Chelsea's prone form.

The blow made Weber lose his grip, even as the subsequent shock made him grasp at the air. Tim caught the weapon as it flew out of his hands. Grabbing their attacker with his free hand, he dragged him away from the women, anger giving him the strength to fling Weber back against the apartment's main entrance. Stunned and electrocuted, he groaned as Tim pulled out his comm. "This is Tim Norris to Dr Flannigan. Come in, Dr Flannigan. This is an emergency."

Weber began to laugh, which soon turned into a coughing fit. "*He* cannot help you, boy."

"Clarrie," Tim called over his shoulder. "Contact the bridge immediately – tell them we need urgent medical assistance and a security team."

She looked up tearfully. "She's dead, Tim."

Tim looked around in dismay and knelt once more beside Chelsea Burnstein. Her heart had indeed stopped. Before any thoughts of cardiopulmonary resuscitation could even be realised, the heavy blow to the back of his head sent him into darkness.

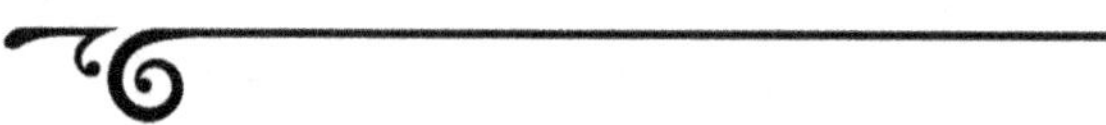

"We must get away from here," Aito hissed urgently. "Jansen, let us take this man to somewhere we can talk – *now!*"

Jansen nodded to Prentice. "He's right. There's more going on here than you know. Perhaps we can help one another. Come with me."

Despite his reservations, Prentice could see no other options – at least, not palatable ones – so he followed, too exhausted to think any more. They ran down the *Heydrich*'s boarding ramp and back towards the APC Jansen had driven earlier. "I'll feel better with some armour around me," Jansen called over his shoulder.

Seeing the main battle tanks manoeuvring all around them, Aito wondered whether they may just as well hide in the toilet for all the protection a lightly armoured APC would provide. At least that way, they might be granted a little dignity when it came time to let go. He followed Jansen inside, with Prentice bringing up the rear and closing the hatch behind them.

"OK, let's hear it," the Yorkshireman demanded.

"Aito, you start, while I get us somewhere safer," Jansen ordered. "Aito? *Aito?*" He shook him. "What's with you?"

"Oh, nothing. I was just thinking about Elvis. Didn't he die on the... never mind."

Jansen's expression was halfway between a pained wince and all-out bafflement. "*What?*" He shook his head. "Just get it together, will ya? Don't tune out on me now." With that, he disappeared into the cab.

After several minutes' drive, Aito's brief story drew to a close. "So that's where we're at. Each time one of the Schultzes' crazy schemes comes crashing down, Heidi builds a new one over the ruins of the last." He called through to Jansen in the driver's seat. "Isn't this, like, their fourth dastardly plan to take over the world, now? I'm losing track. It's a palimpsest of nightmare scenarios. By the way, one of the prisoners who escaped is Heidi's fourth-great-grandaunt from 1940s Munich – also named Dr Heidi Schultz, just to keep things simple. The physical resemblance is marked, too, though she seems possessed of a very different nature."

"She's Heidi's *good* opposite number?" asked Prentice.

"I wouldn't say that, exactly," Aito hedged. "She's stinking rich, spoilt and lazy, but she doesn't seem fixed on world domination or genocide, so I suppose in a way she's... less bad? Who knows for sure, right? That aside, we don't know what *our* Heidi's up to now, either, but with the destruction of the *Heydrich* and some of our complex, she's bound to go for her exit strategy."

"And what's that, then?" Prentice asked cautiously, as yet undecided about whether he should trust these men. He wanted to return Nassaki to his brother – or failing that, to custody – but alone and on a prehistoric planet with no backup, he realised that, for now at least, he would just have to roll with things.

Aito held out his hands, palms up. "I wish I knew."

Prentice couldn't help noticing the appendages were mismatched, one hand being white to just above the wrist.

Nassaki noticed him noticing. "German parts," he elucidated sourly.

In an effort to remain amicable, Prentice suggested, "Still, on the other h— Oh... erm, I mean to say, you know, German reliability and all that?" He flustered as the metaphorical tumbleweed rolled between them. Watching Aito's expression sour further, he changed the subject. "Look, if Heidi's here, we need to stop her, not run away."

"Hey, come and look at this," Jansen called from the cab.

They climbed in behind the driver.

"I've been following these tracks left by the stolen tank," Jansen explained. "Looks like they took a detour here. Let's follow."

"These would be Heidi's prisoners that escaped early this morning and blew hell's bells out of your ship?" asked Prentice.

"Yeah," Jansen replied distractedly. "Let's see where they went."

"You think we might get them on side?" Aito queried with concern. "Surely they won't see us as being any different from their captors."

"Maybe, but they have the only tank that, as far as I can tell, isn't under the yoke of that master control system, so it's gotta be worth a shot."

"There's a master control system?" asked Prentice. "So those things were running on automatic when they..."

Jansen risked a quick glance away from the tracks through the forest. "I'm sorry, Sergeant, but yes. At least, I believe most of them were. I don't know if they were given an instruction to attack your people, or whether you triggered an automated response when you crashed in the middle of our compound. They were swarming everywhere, but the stolen tank never returned."

"How do you know the stolen tank's not still under Heidi's control?" Aito asked again. "They may just be out of range."

"No, they would have got the recall anywhere on this continent. They must've disconnected their vehicle from the network somehow."

"How could they possibly know how to do that?"

Jansen turned a sharp left, following the trail smashed by the tank. "What am I, the oracle? How the hell would I know? Maybe they were just messin' about with every switch they could find and cut the connection by accident. Look, can we just leave this conversation until we have a— *crap!*"

It was Aito's turn for bafflement. "You need to go *now?*"

"Whoa!" Prentice exclaimed.

Their armoured transport rocked to a stop just inches away from the muzzle of a large-bore cannon. Nassaki stumbled forward. Catching himself, he looked up and was forced to concur. "Oh, crap."

"Make it shoot!" H pulled on Badawi's sleeve, tugging him towards the gunner's seat.

"At this range?" he cried anxiously. He had hoped to evade their pursuit at least until darkness fell. This was a most unwelcome surprise. "I don't know if that's a good idea, mis— Heid— er, Dr H," he stumbled over her titles.

"Get us out of here!" Aito pulled on Jansen's sleeve.

"Surely they won't shoot at this range," Jansen cried anxiously.

"They're not tank commanders, Jansen. He's a small-town policeman and she's an expert on obscure Italian Renaissance painters! What if she just hits the wrong button? What if— Oh, this is my *worst* nightmare." Aito's face paled to match his prosthetic hand, as the barrel of the mighty Tiger XII main battle tank depressed enough to point straight in their faces. "*Do* something!"

"Do something!"

"Like what?" Badawi retorted frantically. "If we shoot now, we might take damage ourselves. It's not like they have heavy weapons."

"They will have a radio, you silly little man!"

"*Little?*" Badawi bridled and then frowned. "A radio?"

"You want me to call them on the radio?" Jansen could barely believe his ears. "*Now?*"

"What else can we do?" Prentice raised his voice to cut through the panic of what was shaping up to be their last few seconds on Earth.

"And say *what?*"

"Don't bloody shoot, for a start off!"

"Yes, a radio – for calling for backup? I thought you were a policeman, Apep?"

"I am a— Look, never mind that, you've given me an idea."

"Good!"

"Good!"

"Good, let's do that." Aito's fear was transmitted via his powerful prosthetic hand to Jansen's arm.

"*Ow!* Will you lay off?"

"Sorry. Get on the radio!"

"Alright, I'm on it. Miss Schultz..." Jansen muted the comm. "What's the guy's name?"

"Badawi, Master Sergeant Badawi," Aito supplied. "Hurry!"

"Right, Miss—"

"Doctor."

"What?"

"She's a doctor of something or other. For God's sake, Jansen, you captured her. Didn't you even get her name?"

"I was busy. This is a call to Dr Schultz and Master Sergeant Badawi..." He muted the comm once more. "Who shall I say we are?"

Prentice groaned, holding his head in his hands.

Aito cried out, "Santa Claus, it doesn't matter. Just tell them not to shoot!"

"Right, of course. This is... erm, this is APC 3." He winked at the others, pleased with his cover name. "It would be best if you didn't blow us up."

Prentice looked through the web of his own fingers. "Oh, my God. I never thought it would end like this."

"APC 3, this is... will you give that back to *me?*"

"Get on with it, then!"

With forced calmness, Badawi tried again. "Ahem. This is Master Sergeant Badawi – please state your purpose."

H could not believe her ears. "*Please?*"

"It never hurts to be courteous."

"They're here to capture us, Apep. Why else would they have chased us?"

"They did not chase us, they found us."

"I *know*. That's our problem."

"Don't worry," Badawi placated. "They're under *our* gun. If they give us any trouble, I'll just back us off to a safe distance and fire upon them."

"Why don't you do that now?"

H's suggestion took him by surprise. "I suppose that would give us more options." He switched on the motors and began to back away.

"What's he doing?" Aito asked, an edge of panic in his voice.

Jansen frowned. "I don't know, retreating?"

"Got him right where you want him, have ye?" Prentice commented acidly.

"He's backing up to take a shot." Aito spoke so quietly, they almost missed it.

Prentice fell into the cab's passenger seat. "Follow him, quickly," he pressed. "Don't let him build a safe gap between us."

Jansen started up the APC's diesel engine and crashed through the foliage after them. Although the tank was technically travelling forwards, its turret was reversed and pointed at Jansen, Aito and Prentice.

"Go faster," Aito urged.

H was holding on to Badawi's shoulders. "Slow down."

"Why?"

"Because we've been turning slightly left for a while now and any minute—"

"We are *not* steering left. I will have you know, I have an excellent sense of direction. Survival often depends upon it in the desert—"

"We're not in the desert, we're in the jungle! *And* we're turning left. Any minute now, we are going to— *Stop!*"

The trees made a constant scraping across the vehicle's hull, obscuring its tiny view slots and cameras. They ended abruptly as the tank's nose dropped away, sending a bow wave out across the river. Badawi was already in full reverse, but the tracks merely tore away at the bank while its vast weight pulled it inexorably forward. Seventy tons of steel and laminated graphene, laced with millions of minute solar panels, skipped and slithered sideways into a large tree trunk that swept out at an angle over the river. Out in the sunlight once more, a small beep sounded in the cab to tell the driver that the batteries were indeed charging again. Unfortunately, this was drowned out by the traction control warning and the shaking as the whole machine juddered. The left-hand track bit into the tree and they rocked to a stop, precariously balanced over the water's edge.

"Do... not... move." Badawi's voice was hardly more than a whisper as he gently released the drive levers.

The river ran deep and fast where it narrowed. He knew that if they went in, they might well drown waiting for the water pressure to equalise before any escape was possible. Tanks were not usually watertight. An airlock at the top of the tank might prevent them from opening the hatches at all, under so much pressure.

They looked at one another bleakly.

"I may have been veering a little to the left," he confessed.

"Whoa." Jansen cut their speed right back as the tank in front of them popped out into bright sunlight, only to immediately tip forwards. "Looks like we're back at the river."

Aito leaned over, to see through the small view slot. "Have they gone in?"

"Not yet."

"Happy days," said Prentice, wryly. "If they shoot now, it'll be t'last thing they do. Can you open another short-range communication channel?"

Jansen nodded. "You're on."

"Master Sergeant Badawi, this is Sergeant Prentice. I suggest you get out of there and surrender yourselves to us before you go in – over."

The comm crackled to life once more. "*We're coming out, unarmed – over.*"

"Shall we?" suggested Prentice.

The three men left the APC via its rear hatch and walked around to the front of their vehicle with weapons trained on the tank's top hatch. It flopped open and a pair of hands appeared. "We're unarmed and coming out now," said a man's voice.

Badawi climbed out onto the top of the turret. He raised his hands to show they were empty before reaching down to help H up behind him. As she scrambled out and got to her knees, the tank began to slide.

"Jump!" Prentice shouted from the ground.

The man and woman leapt hand in hand from a height of two and a half metres. As the tank slipped beneath them, the cannon's barrel swiped their legs, twisting them in the air so that they fell into the river after it. H was flung near the edge, where the bank knocked the wind from her chest as her legs crashed into the water. Badawi was thrown further out to land with a splash right behind the tank. The massive vehicle went in obliquely and immediately began to turn over in the river, air bubbling furiously from inside its hull as it rapidly took on water. Badawi flailed helplessly with his arms as the suction from the sinking tank began to pull him down, too.

Jansen ran and held out a hand to the woman coughing and struggling her way back up the slippery bank, so recently torn up by tank tracks. She looked up and recognised him immediately as one of her captors. Despite her predicament, she recoiled.

"It's OK, Dr Schultz. I'm here to help you."

With no other choice, she reached for the helping hand. "You were with my great-grandniece."

"Yes."

"Where is Apep? Was he thrown clear?"

"Badawi? He's..." Jansen pulled her out of the water while searching for her companion. "Let's just get you out first and then we can—" His breath caught as a large sail broke the surface near to where the rapidly sinking tank sat like a temporary island in the middle of the flow. "Oh, no. Some help here!"

Aito appeared at his side, and together they pulled the German woman out, one arm each. She coughed and spluttered, turning to look for her co-escapee. "Apep? *No!*"

Badawi was scrambling with limited success up the side of the tank as it spun over. Shock and terror were taking their toll and he was struggling for breath, his strength failing him. With one last, gargantuan effort, he managed to crawl atop the sinking vehicle.

Prentice placed his hands on his head in horror, helpless to do anything but watch as the tank began to turn over more quickly, like a heavy weight had been attached to its offside. "Jump!" he shouted again. "Jump for your life, man!"

Badawi turned exhaustedly to see what all the panic was about, just in time to see the claws and open jaws of a Spinosaurus aegyptiacus erupt from the river. "Aaaaarrrrgggghhhh!" he screamed.

ROAR! the creature replied. It, too, was struggling to get a purchase on the barrel-rolling tank, though it still managed to swipe for the Egyptian policeman with its heavily taloned forelimbs.

Badawi stepped backwards, two, three, four times – almost running in reverse to counter the spin, while he fought to stay out of the dinosaur's deadly reach. He was not usually a man given to foul language, but when wind from the claws' passage shook the river water from his goatee, he gained a fluency he never knew he had – right up to the point where he fell backwards to disappear below the surface once more.

He popped up a couple of metres closer to the bank. Spinning around to find his bearings, he wasted no time in kicking his feet, eventually moving into the crawl stroke, encouraged by the spectators on the bank.

The tank, so low in the water now, suddenly vanished in a froth of bubbles. Spinosaurus was initially tugged down with it, but soon broke free, the astonishing musculature in its tail and limbs powering it back towards the surface. It emerged in a fizz of carbon dioxide as its nostrils opened, capacious lungs exhaling sharply. Gulping down fresh oxygen, it looked around for its quarry and saw him, just a few metres from the bank. It leaped forward like a sea serpent, over and under again.

Through the splashing of water from his own strokes, Badawi could still hear shouts of encouragement from the bank, though they seemed to have taken on a cadence of panic. He could not make out what was being said among the free-for-all, but the tone told him everything he needed to know. He redoubled his efforts. Between the strong current and the barrel-rolling, he had been carried well out from the edge and into the flow. Badawi was a strong swimmer; growing up alongside the Nile, it made sense, but he was barely holding his own. He glimpsed one of the men attempting to cut a light branch from a tree, but it would never arrive in time. Before he could dwell on that, he found himself rising, straight out of the water. "Aaaaarrrrgggghhhh!" he screamed again as he flew through the air. Now positive this was not his lucky day, he could not have been more wrong. Confused by the bubbling of the sinking tank, the extraordinarily sensitive Spinosaurus snout misjudged his position and distance. The jaws closed just beneath Badawi's belly, while the upward momentum of so many tons on the move thrust the dino's nose straight up into his gut. It knocked seven bells out of him, but nevertheless launched him through the air towards the bank. He landed with a splash just two metres from shore, utterly breathless and back where his ordeal had started.

Prentice looked around. Jansen was still sawing at a small branch with a penknife and Aito was helping the girl. He turned back to reach out over the water with the only thing he had to hand.

Badawi grabbed the end of the rifle's barrel, terrified by what lay behind, and now by what lay in front. "Keep your hands away from the trigger!" he bellowed with the last of his breath, cross-eyed and transfixed by the weapon's muzzle, like he could *will* it not to fire.

Prentice tugged and they both fell backwards onto the bank. He rolled over and jumped back to his feet, grabbing Badawi by his shirt as he ran away from the shore. A roar of frustration followed immediately behind them. "RUN!" Prentice hollered at the top of his lungs.

Jansen dropped what he was doing and ran to Prentice, also grabbing a handful of the policeman's collar as they dragged him away. Badawi was propelled forwards with his legs spinning behind like a slapstick comedian on ice, but they dared not stop to let him regain his feet. All five of them leapt into the back of the APC as the dinosaur crashed through the brush beside it, smashing its way to the rear. The speed with which it had followed shocked them. As the last man dove inside, its monstrous head and long neck followed them.

"Shut the bloody door!" Prentice yelled hoarsely as he dialled up his rifle's stun capacity and fired.

Spinosaurus collapsed, making the front of the carrier jump and throwing its occupants to the deck or into the walls. The shock had not completely knocked the animal out, but it had certainly knocked it silly. Its jaws parted and its tongue lolled into the rear of the APC.

"Great work, Sarge," Jansen called out caustically, rubbing a bump on his head. "Now what are we going to do – swim back for the tank?"

The grotesque tongue extended, unrolling like a slimy party blowout whistle, as it probed for H's leg. She screamed and scrambled across the vehicle's floor to back away.

"Drive forward," Prentice demanded. "Quick! Unload him before he recovers."

Jansen scrambled to his feet and threw himself forward into the driver's seat. When the diesel engine roared to life the dinosaur stirred, clearly aware, if unable to stand. Jansen threw the APC into gear. With the dinosaur's weight added, it dug in at the rear, carving deep grooves in the earth, but as more of the tracks found purchase it began to move forwards. A semi-conscious groan of annoyance left the animal's mouth as the massive head slipped back outside. Prentice sealed the hatch immediately and slumped down against it.

Badawi had fallen to the opposite side of the hatch. He was shaking with shock, his teeth chattering.

Prentice got back to his feet and raided the vehicle's first aid box for emergency blankets. The Red Cross symbol, though synonymous with help and healing, only drew his thoughts back to his failure to secure that help for young Radburn. The dreadful moment, when the teenager had sacrificed his own life to save him and cripple the Schultzes' principal war machine. The fact he had not even been given chance to retrieve the body weighed heavily on his soul.

He clenched his teeth and pushed the memories aside as best he could, while unwrapping and unfurling two silver quilts. He handed one to Badawi, the second to H. "Miss," he offered gently and slumped down again.

The Egyptian policeman managed a stuttered thank you. "I really w-want to g-go home now."

"Aye, lad. Don't we all."

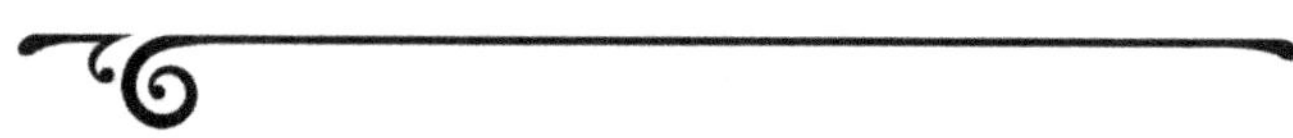

Dr Reid picked up his travel bag and checked his watch. He had just a minute, maybe two, before Heidi returned. He agonised a moment longer and then typed a brief message, encrypted it, and sent it 'eyes only' to a specific contact. His hand hovered over the return key, while his mind raced through the ramifications if he were caught out. In the end, absolute horror of what Heidi planned to do won over his cowardice and he hit the key.

"Are you ready?"

Reid jumped like a spotlit cat burglar.

"Dr Reid?" Heidi asked suspiciously.

"Yes, ma'am," he answered too quickly, speaking around his heart, that was suddenly in his mouth.

"Is there a problem?"

"No, ma'am. I'm just a little nervous about *things.*"

"Come. This will soon all be behind us." She turned and walked from his office.

"Yes, ma'am," he answered darkly. Swinging the bag over his shoulder, he took one last, longing look around his office before he left, too.

The Spinosaurus started to regain its senses, which was as well, because it was blocking their way back. The armoured personnel carrier was a large vehicle, but its weight was but a fraction of the main battle tank's, now lost in the river. It was less powerful, too. If they tried to smash another path through the heavier, denser foliage at the heart of the forest, they risked getting stuck. Jansen suggested waiting the animal out. Now they were locked safely inside, it could no longer harm them, and they could use the time to become acquainted.

Badawi went first as his part was the simplest to tell. He told of a missing girl on a fossil dig in Egypt, that ended with his abduction by Heidi Schultz – the other Heidi Schultz, he hastened to add.

H – also known as Dr Heidi Schultz – took some cleaning wipes from the first aid box and set to work on Prentice's myriad cuts and scrapes while Badawi spoke. She began by wiping the filth from his face. Prentice resisted at first but soon gave up, deciding that, after what he had been through that morning, a little hen-clucking was just what he needed.

"Hmm," H remarked, pleased with the result. "Handsome under all that dirt." Once Badawi had finished his tale, she took up the baton, telling of her life, her family and how she came to be embroiled within her fourth-great-grandniece's machinations, right up to the point where she met Badawi and their escape together.

Jansen's story was somewhat more convoluted, beginning with his recruitment to the Order of the Silver Cross by his uncle Lucas Jansen, latterly known as Del Bond, and his cousin, Lieutenant Audrey

Jansen, pilot of the USS *Newfoundland*. He told of his many hair-raising adventures with Heidi though a world of dinosaurs, egg heists and Nazi megalomaniacs, concluding with their eventual incursion into 1943 Germany and his more recent role as camp security chief.

Aito told them of his student days, how he had become influenced by Sargo Lemelisk – one of the Schultzes' less controllable psychopaths – who falsely set him on his journey towards communism, a journey actually paid for by his father's multinational, capitalist corporation. The irony of that completely escaped a younger Aito Nassaki, as did Lemelisk's true purposes. Blinded by an extremist's zeal in those early days, he had seen oh, so much since then – including how he might change the world from within the Schultz organisation. His chosen path had placed opportunities before him that could never have been realised in his old life, within their original timeline. So he had faked his own death, with Lemelisk's help, and vanished.

Prentice stared searchingly at Aito Nassaki. The crews of the *New World* and *Last Word* had grown close as family over their last decade together. Aito's brother, Hiro, had been a friend for many years now and he could not help drawing comparisons. "Still think you can change the world, Aito?" His question was pointed so that he could gauge the other's response.

"Perhaps," Aito offered cautiously. "Our own time was ending, and clearly things here cannot be left as they are."

Prentice nodded, ordering his thoughts before telling his own story. "What if I told you of a world where man and nature lived side by side in harmony? Sounds like a cheesy pop song, I know, but I've seen it, lad. And I'll tell you summat else, it's worth fighting for."

"And where would this perfect world be?" Aito made little effort to hide his scepticism.

"Not where, lad. When. We left Cretaceous Earth ten years ago – although I know it's only been about seven months for you – and almost made it home. However, call it fate or fortune, we crashed just shy of our own time." Prentice regaled them with tales of daring rescues from castles in the frozen north, with stories of reiver raids under the crisp winter moon, murderous priests and demonic noblemen, even princesses in distress. He had to crack a smile. "I was there, and I still can't believe the half of it, but our crashing in 1558 may have been the luckiest event in the history of our race – though for us, it came with a cost. A heavy one. When we found our way forward again, to 2113, not all of us made it, but here's the twist – the ones we left behind changed the world." He nodded towards H. "The Germany this lass grew up in's proof of that. No Nazis, no death camps, no World Wars. The 2113 we popped into may not be perfect, nothing ever is, but I tell you this – it's damned close."

Aito's scepticism was still plain on his face and Prentice studied him keenly, distrustfully. "I already knew of your past from your brother, Aito. That you jumped from hard left to join a psychotic fascist like Schultz doesn't surprise me at all. I understand, from Hiro, that your own father tried to explain to you that extremists consistently go all the way round to join up at the back – they're the same people, dyed in the wool. The question is, are you willing to leave all that behind now?"

Aito noted Prentice's rifle was ready across his lap where he sat. "And the wrong answer will get me shot, is that it?"

Prentice gave a half-smile. "I'm a soldier, lad. Not a factionalist. And, aye, I obey my orders, but only so long as they're *moral* orders. If you stand in my way, you'll do so as my prisoner – unless you leave me no choice," he added darkly. "I've seen a world worth saving. And even if I can't save it for myself, I owe it to the folks back there to save it for *them*. Don't matter if they never know about it, or us. They're good, open people, willing to share and to learn. Living among them was an experience, I can tell ye. Course, if we work together, we'll all stand a better chance o' getting through this and accomplishing our goals."

Prentice looked to Jansen. "If you're part of t'same organisation as Del Bond, can I assume we're on t'same side?"

Jansen was thoughtful a moment. "I think we *all* are, Sarge. You're telling us that if we play this right, we might actually get to go back, and to proper lives... I can hardly believe it. Sure would be a shame to get myself shot at this stage." He smiled genuinely. "I'd forgotten what hope felt like. I thought the future was lost to us."

"It was, lad." Prentice relaxed to a more comfortable sitting position. "No matter how hard we struggled, our world was full of people fighting against one another and even their common interests. All that mattered was destroying the other side – or the other side's position and standing. We were completely polarised. It was pathetic.

And not only that. Do you remember what the food was like?" His nose wrinkled in disgust.

H's interest in the finer things life had to offer made her curious. "What *was* your food like?"

"Grey slop," the Yorkshireman answered directly. "The resources to provide real food were gone. It kept us alive, but it weren't fit to eat. That all started a hundred years ago for us. Again, should you get chance, our historian, Thomas Beckett, is a mine of useful, if depressing, information. It began with food companies removing ingredients to make their products allegedly healthier – so they weren't sued by their customers."

H frowned in confusion. "Sued?"

"Aye, folk began suing t'food companies, if they had, say, a heart attack or summat. It led to the labelling of ingredients, but the law then deemed people incapable of reading or understanding that, so they started takin' good stuff out o' their grub instead."

"Grub?"

"Food, lass. 'Course, they soon realised that takin' stuff out reduced costs, and saying it was healthy allowed them to charge more. We ended up eating crap as you wouldn't feed to a pig! Aye, and paying through t'nose for it, an' all![15] Eventually, there was so little to go around that, unless you were rich, you were on the grey-enzyme slime."

It was H's turn to wrinkle her pretty, pampered nose. She looked to the others. "We must *do* something."

Jansen ignored her, asking, "OK, so how did your people in the 1500s change all that?"

"Well, I weren't there to see t'changes, but reading the new histories from 1558 onwards, there was a slow change in thinking over the next half century. Actually, comparing the change wi' t'rest of our history, maybe *not* so slow. The world was a big place in those days. Once it opened out, there was less pressure by population, and advancements were made. Our people, having seen fifty billion of us clinging to one rock alone in the universe, must have impressed that on them.

"I'd like to say, baby steps with everyone playing their part had a hand in our development, but knowing some of t'folk we left behind,

---

15   Hiding in the back of an armoured vehicle in mid-Cretaceous Egypt, Prentice may have been about as far from beautiful Yorkshire as it was possible to be, but Yorkshire could never fully be removed from the boy.

they may have introduced the new thinking with a big stick – I can't say for sure – remembering the food we had to eat probably gave 'em extra incentive to stop it all from 'appenin' again.

"They *were* instrumental in working change through the world leaders, I know that, beginning with Queen Elizabeth I. Once t'others started to see the advantages, they must have fallen in line pretty quick. The Holy Roman Emperor had one last stab at a smash and grab in 1588, with the Armada, but we all know how that worked out. Our people must have had a tight hold on the reins by that time."

"How so?" asked Badawi, completely wrapped up in a history he never knew.

"Change doesn't happen overnight. I reckon, if Elizabeth had been given full access to our technology by that point, the Spanish Armada would have had more to worry about than Sir Francis Drake and a few fire ships." He reflected a moment. "Must have been hard to see all that coming and not act. Still, I suppose they knew from our own history that the endeavour would fail. I wonder how it went down this time around?" He lapsed again, into a thoughtful silence.

"So, they told the primitives to keep their numbers under control – what else?" Aito prompted, harshly.

"Oh, no, lad. They weren't primitives. They were a great people. Less advanced than us in some ways, maybe, but not primitive. They lived, they worked, they loved, they laughed, they cried, they invented, they built... they did their best, just like t'rest of us. Obviously, there were a few bad apples, when aren't there? But don't damn a whole people for the time in which they lived.

"As a soldier, I've often seen first-hand where ignorance can lead. My time in the new future taught me a lot. Most importantly, I learnt that history's the best teaching tool we have, but only for those willing to remove their blinkers and take time to understand it all in context, and where possible, from all sides. I never took any interest before, but having seen how it *should* be done, finding out what went wrong became irresistible. Despite what some may think, no one has a monopoly on *anything*. The good and the bad are obvious, all there to be remembered and used to plot a route forward. There's no point isolating and condemning any bits you don't like, lad. It just polarises further, even turning people against, who might otherwise have agreed with you. And what does it leave us with? A tired and endless clip show of repeats that passes for 'news'.

"I count myself lucky to have seen all that I've seen. It's easy to mock from our collapsed ivory tower, but the sixteenth century was a vital period in our history, one where reading was just starting to be encouraged. Again, our historian, Thomas Beckett, explained it to me that the sixteenth century saw the birth of what we'd call t'modern world, and all because people wanted to read t'Bible and understand it for 'emselves wi'out being told what to think by a priest. Some people loved it, others feared it, but though it began with religion, once folks could read... well, the limiters were off.

"As for keeping our numbers in harmony with the natural world's ability to renew itself, well, you've *seen* where overpopulation led us. Aye, and tasted it! Can that point *be* overstated? The human race can accomplish anything when we live in balance with our world – I've seen that, too. There're less than two billion souls in the future we just left behind. It's a place and time where there's plenty for everyone. The rest of our kind live among the stars on other Earth-like planets – it's amazing.

"Our crew in 1558 may have begun the spread of knowledge in the sixteenth century, but more than that, they spread a new way of thinkin', an' all. Turns out, avoiding extremism *can* be a learned behaviour." He looked again to Aito. "According to your brother, your father was a man who would have understood. He would have been proud that his sons had a hand in what would become a *true* new world. Hiro spoke about you often. He loves you. He never gave up on you being alive – despite what 'appened with that dinosaur. I'm paraphrasing what he told me, but I believe your dad advised you both to avoid extremism – for either side – and that's how you avoid hate. Words to live by, eh? Empathy and cooperation follow as a natural consequence, and with cooperation comes advancement – in fact, from what I've seen, I'd say that without cooperation, there's no future... What?" He looked around his audience. "Too namby-pamby? Listen, I might be just a lowly sergeant, and people often think of soldiers as killers, but a *real* soldier's job is to *save* lives. Don't ever confuse those brave men and women with them dickheads who just like hurting folk and think a uniform gives 'em the right. OK, I admit that after the last twelve hours, my emotions may be running a bit higher than usual—"

"No one could blame you for that, Adam," Jansen cut in, compassionately, as a fellow serviceman. He smiled. "And there are no *lowly* sergeants – everyone knows they really run the military. It would grind to a standstill within hours without them."

Prentice nodded thanks and continued, "Sometimes we *have* to use force against an aggressor, I don't deny it – *you* know that – but I tell you *flat,* hatred only gets you killed in war – it *never* works in your favour. If I'd given in to it, I'd have shot Aito and Jansen, here, on sight, when we met. God knows I had cause to hate, after what had just happened to my men, just because we were unlucky enough to be shot down by the Schultzes' machines. Any civilised force would have taken us prisoner and treated our wounded, but if I'd fired in anger at that moment, not one of us here would be alive now. Turns out, we all needed each other to reach this point."

The reality of his statement sank in for them all.

"Sensible words," Aito acknowledged. "I'd even go with 'fine' – and I'm obviously glad you didn't pull the trigger – but all these things have been said before. No one ever listens."

"Aye, but that's just it, lad. I know it's hard to believe, but they *did* listen. Whether initially by choice or under duress, I couldn't say, but the idea took off, either way. Look, I knew some of t'folk we left behind. Most were good people. Others were, well, let's be kind and say they were yet to prove 'emselves. Now, I doubt they won over the sixteenth century populations with kind-hearted liberalism alone – that would only have created another extreme faction, contra to the way people thought. Life was harsher and more brutal back then for most folk. My crew more than likely scared the bejesus out of everybody, by showin' 'em video clips of t'future!"

He turned to Jansen and Aito specifically, with a northerner's forthrightness. "All this is giving me an 'eadache, so I'll make it simple, shall I? The world the three of *us* left behind in AD2112 was nearly dead. I won't let Heidi kill paradise to bring it back." He fingered his rifle in passive threat. Nodding to Badawi and H, he concluded, "These two need to get back to their good lives, in their own times, an' all. So, are you with me or not?"

Aito reached out his left hand to Prentice, then thought better of it. He stood, to offer his right, his real hand, instead. "If this new world is all you say it is, I'm with you."

Prentice stood and took it in his own. "It's the right choice, Aito. We pull this off and you'll see the future. A better world even than the one you dreamed of in your student days, and you'll get your brother back."

Before Aito could answer, Jansen's comm binged. "Could that be Devon?" he asked, hopefully.

"With any luck," Jansen replied, gesturing to Badawi and H. "We haven't heard from him since these two blew the guts out of our ship."

"We're sorry about that," Badawi replied awkwardly. "They seemed evil people."

Jansen shrugged at that. "Some of them are, but like all groups they're a mixed bag. Many of us are here to save the human race from what *was* a rapidly approaching extinction. As Sergeant Prentice just explained, our world was nearly dead. Perhaps we've managed to dodge that bullet somehow, in the future he was talking about."

"*Perhaps* you should open that message," Aito nudged him.

Jansen sighed. Without exactly knowing why, the idea filled him with dread. He frowned. "The message is heavily encrypted."

"What does it say?" Aito pestered.

"Hang on." Jansen read. Eventually, he swallowed. "We have a problem."

"What kind of problem?" H asked, hesitantly.

Jansen dragged his hand slowly down his face as he exhaled. He opened his eyes. "The end of the world kind."

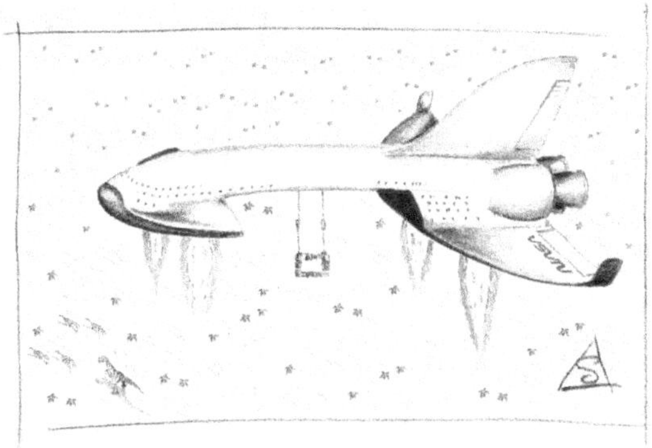

Chapter 13 | Newfoundland

"She's ready to fly, Commander," Dr Harry Bismarck reported to Coleman in her private quarters. "The wormhole catcher is complete and already mounted under her belly."

"You were able to fit it in between the ship and the Pod?" queried Coleman.

"Yes. The Rescue Pods are only three decks. Lowering it to the ground to form part of our perimeter, last year, created a gap big enough for us to work within. When do we leave?"

Coleman stood and winced. Her recently broken ribs were mending, but every now and again she would twist or move without thinking and they would reward her with a great slab of pain. "We don't." She spoke through gritted teeth. "At least, *you* don't. Harry, I'm taking a skeleton crew and leaving you in charge here."

He blinked in surprise. "But Brian Alba is the senior man—"

"*Was* the senior man," she cut him off. "If we don't make it back, I can't leave you in tow to Mr Glass-is-half-empty. Those of you who don't get eaten will be building dugout canoes within a season! No, I need someone to lead with hope for the future. I know how much you love it here—"

"Commander," he interrupted, "it sounds like you're not *planning* to return."

"Oh, I'm planning to return, alright. I'm just not sure it will be possible. There's every chance the *Heydrich* will blow us out of the sky before we even get near enough to be effective. Whatever tale we tell them, it won't change the fact that we flew halfway around the world without orders and abandoned our post. And that's not allowing for any awkward questions about what we're actually doing there.

"Don't worry, Harry. I *know* you can do this. I've left orders in my log stating that you will be in temporary command of Crater Lake Base. If the *Newfoundland* doesn't return, yours will become a permanent post, and the base will fall fully under civilian control with all military personnel answering to the civilian leader – that's you. Are you OK with that?"

A deep sadness came over Bismarck. "But we were in this together. The new world. Now Heidi's lunatics are mostly gone, we have it great here. Can't you just, I don't know, leave them to it in Egypt?"

She smiled bravely. "That wormhole she's opened, Dr Hemmings says it's continually expanding and won't stop until it's consumed everything. It's a threat to the entire planet, and the longer we leave it..."

Bismarck hung his head and sighed. "How did we become embroiled with those people?"

"I take it that's a rhetorical question? We joined them because we wanted to survive. So far, we have."

"But, Ally, we had the whole world. None of this was necessary."

She took his hand. "We knew the sort of people we were getting involved with, Harry. Maniacal despots – some might say, evil. Unlucky for us, they were also the only ones with a plan. No one else would do anything to save our race because decisions that harsh would have been political suicide. You remember how it was. We were so overpopulated, hardly any of us even got to eat real food. Heinrich Schultz's twisted philosophy freed him from troubling over the problem of who dies so that some may survive. Our leaders would have let us *all* die. They weren't completely to blame, of course. Maybe dying with honour is better than living with shame – I have neither the time nor the will to worry about that now. They were paralysed because the practical decisions they needed to make could not have been made *morally.* We'd simply bred ourselves to death."

"I know, I know," he replied miserably. "Our success was our demise, and we failed to speak out against it. I just don't want you to go, Ally. Why should we lose now because of what the Schultzes, and the menagerie of fools we followed before them, have done or failed to do?"

"Because someone has to stop them, and we may be the only ones who can, now. I don't want to sacrifice my crew, this ship, *or* my own life for that matter, but if we don't do this, there will be no future. No future for *anyone*."

Bismarck swallowed. "Ally, there's something I should say before you go."

She brought his hand up to his chest and clasped it with both of hers. "Don't say it, Harry."

"You knew."

She smiled. "If I make it back, we'll talk. If I don't, you should move on. Thank you. For everything. Dismissed, Dr Bismarck."

Dr Harry Bismarck stood with Dr Brian Alba in the large compound off the *Newfoundland*'s starboard side. Aside from the skeleton crew aboard the behemothic carrier, the entire base population stood clear of the launch area to see Coleman off. She had spoken to them all briefly from the roof of their personnel carrier, outlining their plans to prevent the wormhole from creating the worst natural disaster since Earth was struck by a Mars-sized planet, billions of years ago – a collision that quite possibly gave Earth her moon. For those yet to hear of the wormhole crisis, she explained the obvious, that any event on that scale would utterly doom all life.

Bismarck thought she had spoken well, though his emotions dulled his concentration. Alba nudged his arm, gesturing to his own ears. Bismarck nodded and inserted the earplugs everyone had been given.

When the *Newfoundland*'s thrusters fired, the volume was astonishing, even with their protection. The ground shook, even sending tremors out into the lake. Every animal within half a kilometre fled to forest, burrow, the depths, or the air, depending on their kind. Slowly the vast ship began to rise on four fully functional thrusters.

Alba surprised Bismarck by taking him by the hand and shaking it enthusiastically. It was far too loud for any words, but theirs was a triumph. Most never expected the old and much beaten craft to ever fly again. As she gained altitude vertically, she turned further southeast and began to move away. With no Pod filling the void under her belly, she resembled an old-fashioned telephone handset – one with a point at one end and a cluster of massive rocket engines in a diamond configuration at the other. Once at a safe distance from Crater Lake, her main engines fired, shattering the peace for many miles around. She shot forward, vanishing almost immediately. Within seconds, the *Newfoundland* was gone.

"Sergeant, move your security teams in to cover the gaps in our perimeter," Bismarck ordered. "Brian, get your teams to work on the fences straight away. Come on, people, let's move!" He clapped his hands. Once all was in motion, he, too, turned to the southeast, his thoughts following the old ship and her young commander. *Please come back.*

"Have you got a comm on this bucket, capable of sending a signal into orbit?" Prentice asked urgently.

"Sure. What do you have in mind?" Jansen asked in return.

"We're going to need 'elp." Prentice swallowed, stress tightening his chest. "It's looking like I'm the only survivor after t'crash and the attack by those tanks. If any of my people had... Well, they'd have tried to contact me by now. The *New World*'s up there with personnel and equipment we're going to need to find those tanks and stop 'em."

"Use the comm in the cab." Jansen pointed towards the front of the vehicle and Prentice wasted no time in placing a call.

"These tanks," Badawi asked. "What is special about them?"

"Two of them are carrying mixed ordnance," Jansen explained. "Five thermobaric and one nuclear warhead. Heidi had them built to make a 'demonstration'. They were to be part of her planned 1944 world tour, I guess. But now she intends to use them to destroy our compound completely, erasing all evidence of our ever having been here. The fact that it will create an ecological disaster in the region makes no nevermind to her. She must have a plan to get out of here and damn the rest of us."

H's brow creased with concern. "You think she intends to go back to Germany?"

Jansen shrugged. "Last I heard, Heinrich Schultz is still there. Perhaps she has a way to join him, collapsing the wormhole behind her, I don't know any more – she left me out of the loop months ago. But she's so wild, she may have something completely different planned. It's hard to say. There's little love lost between granddaughter and grandfather, not since he tried to lock her away and replace her with Tim Norris. We spent a lot of time together during that period." He shook his head. "No one hates like Heidi – believe me. I'll be more concerned if she chooses *not* to go back to Germany."

"Why?" asked H.

"Because that would mean she intends to leave the wormhole open when she detonates her nukes. Whether deliberately, or because she just doesn't care, hardly matters."

Silence fell. Eventually, Badawi raised his hand to ask another question. "How do we recognise which tanks carry the special ordnance?"

"They *were* parked together, but now the whole fleet has taken up positions around the compound, they're all shuffled. We'd have to check inside each one. They're identical from the outside. I always wondered why they weren't given serial numbers, like any other fleet – seems this was all part of her exit strategy, after all."

"And when we 'look inside them', as you say," Badawi could not let the point go, "what exactly will we be looking *for?*"

"Aside from the two we need to find, all the tanks are armed with standard shells. We're after the ones that also have—"

"Red and blue shells," Badawi completed, closing his eyes and bowing his head.

Jansen stared. Horror ballooned, and like a pricked balloon, he exploded. "You stole a tank with nukes on board?" Jumping to his feet inside the APC, he banged his head. "*Ow!* Goddamn it! Are you crazy? You might have killed everyone when you trashed the *Heydrich*'s hold! You pointed that gun right in our faces! And now it's..." He pointed out through the armoured bulkheads towards the river, unable to finish the thought.

"Don't worry," H defended their decision. "We discussed the pretty, cornflower blue shells and decided we shouldn't use them."

"I was particularly concerned about the red one," Badawi added with chagrin. "Always a warning colour – apply it to a tank shell and, well..."

A loud roar came from outside, followed by a bang that rocked the personnel carrier on its tracks. "Looks like our friend has woken up," Prentice noted as he stumbled back into the rear compartment.

"And it sounds like we've got to go back out there and somehow dive to retrieve those warheads from t'bottom of t'river."

Aito began to laugh, but there was no humour in it. "Oh, I love *that* plan!" Another boom rocked the APC as it was struck by a massively muscular tail. "I mean, what could possibly go wrong?"

Lieutenant Devon waited impatiently, left arm in a sling and right arm over a crutch. His shoulder had connected unexpectedly with a bulkhead and he had twisted his right knee when the *Heydrich* shook from the force of two explosions – explosions now known to have originated from within. The shoulder had been dislocated. Shoving it back in had hurt – a lot – but that had been merely the first attack. While backtracking evidence to find out how the prisoners escaped, it seemed those same prisoners had backtracked themselves, even having the audacity to return in one of the Schultzes' own tanks, no less. Devon still seethed about that.

Then came the second attack; the least damaging, but by far the most worrying. The enemy ship had dropped from nowhere, right into their compound, stretching the definition of 'dropship', while shocking them into realising they were no longer alone. Heidi's suspicions had proved correct.

The third attack was the least of the three, yet had wrought the most damage. Someone had detonated a hand grenade among the *Heydrich*'s computer banks, throwing the ship into instant lockdown. Only now had they finally reached the source of the explosion and Devon paced awkwardly, while engineers tried to lever open the hatch. With one useless arm and the other holding the crutch that nursed his injured leg, powerlessness only added to his fury. So long as he kept most of his weight off the damaged knee, it was not too bad, but the pain from his shoulder seemed to engulf his whole left side whatever he did – it was not helping his disposition. If the *Heydrich* was beyond repair, where would that leave them? Building another would take phenomenal resource. Much of the technology required to *create* the technology would have to be built from scratch before they could even begin.

He fumed impotently and impatiently. Eventually, the hatch was pried open, inch at a time, allowing the acrid smell of spent explosives mixed with electrical burning to spread into the corridor. *Yep, definitely a grenade,* he thought. *Brave, but stupid. And wasteful. They were pushed to this, and now we're about to reap what the fool who ordered an all-out attack on that crashed ship sowed. Damn you, Heidi.* He could not say for sure whether the order came from her, but if not, it would have come from one of the Schultzes' creatures. Devon had been one himself once, in the thrall of Captain Emilia Franke – a zealot to the cause if ever there was one. Now he could see the cracks of division within their people. Some were content to have saved the human race and wanted an end to the relentless ambition of their leaders, others were too far gone to be reasoned with. Hardcore Schultz acolytes. A stand-off was inevitable. He could feel it. Perhaps this latest mess would light the touchpaper and they could just get it all over with.

Smoke still belched from the long, narrow plant room as sparks popped and flew out of the darkness. He leaned against a wall, coughing and wafting it away with his good arm. Eventually he pulled his tunic up over his nose.

"There's a body in here, sir," one of the engineers called.

Devon knelt with difficulty next to the man, several metres from the epicentre of the blast. He lay unmoving. It did not appear that he died in the explosion. Devon assumed he had been trapped by the lockdown, eventually succumbing to the fumes within the enclosed space. With the computers down, there was no extraction, either. They had been fortunate to avoid secondary fires. Squinting in the low light, he glimpsed the young man's other wounds, most notably the gaping hole in his thigh, tied with a tourniquet.

He stooped to check for dog tags. "Bring me a light," he called to one of the engineers. Blood group, service number, surname, initials and religion. Scanning the information, he read the name *Radburn M.* He shook his head. The enemy soldier was just a kid – a teenager. With no expectation, he checked the neck for a pulse. When the body began to cough, Devon recoiled. Flailing with one arm, he almost ended up on his backside. "Get a med team down here on the double!" he barked. "We have wounded!"

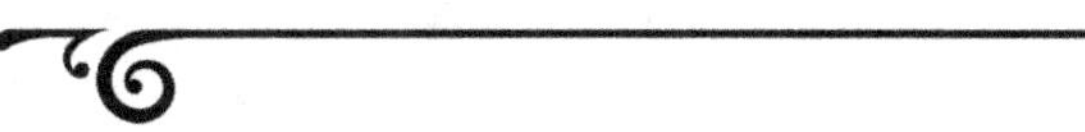

"We still have three dropships, James," Baines explained. "If Sergeant Prentice is right, we can't risk taking the *New World* down there. A nuclear explosion could end everything we're trying to save."

Douglas agreed. "Ah'll go down—"

"You really should stay here, James. I'm the XO[16] on this one, remember? I'll take a team down in one dropship, The Sarge can take another and Gleeson the third – we might need his expertise if we're hunting for explosives. That'll leave Captain Tobias Meritus as your second."

"Got it all planned, have you?" Douglas gave a half-smile. "And what about that beastie down in ma hold? We cannae send her down in a wee dropship, and she's got to go, Jill."

"I've been thinking about that, too. As part of our mission is to remove all potential traces of ourselves from the fossil record, you could drop her off while you re-exhume the bodies from the enemy plateau in Patagonia. If Heidi's planning on launching nukes from a gun, they can't be big ones. At least, not powerful enough to hurt the *New World* from that distance."

Douglas stared intently.

"What?" asked Baines.

"*What?*"

She sighed. "Look, we'll be fine. It won't come to that and the longer we delay here..."

He gave her one of his disapproving looks.

She grinned.

He snorted, ever exasperated by her audacity. "Aye, alright. It'll be easy enough for us to find the wreck of the *Last Word,* although Ah doubt Tobias will be thrilled, but..." His expression clouded.

"What is it?"

"It's just that Ah dinnae feel right about messing poor Arnold and Audrey around for a second time."

She held his hand. "I know. I'm sorry, but we must keep the fossil record clean, so that things can play out the way they're supposed to. Besides, they can be reburied in our time, where we can visit them. That won't be so bad, will it?"

---

16   Executive Officer or First Officer; Captain Jill Baines was second in command of the ship. Captain James Douglas had both seniority and command of the mission. Though of course, when at home, he largely did as he was told.

Douglas exhaled in exasperation. "How do Ah explain *that* to the *other* Arnold Bessel?"

"James, you know Arnie. He'll probably find it amusing and insist on being buried with himself when his own time comes. I can see the headstone now, 'Captain Arnold Bessel, so good they made him twice'. He'll love that."

Douglas threw his head back and laughed. "Most probably, but then there's the little matter of the beer can ring pull that was – or will be – trapped in amber. Jill, how am Ah supposed to find that?"

"You've got me there. But it's something that can be ruled out as an aberration – a freak set of events leading to something being buried stratigraphically out of context. Now, if a young Kelly Marston were to find that on a dig right next to several dozen fossilised Nazis, all buried in a seam of Cretaceous stone, *that* might take a little more explaining."

He chuckled. "Aye, you're right."

"Of course I am." She winked.

"But while we're talking about leaving behind an antiseptic presence, that animal in ma hold is from Egypt. Now, ma geography may be a little rusty, but Ah dinnae think that's in Patagonia."

Baines held up an index finger to forestall him. "I've thought about that, too."

"Have ye now?"

She grinned again. "Knowing how imperative it is that we drop off our guest, I got a little help from our chief expert. Actually, I think I may have gotten him into trouble with Clarrie – I made him late to meet with her family about the wedding. Anyhow, Tim told me that Spinosaurus aegyptiacus is quite similar to the *lovely* Oxalaia quilombensis we met in South America. In fact, there was initially some confusion about whether they might even be the same species, but the distance between the drifted continents boggled even our most brilliant minds, pending further evidence. I suggested to Tim that this palaeontological conundrum may have been caused by the introduction of a Spinosaurus into the mix. Tim rebuffed the idea as absurd, naturally, stating that, no matter how at home they were fishing the rivers, no terrestrial dinosaur could swim across the Atlantic – not even the narrower Atlantic below us."

"So how did ye answer that?"

"I told him it could cross the Atlantic, if it had a spaceship."

He closed his eyes and mussed his hair in agitation. "That's some line you walk."

"It's all in the balance, James. Anyhow, then I asked if he believed it possible for the two species to interbreed."

"And?"

"He thought it might just be possible physically, if not geographically." She smiled broadly. "Palaeontological conundrum solved – and it gets better."

"*No?*"

"Oh, yes. Turns out that Natalie's tests have shown that our lady dinosaur has already laid eggs at least once in the last few years. Her bone marrow shows evidence of old and new medullary tissue because guess what – she's pregnant again! Palaeontological conundrum double-solved! She'll be fine, James."

Douglas' disapproving blue-eyed stare switched to high beam. "Alright, Ah'll get it done," he drawled, sourly. "Just *be* careful."

"You know me."

As she left, Singh chuckled gently.

"What?"

Singh unlocked his pilot's seat and turned it to face him. "Glad you're back, Captain? I bet you missed all this. I'd offer to make you some Earl Grey, but the last time we landed in Patagonia you threw your cup at me."

Douglas could not help but chuckle. "That wasnae me – it *was* ma favourite cup, after all."

"Yes, sir, I felt it break on the back of my favourite head!"

"Captain Baines, this is Sergeant Prentice. Come in."

"*Reading you five by five, Adam. Go ahead.*"

"We're approaching the enemy compound from the south in an unarmed, tracked vehicle. Please don't shoot at us."

"*Understood. We'll be over you in sixty seconds.*"

"Negative, Captain. The enemy tanks will fire on your approach. Give us a little time to disable them and find the nuclear weapons."

"OK, Adam, it's your party. We'll fly a long loop. Call as soon as you're done, and we'll move in to mop up."

"Understood, Captain. Prentice out."

<hr>

"Dr Reid, pack your things aboard our ship and wait for me inside. I will be along directly." Heidi strode away, back towards Reid's laboratory.

He watched her go, heart thumping like a kick drum. He could not take in everything that was going on around him; tanks everywhere, enemy vessels on the way. How had they come to this? The entire world had been theirs for the taking, with practically no one to share it with; it was beautiful. Now it would all end in fire. Taking a shuddering breath, he stepped aboard Heidi's orbital attack craft. The vessel's hold was set up more like a campervan than a troop carrier, and along with its extra fuel capacity, it also packed special ordnance. Reid had serious scruple about leaving such a weapon in Heidi's hands – serious scruple, but insufficient courage to deny it to her.

From the co-pilot's seat, he had a clear view south and watched the approach of an armoured personnel carrier. It threw clouds of dust into the air as it drew closer, taking the track up from the river – a track first cut by Heinrich Schultz's escape pod, jettisoned from the *Sabre* all those months ago. Reid wondered who could be travelling it now. He also wondered if Jansen had received his message. Perhaps that was him returning. He hoped so. Reid did not want to be even partially responsible for Heidi's petulant pogrom. She had sought the Germans out, invading their 1943 as surely as if she were the vanguard of an occupying force, filling their heads with such tales of glory. It was 1944 there now, and the Schultzes were trying to corrupt an innocent timeline – they *were* corruption. He should stop her, but he could not. He was a coward and hated himself for it. So he had sent the message to Jansen – a man who was anything but a coward.

"I wish I'd become an accountant like Dad," he muttered softly, then looked around nervously. There were no internal bugs built into the ship – he knew that categorically – but that did not preclude Heidi from strategically placing 'aftermarket' devices.

The APC arrived at the gates. Two men jumped out to talk with the guards. The remote system for the drawbridge must have been damaged by the recent tank collision. He tapped a few keys and used the ship's optics to zoom in on their faces. Yes, it was Jansen and Captain Nassaki. The temptation to open a channel was hard to resist. He needed to know whether Jansen had got the message. As soon as Heidi started the countdown, they would have just thirty minutes.

He watched the guards lower the drawbridge and the APC trundle over it into the compound. Jansen jumped out for a second time and the vehicle set off again without him, continuing north alongside the ruin of the *Heydrich*. Eventually, it passed out of sight behind buildings, while Jansen headed towards Reid's own laboratory. Watching the man enter the building, he felt a thrill of anxiety. The message must have got through, but if Jansen burst in there now, he would walk straight into Heidi.

Reid swallowed nervously. "I really should have become an accountant."

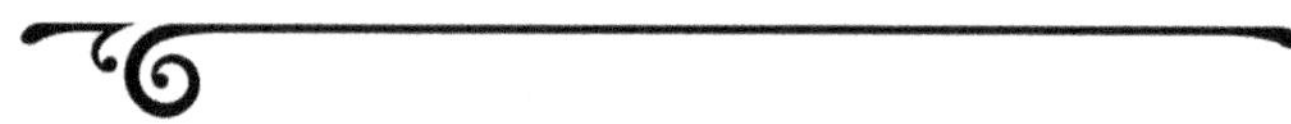

Jansen walked into Reid's laboratory with just two things on his mind. The first was Heidi and the second was how he might undo her twisted schemes. Reid's message had been clear, his panic almost syncopating his words. Jansen knew he had very little time. Heidi had forewarned him to await her call; they were to meet up outside this very building, although she had not called yet. Nevertheless, he knew his time was running out. When he opened the door, he realised his time had come.

"Heidi?" he asked dumbly, struggling to process the scene before him.

She looked up, eyeing him coolly. "Jansen. A necessary precaution."

Her explanation chilled Jansen to his core. "You call *this* a precaution?"

"Indeed." Heidi had her trusty nine-millimetre pistol in hand, silencer mounted to its short barrel. Before her were three dead bodies. One shot in the back of the head, the other two merely in the back as they tried to escape. Jansen recognised them. One was a computer programmer from the *Heydrich*'s crew, the others were Germans from 1940s Munich. "They knew too much. I was just about to contact you," she continued as if they were arranging a drink after work.

"It is time for us to leave. You have been..." She tailed off for a moment, clearly unsure how best to put her thoughts and feelings into words. "You have been most useful during our adventures together."

"*Useful?*" Jansen could hardly keep the disgust and disdain out of his voice.

"Perhaps that is not the right word—"

"Perhaps," he cut her off acidly. "Heidi... what the hell have you done now?"

She kept her gun in hand, not exactly aimed at him, not exactly aimed away, either. "I could not leave these loose ends behind. You will understand once you have command of my whole plan."

Jansen stared wide-eyed at the bodies, bringing his hands together, prayerlike, over his nose and mouth. "Does no life mean anything to you, Heidi?" he asked, eventually. "Does no *one* mean anything?"

She looked away. When she looked back, her eyes bored into his. "You might, perhaps, matter a little."

Jansen was shaking his head in disbelief. "What are you trying to say, you *might* hesitate a moment before murdering me?" he asked, a mixture of disbelief and sarcasm. "Didn't you care about Tim Norris, too? A man you've vowed to kill, even if you have to destroy the whole of causality to do it?"

"That is different. He is family."

A bark of laughter escaped him, unintentionally. "Heidi, what are you about to do?"

She approached. Her manner was not beseeching; the Schultz DNA did not allow for it, but she clearly wanted him to go with her. "I do not wish to be alone," she stated with finality.

Jansen did not like the sound of that. *What the hell is she up to now, the end of the universe?* "Where is Dr Reid?" he asked instead.

"He is coming with me."

"So, not alone then," he countered.

"That is not the same. I..."

Jansen could not believe what he was hearing. Was she offering him some form of a *relationship?* Presumably one other than slave and mistress, although with Heidi, it was difficult to imagine any other kind. Could she be that inept with the basics of human contact? For a long time, he had been secretly confused about his feelings for Heidi and now, as he examined them again, in this charnel house, he surprised himself. He was being offered an incredibly exciting life with one of the most beautiful creatures the devil had ever spawned. Everything he could want, every *when* he could want – a short life, almost certainly, but it would be exciting.

Then Heidi surprised him. She opened her arms wide, allowing the nine-millimetre to hang from her finger by its trigger guard. "The last time I trusted anyone, it did not go so well, I think. Maybe one more time – one *final* time? Well?" she asked, not taking her eyes from his.

Her beauty had always plugged directly into his libido, making him doubt himself, even sicken with himself, knowing her as he did. All his training with the Order of the Silver Cross flashed through his mind; his family, his cause. Even the people of Munich, going about their daily lives as he and Heidi sat by the River Isar together, when they thought they had lost everything. He remembered how she had been found by Coleman, hiding in a cave after the Norris boy's betrayal. He had pitied her then, perhaps even *felt* a little for her. Heidi's first ever brush with love, even if it was just a glancing blow. *Could she seriously have feelings for me, too?* he wondered. Then he looked again at the dead bodies of three young men on the floor and realised it hardly mattered. She was a monster. In a lightning move, he took his own weapon from its holster and held her at gunpoint.

Heidi's expression changed, ever so subtly. Jansen could not read it, but he could not fail to spot it.

"So, you betray me, too, Ben," she stated softly. "It seems I make lousy choices with the men in my life."

Jansen looked her in the eye. "I can't let you go through with..." He realised he did not actually know her plans. "Whatever it is you're going to do," he finished lamely. He had never before seen pain in her eyes. Anger, yes. Fury, usually – along with a whole gamut of contempt. He had even seen disappointment there, but never hurt – not until now. Was it real?

He levelled his weapon a moment longer, staring deeply into her eyes. Eventually, he lowered it. "Just go," he said, looking away.

He felt the pain before he heard the almost silent shot. He dropped his pistol, bringing his right hand to his chest as he crashed to his knees. His agony was inexpressible, not that he was able to talk. He collapsed, breathing hard. The bullet wound to his chest was serious; he could feel life fading with all the colours in the world around him.

Almost out of his wits, he felt something soft touch his lips. He could not see. Why could he not see?

Heidi straightened after kissing him. She had closed his eyes, gently. "An eye for an eye, a tooth for a tooth, a heart for a heart. Goodbye, Ben."

Jansen gasped. He could neither move nor feel his legs, though his mind ran at speeds he had hitherto never experienced. He still had command of his right arm and with it he reached into his trouser pocket for his comm. "Aito." His voice was barely a rasp. Summoning the very last of his strength, he tried again. "Aito. Reid's lab. Come."

He felt his heart stop; it was as sickening as it was surreal. Why was he still conscious? He did not understand. Surely that was not how it was meant to be. It was like he had missed his train and now waited impatiently for the next. Everyone knew the stories about corridors of light, but as the vision behind his lids faded from red to black at the edges, he suddenly found himself standing over a vast chasm. It was so deep that no light reached its bottom. He felt himself fall, but there was nothing to see, nothing to know, nothing to feel. *I'm not ready,* he thought, but it made no difference.

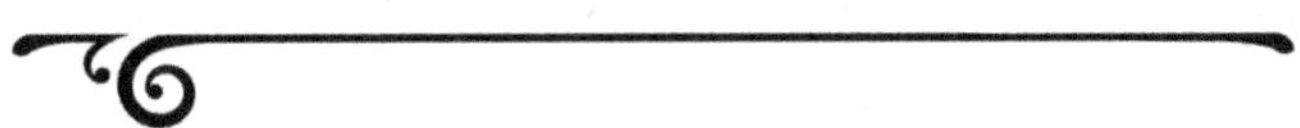

"Take a seat, gentlemen." Colonel Hans Schultz stood at the head of a long table in the Old Academy's boardroom, having packed the young surveyors off to hospital in a military ambulance. "I apologise for the lack of medical care we have so far offered you, Corporal Engel. Please feel free to use the lavatory through that door to at least clean yourself up, if you wish."

Engel saluted the officer and took advantage of what little comfort he could get.

"Why are we here, Hans?" asked Todt when they were alone.

"We are here to meet someone with whom I have had very little patience over the last ten years, but needs must." A knock at the door. "Ah, that will be him now. Come."

A young man of perhaps thirty popped his head around the door. Spotting Colonel Schultz, he entered and closed it behind him.

"Welcome," Schultz greeted. "Fritz Todt, please allow me to introduce Herbert Frahm. I am sure you each know who the other is, even if you have not met."

"We have met before." Todt rose to shake hands briefly with the newcomer. "Herbert Frahm leads what *our* Party Leader, Martin Bormann, describes as one of the fringe parties." He smiled to show that he bore no malice with his words.

"Chief Engineer Todt," Frahm returned the greeting. "Still apologising for the wrong side?"

Todt chuckled and pulled up his seat once more to the table. "So, Colonel, we are not to be interrogated and executed then?"

"You will forgive the formality of my greeting, Fritz," Schultz explained. "After everything you told me I thought we should tread carefully. Ah, Corporal Engel, looking a little more human, I see. How are you holding up? Please, have a seat. You look like you could use a stiff drink, too." The colonel brought a whiskey decanter and four glasses over to the table from a sideboard, on a silver tray. "They have some nice fittings and chattels in this place. I can see why my sister would spend time here."

Engel accepted a glass two-handed, still shaking slightly from horrors so recently endured.

Schultz evaluated him kindly. "We'll keep this as short as possible. I have brought *Herr* Frahm here because we will need popularist support to break the grip my... *descendants?* have over the ruling party. I did not invite any of the major players in opposition, because they are just as likely to be involved in this as our government officials – covering their own ends and agendas, you will agree?"

Todt nodded. "A wise move, Hans. Although I do not believe the broader German government will stand for this. That is why Bormann and his cronies are keeping it quiet as long as they can, in my opinion.

"That aside for the moment, this is Corporal Heinz Engel. He is the man who saved my life and the life of the young lady I journeyed with, through the wormhole. He is also from the future. Not our future, exactly. A parallel future, and one that we hope will no longer come to pass." He looked to Schultz. "You have explained to *Herr* Frahm about the wormhole and our time travelling 'benefactors'?"

"He has," Frahm answered for himself, though his attention was fixed on Engel. "This whole business is monstrous. The German people will never stand for it. Not in this day and age."

Engel took a deep draught of his whiskey and shifted in his seat, awkwardly. "Forgive me for contradicting you, *Herr* Frahm, but you might be surprised just what people *will* stand for. If you'd seen what I've seen, the history the people of my timeline created, you'd see a pattern of turds floating to the top and mankind making all the same mistakes over and over again. Forgive my bluntness, I'm not a diplomat."

Frahm leaned forward intently, linking his fingers on the table. "No apology necessary, Corporal. I've little time for our profession myself sometimes, Heinz. May I call you Heinz?" He smiled disarmingly. "It seems we have all slept too long and it is time to wake."

"To this and other dangers," Schultz added.

"Perhaps," Frahm allowed. He turned back to Engel. "Please, tell us what you can of these Schultzes that are allegedly offering us the world on a platter."

Engel spoke, hesitantly at first, his thoughts ordering around his words. Tiredness made the task more difficult, but knowing the stakes at hand, he refused to give in to it. The colonel ordered them some coffee and sandwiches while Engel unrolled the whole history of the Third Reich, the Nazi movement and its millionfold atrocities. He explained how the people of Germany had suffered, both from insane leadership and from vilification on the world stage, even though so many of them were themselves terrified of the Nazis and their *Wehrmacht*. He walked them through the Nazi resurgence under Heinrich Schultz, all the way to the worldwide network of criminal and militant organisations he had fostered and developed by the early 22nd century. The knowledge, drilled into him since he was young, came as an outpouring of words and emotion, achieving the exact opposite effect to the one its architect had intended.

History complete, he explained about the alternative future in which he had just spent the last ten years, as a civilian. The future he hoped that, by life or death, the people around that table could still bring to pass once more. Douglas' mission would continue in the Cretaceous. They could hope for his success, but theirs was a different path and just as vital to protect the future from the threat posed by Heidi and Heinrich Schultz.

He closed by explaining how the building in which they were seated had been destroyed in the original timeline by Allied bombing in the

Spring of 1944, just a couple of months ago. "I can offer nothing but conjecture on this point, gentlemen, but what if the destruction of this building is what our Captain Douglas calls a 'fixed point'? The wormhole is hidden from the world within these walls. We know it must be closed if this timeline is to escape the ruin I have already seen, the ruin the Schultzes will bring again – no disrespect to the colonel intended."

"None taken." Schultz had to raise a wry eyebrow. He knew all he had heard to be true, though it still sounded like dark fairy tales. "Perhaps I should reconsider having a family."

Engel took his words seriously, considering them carefully. "Hard to say, Colonel. Any children you may have will grow up with very different stimuli to the Schultzes I know – as long as we can put things right."

"Not a believer in the evil gene, then, Corporal?"

"Sir?"

Schultz smiled. "Forgive me. It was not my intention to taunt. It is just so much to take in."

Engel returned his smile, though his was etched with exhaustion. "Every morning, I wake up and it takes me a while to remember which time, timeline and world I'm in. It's nothing short of a miracle I'm so well-adjusted."

All four men chuckled, while Todt poured them another drink. He spoke as he walked around the table. "So, my friends, it will be very difficult to get the evidence we need from the Cretaceous Period to prove all this. We have a witness in the corporal, but he will be telling the Party things they will not want to hear. So, that said, how should we proceed?"

Frahm held up a hand to speak. "I have an idea."

"Jansen!" Aito burst breathlessly into Reid's lab with a pistol in hand, Prentice, Badawi and H following on his heels. "Oh, my God. Help over here!" He cradled Jansen's head in the crook of an arm. Badawi kneeled next to him while Prentice kept guard.

"That bullet wound looks very close to his heart," Badawi noted, sadly. "No pulse."

"Let me give CPR." Aito laid Jansen flat.

"No." Badawi grabbed his arm. "If the heart has been damaged you might cause irreparable harm. Do you have stasis chambers?"

"Do we have what?"

"Medicine wasn't as far along in our original timeline, Master Sergeant," explained Prentice. "He needs surgery. Now!"

Aito wiped Jansen's blood on his trousers and pulled out his comm. "Radio silence be damned. Devon? Devon, this is Aito, come in."

"*Where the hell have you been?*" came a terse response.

Aito sighed with relief. "You're alive, great. Devon... *Devon*, shut up and listen to me! Jansen has been shot. We believe his heart has been damaged. He has no pulse and has been down at least a minute already. We need an emergency medical team to Dr Reid's lab immediately!"

"*We have our hands full over here. Power's out across the entire ship—*"

"Then break out the emergency generators," Aito screamed into the device. "Get a medical extraction team over here *now*, Lieutenant – that's an order!"

"*OK, Captain. On their way.*"

Aito looked around the group. "What can we do for him? His brain's suffocating."

"Do you have refrigeration in this building?" asked Badawi.

"I believe Reid has a small freezer for materials that must be kept stable at sub-zero temperatures. Will that help?"

"It might." Badawi took Jansen's shoulders. "Help me lift him. Now, where to?"

Aito grabbed Jansen's legs and backed towards a large steel door. "H, could you?"

She ran to the door, opening it ahead of them. "Will freezing him help?"

"Not freezing," Badawi corrected, "but the cooler he is, the slower his metabolism will work. Hopefully, we can stave off oxygen deprivation and brain death a little longer, until a medical team can get him onto life support."

Aito looked down at Jansen, sadness clouding his expression. "Right. Sergeant Prentice, watch the door for our med team – give them a yoohoo or whatever you Yorkshire people do to attract someone's attention."

"You *who?*" asked Prentice, baffled.

Aito was not listening. "I need to finish what he started." He took Jansen's comm and ran to a computer terminal. Keying the access codes from Reid's encrypted message, he logged into the tanks' automated control software.

"Have you ever used this before?" asked Badawi, catching up with him.

Aito shrugged. "Not exactly."

"Not *exactly?*"

"Alright, no. How hard can it be?"

Badawi gave him a look that shimmied around the edge of scepticism into frank disbelief.

Aito accessed the system. It was indeed complicated, and like most first editions, less than intuitive. Reid's hastily scripted warning was as low on detail as it was frantic. "I think MC must be the master control... oh."

"What is it?" asked H, joining them and bending over his shoulder to see.

"Turns out, it can be *quite* hard. I've no idea what most of this stuff is. The labelling is terrible. It's all initials and the rest is mostly in German. For crying out loud. What were they thinking? These aren't toy boats in the park!"

H scanned the German instructions in an attempt to help him. "Why has no one ever written a set of help files that tell you anything more than the obvious things even a hamster could work out?" she asked rhetorically, sharing Aito's frustration. "They *never* cover the obvious problems people will come up against that have *no* obvious solutions – like what the jargon words mean in plain German or English, or whatever. Why do the programmers not simply recruit someone to use the system who has never seen it before, and write the help files around their findings, instead of assuming we all understand the in-house terminology they and their three friends have invented? And why do they always hide the menu? Oh, come on!" She banged an anxious fist on the desk.

"Well, at least you don't let it bother you," Badawi noted cautiously.

"Where *are* those medics?" Prentice exclaimed from the door. "I'm going to look for them."

"What's next?" H continued, not listening to either. "Hide the controls on our vehicles, too? So we can admire the swish hieroglyphics as we peruse menu after menu in a desperate attempt to bring the minimised steering wheel back before we die on the Autobahn?"

"They're designed that way to make you buy another one," Aito offered an answer, even though she did not expect one.

"Really? Why would anyone do that?"

"Because you'll have almost certainly put a hammer through the first one you bought. Trust me, I'm an engineer."

"Ah, I see. Ooh, what do you think that does?" H pointed over his shoulder to the word *'Töten'*.

Aito turned to look her in the eye. "You think we should try a button that says 'Kill'?"

"It might be a kill switch," suggested Badawi.

Aito blew out his cheeks. He moved the index finger of his real hand towards the touchscreen. Within five millimetres of contact, a huge bang on the door made them all jump. Prentice ran in ahead of a medical team. "He's in there. Move, move, move!"

"Oh, crap," Aito muttered quietly.

"What?" asked Badawi and H together.

He looked up at them, sheepishly. "I pressed it."

"Stay back!" Weber ordered the Burnsteins as he dragged a stumbling, semi-conscious Tim Norris towards the door. The blow he delivered to the back of Tim's head allowed him to retrieve his pistol. He hit the open stud with his elbow.

The door slid into the bulkhead behind him, revealing the corridor.

"You son of a bitch!" bellowed the Hank Burnstein of yesteryear. "If I get my hands on you, you bottom-feeding—"

"Shut it, Burnstein, or you will join the missus on the floor!" Weber knew he had less than a minute to escape before security arrived.

By moving towards Weber and hurling insults, Burnstein was playing a dangerous game, but he had to keep the gunman's attention on himself, because he knew something Weber was yet to realise. As the door slid open, someone else stood at the threshold, who was clearly just about to knock. With his attention on the family, Weber never saw Woodsey. There was a *thwok* followed by a *fizz* and Weber went down cross-eyed.

"Oh, *man!*"

"What is it? Are you both alright?" Clarrie shouted, the edge of hysteria in her voice.

Woodsey looked down at the bottleneck in his hands, remnant of the champagne magnum he had been carrying. "Do you have any *idea* how much I paid for that?"

Weber groaned and Woodsey bent to relieve him of the weapon, stepping on his face as he crossed the room. "I can't believe that just happened," he continued lamenting over the broken bubbly.

He was barely inside the apartment when Captain Meritus arrived on the run with a four-man security detail. "What happened?" he demanded.

Immediately on his heels, Dr Dave Flannigan arrived with an orderly. He too stepped on Weber as he dashed over to Chelsea Burnstein's side. "Sorry it took me so long, folks." He waved a hand vaguely behind him in Weber's direction. "That cracker-box tied me up. Nurse Smyth has a concussion. Luckily, Matron Runde found us and freed me after you made the call, Clarrie."

Meritus took in the scene quickly, glaring down at Weber with disgust. "What the hell happened to you, Richard? You were a young officer with promise."

Weber was coming back to his senses. "And *you,* Captain Meritus, are a traitor!"

Meritus' lip curled angrily. "Corporal Thomas, take this garbage away."

"Back to his quarters, sir?"

"No. Show him what we have in economy class, Corp."

Thomas grinned. "Yes, sir. Move him down to the cells, lads, come on!"

"Can you help her, Doctor?" asked Clarrie.

Tim pulled her away. "Let him work, sweetheart."

Flannigan wasted no time unpacking his field defibrillator. Placing a self-adhesive paddle on Chelsea's chest and another under her back, he lay her down again quickly. "Clear!" They all heard the *zap* and Chelsea jumped.

"*Mum!*" Clarrie cried out, tears flowing freely, while her father merely looked on in disbelief, a shadow of the man he used to be.

Flannigan adjusted the oropharyngeal airway adjunct before replacing the resuscitator. Happy her airway was open, her tongue not covering the epiglottis, he nodded to the orderly, who squeezed the air bag three times. He watched Chelsea's chest inflate and tried again. "Clear!"

Zap. Chelsea began to cough and gag. Flannigan immediately removed the adjunct from her mouth and throat, easing her into a sitting position. He removed the paddles from her chest and back, gently replacing her blouse. "Hey," he soothed. "How you feelin'? You gave us all quite the scare for a moment there. How many fingers am I holdin' up?"

"What did you do to your poor wrist?" Chelsea asked, dreamily.

Flannigan looked at the marks left by the cord Weber had used to tie him up. A slow grin spread across his face. "You'll do."

Clarrie ran in to hold her mother.

"Gently," Flannigan cautioned.

"It's fine, Doctor," Chelsea managed hoarsely. "Throat's sore. Could I get some water, please?"

"I'll sort it," Tim offered, making his way to the kitchen. When he returned, his fiancée and her parents were in a huddle on the floor, murmuring to one another, while his best friend stood off to one side, like the fourth wheel on a tricycle.

"I, er... better leave you to it," Woodsey muttered, self-consciously.

"The hell you will!" Hank Burnstein barked. "You just saved my whole family from a gun-toting crazy. Get back in here! Tim, get that man whatever he wants to drink."

"Nothing for Chelsea, just yet, Hank," Flannigan advised. "I'm gonna need you to come to sickbay with me, honey. Just to check you're all good. OK? Nothin' to worry about."

"I'll go with her," Clarrie offered. "Tim, look after Dad," she muttered in his ear.

Tim nodded and set about sharing a very large drink with his future father-in-law and best man.

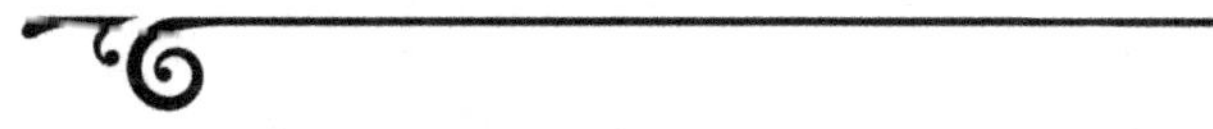

"Oh, thank God," Aito exclaimed with relief as a hidden secondary menu popped open entitled '*Kill-Taste*'. "It *is* a kill switch – I knew it would be."

"Oh, of course," Badawi replied, deadpan. "Will it shut them all down at once?"

"As we're in 'master controls', I have to assume so. Here goes."

They held their breath.

"Nothing appears to be happening," Badawi noted, drily.

"Give it chance," Aito snapped, irritably.

"No 'are you sure you want to shut them down' prompt?" H asked suspiciously.

Aito balled his fists nervously. "No. I told you, first edition. Come on, come on, come on. *Yes!* They're shutting down, all coming to a complete stop." He sat back, heaving a sigh of relief.

"All of them?" Again, H pointed at the screen. "What about that one?"

Aito checked. There was indeed a single tank still in motion. "Why's that one fully operational?" he muttered to himself.

"And what does *that* mean?" she asked again, indicating another menu.

Aito had spotted it, too. The computer was telling them that two of the tanks fell outside the remit of the master control program. One was still within the compound and the other was out of action. After running a quick search for its homing beacon, it was easy to see why – it was at the bottom of the river. Unfortunately, although the vehicle was disabled, its ordnance was not. Neither tank would respond to the controls before him, and both had secondary controls for their armaments. What was worse, the 'special' ordnance could be set by fuse, or timer – they required no impact to detonate them.

"Now, were I a betting man, I would lay odds that those two are the tanks we need to shut down," hazarded Badawi.

"You win a goldfish," Aito retorted angrily, slamming his prosthetic fist down and damaging the desk. "Now what?"

"Can we take control of them directly?"

Aito turned to Badawi. "You're suggesting we get inside them? But we've no idea what they're programmed to do."

"We have some idea," Badawi shot back. "Within an *indeterminate* amount of time from now – I think that is the correct word – they will turn this plateau into a crater!"

"You make a good point."

Prentice returned. "The medics have Jansen away."

"What chance does he have?" asked H.

"They said there's *some* hope, if they're quick enough. The operating theatre is being prepped aboard that ship and gennies are being brought in and powered up as we speak, so..."

"Here's hoping," Aito finished for him.

"Did I hear you say we've got to go out and open up that last tank?" asked Prentice. "Which one is it?"

Aito pulled up a plan view of the site. "The blue icons are now dead – red, there, is the one we want."

Prentice frowned. "All the others look like they've taken up some sort of battle formation, but that one looks like it's hiding. What building is that? The one it's creeping behind?"

"That's our stronghold," Aito explained. "Most of the buildings on this complex are of lightweight portal or spaceframe design. They offer limited protection. Just enough to prevent the avians from troubling the workforce or damaging equipment. The moat and electric fences protect us from the larger, more dangerous animals. That building is of reinforced concrete and designed as a last redoubt should our fences fail. That's why it sits at the opposite end of the compound to the *Heydrich* – our *other* safehold. In an emergency, everyone was to run to one or the other."

"Right, makes sense," Prentice pondered. "So assuming its programmed to hide behind the strongest protection in the area, that must mean the defence of the plateau was meant to be left to the other tanks, you agree?"

"Probably. What's your point?"

"Just that we have three dropships armed to the teeth and full of troops circling this area. If the defence systems are all down, I can call them in to help us."

Aito looked to the others for any objections. Seeing none, he shrugged. "Do it."

Baines checked her instruments. "What the hell is that?" she mumbled to herself. Opening a channel to the ground, she asked, "Adam, this is Captain Baines. Are those people down there expecting company? Over."

"*Not that* we *know of, Captain,*" he responded within moments. "*What do you see? Over.*"

She focused the ship's cameras on the incoming vessel. Whatever it was, was huge. She searched the frequencies for IFF. "I don't believe it," she muttered reverentially. "It's the *Newfoundland!* Thirty minutes out."

Another voice took over the comm. "*Captain Baines, this is Captain Aito Nassaki. Do not engage that ship, they're friendlies – repeat, they're friendlies – over.*"

"What the... Aito? *Two* ghosts in as many seconds!"

"*Ghosts?*" Aito sounded surprised. "*Never mind. Captain Baines, may I suggest you land two of your ships but leave the third airborne for contingencies. Just in case I'm wrong. Over.*"

"Another ship has just taken off from your compound, Captain Nassaki. A small orbital attack craft. Who is aboard? Over."

"*I expect that's Heidi Schultz and Dr Reid. Do not engage them, either – repeat, do* not *engage. If we fail to override the doomsday trap they've set up down here, they may be the only ones who can prevent a major ecological disaster – and our deaths! Over.*"

Baines' sigh travelled across the airwaves. "Understood." She glared at Heidi's escaping ship. If looks could kill, the little vessel would have been in freefall.

Two dropships landed in the compound. Baines and Gleeson moved their troops into position, overlooking the *Heydrich*'s main boarding ramp. They used the stalled tanks and anything else they could find for cover.

Withering fire came from within the ship's hold, though its main weapons were clearly out of commission. Baines was all too aware that most of the *New World*'s actual fighting force had defected with Captain Meritus – people who very likely knew the *other* people they were about to engage. A few shots were exchanged but she could tell there was a reticence to fire on those that were once their own. She could respect that. She opened a channel to Gleeson. "Commander, we need to nip this in the bud."

Gleeson, who had been thinking along the same lines, agreed with her. "*We could try talking them out.*"

"We may not have much time. We know that two of the tanks around us have nuclear ordnance and are not under our control. We're walking on eggshells again, Commander."

An explosion shook the ground around them as a cloud of fire bloomed against the side of Baines' dropship.

"*Looks like they've found the bazookas,*" Gleeson bellowed over the rolling boom. "*Return fire!*" A rattle of fire erupted from all sides, including the heavy, repetitive thud of two tripod-mounted fifty-calibre guns his contingent had hidden either side of a stalled tank. The *Heydrich*'s hangar bay came alive with the spark, clatter and boom of round after round striking the opening and ricocheting inside.

Baines called in to her co-pilot. "Damage report."

"The new armour absorbed it, Captain, but we don't want any more like that!"

"Understood." Baines pulled out her comm. "Adam?"

"*Prentice here, Captain.*"

The *crack* and *pang* of gunshots and further ricochets caused Baines to duck. "Get Aito to talk to his friends in there and tell them they're about to become toast! And make sure he mentions that it's *their* boss with the fork and the marshmallows!"

Prentice greeted Baines with a stiff salute but was immediately enveloped by her hug. "Adam, thank God you're alive. We feared the worst. Are there others with you?"

His expression spoke volumes.

They were joined by Aito, H and Badawi.

"Master Sergeant Badawi?" Baines asked incredulously. "How in the hell did you get here?"

"I may be able to answer both of your questions, Captain." They turned to see a young officer approaching on a single crutch, his arm in a sling. "Lieutenant Devon. We haven't met." He stood and saluted clumsily, trying not to drop his walking aid.

Baines returned the salute casually. "What do you mean, Lieutenant?"

"I mean that we have another of your men in our med bay. The young rascal who I believe was responsible for the death of my ship – at least, he destroyed her computer systems." He handed Prentice a set of dog tags. To Baines, he said, "Heidi captured Master Sergeant

Badawi on a trip to 2122 Egypt, but I'll let him fill in the details when we have more time."

Prentice read Private Mark Radburn's details from the tags and looked up. "Alive?" His voice was barely more than a whisper.

Devon took the sergeant's measure. Despite an attempt to clean his face, he was still caked in dust, blood and who knew what else. A slow smile crept over Devon's lips. "Alive. We saved the leg, too. Though he won't be jumping for joy just yet."

Prentice nodded acknowledgement. "Thank you, sir," he said, heartfelt.

"I'm afraid your other people were not so lucky. The tanks were placed in automatic defence mode from Dr Reid's laboratory. We couldn't override them. We tried, but..." He tailed off. "My sincere apologies."

"How many bodies?" asked Baines.

"Seventeen. Nine inside the ship – we believe they were killed in the crash – and eight without. There's been no time to investigate further, yet."

Prentice did a quick calculation. Twenty troops, plus himself and a pilot. Walker had been killed by the dinosaur stampede the night before, Radburn was miraculously returned to them; that left one other. "Do you have their tags, Lieutenant?"

"Yeah, and according to your Private Radburn, the missing man is a Corporal Heinz Engel. That Radburn is one tough kid, by the way. One transfusion and he was back in the land of the living. As for your other man – would that be the Heinz Engel who shipped out with the *Last Word?*"

Prentice nodded. "Aye. A long time ago."

"I knew him slightly. He was a good man, as I recall."

"Was? He's MIA?" asked Baines.

Devon shrugged uncomfortably. "*Maybe.* Our people guarding the wormhole refused to stand down during the conflict. From the one who survived, we've learned they had special orders from Heidi."

"And you think they got to Engel?" asked Prentice, darkly.

Devon surprised him by brightening. "Actually, I suspect *he* got to *them.* We found three dead, next to the wormhole – Heidi's hand-picked creatures, you understand? Engel was nowhere to be found, and neither was Chief Engineer Todt or his survey team."

"I can help you there," Aito joined the conversation. "Jansen and I sent them back to Germany. Perhaps your man went with them, Sergeant Prentice?"

"Why would he do that?" Prentice spoke to Baines, though his question was rhetorical.

"If he was under fire, perhaps he had no choice," she offered.

Aito's comm binged urgently in his pocket. He retrieved it. "Oh, no. We need to move."

"Move where?" Baines demanded.

"Anywhere far from here. In thirty minutes, this place won't exist any more."

"It's definite about the nukes, then?" She looked to Prentice for clarification, but he could only shrug.

"It's what I've been told, Captain."

"I linked my comm to the control device for those tanks," Aito explained, speaking quickly. "Two of them have nuclear ordnance on board—"

"Yes, but you've stopped the tanks. Haven't you?"

"It's complicated. Heidi had two of them programmed on a separate system. We can't access it. I can see them, but have no control, and most assuredly don't have time to hack them. We could try disabling the nuclear shell in the tank we have here, but if we trip any anti-tamper devices, we're going to look *very* silly. The other tank is even more problematic."

"Explain. Quickly."

"It's at the bottom of the river."

"Nicely succinct. Right, pack everyone into anything that will fly and let's get out of here," Baines ordered. "Captain Nassaki, I suggest you contact your friends aboard the *Newfoundland* and turn them around."

"Negative, Captain."

Baines rolled her eyes and turned back to him. "Go on," she prompted, witheringly.

"She's en route to carry out a secret plan some of us cooked up months ago, to close the wormhole. If we fail, the blast from those nukes will be transmitted through to 1944 Germany. They're not Nazis, Captain. The future is all messed up—"

"Messed up for the better. I was there," she interrupted him. "So what's the *Newfoundland*'s plan?"

Aito explained as quickly as he could, finishing by saying, "Our main hope is to disconnect it from its power source. After that, it should collapse – again, *hopefully.*"

Baines was almost afraid to ask. "Its power source being?"

"The planet's core."

She hung her head. "What is *wrong* with you people?"

"Twenty-seven minutes, Captain," Aito reminded her.

Thinking quickly, she reached a decision. "OK. Let the *Newfoundland* do what they've got to do. Do you have *anything* here that will fly? We came fully loaded. We might be able to squeeze in a few, but not enough. How many people are here?"

"Roughly a hundred or so Germans from Munich," Devon interjected. "And about forty-five of our own. I suggest we start an emergency evacuation of the Germans immediately. We can send them home – the *Newfoundland* is still fifteen minutes out."

"Do it," Baines dismissed him and turned back to Aito. "And your ships?"

"Incomplete," he admitted. "Some may manage limited atmospheric flight, but I know they're not ready for vacuum."

"Oh, no," she groaned as realisation struck.

"Captain?"

"That was the reason Heidi only sent five birds against us around the moon, wasn't it? We suspected as much. Trouble is, we took captives. Captives that belong in 1944."

"Can you get them down here in a shuttle?"

"Bit of a problem there. Captain Douglas has taken the *New World* to South America to clear up our mess from the fossil record. No way could he get them here in the next fifteen minutes."

"Twelve minutes."

"Great!" Another thought struck her. "How *did* you find your way to 1944?"

"1943, actually. We shot every Spinosaurus we could find in the north of the continent with a radioactive isotope—"

"Strontium and uranium?"

"Yes, how did you know?"

"Never mind, Aito. Please continue. I have an idea."

"We were able to track them by sending the isotope forward the long way around, through natural time, and tracking it via a continually open wormhole. With a little triangulation from the moon, we were able to pinpoint the exact location of the dinosaur remains in the Old Academy, Munich, November 8th, 1943."

"Ingenious," Baines had to admit. "So, in theory, and assuming *that* dinosaur's remains are still in 1944 somewhere, couldn't we do the same to send those people back?"

"We plant an explosive device at this end of the wormhole," explained Herbert Frahm.

"In the middle of the city?" Todt exploded. "I can see Bormann underestimated how dangerous you are!"

Frahm shot to his feet. "If the Party are planning a murderous rampage through Europe and beyond, they must be stopped – by whatever means."

Todt rose, too. "Not the *whole* party, Herbert. Remember with whom you speak. We are not all bent on world domination and enslaving the lower classes, despite what you write in that *rag* of yours – Willy Brandt[17]! Ha! How do you like that? You thought we were unaware of your little pen name, yes?"

"That *rag,* as you so derisively call it, is a working model for a fair, classless society!"

"Gentlemen, please." Colonel Hans Schultz raised his hands for calm.

"He writes them in crayon!" Todt appealed to him.

"Let us lay politics to one side for now, Fritz," Schultz replied calmly. "Perhaps planting an explosive is not *so* insane."

Todt rounded on him in disbelief. "This is the Old Academy we're talking about. Some of these exhibits are priceless!"

An alarm sounded, ending their discussion. A knock at the door revealed Lieutenant Gunther Sonne, the young man who greeted Todt and Engel after their trip through the wormhole. "Forgive me, Colonel," he stuck his head around the door, "but we have incoming."

---

17 Herbert Frahm, later known as Willy Brandt, famously opposed Hitler and the Nazi regime from exile after being stripped of German citizenship in 1938. He planned extensively for the peace to follow, after the Nazis were militarily defeated.

"Through the wormhole?" asked Todt.

"Yes, sir."

"Who is it, Gunther?" demanded Schultz.

"Looks like everyone, sir. Our whole complement – they just keep coming."

The men around the table looked at one another in confusion. "What is going on?" Todt spoke the thought aloud.

"There is more, sir," Sonne continued. "They are talking about a nuclear device that is about to explode just the other side of the wormhole, in the Cretaceous, sir."

Todt blanched. "What has she done?"

"My sister?" asked Schultz, anxiously.

"No. The other Heidi Schultz. The one that... Look, that does not matter right now. With reticence, I am forced to agree with your demolition plan. Our only chance, and it's a slim one, is to collapse this building on top of the wormhole, hopefully dampening the force of any explosion that might be transferred through it. I'm no astrophysicist, but maybe if we interfere with the event horizon – break it down somehow – we can reduce the amount of matter transmitted through." Todt turned back to the young lieutenant. "Sonne, did they say how long we might have?"

"Just minutes, sir."

"Minutes?" Todt turned back to Schultz. "Can we get demolition charges here in that time?"

The colonel blew out his cheeks. "Doubtful. But if we placed just one device of a suitable size at the event horizon, might that do it?"

"Hang on," Engel interjected. "Trust me when I tell you that detonating a bomb at the event horizon of a wormhole is a *bad* idea."

"Worse than losing half the city?" Todt bit back frantically.

Engel kept his gaze on Schultz as the officer in charge. "Maybe," he argued seriously.

Schultz shook his head. "I doubt we have anything of suitable scale here anyway, and with our nearest base several kilometres away... Gunther, what ordnance do we have on site?"

"We have this," a new voice joined the conversation. A female voice.

Sixty seconds and a hundred million years earlier

"Though I wish it were possible, I cannot come with you," Badawi explained with a heavy heart. "I must return to my own time. Heidi left one of her locator beacons in a valley near my home town. She might pop up there at any time, bringing who knows what dangers with her. My people will be caught completely unawares. Defenceless."

Tears ran down H's face. "I wish things were different for us."

He smiled. "Me too. But you must save your people *and* my future. If these Schultzes are loose in your world, mine might never come to be." He leaned in and kissed her. "Goodbye, Miss Dr H."

She laughed, tearfully. "Goodbye, Apep." She stroked the stubbled cheek around his goatee tenderly and kissed him back. "By the time you get home, I will be more than a hundred years in my grave."

He placed a hand to her soft cheek in return, so full of life and beauty. "Not to me. Now, take this," he said gently, handing her the device Captain Baines had provided. His eyes glistened, though his smile was full of warmth. "You always were a bombshell."

Now

"Heidi?" Colonel Schultz began to walk around the table, but hesitated.

"Brother," she replied coolly. She had obviously been crying. "You will know what to do with this, I assume – something always more in your line than mine." She handed him the device. "Gentlemen, I have been told we should detonate this bomb without delay. We have just minutes to clear the building and set up a perimeter." Returning her gaze to her brother, she spoke quietly. "Hans, do not hesitate."

"Will that be enough to stop a nuclear blast?" asked Todt.

"People are working on the other side of the wormhole to save us. This is our part of the plan to carry out. Gentlemen, *please,* we must go. We can talk later."

"But if they're working to stop the explosion," Todt could not let go, "then we could avoid the destruction of this museum and gallery."

"And if they fail," H countered, "we will lose the city. Whereas, if we sacrifice the museum and the worst happens, destruction may be limited to a few city blocks. Perhaps less, if we are fortunate. We cannot take the chance."

"Right, enough talk!" Colonel Schultz burst into action, barking orders. "Everyone out. Move, people!"

"Sergeant Jackson?" Baines called into her comm. "Sarge, it's Baines. Tell your pilot to keep a close eye on the ship inbound. The *Newfoundland* has been pressed into service to take the wormhole away – at least, that's our hope – but with Schultz's people, who can say for sure?" She jogged over to the *Heydrich,* where Lieutenant Devon ushered the ship's crew down the main boarding ramp from the ruined hold.

"Take only what you can carry!" he barked.

"Lieutenant." Baines took his elbow, making him wince. "Sorry. I need you to contact the *Newfoundland* and issue new orders."

"We don't have much time, Captain."

"I know. And it gets worse. Captain Nassaki has just informed me that only one of your ships is flightworthy. He says it will carry no more than twelve. That leaves about thirty people with nowhere to go. We might be able to squeeze half of them into our three dropships, one of which has yet to land, but..."

Devon frowned, thinking hard. "Hmm, I see your point. You think the *Newfoundland* should land? If she does, we won't have time to execute our plan and that could lead to thousands upon thousands of casualties in 1944 Munich."

Baines pulled out her comm. "Baines to Nassaki."

"*Nassaki. Go ahead, Captain.*"

"Aito, will any of those ships get off the ground?"

"*Maybe, but they won't get far. The management systems for the main engines are yet to be installed. They're thrusters only. What's your plan?*"

"That will be enough. Like the original *New World,* the *Newfoundland* has a shuttle bay in the bow section. It's empty – or was. With care, three of those attack ships should fit. Presumably the *Newfoundland* will hover while they collect the wormhole?"

"*That's worth a try. Thank you, Captain. Please take as many as you can and tell Devon to bring the rest over here.*"

"Wilco. And, Aito, I wouldn't hang around! We'll rendezvous in orbit. Baines out." She turned back to Devon. "Get all that?"

"On my way, Captain. I'll call Commander Coleman on the run. What about the wounded? We have two men on gurneys."

"We'll take them. It'll be cosy, but our ships will be more reliable. Go."

Devon saluted and led his party in a high-speed hobble towards the grounded vessels.

"Captain!"

Baines spun round to see Sergeant Jennifer 'Iron Balls' O'Brien waving her over to the compound's main entrance. She arrived breathlessly. "What is it, Jen?"

"Look who I found, Cap." O'Brien pointed across the moat to their *Afromimus* dinocam. "The geeks call him Rhubarb. Should we take him with us?"

"There's not much room. Still, Hiro will be in mourning if we leave it to be incinerated. Alright, bring it, but if it comes down to a choice between the robot and a passenger, it'll have to stay."

"Captain Baines!"

Baines turned yet again to see who was calling her this time. Back at the entrance to the *Heydrich,* a middle-aged woman in a lab coat stood alone in the wake of Devon's evacuation. "Everyone keeps shouting. Why am I the one running? Take care of it, Jen. I'll go see what this is about." Baines took a deep breath and set off again.

"Captain Baines?" Dr Hemmings asked again.

"Yes. And you are?"

"Anne Hemmings. I wish to travel with you."

"Do you, now? And why would that be?"

"Because I wish to know what actually happened to my daughter, Elizabeth."

Baines studied the woman. She had only met Special Agent Elizabeth Hemmings in the alternate future, yet the resemblance was clear. "Lieutenant Elizabeth Hemmings?" she queried.

"You knew her?"

"Only by reputation. My husband says she was one of the bravest people he ever met. If you really wish to know what happened, I'll be glad to introduce you."

Hemmings frowned. "And your husband would be?"

"Captain James Douglas."

Hemmings' expression hardened. "I was told he killed her."

"I'm sure you were, but that was not the case. Once you've met James, you'll understand. Come, we must go immediately."

Her last words were drowned by three orbital attack ships launching on thrusters, and the noise *they* made was drowned completely by the arrival of the *Newfoundland*.

Baines looked up wistfully at 550 metres of NASA engineering. In the vast space between the bow and aft sections hung a strange device that looked like an enormous, old-fashioned speaker coil. "Time to go," she shouted, manhandling Hemmings towards their ship.

Heidi and Reid looked down on the planet below, watching movements within their base via a satellite feed. Heidi was pricklier and more brittle than Reid had ever known her, which was something to behold. Almost afraid to speak or even breathe, he could not help but exclaim, "What on earth are they doing down there? Is that the—"

"*Newfoundland,* yes," Heidi spoke without looking away from the monitor. "It seems their betrayal ran deeper than I suspected." She had forced Reid and Hemmings to work in parallel, yet against one another, neither having full knowledge of what the other was doing. Now, she was forced to question the wisdom of that strategy. Reid, after all, had always been loyal – or rather, too afraid to cross her.

Her suspicions about Coleman, too, had not been groundless. When she visited Crater Lake, Commander Coleman and her pet engineer had played her. Just hours ago, for everyone else, Heidi had travelled thousands of kilometres, crossed between timelines and even geological periods in that time. She was exhausted, but that was no excuse – it was certainly no time to rest.

She slouched in her seat, watching the chrono count down below five minutes. It would all be over soon. Whatever they were planning down there would fail, and if her grandfather was still in Munich, this would be his last four minutes and forty-three seconds, too.

She could not smile, nor take any satisfaction from what was about to unfold. That would be to celebrate failure on the grandest scale. Though the failure was not hers. She had been betrayed at every turn, since the very beginning. Betrayed by family, by colleagues, by underlings, even by the man she desired. It was time to clear the game board, Etch A Sketch style – but the shake-up she planned was one the people below would not survive.

"They're powering some sort of device," Reid broke into her thoughts. "It's slung beneath the *Newfoundland* and generating a massive magnetic field."

Heidi sat up. "Could they be trying to move the wormhole? Is that possible?"

Reid tugged at his collar uncomfortably. "Maybe. Hemmings was working on that, I believe. Did she reach a conclusion?"

"It seems so. Look at the monitor! Think, Reid. How would a strong magnetic field affect a wormhole?"

He thought quickly, suspecting his life might hang on the quality of his explanation. "Erm." Bad start. Heidi turned to glower at him. He swallowed, wringing his hands. "I took some *initial* readings from the wormhole, before my attentions were diverted elsewhere," he began, reminding her that she had taken him away from the project. "As you know, it continues to grow – slowly, but at a rate that is accelerating."

"I know that."

"Of course, ma'am, but did you know that it also spins?"

Heidi calmed slightly. "I did not. Continue."

"It spins very, very slowly, but enough to generate a low electromagnetic field – a consequence of the motion of any charged particles within. If I'm right, a slowly rotating wormhole could also affect a certain volume of space around it. Charged particles, that is, electrons—"

"You would be advised not to dumb your explanation down too far, Doctor."

"My apologies, ma'am. Anyhow, these *electrons* are also gravitationally attracted, and as the wormhole rotates, it drags the cloud of electrons with it. It's known as 'frame-dragging'."

As an MD, astrophysics was not Heidi's strongest suit, but she remembered how the wormhole had followed her – or at least, her device – during her first journey through a personalised time portal. She wondered if that was a consequence of, or related to, the effect he described.

"And in that," Reid continued, "it bears a certain similarity to the effects of a slowly rotating compact star on surrounding stellar plasma.

Though without proximity to a star, we avoid the contrary effects of extreme gravitational and electromagnetic fields on particle trajectory."

"Hmm. Perhaps you might dumb it down just a little, but do not take me for a fool."

"By no means, ma'am. Perhaps I should skip to the end? I theorised, initially, that a large enough magnet placed near the wormhole, and polarised to attract, could produce a relocation relative to the magnitude of the field created."

Heidi digested his explanation. "So the answers to my questions – could they be trying to move the wormhole? Is that possible? – are yes and yes."

"Yes, ma'am."

"Damn!" She slammed her fist down on the console.

"But they have less than three minutes to not only take hold of an active wormhole, but to transport it to a safe distance. Which, by my calculation, would be about two kilometres – if both devices detonate together. I mean, we considered moving the wormhole, of course, but what difference would it make – other than making it more difficult for us to control our meta border with Germany? No matter where you moved it on Earth—"

"The *Newfoundland* is a spaceship, you fool!" she hissed waspishly.

"But... but they surely don't have time to..." Reid blustered but Heidi was not for placating.

"Can we launch a missile at them from here?"

"No."

"No?"

"You require a longer explanation on this occasion, ma'am?"

Heidi sighed. "So, we're out of range, yes?"

"Oh, no. It's not that. It would simply take too long to reach them from this orbit. By the time our missile arrived, they would either be long gone or incinerated by our ordnance on the ground."

Seething impotently, Heidi glared at the chrono, willing it to speed up.

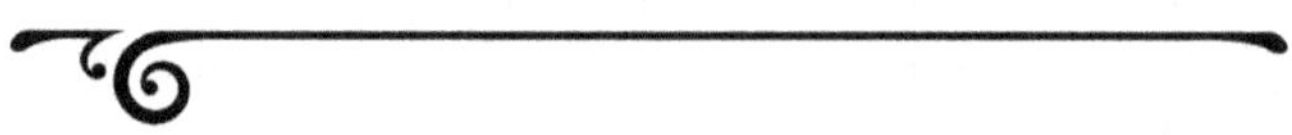

Colonel Hans Schultz and his men, joined by the German workers returned from the Cretaceous, used what little time they had to clear the streets that bounded the Old Academy in the city of Munich. It was pretty much all they could do to make people run away, often firing into the air when people were slow to catch on. Schultz decided it would be easier to apologise later than simply allow people's stubbornness or nosiness to get them killed.

When the explosion came it was subdued, as they had hoped, by the Old Academy's heavy, late 16th century fabric; masonry that had stood since the days of the Spanish Armada. The destructive effects were further broken by the building's courtyards, which sprawled over an entire city block. Flying glass was Schultz's chief concern as people packed the street, still moving far too slowly.

As the beautiful old building shook, the sounds of collapse and structural torture were enough to make even the worst architectural philistine wince. A choking dust cloud engulfed the city centre, as the airwaves choked with reports of an explosion and screaming sirens.

Hans and Heidi Schultz looked at one another as they had not since they were children. "We are going to be in *so* much trouble for this," H announced.

Hans grinned. "We're alive and we saved a great many other lives. We will just have to explain that to the government. Knowing how much *they* have to cover up at the moment, I do not believe they will want to incur our enmity just now."

"We're alive *so far*," H added the caveat. "The rest will depend upon the people a hundred million years ago in Egypt."

"Once upon a time, in a timeline far, far away, that may have sounded strange to me," Engel chipped in. He coughed and tied a scarf around his face to help stop the dust.

H took his arm. "I am sorry you cannot go back to your people."

"Me too. Still, I am in Germany, so at least I am home in a way."

"Trust me," Todt joined them, "if this works, you can stay at my place."

In this 1944 Munich, there was no Allied bombing, just a fixed event that echoed across the multiverse, retying a fray, and though the event came a couple of months late, it proved to be the one stitch in nine, that saves time. Yet healing comes with a cost and always leaves a scar. As the Old Academy collapsed, it covered the wormhole, but also destroyed Ernst Stromer's collection of mid-Cretaceous, North

African dinosaurs – including the most complete remains ever found of Spinosaurus aegyptiacus.

"The ships are docked aboard, Commander. Sealing the hatch," Coleman's pilot reported.

"Excellent. Tell Lieutenant Devon to secure his people well. We won't be able to give any warning when we go, and we'll be pulling serious Gs." She pointed to another officer on the bridge. "Wormhole device? Quickly!"

"We have it, ma'am," she confirmed. "I think..."

Everyone looked at her.

"I'm sure, I'm sure. Go, go, *go!*"

"Lieutenant, get us out of here," Coleman barked. "And don't spare the horses!"

"No! *Stop!*"

Coleman turned once more to the officer controlling the wormhole collector. "What's going on?"

"Ma'am, the wormhole... It's *moving!*"

"Explain."

"It's like we're pushing it across the ground. It just passed right through the wooden enclosure." She turned. "Commander, it's like the wormhole just ate its way through the timbers – there's literally nothing left, where it passed."

Coleman frowned in concentration.

"T minus one minute, Commander," the pilot called.

"Open a channel to engineering," Coleman ordered.

"*Engineering.*"

"Sergeant, we're repelling the wormhole, rather than attracting it. Can you switch the polarity?"

"*Only by manually swapping the connections, ma'am. The system is rough and ready—*"

"How long?" Coleman demanded, interrupting him.

"*A couple of minutes?*"

"You have thirty seconds or we're all dead!"

"*I'm on it!*"

Coleman sighed deeply, gripping the arms of her captain's chair that once belonged to Captain Arnold Bessel. *Damn our luck! I suppose the polarity was always going to be fifty-fifty,* she thought, forcing herself to breathe normally. *That just leaves the one in a thousand chance of us pulling off the rest of this crazy scheme!*

Thirty-two seconds later, the engineering sergeant came back to the comm and calmly reported that they should try again. Coleman, also hiding her fraying nerves, nodded to the officer controlling the device.

"Twenty-five seconds," the pilot continued to count down.

Come on! Coleman thought frantically. She knew they would have to engage full power immediately if they were to stand any chance of escaping now, and could only hope their ancient and mighty damaged ship survived the stresses.

"Twenty seconds!" Terror shook the pilot's voice now and Coleman could hardly blame him. If necessary, they would just have to save themselves, but she would give the people of Munich every last second she could spare before doing so.

"Got it! We have the wormhole, Commander!"

"Get us out of here!" she roared at the pilot.

He did not need telling twice. Despite inertial dampening, the blast of power from the *Newfoundland*'s four rigged, and re-rigged, main rocket motors was crushing. The old ship creaked and groaned in protest, but answered her helm and shot forwards and upwards, unstable payload swinging beneath her belly as he set course for the stars.

At an altitude of six thousand kilometres the wormhole faltered, as power from its geothermal source began to fluctuate. Secant line between Egypt and Munich broken, the event horizon was already losing coherence when the explosion came. Compressive force from the detonation in Munich travelled in waves, only partially emerging into the minimal atmosphere high above the Cretaceous Earth. The device, built by Doctors Harry Bismarck and Brian Alba, flash-melted so quickly that the black copper oxide was spread through the thin atmosphere by the final pressure wave from the collapsing wormhole. Equally sudden cooling turned it back into copper and water, to rain down over the continent below.

The steel cables securing the device from the *Newfoundland*'s cargo winches were cut cleanly, their ends necked and glowing as they flailed violently until the atmosphere grew so thin that friction no longer acted upon them.

Coleman gripped the arms of her captain's chair even tighter as the old vessel shuddered. "What the hell just happened? Damage report."

"Minimal to the ship, Commander," the pilot reported.

"And the wormhole?"

Her bridge crew looked from one to another, baffled.

"We've lost the device, Commander," stated the officer in charge of the wormhole catcher. "It's been..." she checked her instruments again, "incinerated, ma'am. It's like an explosion occurred at the other end and travelled into our space–time."

"Wouldn't it have been nice to be informed about *that* part of the plan!" Coleman spat, crossly. "And the explosion closed down the wormhole?"

"No, ma'am. That was never possible. If we had been at a lower altitude, with the wormhole still drawing power from the planet's core, it would certainly have closed us down, though!"

Coleman slammed her fist down on the arm of her chair. "That's it, I've had enough. Lay in our course. It's time to get the hell out of here."

Carcharodontosaurus saharicus turned towards the light. The sun was already well in the west when a second lit up the east. The apex predator growled softly, sensing something was wrong. He was alone – few remained in his presence that wished to live, but this was different. Even the birdsong had ceased. It was as though every living creature were hunkered down or in hiding.

Carcharodontosaurus blinked, eventually turning away from the painful brightness. Six beats of his massive heart later[18], a colossal wind tore past him, around him and over him. He staggered to regain his feet and turned away, allowing it to propel his eight tons along, in a forced march.

The brightness faded, the wind reducing to a mere gale. The giant stopped and turned back, blinking against the flying dust, ash and

---

18   About seventeen seconds by reckoning of the monsters who gave the world a 'new clear' reality.

debris. Behind, a vast cloud rose impossibly high into the eastern sky, broadening at the top to resemble a tree made from nothing but smoke. The animal's racial memory equated it to a volcano. Though he had never seen one, his very existence stood as irrefutable proof of the wide berth his ancestors had given to such events. He roared at the monstrosity that had lain waste to his kingdom, but it was a cry against the inevitable, for nothing lasted forever.

Turning away from the blast, he faced an uncertain future, full of strangers against whom he would soon be tested. An entire life spent carving out his place in the land was all to do again; new territory, new resources. The wheel had turned, as it would continue to do until the last star went out in the universe, and Carcharodontosaurus saharicus, despite his vast size and power, was no more than a child in its thrall.

He flicked his tail and *roared* – a warning to the world that he was coming, ready or not. The world would have expected nothing less.

Devon evacuated the shuttle bay. Herding their people along the *Newfoundland*'s corridors, he could not help stopping at a porthole to admire the planet below them. Directly below, it was still possible to make out the plume of the atomic explosions they had narrowly escaped. The two were so closely grouped that it was impossible to separate the mushroom clouds from a single event. He remembered Jansen mentioning that Heidi's scientists had a theory, something about a localised extinction event that was taking place in the region around their base. He tried to recall. A series of volcanoes on another continent to the north was altering the weather patterns, forcing rain clouds over the African continent further south. Decreased rain meant no monsoon, and no monsoon meant a reduction in vegetation, which in turn meant fewer vegetarians. From there, it was easy to see how that would lead to a short-term overnumerousness among the carnivorous species. Many had survived thus far on fish, or each other, but surely this man-made disaster would change everything in the fossil record – or would it?

He struggled to recall a name. Stromer, Ernst Stromer, that was it. The early 20th century palaeontologist who had found the remains of the dinosaur Heidi used to piggyback her journey to the 1940s. Stromer had puzzled over the high ratio of carnivores in the area. Might this debacle have just put history back on track?

Devon shuddered. These were big events, big questions. *Oh, what the future holds,* he pondered, taking a deep breath. Whatever it might mean to the future, for him and his fellow survivors, it had been a very close call, and now it was time to thank their saviour.

Packing his staff into the officers' mess, he and Aito set off for the bridge to congratulate Commander Coleman on her timely rescue. Unsure whether the old ship's internal transport system was working, they took the safer, long way around. It would have been enjoyable; a leisurely stroll after what had been one hell of a day, but unfortunately Devon's knee and shoulder made it just another penance. Eventually, they arrived outside the bridge and pressed the door comm.

Nothing.

Devon turned to Aito, who shrugged. He pressed it a second time.

Again, nothing.

Slightly perturbed, Devon put it down to a technical failure. After all, he had to concede that it was a miracle this ship was even flying, let alone in space. Rather than pressing call, he pressed open, instead. The hatch doors parted for him to step inside, whereby the greeting died on his lips. The *Newfoundland*'s bridge was deserted.

It was a warm evening at Crater Lake. Balmy and somnolent. Spring in Cretaceous Britain was more like a particularly good August in the Northern Europe Bismarck remembered. He strolled along the beach at his leisure, the waters of the lake lapping gently. The temptation was to sit against a palm tree and watch the sun go down behind the mountains in the west, maybe allow himself to nod with a tall glass in hand. Of course, that would be suicide, and though he was feeling depressed, he was not that far gone.

He pulled the strap further up his shoulder to stop it from slipping. This was a beach where one walked, not with a stick or a dog lead in hand, but with a high-powered assault rifle. Bismarck sighed. Other than that – and the fact that, even if she were still alive, he would never see the woman he cared for again – it was perfect.

His comm beeped. He took the small device from a pocket and stared balefully at it. The damned thing felt like *his* dog lead. Bismarck had grown up in a world where cables were almost entirely a thing of the past, yet people were more tied down than ever. Even in the Cretaceous Period, it seemed there was little freedom to be had.

It beeped again. Someone on station aboard the Rescue Pod, within their new command centre, seemed particularly anxious to get hold of him. He toyed with the idea of ignoring it, but who was he fooling? Switching the device off could be personally dangerous in that location, and there was no way the wretched thing would shut up on its own. He blew out a deep breath of annoyance and answered, "Bismarck."

"*Dr Bismarck, I've been trying to reach you.*"

Bismarck rolled his eyes at the barely veiled reprimand. "Now you've got me. What is it?"

"*We have incoming, sir. A ship.*"

Hope stirred in his chest. "The *Newfoundland?*"

"*Negative, sir. It's a small orbital attack ship. ETA ten minutes.*"

Silently cursing himself for not answering more quickly, he walked and talked. "Get a full armed response team kitted out and deployed around the compound. They're to use whatever cover they can find, but tell them to stay out of sight. We have no *idea* what this might be about. They may be here to carry out some form of punishment for Commander Coleman's journey to the wormhole."

"*Understood, sir.*"

Bismarck closed the connection and set off at a jog.

In Patagonia, it was still the middle of the afternoon. The *New World* came in low over the clearing its crew had once called home, ten years earlier. Douglas smiled, despite himself. "Ah never thought Ah'd see this place again."

"Thought or hoped?" asked Singh, reasonably.

"Aye. Bit of both, Ah'll no deny it. Ah have to say, though, this is a beautiful world."

Singh flashed his perfect smile. "But if it goes to the vote, I don't want to stay!"

Douglas chuckled. "Nae fear of that, laddie."

"I'm going to put us down over the footprint of the old *New World,* sir. Because we know the ground there."

"Ah dinnae remember that ground being so stable?"

"Yes, sir, but elsewhere might be even worse."

"Good point. Very well, land us, please, Lieutenant-Commander Singh, before that beastie in ma hold starts taking runs at the door."

"Yes, sir." Singh remained quiet for a few minutes, concentrating. The massive bulk of the *New World* defied gravity as its namesake had once before, all those years ago. It may have been a decade for Douglas and his crew, but only a year had passed in the clearing below since that storm-wracked night. This time there was no storm, there was no rain, it was not even dark – there was practically no drama at all.

"Perfect landing, Sandy."

"Yes, sir. Shall I give Dr Pearson the good news?"

"Aye. Tell her Ah'm on ma way down there, too. I dinnae want ma ship all bashed aboot."

As the most likely target for any assault, Bismarck emptied the Pod of personnel and now stood alone in the compound, where Heidi had landed that morning. He hoped to greet their visitor or visitors with civility, but should they have other ideas, at least his strategy would prevent them from taking out all his people at a stroke.

The ship was now visible with the naked eye. He breathed deeply, straightening his tunic in preparation for he knew not what. If it was Heidi again, what would he tell her – he was only following orders, and only Coleman knew the plan? Firstly, that would be a betrayal, and secondly, he doubted she would believe him. If only Crater Lake Base could break away from the Schultzes and their faction. He thought about little else these days. This was now his home; he had long ago admitted that to himself. Perhaps it was time to fight for it? He checked his rifle; it would not do to have the safety on should he have to respond quickly. No one would question his being armed – they lived in a flooded, extinct volcano in the time of the dinosaurs, after all. He snorted gently. *I've got* that *going for me, at least,* he thought wryly as the ship drew nearer.

The roar of its engines entered the crater a split second after the ship itself, growling around its mountainous rim. The small vessel was slowing. Bismarck relaxed slightly. *Not an attack run then,* he conjectured.

The IFF registered it as a Schultz vessel. Again, new to them, but not the one Heidi had used earlier – another plus. Their hails had gone unanswered. Could that represent a technical problem, or were they just anxious to keep the airways clear? He began to sweat; a combination of humidity and nerves. Covering his ears, he watched the little ship come to a stop right above the compound where he stood. Gradually, it lowered vertically to land just twenty metres away.

As the rocket motors shut down, the silence flooding in seemed temporarily unnatural. Bismarck walked forward hesitantly. Five metres out from the ship, the side hatch opened. He froze, raising his rifle.

"Nervous," announced a voice he recognised well.

"Ally?"

Coleman stepped out ahead of her skeleton crew and walked towards him, beaming.

Bismarck released his weapon, allowing it to hang by its strap while he slumped, his hands on his knees. Recovering, he straightened. "*That* is *not* the vehicle you were driving earlier. Did you crash the *Newfoundland?* Because if that's the like-for-like courtesy ship, we need to check our policy!"

Coleman laughed. "We were successful. We moved the wormhole into space and it closed down on its ow— *mostly* on its own."

He looked at her quizzically.

"I'll tell you later, over whatever delights you're going to cook for me – something celebratory, I think. All I'll say for now is, we left the *Newfoundland* safe in orbit, with most of the *Heydrich*'s crew aboard."

"They let you go?" Bismarck was astonished.

"Not exactly. I left Captain Nassaki a note. It will be up to them whether they keep our secret or not."

"Secret? From whom?"

"Douglas' people are back. I've seen them. They'll retrieve Devon and Nassaki from the *Newfoundland* and take them back to the future. If they keep their mouths shut, then maybe we'll be able to retrieve the *Newfoundland* at a later date, now we have this little ship."

Bismarck blew out his cheeks. "They must be thrilled to be going back to that hell hole."

"From the limited conversation I had with Captain Nassaki, it might not be as bad as all that. The future is... Look, there's a lot to explain. Shall we go in? We're not safe yet. Heidi has done something terrible – no surprise – and we don't know what Douglas' response will be."

"Devon, look," Aito called from the captain's chair. "They left us a note."

"A note? What, like a 'Dear John' or something?"

Aito huffed. "Pretty much. Coleman and her staff have... son of a..."

"What? What have they done?" Devon demanded anxiously.

"They've taken our ship. The one of the three that was almost complete and mostly, actually worked. That means we're stranded up here!"

"Oh, I wouldn't say that," Devon commented, softly.

Aito looked up to see him staring out of the front viewport. Before them was one of the *New World*'s dropships. Though her weapons were not live, the feeling of being under her guns was undeniable.

Devon sat in the pilot's seat with a grunt, holding his injured leg straight, and opened a channel. "This is Lieutenant Devon. Glad you made it."

"*Wouldn't have missed it, Lieutenant. This is Sergeant Jackson of the* New World."

"Where are your other two ships, Sergeant?"

"*On their way to rendezvous with the* New World, *sir. I understand some of their passengers require urgent medical care. Once they drop off our personnel, Captain Baines will be back to dock with the* Newfoundland *and collect your crew.*"

"That's good to hear, Sergeant, but if you're fully loaded, why didn't you go with them?"

"*I'm here to make sure you don't get* lost, *sir.*" The Sarge's voice, carefully neutral as it usually was when he addressed an officer, carried just the slightest cadence of contempt over the word 'lost'. The threat found its mark.

"Understood, Sarge. Thanks for caring."

"*It's my way, sir.*"

Devon closed the channel. "It seems we have a comedian watching over us."

"Funny you should say that. When I met him, during my time aboard the *New World,* he seemed to have no sense of humour at all. No surprise that he was a close friend of... Oh, *man...*"

Devon frowned. "What is it?"

"I've just realised I'm going to have to face my older brother again. And after what Heidi has just committed, he's going to be unbearable. Hiro, my hero," he added sardonically. "I should have taken my chances with the nuke!"

"Nukes. There were two of them, remember?"

"Yes, well, luckily, I only have *one* brother, but he more than makes up for it." A thought struck him. "I wonder if our older sister, Himari, is alive in the alternate future Douglas' people created?" She had been all their father, too, running the family business after he and Hiro left. He shook it off. "You see, my brother got all our father's sanctimoniousness but none of his drive. Of course, he would call it father's 'sense of honour'."

"And what did you get from him?"

"I got away."

Captain Douglas and Dr Natalie Pearson nudged their small armoured vehicle up to the cage that held the captive Spinosaurus aegyptiacus. The main hangar had been cleared of personnel and the inner hatch to the vehicular airlock stood open in readiness.

Natalie looked to Douglas. "I was glad to hear Captain Baines is safe, Captain."

"Aye, and The Sarge, too," he acknowledged kindly.

"Oh, I think *he's* indestructible."

"With your penchant for playing with ferocious animals, he needs to be."

She grinned. "Are we good to go?"

A whine from behind their seats suggested that someone was. "Reiver, shh."

Douglas linked the vehicle's sensor suite to the ship's exterior cameras. "Aye. The compound looks clear. Unlock the cage, Natalie. Opening the outer hatch now."

They hit the remote controls together and Douglas backed their vehicle away slowly, his concentration slightly marred by a *presence,* leaning heavily on his thigh. He looked down into a furry, black and white face, whose brown eyes were staring back up at him, unblinkingly. Douglas got the impression that he was somehow in The Sarge's seat, and that he had better get this right and mind his manners. He gave Reiver's ears a friendly tousle, but the scrutiny remained.

As the cage split apart, its sides hinging away from the dinosaur, the torpid animal suddenly found her mojo and jumped to her feet, knocking the bars aside. She moved free of her enclosure and roared, stretching cramped muscles. It would have been deafening within the enclosed space without the protection of their vehicle. Fortunately, Reiver filled their cab with barking, instead, lest they miss out. "Reiver, *shush!*" Natalie shook her head anxiously as she watched the Spinosaurus. "Ooh, she's not happy."

"Neither am Ah. Why is she no' leaving ma ship?"

"Give her a moment, Captain. She's disoriented, but she'll soon smell the outside air. I'm sure she'll get her bearings... What?" Natalie could not help noticing Douglas' look of alarm.

"Och, nothing. Ah'm just filling out the insurance claim in ma hid, that's all."

"Shh, she's moving. Look." Natalie failed to register Douglas' consternation after being barked at, shushed and effectively switched off. "Now, take us in behind her," she continued handing out her orders, oblivious.

Douglas swallowed his pride and crept the vehicle forward. The dinosaur roared again, but unsure of herself, backed away towards the airlock. Eventually, she turned into the sunlight and set off quickly, out into the D-shaped, palisaded enclosure.

Once upon a time, those earthworks and defences had protected their crew from the Cretaceous wildlife. The ferns were growing well; even the ramps leading up to the rear of the wall walk were overgrown. "It doesnae take long for Mother Nature to take back what's hers," Douglas muttered softly, casting about. Even the heavy wooden palisade was showing signs of growth, and then he saw it. "Damn."

Natalie looked at him, sharply. "What is it?"

Douglas closed the massive outer airlock doors while opening a comm link to the bridge.

"*Singh here, sir.*"

"Sandy, how accurately did ye put us down over the footprint of our old ship?"

"*Nice and tight, Captain. Her plan shape is a little different from* USS New World, *but I still managed to nudge her in close. Why?*"

"Are we sealed up to the ends of the enclosure walls?"

"*Yes, sir. Tight as a drum, both ends, just as I said.*"

Douglas sighed.

"*Sir?*"

"The dinosaurs are meant to be on the *outside*, Sandy. We didnae open the damned gates!"

Unable to help himself, Singh began to laugh.

Natalie chuckled, too. "Well, you were wondering what to get Tim and Clarrie for a wedding present, Captain."

"That's no' funny! And we're no' staying here one minute longer than we have to, either."

"*We have incoming, Captain,*" Singh chortled. "*It's Captain Baines.*"

"Och, great. Ah'll never hear the end o' this now."

Twenty minutes later, Douglas shook the Australian builder's hand. "Thanks for doing this, Bluey. Natalie thinks moving the ship might hurt the dinosaur – perhaps even give it a heart attack, not to mention deafen it."

"You're asking me to go out there and you're worried about giving *it* a heart attack?"

Douglas winced, but Bluey only laughed cheerfully. "I'm messin' with ya, mate. After going to this much trouble, it'd be a shame to kill it. Besides, it's not like the old days, with our jerry-rigged machinery. These diggers are military spec. That ugly rooter out there won't be able to get to me, even if it tries."

"She."

Both men turned.

"She," Natalie repeated. "*It,* is a she."

"I'll take ya word for it, missus," replied Bluey. "I'll be driving a tank with a shovel and a back actor anyway, this time – just in case she tries any of her feminine wiles."

"Ah hope the gate draw bars will still slide," Douglas mused.

"They'll go," Bluey assured him. "If not, I'll just have to knock the gates down."

Douglas shrugged; there was that.

"No. Don't damage the enclosure."

Douglas turned to see Tim Norris approaching, along with his fiancée and Douglas' own wife – who wore a broad grin. He slumped. "What now? Bluey, ye'd better get going. Good luck, laddie, and thank ye."

Bluey moved the military excavator into the airlock, closing the heavy doors behind him before opening the outer hatch.

They all stepped up onto a high walk that led to an observation lounge above the vehicular airlock. It was a useful feature their old ship had lacked, designed as she was for a completely different purpose. There was no dangerous wildlife on Mars, after all, but with this ship they had known what they were getting into.

"Look at her pacing the digger," Tim commentated enthusiastically.

"Aye, Ah reckon Bluey would have had the wind up him by now, were he driving one of our old JCBs."

"It's like she's trying to work out what it is," Tim continued, almost to himself and not really listening. "It doesn't smell like food, but is it a threat? Look at her, working it out – checking it from different angles. Beautiful."

Douglas raised an eyebrow, and then remembered who he was talking with. He patted Tim affectionately on the shoulder. "Aye. 'Course she is. Just keep taking the tablets, laddie."

Bluey expertly manipulated the tree trunk draw bolts and pushed one gate open, wide enough for the animal to pass. He reversed out of the way and waited.

The dinosaur stayed where she was, staring.

"What's she doing?" asked Clarrie.

"I'm not sure," Tim was forced to admit. "You know the way we look back to our history, and often think, why did people speak or act that way? It seems weird to us, yeah?"

"What's your point?" asked Baines, curious.

"Just that, no matter how much we equate these creatures to sparrows and swans – eagles, even – they're not. They're non-avian dinosaurs, and try as we might, there's no way to truly comprehend them from a few bone-shaped rocks. They're more incredible, more diverse and more unknowable than we can possibly imagine. And having been lucky enough to live with them for a while, I have to say that the last is what I love about them the most."

Clarrie swooned a little. "Oh, Timmy, and that's why I love *you* so much."

A colossal roar tore across the enclosure. The Spinosaurus was lunging and fading at Bluey's machine. Not actually attacking. "She's decided it's a threat," Tim explained, completely oblivious to Clarrie's show of devotion. "Or might be."

Baines bent close to the ear of the young bride-to-be and whispered, "It's a woman's lot in life to be taken for granted, honey. May as well learn it early and be careful not to confuse it with 'he doesn't love me'. It's almost never that. Mostly, they're not cruel, just hopeless." She winked, conspiratorially.

When the excavator failed to respond to the dinosaur's threats and posturing, she continued to lunge but all the while making her way closer to the open gate. Eventually, she felt secure enough to turn and flee.

From their vantage point in the observation lounge, the spectators watched the giant make her way through the open gate and out onto the plain. Once outside the walls, she turned, checking that her dumb adversary was not giving chase. She seemed to take a moment, rising up on her hind legs to sniff the air abouts. After examining her new surroundings, she made straight for the river. Several crocodiles were basking on the bank. She roared, a terrifying, blood-curdling cry that sent them scattering in all directions before her, as she slipped into the water – not so much a 'home from home', as a 'home at last'. Tim watched with tears in his eyes. "After all we've seen together – time travel, pyramids, space battles, even a donkey – goodbye, old girl."

"You're sad to see her go?" asked Baines, gently.

He nodded, watching the waters settle in her wake. "I'm also mindful that poor Simba, one of my research students, is now part of her forever." He wiped away a tear and, returning to the now, smiled down at his future wife. "Shall we ask him?"

Clarrie hugged him and then nodded, enthusiastically.

Douglas gave Baines a suspicious sideways look, but she gave nothing away. "Ask me what? Does this have something to do with saving the integrity of the compound?"

Tim turned to face him. "Yes, Captain. Clarrie and I have been talking it over and we've decided that..."

"Go on." Clarrie shoved him.

"I'm doing it, I'm doing it." He rubbed his arm, petulantly. "We all remember the funeral pyre built for Sergeant Bud O'Neill, Privates Jack Dorset and Andreas Paolo, Dr Jamie Ferguson and, though we had only a wreath to cremate, Engineer Mario Baccini, too."

Douglas nodded sombrely – he had not actually been present, being Heidi's hostage at the time, but he would never forget them.

"Ahem," Baines hinted.

"Oh, yeah. Sorry, Captain. I forgot you weren't there. Well, I thought – that is, *we* thought – that to honour their memory, it would be the ideal place for you to marry me. Er, us, I mean. For you, Captain Douglas, to marry Clarrie and me."

"Yes, Ah think Ah understood—"

"You see, Captain," Clarrie interrupted, losing patience with the slowness of Tim's delivery, "right here, was also the first place we—"

"It was a different ship," Tim butted in. "And a different main hangar," he added for clarity.

"Yes, I know that – I *was* there," she shot back tersely. "Right here – *more or less* – was the first place we kissed."

Douglas slumped. "Oh, thank God."

"Captain?" asked Tim.

"Nothing, nothing. Ah just thought the lassie might be going somewhere else with that tale."

Baines began to giggle.

"So, will you marry us here, Captain, out in the enclosure where we spread the ashes of our friends?" Clarrie looked up, her gaze locked with his, eyes impossibly large and pleading.

Douglas glared accusingly at his own wife. "Ye knew about this, didn't ye?" Turning back to the betrothed, he placed a fatherly hand on each of their young shoulders. "Clarrie, Tim, are the pair of ye out of yer minds?"

"*James!*" Baines elbowed her husband in the ribs.

"Ouch!" He turned back to her crossly. "We're in the middle of a dangerous mission here, at one of the most dangerous times and in one of the most dangerous places in the history of the world!"

"We've a hundred million years to get home, Douglas." Baines' smile was brittle and she spoke quietly. "So I suggest you reconsider, darling. Unless you want to find your new car shares out on the lawn with the rest of your gear when we get there." She looped an arm through her husband's and beamed at them. "Tim, Clarrie, of course he'll marry you here, won't you, dear?" She released Douglas' arm to embrace the young couple fondly. "So long as I get to help with the arrangements!"

While Baines and Clarrie huddled to discuss things no man should ever have to consider, Douglas pulled Tim close. "Doing as you're told is a man's lot in life, son. Ye may as well learn it early. It's easier all round. The trick is to make decisions without them noticing." He winked conspiratorially.

Clarrie pulled Douglas away, squeezing the life, and at last forcing a smile, out of him. "Oh, aye, it's a madhouse, sure enough," he muttered.

High above, in orbit around the other side of the world, Heidi looked down balefully. Both nuclear weapons had fired and the blast area was clearing now, the electromagnetic field dissipating enough for them to take readings. "They closed the wormhole, then?"

"So it would appear, ma'am. Quite a feat of cleverness and courage at the eleventh hour, wouldn't you agree?"

She glared at him.

"B-but, surely, you didn't want the wormhole to eat the world, ma'am?"

"Perhaps," she agreed icily. "But I required its use a little longer."

"But we can travel anywhere we wish—" Heidi's fierce stare closed his mouth.

"Release the satellite into a retrograde orbit and bring it online," she ordered at last. "It's time."

He hesitated.

Heidi turned her fierce glare on him again. "Activate the system – what are you afraid of?"

"Everything, ma'am. That is, the... *end* of everything."

"You are guessing. I do not need you to carry this out, so ask yourself *this* question, Reid – do you want to die like the team of scientists who helped you build the device, the ones whose remains were just incinerated below us on the planet, or would you rather live to see what happens next?"

"But we saw ships leave the surface," he replied, uncertainly. "Surely, my team escaped."

She smiled coldly, and in that smile, he clearly saw the demon within.

"You *killed* them?" Even after everything, he could hardly believe it.

"They knew what we have built."

Reid had known those people, had worked closely with them for months. Heard stories about their families and friends, listened to their dreams for the future, watched them play harmless pranks on one another. He swallowed his nervousness. He had to speak out. "They would have gone back to 1944. They could not have harmed your plans from there or then."

Heidi lost patience. "I said, activate the system and launch the device."

Reid typed the commands and then straightened in his co-pilot's seat. "I won't."

"*What?*" Heidi's voice was barely more than a whisper.

"I'm sorry, ma'am, but what you're trying to do... I can no longer go along with it."

She leaned closer to him, pulling her sidearm from its holster. "Well, *I* am sorry to hear that, Dr Reid."

"You c-can't fire that in here," he stuttered, tremulously. "You'll kill us both."

"True. Perhaps I should launch you into space for insubordination instead, hmm?" Not waiting for an answer, Heidi struck Reid hard across the temple with her pistol grip and her last reliable minion slumped over his controls. She pulled him back, eyes suddenly brimming with tears of fury. "Curse you, Douglas," she spat, vehemently.

Reid's system was all set. Heidi had only to hit return to execute, yet she hesitated, finger hovering just above the key. Somehow, Douglas had taken control of the Schultz satellite net and was confusing it to hide his ship. She may not be able to get a fix on it, but it surely stood to reason that somewhere below her, Tim Norris was back once more among his beloved dinosaurs and that gave her an idea. She wiped an angry tear as a cold smile crept over her lips.

"If dinosaurs are what you love, dear cousin, then you shall have them." She chuckled softly to herself. "Now, I am God." She hit return... and the whole natural order ended.

Epilogue

AD1559, Anglo-Scottish Borders

"We agreed to keep a low profile and build our wealth quietly, Allison." Erika Schmidt stood with hands on hips, glaring down at Cocksedge with annoyance.

Seated by the bastle's hearth, Cocksedge opened her arms expansively. "I don't know what to tell you... I'm bored! It's almost February, we've been here three months and after half a winter in this place, I've had enough. Can you honestly tell me you feel differently, Erika?"

"Feelings are irrelevant. Not all of Douglas' people left with the others and they still hold the power in this land. We must adjust that balance if we are to remain here."

"What can we do in the dead of winter? You won't get these people to even leave their hearths in this weather, and who can blame them? I wouldn't send a penguin out there. Look, I spent a good deal of my time reading up on the politics of this period – while ensconced at Douglas' pleasure. I've put a lot of thought into this and now have a plan that is bolder and more far-reaching than simply stripping wealth from this rather *poor* region."

Schmidt rolled her eyes. "Have you?"

Cocksedge met her disdain with a smile. "Indeed. Aila. *Aila,* come here, girl."

Their Scottish captive-cum-chambermaid scuttled obediently to her new mistress.

"Aila, tell me, how would you like to see London?"

The girl's eyes widened excitedly

Schmidt's widened with disbelief. "What are you suggesting?"

"My dear Erika. Our young queen made quite the impression on King Phillip II of Spain while he was married to that awful sister of hers. Hardly surprising, really – a vital young man saddled with that old trout."

Schmidt leaned back slightly, pot and kettle crossing her mind, but she listened in silence, nonetheless.

Cocksedge continued, oblivious, "However, he'll be far less enamoured once he realises that he can't bully her into returning England to Rome, or indeed, into marrying anyone who might. Now,

I suggest we have a word with young Phil and make him a more appealing offer."

Schmidt gave her a sideways look. "An offer?"

"Indeed. We know – more than that, with a little theft from the *New World*'s archives, we can *prove* – that she will die without issue. She will never marry. She will never breed. Eventually, the throne will fall to a Scot, James, and we really don't want one of these ruffians hereabouts on the throne, do we? Besides, having lived up here, we know Scotland's in France's pocket. A good many Scots hate it, but like *that* matters to their great 'ally'." She dusted off the inverted comma bunnies. "I reckon King Phillip won't be thrilled by the sideways succession, either. As it happens, James will spend most of his time in England, but only *we* know that. At the moment, the future is whatever we say it is. Even if the future James I did take England back to the Pope – and we also know that he won't – Phillip will assume that England will most likely cosy up to the French, rather than Spain. At least, that's how *he'll* see it. We can reinforce his concerns, play on them, and then offer a solution – a third choice, so to speak."

"Go on."

"A regency, in the name of Spain. Someone more... *sophisticated* than they're used to should take the helm. After all, it would be for the best. The royal line will be severed and option three will give Phil direct control over England, and more quickly, too. Of course, we'll oversee the day-to-day running of the nation, offering crucial insider advice, while he creates a *new* royal line. I'm sure we can come up with all kinds of 'genuine documentation' to support whatever will suit us best in that regard – these people will believe anything. *We* will hold the reins, the actual power, and if we can't skim a little off the top, sides and bottom from that arrangement, my girl, then we don't deserve to."

"When you say *we*, Allison, you are actually proposing yourself for the regency?"

"Why not, my dear? And with the most beautiful woman in all Christendom at my side, the monarchs of Europe will be tripping over themselves to win our favour. They're only *men*, after all – and who knows, maybe the women, too." She smiled her politician's smile.

Schmidt raised a wry eyebrow, which merely punctuated the perfect symmetry of her features with added interest. "Flattery?"

"*Strategy,* my dear. We use the gifts we have. Now, come. Sit with me beside the fire and let's compose a letter to our new friend, Phil. If he sends a fleet to invade, we could perform this coup right under the noses of those blustering cretins that make up the English court."

Schmidt took a seat, accepting a glass of mulled wine from Aila. "You do think big, Allison. I will credit you with that. You feel sure about this?"

Cocksedge smiled again. "My dear, I hoodwinked those fools' progeny for a *living,* back in the twenty-second century. Right now, the so-called English nobility are already cowering under a slip of a girl – just wait 'til they get a load of us..."

AD1944, Bavaria, Germany

Even in June, the Austrian Alps were capped with snow. Heinrich Schultz sipped a particularly fine white as he handed the photographs to his companion.

Reinhard Heydrich accepted them from his guest. "These are warships?"

"They are much more than that, my friend. The *Last Word* was an interstellar battleship able to fly through time itself. She also packed the capability to destroy anything your military has to offer. Even without nuclear ordnance, she could wipe out your entire navy from space without taking a hit. Though, I believe the smaller vessel might be of particular interest to you. She is called the *Heydrich.*"

Heydrich looked up sharply.

"Oh, yes," Schultz continued easily. "You were quite the hero of our cause in my own timeline, Reinhard. You have seen some of the footage?"

Heydrich nodded. His demeanour remained cool but his mind was ablaze with possibilities. "And you can give me the plans and information I need to build more of these?"

"I can. You have the necessary command of materials technology in this time. You lack only the superior knowledge of my century."

"And what is it that you want in return?"

"Oh, I'm sure we'll come up with a suitable reward. This house, for instance."

A flicker of surprise crossed Heydrich's face. "You want the Berghof?"

Schultz stood and stretched languidly. He took a few steps to lean on the parapet wall that circuited the lofty residence, breathing deeply of the purest mountain air. "I used to have a fortress in South America, looking out across one of the last remnants of the rainforest. In many ways, it was not dissimilar to your beautiful holiday home, Reinhard. Although, I must say I prefer both your views and your climate." He turned, treating Heydrich to one of his cool smiles and penetrating stares. "Your reconstruction and renovation work on the place, a few years ago, was first class. Yes, indeed, very nice. Shall we call it a small, a *very* small, down payment for what I have? You are, after all, one of the richest men in the world and I am, *after all,* offering the world itself."

Heydrich studied the photos again – he could build another mountain court. Perhaps he would build another here, higher up, overlooking this incredibly dangerous new business acquaintance. *Yes,* he considered, *common prudence would suggest that I keep this old man under* constant *surveillance.* "Very well, Heinrich. I will need some proof of the technical documents before I hand over the deeds, you'll understand, but in principle—"

A servant delivered a note upon a silver tray, interrupting him. Heydrich opened the missive, written on his own stationery and closed with a most peculiar three-way fold – a fold he recognised as unique to just one man. His cold eyes brightened, almost happy. "Ah, it seems my other little science project is about to pay dividends. Would you care to join me, Heinrich?"

The two men stepped inside a large outbuilding, set into the mountainside just below the Berghof. "Heinrich, may I introduce you to one of my most eminent scientists, Josef Mengele. Josef, Mr Heinrich Schultz. He has offered us some very, very advanced technology."

The two monsters shook hands like gentlemen. Schultz, cultured as always, smiled coolly. Mengele's smile was of the more manic kind. The old man studied the two younger men, each with potential to join the ranks of the most heinous war criminals in history, though in this timeline, at least, neither had accomplished any great evil, yet. He compared them.

Mengele's eyes crinkled at the corners as he smiled, but not with joviality so much as with insanity. Black drowning pools leading to a Lovecraftian abyss where 'no lives matter'. Heydrich's smile was as frigid as the Arctic tundra. Chaos and law, shoulder to shoulder with one another, and with evil itself.

Schultz was, for the moment at least, a far more accomplished villain than either this young scientist or his state oligarch patron. More than twice their age, he already had more blood on his hands than even *he* realised. Indeed, by June 1944, Reinhard Heydrich was already two years dead in Heinrich's own timeline, and yet even a sociopath like himself could feel the power of evil that radiated from these two young men. Power he could use.

"You are just in time for our first arrival, gentlemen." Mengele ushered them towards an antechamber where several white coveralls hung from a rack, along with boots and masks. He invited Heydrich and Schultz to don the protective clothing before leading them into an atmospherically sealed cleanroom.

Three incubators sat on wheeled stands in the centre of the floor, each facing outwards from one another in a triangular formation. Schultz raised an eyebrow in surprise as he walked around them, looking into each in turn. He glanced to Heydrich. "I see you have met my granddaughter, Reinhard."

Heydrich's voice was slightly muffled through the mask, but easily intelligible. "I have not had that pleasure personally, Heinrich. One of my intermediaries procured the items. There are but three in the entire world."

Schultz was impressed – he knew how much Heidi had charged for this merchandise. "And here they are," he answered, noncommittally.

Greed glinted in Heydrich's eyes like sun on steel. "Call me a collecting fool, but I just had to have them all. That way, Josef will be able to conduct experiments on the spare, in order to make more. Is that not so, Josef?"

Mengele smiled his manic smile, visible through the transparent mask. "With the full genetic code, I can make as many as you like, Reinhard."

Heydrich turned back to Schultz. "Can you imagine the terror and disruption to a population, should they be dropped in the middle of a city, Heinrich? Or, on the other hand, just how much people would pay to come and see them?" He chuckled softly. "No, I have no fears for my investment."

Schultz was reminded that, while it was only 1944, Douglas' meddling had accelerated these people's understanding by at least a century. Yes, these men he could use.

Mengele drew their attention back to himself with two simple words. "It begins."

Author's Notes

Many of the dinosaurs in this book have been discussed previously. There was, of course, a whole ecosystem's worth of wonderful creatures in Cretaceous Egypt, but as those elements of the story took place over a relatively short period, many of the animals that appeared in the last three books are not merely the same species; often they were the same animals – locals, as it were. For example, the giant *Carcharodontosaurus saharicus,* the giant crocodilian *Sarcosuchus imperator* and the rowdy pack of *Rugops primus.*

Carcharodontosaurus saharicus, suffice to say, was another of the large theropod carnivores discovered by Ernst Stromer during his remarkable Egyptian excavations of 1911-14. Just to give a basic mind's eye picture, it was broadly shaped and sized comparably to *Tyrannosaurus rex,* although not directly related. *T rex* joined the fossil record more than thirty million years later and was overall, a stronger, more advanced and dangerous animal.

Rugops primus – it is perhaps worthy of note that no actual evidence exists to prove that they were social or moved about in packs – at least, not at the time of publishing. As Rugops was comparatively weak in the jaw, I took a liberty and made them hunt, or scavenge, in numbers. From a fictional storytelling perspective, I think this makes them a scarier proposition, too. If they really did go about in groups a dozen strong, they would have been a right handful!

Spinosaurus aegyptiacus, a dinosaur that probably requires little introduction these days. Apologies if it seemed like 'icon mashing', but I just couldn't resist draping one across a pyramid – two ancient fascinations for the price of one, with a later nod to Agatha Christie's 'Death on the Nile', for good measure!

Paralititan stromeri were large sauropod dinosaurs – sauropods were the long neck, long tail varieties. They were titanosaurs related to Argentinosaurus, and others, from earlier books in the series. They were probably a little smaller than Argentinosaurus, but still huge. Only fragmentary evidence exists for this once extraordinary species, so estimates vary wildly between 20-60 tons in weight and 20-32 metres in length. Hopefully a more complete specimen will be found in the future to fill in the gaps. Dispersed over several continents, the titanosaurs presumably shared common ancestors from before the breakup of Pangaea into the continents we recognise today. A process that began back in the Triassic Period, a hundred million years or more before the Cretaceous setting for this story. Again, as the name suggests, they were discovered and named by Ernst Stromer. He must have won the dino-lottery during those brief years of the early 20th century. Sadly, the majority of his finds, including the most complete remains yet discovered of the mighty *Spinosaurus aegyptiacus,* were destroyed in the Allied bombing of 1944. As the song says, 'War – what is it good for? Absolutely nothing!' Well, at least it stopped Hitler, eventually. Pity it didn't end there.

Afromimus tenerensis, small and ostrich-like, this little creature was an ideal choice for a dinosaur-mimicking robot spy. Extremely fast and a relative minnow in the age of giants, it would have been easy to overlook. *Afromimus* was an earlier North African relative of the more famous *Ornithomimus velox.* They must have been graceful, bird-like creatures, as implied by the name.

Ouranosaurus nigeriensis I also mentioned in a previous book. However, aside from being an ancestor to the hugely successful duck-billed dinosaurs, who mainly came later, I find these creatures interesting in that they share such a similar (at least, superficially) sail on their backs with *Spinosaurus. Ouranosaurus* was herbivorous. (As you will no doubt have gleaned from this book, *Spinosaurus* wasn't!) That both had a similar body plan and were from the same area raises the question of perhaps another common ancestor. Perhaps divergence came as a necessity of lifestyle – although *Spinosaurus aegyptiacus* was far larger and a whole lot meaner! The dorsal sail has long been pondered by experts, some believing it functioned as a thermoregulator for heating or cooling the blood – dogs use a similar process, instead passing blood through the pads in their paws to cool themselves down. (Quite often, the little darlings get too excited to drink cool water, even when they should, so cooling their paws on a cold surface or in a stream is a good idea if they're overheating. Health and Safety Notice: DO NOT TRY THIS WITH A SPINOSAURUS!) Other scientists have suggested that such a skeletal construct may have supported a hump of muscle or fat rather than a sail, and like a camel, it might have been used for energy or fluid storage in times of scarcity or drought. There's still just so much to learn about dinosaurs.

We've barely scratched the surface, and I think that's a large part of the fascination for so many of us – once you recover from how vast and dangerous some of the dinosauria were.

Sarcosuchus imperator. Again, closely related and contemporaneous with South America's *Sarcosuchus hartti* from earlier books in the series, suggesting common ancestry. These giant crocodiles were easily large enough to dispatch an unsuspecting carnivorous *Rugops,* or herbivorous *Ouranosaurus.* Each prey animal growing to roughly seven metres long, the deadly *Sarcosuchus* would have possibly preyed on both – quite probably when they needed to drink, as crocodiles do today. Imagine, if you will, *Sarcosuchus imperator* hiding just below the surface, or maybe looking like a log floating downstream. Well over twice the length and many times the size of even the largest modern-day saltwater crocodile (*Crocodylus porosus*), they would have guaranteed that no one *ever* wasted time on idle chatter around the water cooler in Cretaceous Africa! It's believed that the comparatively slender nature of the *Sarcosuchus* jaw would have made it impossible to 'death roll' its prey, as modern crocodiles do. Rather, the jaw structure leads palaeontologists to believe that *Sarcosuchus* hunted large prey, such as dinosaurs, killing with brute force rather than shaking them apart, like their modern descendants.

*Corporal Heinz Engel is introduced to the series in **ENGEL | REVENGE EXTRA**. See also **MAPUSAURUS | DINOSAUR EXTRA** in the **New World Series Short Stories** collection. More information at **www.stephenllewelyn.com**

Geek alert: Name change from *São Paulo* to *New World – São Paulo* was the original name for the second *Defiant,* in Star Trek Deep Space Nine – my homage (Starfleet's famous engineer, Chief Miles O'Brien, hated the new carpets, too).

On the subject of ships, the 800-ton Spanish galleon, *San Juan de Sicilia,* really did explode and sink on November 5th, AD1588. (It's unrelated, but perhaps ironic, that we celebrate Guy Fawkes Night [Bonfire Night] on November 5th in Britain, to commemorate the Gunpowder Plot of 1605 which *didn't* actually go off!) The late 16th century, and especially 1588, was marked by turbulent North Atlantic storms. They're believed to have been an effect associated with a period that has become known as the 'Little Ice Age'. Despite the purposes of the Armada, far more sailors were killed by the weather than enemy action. Near the end of September 1588, the *San Juan de Sicilia* anchored off the west coast of Scotland, near the Isle of Mull, in Tobermory Bay. Though she was as yet undamaged, her crew were short of water and supplies. Her senior officer, Diego Tellez Enríquez, made a deal with a local Scottish lord, Lachlan MacLean of Duart. MacLean would provide the supplies the *San Juan de Sicilia* badly needed and Enríquez would provide armed men to help settle MacLean's feuds with his neighbours. Enríquez was no fool – unwilling to trust a man who attacks his neighbours, he insisted on hostages to guarantee the Scottish lord's good faith. The *San Juan de Sicilia* remained in Tobermory Bay for a little over a month, during which time Enríquez's Spanish troops attacked and ravaged the islands of Rùm, Eigg, Canna and Muck, going on to lay siege to Mingary Castle on the mainland. At some point during this period, it was discovered, or assumed, that one of the merchants charged with the reprovisioning, John Smollet, was actually in the pay of Sir Francis Walsingham – Elizabeth I's 'spymaster'. The *San Juan de Sicilia* never actually set back to sea, for on November 5th she exploded while still at anchor, killing almost everyone aboard, including the hostages. The fifty or so survivors continued in service to MacLean until he finally had them shipped back to Spain a year later. Details of the ship's destruction are sketchy, its actual reason, unknown – though the wreck still intrigues marine archaeologists to this day.

The Old Academy, Munich was destroyed by Allied bombing, as mentioned above. It was actually destroyed in the April of 1944, rather than the June explosion described in this story – it would have been nice to tie in exactly, but it just didn't quite work with the timeline for the rest of the story.

The Nazis did indeed invade the Netherlands on May 10th, 1940, despite the Netherlands being neutral at the time. The occupation began *comparatively* softly, with trade deals from the hand wearing the velvet glove, but deteriorated throughout the war to a point where the population were starving by 1945. 70% of the Netherlands' Jews were killed during the Second World War. Active resistance, which began with just a handful of fighters, grew throughout the occupation – perhaps unsurprisingly. From this came the idea for my 'Order of the Silver Cross' Nazi hunters, to honour the courage of those concerned.

The Order in my books was not real, just a device I used to tie various characters to an overall thread throughout the story, but there certainly were real heroic groups who fought with whatever they had, to free their people from tyranny.

Reinhard Heydrich was one of the principal architects of the Holocaust. As previously discussed, he was a monster, arguably the worst of Hitler's entire regime. Mortally wounded in Prague on May 27th, 1942, he was ambushed by Czech and Slovak soldiers sent by the Czechoslovakian government-in-exile, whose troops were trained by the British Special Operations Executive. Heydrich died from his injuries a week later, but the Nazi response, wreaked erroneously on villages thought to be linked to the attack, and a wider resistance, was terrible. Indeed, Heydrich probably deserves more 'infamy' than he actually receives. Hitler, looking for a pretext to invade Poland in 1939, tasked Heydrich, Himmler and Heinrich Müller with designing a false flag operation. The dastardly scheme they cooked up involved a fake attack on a German radio station at Gleiwitz on August 31st, 1939. Wearing Polish uniforms, 150 German troops carried out several attacks along the border with Poland. Heydrich masterminded the plan, giving Hitler his excuse to invade Poland and the rest, as they say, is history – although you might be forgiven for thinking it sounds familiar.

Josef Mengele is a name most will already be familiar with, I'm sure. He is also remembered under the quaint moniker of the 'Angel of Death' – more than just a Slayer song. His penchant for carrying out genetic experimentation on twins was revealed in a recent documentary that followed the life of a Holocaust survivor. He would use one for his sick experiments until that twin died – and these were often children – whereupon he would murder the other twin to compare their anatomies as part of his 'research'.

Briefly following on from that, it's so difficult to imagine such atrocities and yet... with war crimes practically accompanying our TV dinners right now, almost a century later, the original plot I had noted for this part of the story arc fast became unpleasant to write. It was just too 'close', as I mentioned in the preface at the beginning of this book.

That said, some people simply found themselves on the 'wrong side' because of where they were born. During the Second World War, Erich Alfred Hartmann, or 'Bubi' (roughly translated, 'The Kid'), was a German pilot and the most successful fighter ace to date. History remembers him as a skilled pilot and an honourable serviceman, unlike the Nazis shamed above. A master of stalk-and-ambush tactics, he honed the technique of ambushing and firing at close range, rather than dogfighting. "Fly with your head, not with your muscles," was the famous advice he passed on to new recruits, after a rude awakening which would have gotten him killed had he not been confined to barracks. During his time with the *Luftwaffe,* he flew 1,404 combat missions and engaged the Allies in aerial combat 825 times. He was credited with 352 kills; 345 Soviet and 7 American. Hartmann survived 16 crash landings, the causes being mechanical in nature, or damage due to impacts with flying debris from aircraft he himself had shot down. He was never brought down by direct enemy action. He was highly decorated and by 25th August, 1944, Hartmann had earned the coveted Knight's Cross of the Iron Cross with Oak Leaves, Swords and Diamonds for 301 aerial victories – at that time, Germany's highest military decoration. As discussed within this story, he was tried by Russia for war crimes against civilian targets, which he denied all his life. He seems to have been convicted for the costs to Russia in 'expensive' aircraft and for what must have been quite a dent to Russian pride – after all, he had shot down a lot of their planes. Apparently, the judge at his trial said his attempts to defend himself were "a waste of time." He was initially sentenced to 20 years' imprisonment, later increased to 25. He actually served 10 of those years, in various Soviet prisons and Gulags until his release in 1955. In 1997, the Russian Federation exonerated him of all charges during the democratic Yeltsin years. Sadly, this was a posthumous admission as Hartmann died in 1993. Of all his accomplishments, he was most proud of the fact that he never lost a wingman – although, technically, he did lose Major Günther Capito in 1943, who nevertheless lived on to fly again, until the end of the war. Now Erich Hartmann is cut off from his native 1944 Germany and ensconced aboard the *New World,* it will be interesting to see where he 'flies' next.

I hope you've enjoyed this sixth book of the series, and wish you all a bright and hopeful future, wherever you are in the world. Thank you so much for reading,

Stephen Llewelyn.

Coming soon:

COLLISION
THE NEW WORLD SERIES | BOOK SEVEN

BOOK 1
DINOSAUR

BOOK 2
REVENGE

BOOK 3
ALLEGIANCE

BOOK 4
REROUTE

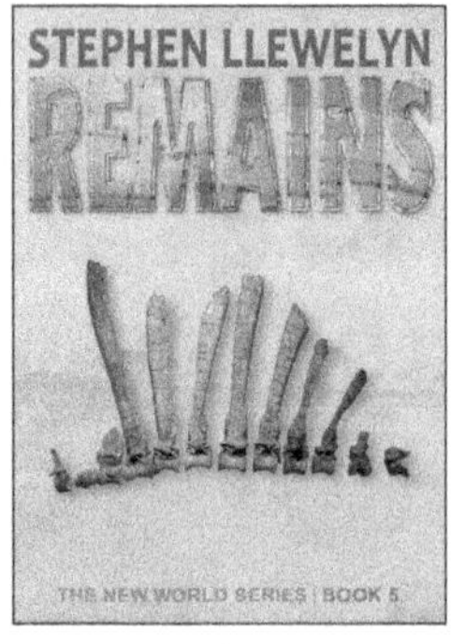

BOOK 5
REMAINS

BOOK 6
CURSED

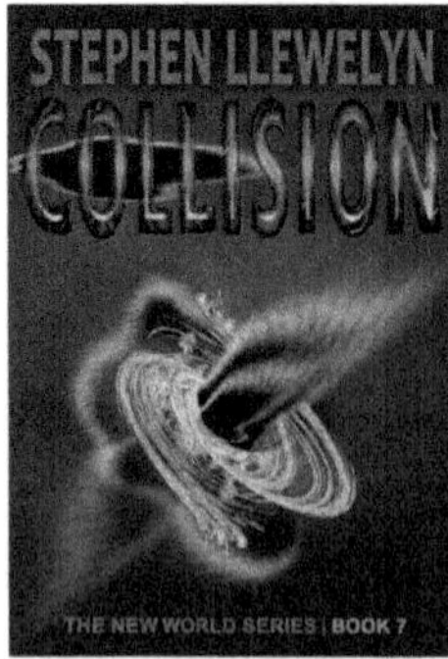

BOOK 7
COLLISION

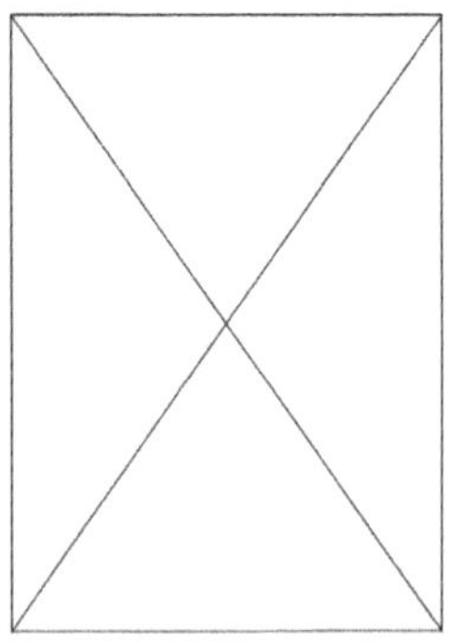

NEWFOUNDLAND

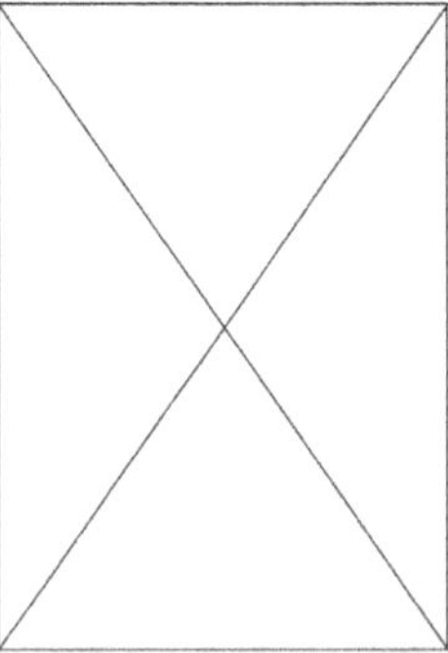

REBIRTH

www.stephenllewelyn.com/books/

DINOSAUR
audio performed by

CHRIS BARRIE
(Red Dwarf, Tomb Raider)

www.stephenllewelyn.com